P9-DNP-637

Whisper the Dead

ALSO BY ALYXANDRA HARVEY

The Drake Chronicles
Hearts at Stake
Blood Feud
Out for Blood
Ruling Passion
(Bind-up of *Hearts at Stake*, *Blood Feud*, and *Out for Blood*)
Bleeding Hearts
Blood Moon
Blood Prophecy

Haunting Violet

Stolen Away

The Lovegrove Legacy
A Breath of Frost

THE
LOVEGROVE LEGACY

Whisper the Dead

ALYXANDRA HARVEY

BLOOMSBURY
NEW YORK   LONDON   NEW DELHI   SYDNEY

First published in the United States of America in October 2014
by Bloomsbury Children's Books
www.bloomsbury.com

Bloomsbury is a registered trademark of Bloomsbury Publishing Plc

For information about permission to reproduce selections from this book, write to
Permissions, Bloomsbury Children's Books, 1385 Broadway, New York, New York 10018
Bloomsbury books may be purchased for business or promotional use. For information on bulk purchases
please contact Macmillan Corporate and Premium Sales Department at specialmarkets@macmillan.com

Library of Congress Cataloging-in-Publication Data
Harvey, Alyxandra.
Whisper the dead / by Alyxandra Harvey.
    pages   cm   —(The Lovegrove legacy ; [2])
Summary: In 1814 London, Gretchen must put aside annoyance at the constant buzzing caused by being a
Whisperer, concern about her twin brother, her growing feelings for a member of the Order of the Iron Nail,
and the boredom of being a debutante when a new menace threatens Mayfair.
ISBN 978-0-8027-3750-2 (hardcover) • ISBN 978-0-8027-3751-9 (e-book)
[1. Witches—Fiction. 2. Magic—Fiction. 3. Love—Fiction. 4. Brothers and sisters—Fiction.
5. Twins—Fiction. 6. Cousins—Fiction. 7. London (England)—History—19th century—
Fiction. 8. Great Britain—History—George III, 1760–1820—Fiction.] I. Title.
    PZ7.H267448Whi 2014   [Fic]—dc23   2014005626

Book design by Amanda Bartlett
Typeset by Westchester Book Composition
Printed and bound in the U.S.A. by Thomson-Shore Inc., Dexter, Michigan
2 4 6 8 10 9 7 5 3 1

Beware! Now I know a language so beautiful and lethal
My mouth bleeds when I speak it.
—Gwendolyn MacEwen

Whisper the Dead

Chapter 1

Gretchen was on her way to the Worthing musicale when her head exploded.

She finally knew exactly what a ripe melon felt like when it burst open. Frankly, it was knowledge she could have done without.

She'd told her chaperone that she was leaving for Lady Worthing's annual musicale from the Rowanstone Academy, she'd told the school she was leaving from home, and she'd avoided her mother altogether. All to snatch a few minutes alone without a hovering chaperone or a lady's maid who would tattle her every deed to her parents. Gretchen fancied herself rather clever at subterfuge. But now, clearly as a punishment for lying, her head was exploding.

And it still wouldn't excuse her from another tedious evening, more's the pity.

Magic burned inside her like embers, just waiting to catch. But instead of doing something exciting with it, she was on her way to an event where young ladies were expected to sing and perform for eligible young men of the aristocracy, dragged there by their own mothers. In the last two weeks alone, she'd attended three balls, the opera, the theater, and two supper parties. She'd danced the quadrille with a perfectly polite peer's son, curtsied at duchesses, and only hidden in the library twice. A girl could only take so much.

Not that her current magical state was much of an improvement.

She pressed her brow against the cool glass of the carriage window and tried to figure out what was happening. She caught glimpses of gargoyles crouched over rain gutters and roof corners, but they remained still and unanimated. No dark magic had awakened them; there were no warlocks roaming the sidewalks and no Greymalkin Sisters, who had so recently terrorized London. There was only a group of gentlemen with ivory-handled walking sticks gathered outside a chophouse, and a woman hurrying home with an armful of paper-wrapped packages.

Gretchen pounded her fist on the roof until the coachman stopped. She stumbled out onto the pavement. "Just need some air," she croaked. "I'm not well." She must have looked as green as she felt, because he didn't protest.

There was an odd grinding in her head, like the rusty cogs of some invisible clockwork. Her magical gift, called Whispering, was most unhelpful. It warned her when a spell was going badly, but unfortunately that warning came in needles of sound and pain. She still hadn't learned to decipher it or control it. She'd barely learned not to be ill when it pressed down on her like this.

She stepped onto the pavement and wrapped her hand around a lamppost to steady herself. Another surreptitious scanning of the area didn't make her present predicament any easier to understand. The cold iron was weathered under her hand, scraping slightly at her palm. Her witch knot flared once. All witches had the symbol on their palm, visible only to other witches. Gretchen already noticed it tended to itch when magic was being worked. A closer look revealed a sigil scratched into the lamppost. It was mostly lines intersecting with small circles. She didn't know what it meant. The black paint flaked off as she traced the pattern, altering one of the lines.

The lantern above her shattered.

Glass rained down as one of the gentlemen gave a shout of alarm and rushed forward. "Are you well, miss?"

Gretchen nodded mutely. She might have been pelted with shards of broken glass, but the respite from the awful buzzing sound in her head was well worth the risk. Whatever prompted the lantern to break had also silenced her inner magical storm.

He frowned at the broken light. "I know they say gaslights are safe, but that's the third one this week I've seen shatter."

Gretchen knew perfectly well the gas lamps weren't faulty. Something magical was at work. The sudden and blessed quiet in her head attested to it.

"May I escort you home?" the gentleman offered, bowing politely.

"My carriage is waiting just there," Gretchen said, "but thank you."

She waited until he'd rejoined his friends before circling around the lamppost. There were no other symbols, nothing to suggest spell ingredients anywhere else in the vicinity.

Her familiar pushed its wolfhound head out of her chest and leaped down on the pavement. The giant dog was the form her magic took, glowing like moonlight through an icy lake. All witches had a familiar they could send outside of their bodies to various magical ends. As he closed his misty teeth around her hem and tugged, Gretchen assumed most familiars were better behaved than hers.

"What now?"

Another glowing wolfhound raced toward her, barking. His dark eyes were sad. It was her twin brother Godric's familiar, but he rarely sent it out. He said it made him feel nauseous. The dog gave another low woof and then both familiars raced away. If Gretchen concentrated very carefully, she could see what her wolfhound saw, though the lights glowed brighter and the colors were exaggerated, and all of it was smeared like a chalk drawing in the rain. Still, she recognized enough of the buildings and their soaring columns to know he was running down Bond Street faster than any regular animal could run. He turned onto Piccadilly and down to the Strand, following it all the way to the area around London Bridge.

Either Godric had sent his wolfhound to fetch her, or else it had come looking for her of its own accord.

Either way, her brother was in trouble.

. . .

The goblin markets were as crowded as a midsummer fair. Witches mingled with warlocks, goblins spat on cobblestones, and changeling children pilfered magic trinkets from shops pressed together like disreputable lovers. This was the London Bridge ordinary folk never saw. Under the pomegranate lanterns, pegasi were as common as draft horses, and strange ingredients filled glass jars at every turn. Every rooftop, no matter how flimsy and poor, was crowned with a gargoyle crouching protectively, ready to gobble up stray magic.

Cautious witches draped themselves with evil-eye beads, carried white-horse banishing powder, and filled their pockets with salt and iron nails. All of these ingredients could be had at any booth, but the stronger, and slightly more illegal, items were purchased from a Rover. Or a hag, but hags were even worse than the scarred, belligerent Rovers, who swaggered down the bridge, fighting and stealing and generally making a nuisance of themselves. They weren't quite warlocks, but they certainly flirted with the boundaries of magic and good sense.

Tonight Moira was alone under the bridge. The other Madcaps had scattered as soon as the Order doubled its patrols. The rooftops were barely safe, never mind now that the Greybeards were even more insistent on claiming every witch for their own. Especially Madcaps, since they had a way with gargoyle magic. But a Madcap would not be claimed, not in life or in death. Moira would make sure of it.

Madcap funerals were rare—too often a Madcap witch went missing, her bones never to be found again. But Moira had held her friend Strawberry when she died and knew exactly where the body was taken. She'd stolen it herself from the back of a Greybeard's cart, still wrapped in a preserving spell to keep it from decomposing.

It was bad enough that Strawberry was murdered by a bleeding debutante for the warlock Greymalkin Sisters. She deserved a better send-off than what the Order had planned for her. The bones of witches ground down to a powder made an excellent ingredient for protective charms or more nefarious magic. They wouldn't use a lady of quality for that kind of thing, only a raggedy orphan like Strawberry. If anything, Moira was even more determined to have a proper, traditional Madcap funeral, the kind rarely seen in London since the Order closed its iron fist around the city.

The soles of her feet itched, but she didn't need her warning magic to tell her she wanted to be anywhere but here. Sensing her mood, a fat little gargoyle circled her head like a bumblebee. She'd spelled him back at the Greymalkin House to distract the house gargoyle so she and the Lovegrove cousins could get in. But now it wouldn't go back to sleep. "It's time," she whispered to it.

The moon was bright enough to outline ships, rowboats, and mudlarks farther down the river, scavenging for lost trinkets and dead bodies. Dead bodies sometimes came with gold teeth or buttons. Strawberry's bones would only come with Madcap magic and a gargoyle guard.

Her friend lay in a tiny, splintered rowboat, her blond hair spread out and woven with ribbons. She was sprinkled with salt, and there were apples, a cheap clay gargoyle, and an iron dagger for her journey through the Underworld to the Blessed Isles. Not that Strawberry would even know what to do with the dagger regardless of which side of the veil she inhabited.

The side of the boat was painted with a single blue eye and hung with an illusion charm to keep the funeral hidden from those without the magic to see it for themselves.

Moira sprinkled the flower petals into the black oily water of the Thames. Boats glided past, lanterns hanging on prows. She wished she knew the old farewell song free witches sang, before they were reduced to a handful of coal-stained Madcaps.

"May you find your way to the Blessed Isles," she whispered instead. The torch in her right hand flickered wildly, searing the water, the white sheet, the staring painted eye. She refused to let tears fall, no matter how her throat burned. She lifted her left palm, displaying her witch knot in salute.

"Oi, you're wasting good magic," someone barked suddenly behind them.

Moira learned long ago to react first, question later. She tossed the torch but it missed the boat. Still, she managed to fill each hand with a dagger. She threw one, and it slammed into the shoulder of a Rover. He fell back, cursing. The others pushed closer, teeth flashing in angry sneers.

"Back off and we won't gut you like a fish," one of them said.

"Back off and *I* won't feed your liver to my gargoyle," Moira shot back. Her familiar, a russet tabby cat with a bent ear, leaped out of her chest, hissing. Rovers rarely traveled in packs. No one liked them, not even other Rovers.

"I knew this would end badly," she muttered.

"Take me to London Bridge," Gretchen directed her coachman.

He twisted to glance at her. "Are you daft?"

"I have ten shillings in my reticule. It's yours if you'll do it."

"And what will you offer me widow when your mam kills me dead?"

"A guinea, then! And it's only for a moment; you can cart me off to the bloody musicale afterward," she assured him, the wind snatching at her short hair as she ducked back inside the carriage. "It will drag on for hours. I won't miss a thing."

"Get back in there before someone sees you," he grumbled, but he continued down Bond Street instead of turning into the residential neighborhood where the Worthing mansion reigned. He pulled the horses to a stop at the edge of the bridge. "Fresh Wharf and London Bridge at this time of night?" he asked. "You shouldn't—"

But Gretchen had already hopped out and darted into the thick shadows with a carefree, "Won't be a moment!"

Gretchen had no idea what Godric was doing down near the bridge, so close to the goblin markets. He might not deny his magic the way their mother did, but he certainly wasn't keen to embrace it. There was just enough moonlight to make out the masts of ships, the looming shadow of the Tower, and a collection of warehouses.

Godric's familiar dashed ahead of her and then back to make sure she was following and then ran ahead again. Walking alone at night was dangerous business, never mind in a white silk gown and an emerald necklace. She didn't exactly have anywhere to hide a dagger or a pistol on her person. Voices drifted out of taverns, and torches burned, leaving soot on the walls.

She was already having more fun than she could ever manage at a musicale.

Even when she found her brother in a stone alcove permeated with the unfortunate stench of the river. She'd expected him to be cornered by some strange magical beast, or at the very least fighting off a gang of thieves. Not drinking whiskey from a flask and holding a bundle of what looked like bird bones. "Oh, Godric, honestly." She sighed.

He blinked blearily. "What are you doing here?"

"You sent your wolfhound to fetch me."

"I did not. I sent him to find more port."

"Well, then, your familiar is smarter than you are," she said. "And I'm pretty sure magic dogs can't fetch liquor."

"Worth a try." His blond curls fell over his forehead, and there were grass stains on his sleeves. This wasn't her cheerful, clever brother. She pinched him hard.

"Ouch!" he squeaked. "What the bloody hell was that for?"

"You know what." She pinched him again. He was too drunk

to evade her; he just looked mournful. It was like pinching a puppy. "You smell like a tavern."

He scrubbed his face. "I can't stand it, Gretel," he said, using his old nickname for her, from when they'd played at being Hansel and Gretel trying to escape the witch's house. Before they'd found out they were witches themselves.

"You're going to have to get a handle on it eventually. You can't go on like this. It isn't healthy." She kept her tone brisk. If she showed the barest trace of pity, she was afraid he'd dissolve away right before her eyes.

"The Prince Regent can drink fifteen bottles of port in a single day."

"The Prince Regent is sweaty and smells like the bottom of a wine bottle. Is that what you want?"

"You used to be nicer," Godric complained.

"You used to be sober," she returned, grabbing his arm when he started to tilt to the left rather dramatically. "I can't believe— *gah!*" She'd forgotten that Godric's talent for seeing spirits transferred to her if she was touching him.

The broken body of a man in a Roman toga sprawled on the cobblestones, the ragged chafing of rope burns around his throat. The back wheel of a carriage rolled over him. He didn't notice, only stood up and crossed the pavement to the nearest house and walked through the wall. She caught a glimpse of him on the roof moments later, a glowing rope in his hand. He was stuck in the ghostly loop of his own suicide.

A second ghost, a woman in a Tudor-style gown Gretchen's cousin Penelope would have coveted, glided over the sidewalk, the pearls around her neck gleaming sharply. She left a trail of frost like a lace train behind her and seemed perfectly happy to be a spirit. She even tossed a smile at Godric. He clenched his jaw and looked away.

He pulled back from Gretchen, severing the magical connection. "They're everywhere. You have no idea how crowded London is."

She couldn't see the ghosts anymore, nor the winter they left behind. She noticed the scorch on his sleeve and the raw burn on the side of his hand. Ghosts pulled so much energy from the world around them that their touch scalded even as their presence froze everything else. The Greymalkin Sisters' spirits had done the same thing when they attacked, only they were powerful enough that any witch felt their touch. These ghosts were just on regular ghost business, haunting their graves or whatever it was ghosts did instead of traveling on.

"What are you doing here anyway?" she asked. "Besides feeling sorry for yourself?"

"The Order is sending Ironstone students to reanimate the remaining gargoyles that fled the city last month. After that night with the Sisters, no one wants to take any chances. We need all the extra protection we can get." He didn't sound impressed. She was wild with envy.

"That is deeply unfair," she grumbled. "Rowanstone girls don't get to have any fun. I'm meant to learn embroidery. And rhyming couplets." She shuddered.

Godric laughed so hard he had to grab his head when the sound clattered like knives.

"Serves you right," she said primly. "Anyway, why are they sending *you*? You're not a Keeper and you've only been an Iron-stone student for a few weeks."

"Most of the experienced Keepers are overseas fighting old Boney."

"They're fighting Napoleon with magic? Brilliant."

"All it's done so far is leave London vulnerable to the Sisters."

"But Napoleon was captured just last week," Gretchen pointed out. There had been an impromptu parade with burning effigies and barrels of gin liberated from some poorly locked tavern. Godric told her all about it. "The Keepers should come back soon enough, shouldn't they?"

"I suppose so." He blinked. "Why is your hair glittering?"

"It's glass dust."

He blinked again. "In your hair? What for?"

"I found a magic sigil on a lamppost and it very rudely exploded."

He didn't look surprised. "Again? We're run ragged trying to keep control of all of the magical wards in the city lately."

"So the Order already knows about it?"

"Of course."

"Prats," she muttered, because she couldn't resist a good insult at the Order's expense.

Godric shrugged and nearly toppled over.

"Oh, honestly, Godric," she added, keeping her tone to that of an annoyed little sister to hide the worry. "Is it really worth it? Being in your cups all the time?"

"It only hurts when I stop."

She kicked him in the shin. "Don't be such an arse."

"Ouch. Can't you let me die in peace?"

"Certainly not. Now where's this gargoyle?"

He walked out of the alcove with the exaggerated care of one who is not entirely steady on his feet. He pointed to the rounded dome of the alcove, on which crouched a stone gargoyle with monstrous teeth and surprisingly delicate wings. "I was trying to find a way to climb it without landing on my head."

"No wonder you've been out here so long." Gretchen had always been the one to scamper up trees and ladders, whereas Godric went green if he looked out a second-story window. "How do we animate it?"

Godric nodded to the wooden box on the bench inside the alcove. When Gretchen opened it, the smell of cedar and honey fought the iron and dead fish of the Thames. Inside the box were dozens of gray silk pouches. She opened one carefully, unfolding the edges to reveal the pale bones of birds. "That's barbaric."

"Apparently, the bones are from birds that led happy lives, raised by Bird Witches on the coast of Dover. They died of natural causes." He shook his head before remembering that he was drunk and it might fall right off. "This magic is rather rum business, wouldn't you say? I mean, can you see Mother chanting over dead birds?"

Gretchen grinned at the image. "I suspect that's the real reason she turned her back on the witching world. It's too messy." She tried to use the cracked stone as a foothold but her gown was too constricting. She glanced at her brother. "Godric, make yourself useful."

"I'm not talking to anything dead."

She rolled his eyes. "Just give me a boost, muttonhead."

He handed her the silver flask first. "Apparently, they need whiskey as well." He laced his hands together and she leaped up onto the makeshift step. He'd been lifting her for years, especially inside the pantry to steal biscuits. She steadied herself on the curve of cool stone and then clambered up, stretching to jam the pouch into the gargoyle's mouth. The creases of the stonework were dark with soot and one of its nostrils was chipped. She added a splash of whiskey. Godric released his hands, and she dropped back down to the ground.

"That's it?" she asked.

"For now. At midnight, another witch will animate it."

"Why can't they feed it too?"

"She's eighty-seven years old, to begin with," Godric told her.

"Oh. Well, that was brilliant, but I'm already late for the musicale."

"Mother will marry you off to some old man without his own teeth if you insist on provoking her," Godric said as he bent to retrieve his hat. The brim was slightly dented.

"Mock all you like," she said. "She'll marry you to a girl who giggles and doesn't know where India is on the globe."

"There are worse things, if she's pretty."

Gretchen ignored him, knowing he was joking. He didn't want to be forced into a marriage any more than she did. The difference was, he was so much more amiable and disposed to like people; the odds were in his favor. And, more importantly, he would retain his autonomy and wealth after marriage. Gretchen was legally and socially expected to obey her husband.

Obey.

"I bloody well don't think so," she muttered. She must have looked a little wild-eyed as Godric nudged her with his elbow.

"Don't fret," he said. "You know I won't let them bully you." He paused, frowning. "Did you hear that?"

"We only want the girl," one of the Rovers said, as though it was perfectly reasonable. "She's already dead, what do you care?"

"Go to hell," Moira seethed, grief and rage leaving a sour taste in her mouth. She could have spat fire. "Because I *care*."

He lunged for her. He was built like a bull, with shoulders wide enough to rightfully belong to three people. She dodged to one side but didn't have anywhere to go, not if she meant to stay close to the boat. His fingers closed in her hair. She'd left it loose, as tradition demanded, to ensure magic wouldn't get caught in her braids. She'd wanted to save every whisper for Strawberry.

The Rover jerked her to a halt, and her scalp prickled painfully. She angled her elbow up and smashed it into his nose. It barely stopped him, even when blood dripped from his left nostril. Her little gargoyle attacked, leaving more gashes. She jabbed backward with her boot, aiming for his groin. He grunted in pain and cuffed her on the side of her head. She fell to her knees, ear ringing. His friend handed him an iron chain that glowed like blue fire, a contraband jet-inlaid iron spoke pendant on one end. No one made a binding charm like the Order, even in the hands of petty magical criminals.

The other Rovers turned toward Strawberry's body, the boat bobbing on the end of a frayed rope.

"Gretchen, wait!" Godric stumbled after her, cursing. From beneath the bridge came battle sounds and worse, the sound of a girl fighting off someone far larger than herself. Gretchen barely made out their silhouettes, a rowboat, and a torch sputtering on the ground. She had no idea who she was supposed to be rescuing since the girl with blood on her teeth was laughing.

"I need a weapon!" Gretchen demanded. She was never attending so much as a tea party without a dagger again. Her mother had confiscated her reticule because it was too bulky. It was bulky because it was filled with iron nails, a dagger, and packets of protective salt. Useful things. Not smelling salts and dance cards as her mother insisted was a reticule's proper contents.

"Wait for me, damn it," Godric said, but he tossed her the iron dagger he was given when he first joined the Ironstone Academy. When Gretchen joined Rowanstone, she'd received a ring set with tiny pearls and painted with an eye to ward off the evil eye.

Fat lot of good it did her now.

"Rovers," Godric warned. "Watch yourself."

Gretchen recognized the girl as Moira, the Madcap witch who had helped them defeat the Sisters. Moira leaped to her feet, flipping over one of the bodies on the ground and kicking a Rover in the face as she landed. Gretchen jumped into the fray, smashing the hilt of her dagger on the back of a Rover's head.

He grunted and fell. Godric was suddenly beside her, ducking punches.

Gretchen knocked a Rover into the river. The resulting splash arced black water into the air. Two more Rovers thundered down the slope toward them. Gretchen whirled, enjoying herself immensely. Every lesson in pugilism and fencing that Godric had ever taken, he'd passed on to her. Her curtsy might be dismal, but her right hook was sharp as a bloody embroidery needle. Better than Godric's right hook, it had to be said. A Rover sidestepped his assault and retaliated so viciously Godric sailed through the air, bleeding. He landed hard and rolled out of the way of the next strike.

"Don't die!" Gretchen shouted at him, kicking the Rover in the back of the knee. "That's an order!"

"You always were bossy," Godric muttered, getting back to his feet. He winked at her, catching her worried expression. "That was my favorite hat," he said mournfully as Moira knocked an angry Rover into another equally angry Rover.

The last Rover cursed and made a run for it.

Moira pushed muddy hair out of her face. "Brilliant timing. Gretchen, inn't it? You've torn your gown."

Gretchen grinned. "Good. It's hideous."

"Who's he?" she demanded.

"That is my idiot brother," Gretchen said.

"I prefer to go by Godric Thorn, Lord Ashby, actually," he said formally, with a perfectly executed bow. "How do you do?"

She looked at him as if he were addled. Her eyebrows lifted when she realized he was serious.

"What did those Rovers want?" he asked. "Should we summon the Order?"

Moira bared her teeth at him. "No Greybeards. And they wanted Strawberry's bones."

"Why?" Gretchen frowned, recognizing the name as one of the victims Sophie had murdered to summon the Sisters.

"That's the real question, inn't it?" Adrenaline made Moira's hands shake as she picked up the fallen torch. It was more smoke than fire.

She waded into the spring-cold water, steadying the boat as she lowered the torch. The hay packed under Strawberry's body caught instantly, hissing smoke. Moira gave the boat a shove and magic pulled it along, flames licking up the sides.

When Moira lifted her hand to display her witch knot, Gretchen and Godric did the same, not sure of the etiquette when it came to crashing a Madcap funeral.

Silently, they watched it drift away until it was a column of fire, golden flames snapping and flickering at the night sky. It finally collapsed, sinking into the dark river, far outside the borders of London. The smoke lingered, fennel-scented and thick as fog.

Moira clenched her fist around her witch knot. "Farewell, Strawberry." She turned, chin up and eyes ruthlessly dry. "Thank you," she said to Gretchen and Godric before walking away.

"She was magnificent," Godric said, if not precisely sober, at least less befuddled. "She smelled like mint."

"She probably picked your pocket too," Gretchen pointed out. "Even with all that going on."

Godric patted his pocket. "Hell. Never mind," he added. "I don't care. She can have all my gold." He watched Moira stride away. She didn't look back.

Gretchen nudged him with her shoulder. "Say good-bye, big brother."

He just smiled. "We'll see, little sister."

Chapter 2

"Are you sure about this?" Cormac asked. "You've only been back in town two days. And double duty is a lot, even for you."

Cormac and Tobias were an incongruous pair—the charming Keeper with no magic of his own and a certain disregard for the rules, and the proper Keeper who followed those same rules with a nearly religious devotion. Still, they had been partners for a year and used those differences to save each other's lives.

"I'll manage," Tobias replied, his ivory-handled walking stick tapping the pavement as he walked. "And the house is rather crowded," he admitted.

His family was rarely in town, preferring the country to city life. Town was too constricting for them, with its corsets and commandments and courtesy. It did not fit them, but it fit Tobias like a perfectly tailored coat.

He loved the Roman statuary, the cobblestones, carriages,

Corinthian columns, and shining gas lamps. He loved the restraint and the constancy, and the rules of proper behavior that made everything simpler. The Thames stank, but it always stank. It, too, was reliable, in its own way.

His mother's country house might smell like beeswax candles and the pine branches his little sister insisted on hanging everywhere, but it was disorganized and chaotic. No one else seemed to mind. They liked dog fur on the furniture, muddy boots in the foyer, and half the chandeliers' crystals cracked from the relentless wind whipping through the constantly open windows. Sometimes, Tobias thought they may as well live in the forest, which he supposed was the point.

He preferred his feather mattress and a valet who knew the intrinsic worth of a properly knotted cravat.

Cormac snorted, well aware of Tobias's family secrets and preferences. "I heard your brother is still running with a bad crowd."

A muscle twitched in Tobias's jaw but all he said was, "Yes."

"Do you remember those goblin brothers?" Cormac grinned.

Tobias smiled back, despite himself. "You mean the ones who drank so much black ale they grew black witch fungus and had to be packed in salt for three days?"

"As I recall, it was you who trapped them in that barrel of ale in the first place."

"Only because they—" Tobias glanced up sharply.

Cormac recognized the look. "Have you found something?"

He frowned, shaking his head. "I'm not sure." Rain pattered down, spotting the pavement. "Too faint to be sure."

Uncontrolled magic scratched at Tobias's inner wards, and he pushed back until sweat glistened on his forehead. Denying his inherited magic was proving more and more difficult. Claws scraped him raw on the inside.

Cormac slanted him a knowing glance. "You can't keep doing this to yourself," he said. "And for what?" Having no magic of his own in a powerful witching family, he couldn't understand why Tobias refused to give in to his lineage. They argued over it at length. Especially as it might have saved his life the night the Sisters first attacked. Tobias thought the opposite: the added burst of magic might have made them strong enough to kill Cormac.

"I'm fine," Tobias said. He sounded cold and unemotional. It had taken him years to be able to speak at all when the wolf woke. Control was a finely hewn sword. "It's gone now at any rate."

Greymalkin House sat in gloom across the street, the garden choked with weeds and windows grimy with dust. It had sat empty and derelict for decades, unseen to all but witching folk. Malevolent magic still pulsed within, leaking out tendrils of anger, despair, and sorrow. The Keepers set to watch it day and night always came away in need of saltwater baths and purifying sage smoke.

Footsteps sounded behind them as one of those Keepers emerged from a concealing tree. Cormac turned his head, his expression dangerously bland.

"I thought you were meant to be watching the house, Virgil," Tobias said mildly, knowing Cormac wouldn't be able to say anything mild at all. Virgil took too much delight in antagonizing him.

"I was watching it." He flicked imaginary dust off his cuff. "Some of us not only have magic, we also have the good sense to get out of the rain." He nodded pointedly to Cormac's wet hair.

"And some of us take pride in our work," Tobias said coldly. "Regardless of the weather."

Virgil's smile turned ingratiating. No wonder Tobias spent so much time convincing Cormac not to punch him. "Of course, Killingsworth. No one denies you're an ace Keeper. Especially considering Cormac's dead weight you have to drag about. Don't know why they keep you on, Cormac. You're useless without magic."

Tobias looked down his nose disdainfully, knowing it infuriated Virgil. "Your intolerance is rather gauche, Virgil. Perhaps you ought to carry on with your duties."

He sniffed, bowing sharply. As a viscount in line to inherit an earldom, Tobias outranked Virgil both in the Order and in regular London society. "As you say. I'll continue my rounds."

Tobias frowned. "Did you see how dilated his pupils were?" he said to Cormac when Virgil had walked stiffly away. "I haven't seen eyes like that since my brother stumbled into that opium den. We'll have to keep an eye on him."

Cormac glared down the street after him. "I intend to."

When a howl ululated across the foggy London streets, Tobias swore. There was a long pause of silence before a dog nearby began to bark fearfully. "Not exactly subtle," Cormac remarked.

"People will assume it's a dog." Tobias said wryly. "There are no wolves in England, of course."

"Of course," Cormac returned, equally wry.

The answering howl was piercing.

And much, much closer.

"That one came from the park." Tobias dashed across the street, narrowly avoiding two horses pulling a cart piled with empty bottles. Hyde Park was dark as an ink blot and full of whispering leaves and animals.

Not just animals. Wolves.

There was a crunch of bones as someone shifted into wolf form and the bark of wolf to wolf, messages howled from the other side of London. Tobias broke through the trees, rabbits and mice fleeing at his approach. His nostrils flared as he cataloged the layers of scent on the night wind: lilac, earth, a badger's den, iron, musk, wolf.

Not just any wolf.

His brother.

"Ky's here," he told Cormac.

"Bloody hell," he replied wearily, knowing exactly where this was headed.

Tobias melted into the shadows, assessing which direction the pack was going. He circled an oak and crouched low in a blackberry thicket, viciously controlling his inner wolf, who longed to join the others.

Moonlight fell through the leaves as they approached, glinting off sharp teeth and the whites of too-human eyes. Tobias knew perfectly well his brother was at the front. There were at least four of them, possibly five. He heard the snap of twigs, the panting breaths. The first wolf to turn the bend and charge into view was tawny, with a patch of white on his chest. His long strides ate up the ground until he could have been flying.

Tobias lunged out of the bushes. He stabbed his walking stick into the ground at a sharp angle. Startled, the wolf didn't have time to alter his course. His legs splayed, scraping through mud. He slid sideways and somersaulted.

The rest of the pack charged at Tobias and Cormac, growling. They stood shoulder to shoulder, with the wolves circling. Ky sprawled on the ground, cursing viciously as he completed the shift back to human form. He had dark blond hair, a well-defined jaw, and not a stitch of clothing.

"What the hell, Tobias?" He spat leaves and rolled to his feet.

As the wolves pressed closer, a young boy, fourteen at most, stumbled into the clearing, dropping a pack with a greatcoat pulled through the straps at Ky's feet. He had three more packs slung over his shoulders and across his back. He still had pimples on his chin, and he was as thin as a sapling under his shirt.

"Isn't he a little young to be a Carnyx?" Tobias asked. Carnyx were named after the Celtic war trumpet used to instigate fear in the enemy. The group protected the packs from Wolfcatchers and hunters, and occasionally they protected other shifters as well.

The boy pulled himself up proudly. "I'm in training."

"You carry their things."

"For which we're grateful," Cormac cut in with his charming smile. "I, for one, am quite relieved not to have these ugly sots roaming naked through the streets." Clothes were not forgiving, and shifting between forms usually resulted in a naked human.

"We were answering a warning call before you interrupted us, big brother." Ky fumed. "I'm sure you heard it."

"I did." By contrast, there was no inflection in Tobias's voice.

"Some of us don't ignore our brothers," Ky sneered. One of the wolves gave a yip like a laugh.

Tobias kicked his pack over. "Get dressed, little brother. And let the Order handle it."

Scowling, Ky shrugged on a pair of breeches with a belt hung with daggers and pouches. "The Order has no business dealing in wolf matters."

"You have no way of knowing if this is a wolf matter," he pointed out with cool and precise patience. "You just want an excuse to run wild, and you're too old to indulge in theatrics, Ky. Now call off your mongrels," he added when one of the wolves snapped at Cormac, hackles raised. "You know as well as I do that Cormac isn't a threat."

Ky nodded to the suspicious wolf. "He's right." The wolf backed off but didn't shift back to human.

"Are you mad to shift?" Tobias snapped coldly. "Anyone could have seen you."

"In the park?" Ky scoffed. "And at night? I doubt it."

"You know better."

"I won't be shackled like a lapdog, Tobias," he said. "I'm not afraid of what I am. Unlike you."

"You're a fool, Ky."

"And you're a coward."

The air fairly sizzled. Barely leashed magic sparked between them like static electricity.

"As a Keeper, investigating these matters is what I do, *little brother*." The brothers were nearly nose to nose.

"By turning your back on your wolf," Ky returned, "*old man*."

"Lawless family reunions are always so pleasant," Cormac said lightly to the boy holding the packs, who cringed, turning his body sideways in subconscious submission. Cormac glanced at Tobias, his expression deceptively casual. "Shall we carry on, Killingsworth? I don't fancy having one of these beasts piss on my boots. They're new."

Some of the tension cracked. Ky was still sneering and Tobias was cold as a marble statue, but they stepped apart. Ky stalked off, the wolves following him.

"I hate to add insult to injury"—Cormac clapped Tobias on the shoulder—"but if you mean to carry out your new orders, we have a musicale to attend."

"My mother looks as though she is longing to stab me with her fish fork," Gretchen murmured to her cousin Emma.

Candlelight gleamed on enough silver to dazzle the eye, along with plates painted with delicate blue flowers, crystal wine goblets, and the fattest pink peonies Gretchen had ever seen. They bobbed their heavy scented heads, looking as bored with the whole affair as she was. Petals drooped over dishes of veal with olives, sweetbreads, stewed celery with beetroot pancakes, asparagus, potted venison, and ratafia cakes. An enormous silver soup tureen sat in the center, handles shaped like griffins with leaping hares all along the edges. As if one wanted rabbits running through their soup.

The guests were stylish and polite; the ladies ate small morsels, and the men wore collar points, some so starched they could barely turn their heads. Conversation was a dignified murmur over the clink of silver cutlery. It was all very elegant and sophisticated.

In other words, torture, pure and simple.

Her mother, the very proper Lady Cora Wyndham, sent her another scolding glance. Even the sharp gleam of her impressive diamonds judged her.

"Emma, distract my mother. Make it rain from the chandelier or blow that ridiculous wig right off Lord Chilcott's head, won't you? Preferably right onto my mother's plate of sweetmeats."

Emma paused to consider. "Better not," she decided with a regretful grin.

Lady Worthing, their hostess and a dear friend of Gretchen's mother, rose gracefully from her chair. "Ladies, let us leave the gentlemen to their port and retire to the parlor."

Gretchen leaped up like a salmon fighting its way upstream. Her chair scraped with an indecorous groan across the parquet floor. A footman caught it before it toppled backward. As she passed, her mother rapped her across the knuckles with her fan. Hard. "Decorum, Gretchen, if you please."

She insisted on acting as though the only thing of any great importance was training her son to be an earl, marrying her daughter to an earl, and acting like the perfect wife to an earl. Gretchen's father wasn't a witch and knew nothing about the secret London Gretchen was just beginning to navigate. Her mother wanted no part of the world of witchery, even though she was born into a family steeped in magic since the fourteenth century. Even now, after her daughter and nieces defeated the Sisters, she pretended it never happened. She was more concerned that Gretchen was unfashionably tanned.

"What have you done?" her mother snapped, blocking her entry into the parlor.

"What? Nothing!" Gretchen glanced down swiftly. She was wearing a perfectly lovely silk gown that floated around her ankles. If the dress was meant to be simple and evoke classical lines, why was she forced into constrictive stays? Shouldn't she be able to breathe? Shouldn't her liver not be quite so well acquainted with her spleen?

"Your hem is *dirty*. And why were you late?" her mother asked. "You will answer me."

"I . . . um."

"Gretchen, I have been your mother your entire life. You cause more trouble than a houseful of adolescent boys." She sniffed, looking horrified. "And you reek of magic."

She winced. "It's only a little magic, *Maman*," she said in what she hoped was a soothing voice.

"It makes you a target, Gretchen," she snapped, not sounding the least bit soothed. "Surely you must realize that by now."

She wasn't wrong.

"I think we should pull you out of that school," her mother added suddenly. "You would benefit more from a proper finishing academy."

She was already pretending to attend lessons at a finishing school, instead of the Rowanstone Academy for Young Ladies. To the Beau Monde she was learning how to draw, speak French and Italian, play a harp, and embroider. In reality, she was learning the history of the witching families, how to work spells, and how to send her wolfhound-familiar out into the world. And also, sadly, embroidery. Adding hours and hours of actual curtsying, elocution, and deportment? She shuddered. "You can't be serious."

"What has magic ever done for us?" her mother asked bitterly. "Besides poison my sister's mind and divide my family?"

"I know all about Emma's mother," Gretchen said quietly. "It wasn't like that."

Lady Wyndham lifted her chin, retreating behind her customary haughty disdain. "She made her choice. And I made mine."

Gretchen wanted to say that Theodora made her choice in order to protect Emma, but her mother wouldn't understand. She'd never see past a baby born on the wrong side of the blanket, never mind to a Greymalkin warlock. "It's not that simple," she said instead.

"I'll tell you what's simple, Gretchen. Find yourself a husband before it's too late. Social power is the only real power left to a woman. Use it."

"You can't keep me from the academy," she argued. "*Maman*, I'm a Whisperer. It's already . . . uncomfortable."

"All the more reason to turn your back on that world."

"That's not an option anymore. Aunt Theodora's binding

spell wore off. I am who I am, now, *Maman*. Whether or not you approve."

She pulled away and slipped into the parlor before her mother responded. Penelope slid her arm through Gretchen's. "Do you want me to play a pirate's song?" Penelope was an accomplished singer and already famous for her performances at the pianoforte. Lady Worthing's dinner party was to be followed by the arrival of more guests for the musicale.

"Tempting, but my mother would smack you with more than her fan," Gretchen said.

"She didn't even notice last time." Penelope grinned.

"Girls," Lady Wyndham snapped from the doorway. "Mingle!"

"Honestly, my mother should work for the Order. She's worse than a Keeper when it comes to tracking. I'm starting to feel like a wounded deer."

Emma snorted, joining them. "Try having antlers on your head."

"I thought One-Eyed Joe gave you a cameo for that very purpose," Gretchen said as they wandered farther into the drawing room.

"Your mother made me take it off before we went in for supper. She said it wasn't appropriate evening wear." She grinned. "I told her neither were antlers, and then she got all quiet and scary so I worked the Fith-Fath glamour to hide them myself."

The end of the room was cleared of furniture except for rows of chairs facing the pianoforte and harp in one corner. Beeswax candles dripped in silver candelabrums and sconces set

into the cream-colored walls. The ceiling was a mosaic of frol-
icking lambs and rosy-cheeked cherubs. "Gah," Penelope said,
when she glanced up. "That's ghastly."

"Why are there so many moths about?" Gretchen fanned
one away from her face.

"It's been a bad spring for them," Emma agreed. "My windows are covered at night."

"Insects in the drawing room." Gretchen grinned. "My mother
will turn rabid."

It was another half hour before the men joined the party in
the drawing room. The other guests trickled in, trailing the
scents of rain and the yellow London fog pressing at the windows. When Cormac, Viscount Blackburn, arrived, Penelope
glanced at Emma. "If you and Cormac are still trying to pretend you barely know each other, you should probably stop
looking at each other like that," she pointed out. "Not to mention, you're in very great danger of setting the carpet on fire.
I'm positively blushing."

"You are not," Emma said, though her own cheeks were
pink. She looked away. Cormac and his friend crossed the room
to greet their hosts.

"Who's that with him?" Gretchen wondered. The tall blond
man looked so icy and proper, she felt an instant need to wrinkle
him. His cravat was white and spotless; it may as well have been
made out of snow. Despite the chiseled Grecian-statue perfec-
tion of his features, there was something slightly dangerous
about him.

"That's Tobias Lawless," Penelope said, her long black curls sweeping over her shoulder as she tried to turn subtly on one heel to get a better look at him. "He took off his jacket the night of the fire at the Pickford ball, remember?"

"No," Gretchen said crisply. His blue eyes snapped onto hers as if he had heard her. The blasted man was looking down his nose at her. "I don't." He looked away dismissively. That was even worse.

"Pity." Penelope gave a little sigh. "He has lovely shoulders."

"You're incorrigible." Emma grinned, nudging her.

"My mother says the human body is a beautiful miracle to be appreciated."

"My mother says the physical body is something a lady ignores." Gretchen rolled her eyes. "Of course she only says that when my nose is itchy or I'm starving for cake."

Emma's mother, having recently turned herself into a deer, didn't say much of anything at all.

"Why is he staring at us?" Gretchen grumbled. "Surely he's seen the Lovegrove witches before."

"He's not staring at us." Penelope smirked. "He's staring at *you*."

"Don't be daft," she said, dismissing the very notion. She winked. "I haven't done anything worth staring at yet."

"And you'll keep it that way, Gretchen Thorn," her mother snapped from behind her shoulder. "Tobias Lawless, Viscount Killingsworth, is heir to the Starkwood earldom. So if he's looking at you, you'll smile prettily."

It explained why all the ladies watched him over their fans, but not why he was watching *her*.

"And he is unmarried," her mother announced in a fervent whisper best suited to declarations involving kings and kingdoms.

"Oh, mother," Gretchen groaned. She met Emma's sympathetic glance. Penelope was too busy looking curiously at Tobias.

"Lord Gilmore is also unmarried."

"He's thirty-seven!"

"And he has a duchess for a sister," her mother replied, as if it negated all arguments. "Choose, Gretchen. Or I will choose for you." She sailed away as conversation quieted and the guests were urged to take their seats.

Someone's marriageable young daughter sat at the harp and sang with the enthusiasm of a cat trapped in an icehouse. Her father eyed all the young men hungrily.

"Hide me, won't you?" a young man asked, sidling up to Penelope. He glanced imploringly at the cousins. His eyes were strikingly moss green. "He keeps staring at me with his quizzing glass. I feel as though I'm sitting exams again."

Penelope chuckled. "Are you married?"

"No."

"Then Lord Herringdale is most definitely looking at you."

"He's rather fearsome. Am I to assume that is his unmarried daughter currently abusing the harp?"

"Yes, but she's harmless."

"Good to know. And I do beg your pardon," the young man added with a bow. He was very handsome. Penelope was already starting to melt. "We haven't been properly introduced but I was feeling rather desperate. I am Lord Beauregard. And you have quite saved me, Lady . . . ?"

"Penelope Chadwick," Penelope replied. "And my cousins, Lady Emma Day and Lady Gretchen Thorn."

"I am in your debt." His brown hair tumbled over his forehead and his crooked smile was charming. He bowed again, wine sloshing over the rim of his glass. Drops splattered onto Penelope's pink gloves, staining them across the knuckles. He flushed, mortified. "I am very sorry, Lady Penelope," he apologized. "I have the manners of a beast. Please, allow me to have those cleaned for you."

Penelope only smiled. "They're only gloves, my lord. I'll have them dyed burgundy and start a new fashion."

"You are as kind as you are beautiful."

Penelope blushed. Emma and Gretchen grinned at each other behind her back, turning slightly away so as not to intrude. After a few minutes, Emma drifted away, mumbling something about tea, and Gretchen eased back into the shadows of a large potted palm tree.

By the time Penelope took her turn at the pianoforte, Gretchen had reached one of the side doors. She stepped back swiftly into the safety of the hall, narrowly avoiding knocking over a passing footman. "I'm very sorry, miss," he said, even though she was the one flying out of nowhere.

She helped him steady his tray before vanishing into the library. It was full of leather-bound books and shadows. A candle burned in the far window, and another on one of the tables. The scent of dust clung to her as she eased deeper into the comforting darkness.

She didn't hide in libraries because she was a bluestocking like Penelope, forever prattling on about poetry, but rather

because at most musicales and balls, it was the room least likely
to be occupied. Couples were more interested in stealing kisses
in conservatories, and old ladies sleeping off too much brandy
generally escaped to the parlors, which left the libraries bless-
edly abandoned.

And luckily she knew the Worthing library as well as her
own, right down to the popular novels hidden on the back shelf
by the balcony. Good thing too; just last week she'd been trapped
in the Brookfield library for hours with nothing to read but
tracts on sheep shearing and the benefits of rotation crops. She'd
fallen asleep somewhere between lentils and Egyptian onion
farming.

The contrast between fighting off the Rovers and pasting a
polite smile on her face for the single sons of earls was too stark.
Residual magic burned through her. She was surprised the air
around her didn't crackle. Her mother shouldn't begrudge her a
stolen moment in the library, not if the alternative involved
magic shooting off the ends of her hair. Hardly subtle.

Not to mention hardly marriageable material.

On second thought . . .

Better not. She'd already pushed her luck by going off with
Godric.

Egyptian onion farming it was then. She walked along the
book shelves, reading titles and glancing into the glass-fronted
cabinets displaying painted globes. It was dull and dusty and
soothing. Her witch knot stopped aching.

Until someone grabbed her arm, yanking it behind her back
and spinning her around. Her cheek pressed to the cold glass of

a curio cabinet. Pain shot up to her elbow when she tried to move. "Who are you?" a man asked, his voice quiet and cold in her ear.

"Who am *I*?" she barked back. "Who the hell are *you*?" He evaded the kick she aimed at his most sensitive parts. Her skirts wrapped around her knees, hobbling and infuriating her. He turned her roughly around.

Tobias Lawless.

She wasn't sure which of the two of them was more surprised.

Someone so chilly and perfect and wearing such a flawless cravat shouldn't be mauling ladies in dark libraries. He also shouldn't have several short iron daggers tucked inside his cutaway coat. It probably said something unsavory about her character that the sight of those daggers made her like him a bit more. But only a little bit.

"Let me go." She yanked down savagely, breaking his hold. He didn't move back, and his body continued to block her against the cabinets. The glass rattled.

"What are you doing?" He stepped closer still. She had to tilt her chin up.

"I am currently being accosted," she snapped, driving the heel of her shoe into the top of his foot. He fell back a step, growling in his throat. Growling. He really didn't seem the type.

She made a proper fist, not like the ones girls made when they hadn't practiced before. She'd already punched a Rover tonight. She was very comfortable punching Tobias, Lord Killingsworth. Eager, in fact.

"What is *wrong* with you?" she asked finally. "Are you drunk?"

"Certainly not."

She raised an eyebrow. "I'm the one being mauled and yet *you* take offense?"

"I can smell it on you," he answered, which was no answer at all. "There's no use prevaricating."

"I don't usually bother lying about perfume," she replied, now more bewildered than concerned.

"Not perfume," he ground out, as if *she* was the frustrating one. "Dark magic."

Her eyes narrowed to angry slits. "I beg your pardon."

"As you should."

She aimed for his head. It was big and fat and so perfectly groomed, how could she miss?

He caught her wrist and squeezed. Hard. He shouldn't have been fast enough.

An iron-nail pendant in the shape of a wheel slipped out from under his collar. Gretchen stared at it, then transferred her glare to his haughty, unkindly beautiful face. "I knew it." Her smile was better suited to one of the animals in the zoological gardens. "You're a bloody Keeper."

"Which is how I knew you've been playing with magic beyond your ken." He leaned in slightly. "I can smell it all over you."

"What you smell," she returned, drilling her finger into his chest until he stumbled back a step, "is some poor witch's funeral nearly ruined by a bunch of Rovers. Who the Order is meant to keep controlled, if I'm not mistaken."

And now he was *sniffing* her.

Oh, he was being very subtle about it. Some other girl might have thought he was interested in her, that he was flirting or leaning in for a kiss. But she knew better.

"*Now* what are you doing?" she asked, exasperated.

He froze. "Ascertaining the truth."

"By flaring your nostrils?" She rolled her eyes. "Honestly, does that work on all the girls? You can't gull me, Killingsworth. You're not the first Greybeard I've met." She shoved him, mostly because she could. "Now stop it."

"You're a Whisperer," Tobias said.

"So?"

"So Whisperers collect strange things for their spells. Bones and teeth and poisonous flowers. Unclean things."

"Not me," Gretchen replied grudgingly. "Though frankly, it sounds more interesting than the embroidery they keep insisting I learn. I told you, what you're smelling is Rover magic and a binding pendant. So if it's unclean, blame the Order. And if it's that noticeable, I'm going straight home for a bath."

He stretched out an arm on either side of her, caging her in. His blue eyes were very intent on her. It felt as though he were sorting through the drawers in her bedroom cabinets. She had to fight not to squirm. "I'll see you back to the drawing room," he finally murmured, apparently satisfied with whatever it was he saw there.

"I think I can manage five feet of hallway on my own; thanks all the same."

"It wasn't a request."

She crossed her arms. "And yet still I repeat, no thank you."

He looked briefly irritated. It was the most human emotion she'd seen on his face so far. "No one told you."

"Told me what? That you're mad? I've figured that out all by myself."

He looked down the length of his patrician nose. "That I was sent to watch you."

She listened for the buzzing sound that told her a spell wasn't working and, incidentally, when someone was lying to her. There was nothing but their breath in the quiet room and the faint strains of the harp from the parlor.

"For your protection," he added.

The buzzing was so loud it was like a slap to the face.

He was lying now.

Whatever he was doing, it had nothing to do with her protection.

Chapter 3

Returning to the Rowanstone Academy instead of her father's townhouse a few streets away still felt strange to Emma.

Though in all honesty, she preferred it.

She liked walking through the front door with the other girls who had attended the musicale, even if few of them spoke to her. They'd grown accustomed to the sight of her antlers, but not to the fact that she'd been inside Greymalkin House.

Still, she loved the academy—from the grand staircase carved with rowan leaves and berries to the long draughty upstairs hallway to the ballroom full of dents and marks from spell class. She was rather proud of the new burns in the floor from the ghoul she'd dispatched with lightning just a few weeks ago. All of it, down to the apothecary closet with its odd collection of flowers, crystals, animal teeth, feathers, and holed stones was more welcoming than her father's opulent and empty house.

The gleaming marble, crystal vases, and gilded table settings couldn't disguise the fact that Emma had regularly gone days without saying a single word beyond "thank you" to the servants, who were not permitted to reply.

She slipped a leg over the windowsill, scooting down to her favorite part of the roof. A moth floated past her, denied the tempting light. She lay back on the shingles and the clouds directly above thinned to reveal a scatter of stars. One street over, rain pelted the gardens and hissed at the torches. There were certain advantages to her particular magical gifts.

There was a sound behind her, and then Cormac blocked the stars for a brief moment before he sat down at her side. He put a finger to his lips before she said a word. He pulled two charms out of his jacket pocket, one shaped like an ear, the other round as a marble and painted to resemble an eye. He placed them on the shingles and smashed them with the side of his fist. She felt, rather than saw, the magic billow around them. It was like sitting in a pocket of mist, except she could still see the sky. One of the nearby gargoyles made a small sound, like a sneeze.

"No one can see us or hear us now," he said. "Not even the Keeper they've assigned to watch you."

"Not you, then?" she asked, disappointed but not surprised.

"Virgil," Cormac replied, jaw clenching. Emma winced. They'd hated each other since their school days, and Emma knew perfectly well Virgil wouldn't hesitate to use her against Cormac if he suspected their attachment. It was that much more vital that they keep each other secret.

"Well, he's not very bright," Emma said lightly. "So I'm not too worried."

A smiled flickered at the corner of his mouth before he went serious again. "But he's ambitious," he said. "So have a care."

She slipped her hand into his, their fingers entwining. She smiled shyly. His dark hair tumbled over his forehead as he turned his head toward her, willing to be distracted. "It was torture being so near you all evening and yet so far," he said hoarsely.

She met his eyes and tried not to blush. A normal girl would have known what came next: Cormac would court her with rides in Hyde Park and stolen kisses in ballroom gardens. He would eventually ask to speak to her father, and they would marry by special license one morning at St. James Church, where her own parents were wed.

But she wasn't a normal girl. Not anymore. She was a witch with a family secret that could get her banished from society or trapped inside a witch bottle. Cormac reached out to smooth the frown lines between her eyebrows. "You think too hard." She didn't disagree. He half smiled. "And you worry too much."

"Perhaps," she allowed. "You're taking an awful risk."

"It's worth it." His hands closed around her shoulders, bared by her evening gown.

"But I'm technically a Greymalkin," she said, whispering even though she knew the charms shielded them. "You've worked so hard to prove yourself to the Order. I could undo it all."

"Then it wasn't worth doing." He sounded very sure of

himself. He raised an eyebrow, drawing back slightly. "Have you changed your mind, Emma?"

"No, of course not."

"Then nothing else matters."

He kissed her; his lips were warm and clever. She leaned into him, kissing him back until his fingers tightened in her hair. He eased her back onto the shingles and the rest of London disappeared. When his tongue touched hers, the entire world vanished. She felt as if she were floating away or falling, she couldn't be sure. She gripped his coat to hold on. His breath was hot and ragged in her ear, sending delicate shivers down her neck and over her collarbone.

They could finally lose themselves to each other. She could let go of the Order's surveillance, the worry over her father in the Underworld, her mother in the forest. Cormac could put aside the lack of magic burning inside him, the lies he told the Order daily, and the fear that it wasn't enough to protect her.

For a little while, it was only two mouths and two bodies and a certain singing in the blood. His hand was at her waist and his leg pressed along hers when the rain started to fall. Within moments the sprinkle turned to cold, fat drops that pelted them. By the time they'd dashed to the relative cover of the attic window gable, they were already soaked through. They laughed, wiping water off their faces.

Emma felt her hair come down out of its chignon. She wrinkled her nose. "Sorry about that." Cormac grinned. She fought another blush. They both knew it was raining because she'd gotten carried away by his kisses. It still proved difficult to control her magic sometimes.

He tossed his damp hair off his face. His cravat was wilted around his neck, so he yanked it off, revealing a slice of bare skin. "I have to go anyway," he said. "I'm due back at Greymalkin House."

"I'm sorry about the rain," she said. "You'll have a miserable night now. Have you found anything?"

He shook his head, bewildered. "Nothing at all. The house hasn't changed."

She suppressed a shiver that had nothing to do with her wet dress. His arm slid around her shoulder, and though his touch was gentle and protective, his voice had an edge of bitterness. "I should have been able to protect you."

"You were the reason the Lacrimarium's witch bottle didn't trap me the way it trapped the Sisters." She had nightmares about it sometimes. "You did more than even the First Legate could." All without magic of his own. She didn't have to say it.

Cormac didn't look convinced. She knew it took great effort for him to smooth his scowl and smile his most charming smile. It was the same one he used on countless girls and women. She didn't smile back. "Don't," she said softly.

He didn't pretend to misunderstand. "I'll find a way to protect you, Emma."

She watched him disappear into the dusty darkness of the attic, rain dripping off her antlers. "And I'll find a way to protect *you*," she promised quietly.

Later that night she woke to find the bedroom floor inches from her nose. Her palms stung and she'd wrenched her left knee. The nightmare was particularly violent, and she'd evidently flung herself clear out of bed.

She pushed herself into a sitting position, her heart beating in her chest like thunder trapped in a bell jar. She lit a candle with trembling fingers, reminding herself that she was safe in her chambers at the academy. Her fingernails were blue and her teeth chattered, recalling with perfect clarity the searing cold of the Greymalkin Sisters.

In her dreams, she was back in the Greymalkin House or running barefoot through London while birds dropped dead from the sky. Always the Sisters stalked her, ice spreading from them as inexorably as spilled ink on paper. They reached for her and no matter how fast she ran, it was never fast enough.

And when she was lucky enough to dream about something else, she dreamed of her father. Ewan Greenwood, banished to wander the Underworld, never reaching the Blessed Isles, where the dead met their loved ones. The Order's spelled arrow robbed him of that basic right, and it filled Emma with the kind of black sorrow that woke her with tears on her cheeks instead of the perspiration of fear.

She wrapped her blanket around her shoulders against the cold still trapped in her bones. She couldn't do much about the nightmares of the Sisters, but she could do something about Ewan. She had to find a way to save him. He'd sacrificed himself to help close the last portal and he shouldn't be punished for it. Not to mention that he'd been killed and banished in the first place all because of his mother's last name, not any crime of his own.

It wasn't right.

And she knew full well the same would happen to her if anyone in the Order discovered her secret. They already suspected her and her cousins because of their presence at the Greymalkin House the night the Sisters were defeated, but they had no actual proof.

She pulled out books she'd borrowed from the school library and hidden in the chest at the foot of her bed. They were all on the same subjects: the Underworld, portals, the Sisters.

She didn't know how but she was going to find a way to reverse Ewan's banishment if it took her decades to do it. She couldn't save her mother from her own madness, couldn't even find her now that she'd turned herself into a deer, but she would damn well find a way to get Ewan out of the Underworld.

No matter what it took.

When Gretchen stepped out of her house the next morning, Tobias was waiting on the front step.

The dark blue of his coat and the stark white of his cravat made his pale eyes even more arresting. His cheekbones were as aristocratic as his impressive family lineage, but the shape of his lips was wicked. Too wicked to belong to such a proper lord. He was too handsome for his own good. She scowled at him. He didn't even have the decency to scowl back, only bowed crisply and politely.

"What are you doing here?" she demanded.

"I am escorting you to the academy, of course," he replied neutrally, though his eyes glittered.

"I have my own carriage." She crossed her arms, thoroughly vexed. "Go away, Tobias."

"I rather think not." He leaned in close, so close she smelled the soap on his skin and could see the curl of hair that refused to stay pinned under his hat. It was endearing. *Irritating*. She meant *irritating*, of course.

And just when she wondered how close he intended to get, he reached around her to push the door open. "Please tell Lady Wyndham that Viscount Killingsworth is here," he said to the butler.

"What are you doing now?" Gretchen whispered, aghast. "You can't talk to my mother."

She was trying to forcibly drag Tobias to his carriage when her mother's heels clicked on the marble of the foyer. "Gretchen, stop that immediately."

Gretchen groaned. "I'll get you for this," she muttered to Tobias under her breath. She swore he was fighting back a smile. *Now* he chose to smile.

He bowed to her mother. She inclined her head. "Lord Killingsworth."

"I wonder if I might beg the honor of escorting Lady Gretchen to the academy this morning."

Gretchen smirked. Her mother would never agree. It was too scandalous.

"I've brought my open-top barouche and it's a fine day," he continued smoothly.

Gretchen's smile died. That was far less scandalous. Anyone could see them. The gossips would launch into a frenzy, but there were no indiscretions possible in such a vehicle in town.

Her mother looked pleased. It was clear if she could have stuffed Gretchen into a wedding gown and shoved her at the poor man, she would have. "Certainly, you may."

Gretchen wondered what magic was good for, if not to create a hole big enough to hide in.

"I've already summoned the carriage," she said, even though she knew full well the attempt was futile.

"Don't be silly, Gretchen," her mother said sharply. "You'll go with Lord Killingsworth. He is showing you great favor."

Tobias offered her his arm. Gretchen took it, afraid her mother might actually chain her in the cellar if she refused. "You know, he's only doing this because the Order has set him on me," she said.

Her mother pursed her lips. That was never a good sign. "Let's go," Gretchen added, dragging Tobias down the steps. Her only comfort was that he would suffer as much as she. He clearly didn't like her; his face got all pinched and haughty whenever he even glanced her way. At least his barouche was well sprung and he handled his horses well, urging them to go faster than she'd have assumed he was comfortable with.

Once they reached the school, she stepped down without waiting for his help and hurried away, not waiting to see if he followed. She found everyone gathered in the back where the gates between the gardens of the Rowanstone Academy for Young Ladies and the Ironstone Academy for Young Men were opened to create one large open space. Students from both academies flooded onto the lawn, eager for the demonstration. Gretchen remembered Mrs. Sparrow saying something about the Order and a traditional tournament. She'd love to get her hands on a lance.

She found Penelope and Emma under an ash tree. "It's so romantic," Penelope said, standing on her tiptoes to get a better glimpse of the older male students waiting in the circle of stones. "Like a tournament out of a King Arthur story. But I do wish Cedric could see this," she added. "It's dreadfully unfair that he's left out of everything just because he's the grandson of a coachman."

Gretchen and Emma exchanged a knowing glance behind her back as they wound through the crowd. "There's Godric." She pointed to her brother, sprawled on a marble bench. She marched through the girls floating on satin slippers. Her riding boots made a satisfying slapping sound on the flagstones. Godric's eyes were only half-glazed, and he smelled like cologne instead of wine. She tilted her head. "Is that a bird in your pocket?"

He adjusted his coat hastily. There was a strange flutter and a flash of cream-colored parchment. "No. It's nothing."

The cousins advanced as one, smiling. His gaze darted back and forth, but when he realized rescue wasn't forthcoming, he sighed. "Stop it."

"Not a chance," Gretchen said cheerfully.

"It's a poem," he mumbled. "Folded into the shape of a bird. I'm trying to spell the paper to fly."

She climbed up to sit on the back of the bench beside him. "You're trying to send it to Moira, aren't you?"

His ears went red.

"Let me read it," Penelope insisted.

He snorted. "Not in this lifetime or any other."

She pouted. "Why not? I love poetry."

"Yes, and you're vicious in your opinions." He folded his arms protectively over his pockets.

A bell rang loudly before they could tease him any further. The sound shivered through the spring gardens, silencing the students. Mrs. Sparrow stepped onto the lawn, next to the headmaster of the Ironstone Academy. He was handsome enough to have most of the girls sighing. Penelope fluttered until Gretchen pinched her.

"Welcome, students," Mrs. Sparrow said. She didn't raise her voice but no one dared talk over her. "As you know, the Order has recently closed several gates to the Underworld and banished and bottled the three Greymalkin Sisters."

"The Order didn't bottle them," Gretchen felt the need to mutter. "Emma did."

"The kind of magic the Greymalkin family deals in draws only the most restless and hungry of spirits," Mrs. Sparrow continued. "As such, spells and wards may be particularly volatile. The Order will, of course, maintain your security, but you must be on your guard."

A Keeper standing next to the headmaster frowned. Gretchen felt certain Mrs. Sparrow was advised not to worry her girls.

"And as you no doubt also know, every summer we hold a demonstration of the Ironstone graduates for the Order to assess where they might be most helpful. After recent events, Mr. Whitehall has decided to have his students exhibit some of their skills to better reassure you of your safety."

"How's that going to make us feel safer?" Gretchen whispered, disgusted. "Do you know what would make us feel safer? Learning to do all of those things *ourselves*."

"You can take my place," Godric muttered. "I beg you."

The lawn cleared and two students stepped into the ring created by stones and students. One held an energy shield so well spelled it looked real, except for its faint blue glow. His opponent held a dagger made entirely of iron nails.

"Oliver Blake and Finnegan something-or-other," Godric told the cousins.

"Lady Daphne, if you please," Miss Hopewell, one of the teachers, called out. Daphne stepped into the circle, graceful in a dress edged with pearl embroidery. Her hair shone like honey.

"As Rowanstone's top student, Lady Daphne will play the part of the damsel in distress," Mr. Whitehall announced.

Gretchen huffed. "If she's the top student, shouldn't she be fighting?"

"That's not what Rowanstone girls do," Olwen, one of Cormac's sisters, murmured from the other side of the tree. Gretchen stood up on the bench, looking thoughtful.

Penelope groaned. "I wish you hadn't said that, Olwen."

The mock battle began before Gretchen could hurl herself into it. Oliver was charged with defending Daphne, who had draped herself artfully over a nearby statue of Hercules. Finnegan attacked with elf-bolts he created out of nothing at all. They slammed into Oliver's shield like wasps. Oliver grinned when some of the girls shouted encouragement.

Finnegan prowled the lawn. He threw a smoke bomb, which made everyone cough. Oliver pierced through it by gathering the light from the torches and focusing it like a sunbeam. Finnegan retaliated with whips of fire. Oliver stumbled to one knee. Someone gasped loudly.

Finnegan flung his dagger. It came apart as it whirled toward Oliver, sending iron nails flying like arrows. They left a trail of blue sparks and the smell of burning apples.

Oliver threw his shield up to take the brunt of the attack. He spun around, clasping Daphne around the waist and depositing her safely behind the statue. The iron nails not already embedded in the shield targeted them. Oliver blocked, flinging his hand up. The nails hovered, vibrating for a long, quiet moment. The invisible wards he'd raised held strong. The nails clattered harmlessly to the ground and applause erupted.

Oliver and Finnegan shook hands and bowed. Daphne curtsied. Gretchen made rude noises.

Once the applause faded, poppets of birds were tossed into the air, animated with magic. They flew fast and erratic, purple-and-blue sparks shooting from their feathers. They dove, pecking at the Ironstone students standing in a row and the girls clustered behind them.

The Ironstone boys showed off their aim and skill one at a time. The first used a slingshot, whipping a charm shaped like a glass marble at the nearest poppet. He clipped its wings and it plummeted, spinning. When it hit the ground, it dissolved into rose petals.

The second student used an iron-wheel pendant, looping it

around the neck of a poppet. He tugged and it fell, catching fire as it went down. His feat was followed by elf-bolts, levitating pebbles, and fiery Catherine wheels. Familiars darted in and out of the melee. There were three cats, two toads, a heron, a fox, a rabbit, and a hummingbird.

The poppets vanished one by one, until all that was left was a wolf made entirely of magical energy. It prowled the circle, dodging a combination of charms, amulets, and a spell in the shape of a goblin. Magic crackled and sizzled like fireworks. The wolf was faster than all of the amulets combined, dodging between them, blurring white as the tail of a comet.

He wasn't faster than a bullet.

It tore through him and he fell apart in a flurry of stuffing and thread. Everyone swiveled, trying to find who had done it. The Ironstone boys gaped at one another.

Gretchen stood on the bench, her brother's pistol in her hand and a cocky smirk on her face. She bowed theatrically. There was a lot of blinking and a smattering of applause.

Unfazed, Godric reached up to reclaim his pistol. "Give me that." He snatched it out of her hands, but he was grinning the same smug grin as she was. He'd taught her to shoot, after all.

Magic sparked in the air as the remains of the wolf smoldered. Tobias stepped forward and snapped, "*Finis.*" The magical traces vanished until only smoke remained.

"Thank you, Lady Gretchen," Mrs. Sparrow said. "That was very proactive of you." She didn't sound angry. In fact, she rather sounded as though she was trying not to laugh. She nodded once at the students. "You are dismissed."

They dispersed, whispering frantically to one another. A blistering kind of excitement went through them the farther they got from the scorched lawn. Groups clustered together, taking advantage of the proximity of the students from the other school.

"I didn't know you could shoot like that," Olwen said. "Does Colette know?" she asked, referring to one of her sisters.

"I don't know. Isn't she here?"

"No, she was expelled before Christmas."

"What for?"

"That was a crack shot," Finnegan interrupted, elbowing his way through the crowd toward them. "Well done." Gretchen offered him her most feminine curtsy. He chuckled. "If they'd let you join the army, old Bonaparte would be dead by now."

"That's the nicest thing anyone's ever said to me." She beamed at him.

"You shouldn't encourage her," Tobias interrupted frostily from behind her left shoulder. "Pistols are useless in most magical battles. And that kind of recklessness is dangerous."

"And *that's* the most *boring* thing anyone's ever said to me," Gretchen said. "We're not all damsels in distress waiting to be rescued, my lord," she added scathingly. "And since I'm on school grounds, I don't believe your spying services, or your opinions, are currently required."

"The Order set you to watch her?" she heard Olwen ask as she stomped away. "Have they completely lost their minds?"

• • •

Gretchen had stabbed herself in the finger more times than she cared to count. Embroidery ought to be classified as blood magic, she thought. The white handkerchief on which she was attempting to replicate a passable witch knot was hopelessly spotted with blood. She poked herself again when the needle stuck in a tangle and she yanked too hard.

Miss Teasdale looked up from her flawless rendition of Aphrodite emerging from a clam shell. She made it look easy. And she never smeared her threads with blood. "Gretchen, not again. You must be gentle." Her eyes were the eyes of a wounded rabbit, wide, dark, and bewildered. Gretchen may as well have stabbed her, as mangled her embroidery.

She abandoned the handkerchief to pace. Miss Teasdale's parlor was famous for its calming effect. The soft carpets were the color of soothing mint tea. Everything was pretty and perfect, designed to uplift and encourage genteel instruction. Gretchen was a feral dog among perfumed poodles.

Two younger girls sat under the window, peacefully working at their sewing. They never cast longing glances outside. Gretchen's familiar was already out on the lawn, racing in happy circles. The ache to join him was physically painful.

"Can't I learn ax throwing?" she asked, turning her evil-eye ring around and around her finger. "Or archery?"

"Those aren't necessary arts for a Whisperer," Miss Teasdale replied as Mrs. Sparrow strode into the drawing room. Her white-streaked black hair was in its customary bun. "You need to learn all aspects of spellwork first. How else will you be able to create your spells?"

"Instinct."

"Instinct is for animals, dear," Miss Teasdale replied. "You're a lady."

Mrs. Sparrow glanced at Gretchen's clenched fists and the decidedly unladylike turn of her mouth. "Hmm. Even ladies require exercise," she said. "Come with me, Gretchen. Let us take a walk."

Gretchen all but ran from the room. She didn't care if Mrs. Sparrow scolded her, as long as she did so without a needle and thread in her hands. They crossed the stones to follow the path around the fountain. Peonies bloomed all around them.

"Whisperers are very rare," Mrs. Sparrow said. She didn't sound particularly cross.

"Yes," Gretchen replied, mostly because she felt she ought to say something.

"There have only ever been two Whisperers at this academy," she continued. "While the boy's school has had five Whisperers. And they feel quite superior over it." Now she sounded cross.

Gretchen felt the fire of indignation before she realized the headmistress had expected it. "Well done, Mrs. Sparrow," she said with reluctant admiration. Even knowing she was being manipulated didn't take away her desire to prove herself as good, if not better, than any Ironstone student. Past or present. Especially past. And especially if that student was named Tobias Lawless.

"What happened to them?" she asked. "Are they still here at the school?"

"One is in her first year. She's barely thirteen years old."

"And the other?" she asked as they came to the life-sized statue of Hecate, bronze dogs straining at her leashes.

"She went mad."

Gretchen came to a halt. "What? No one ever told me that!"

"She couldn't cope with the buzzing. It built and built until it was all she heard. Her family took her to a secluded Scottish island, but it was too late to regain all of her faculties, I'm afraid."

Gretchen sat down on the marble bench. She thought of Emma's mother, mad in the woods. "Does it seem to you that there's an awful lot of mad witches about?"

"Everything has a price," Mrs. Sparrow replied. "Especially power."

"Even yours?" she asked. "I should dearly love to be able to put my mother magically to sleep every time she mentions finding me a husband."

"For every moment of sleep I conjure on another, that same sleep is stolen from me. It becomes . . . uncomfortable. Magic is never to be taken lightly," Mrs. Sparrow added. "It's a force. And like a wild horse, if you don't tame it, it will trample you to death."

Gretchen blinked. "That's hardly an inspiring speech."

Mrs. Sparrow smiled briefly. "You don't need soft words, Gretchen. You need truth."

"Whispering used to be just another word for spellcasting," she continued. "To the untrained eye, a witch reciting a spell looked like she was muttering to herself. After a few years of being hanged or burned at the stake for it, we learned subtlety," she said wryly. "But Whisperers such as yourself can still hear those spells being cast. That's what the terrible sound you hear is. Hundreds of witches over hundreds of years all casting their spells at the same time."

"That explains why it makes me feel so odd," Gretchen said. It didn't feel any less odd to think that she was hearing voices of dead witches. No wonder Godric drank so much.

"Yes, but with discipline, you can focus on the spell you need. At the very least, you'll be able to quiet the thunder to an actual whisper."

"I didn't know that," Gretchen murmured. To be fair, she hadn't thrown herself into learning the history of the witching world like Emma had.

Mrs. Sparrow led them back inside to her personal study. The shelves were stuffed with books and jars of evil-eye rings and rowan berries and was far less tidy than expected. The desk was sturdy and simple, nothing like the scrolled and gilded desk her mother preferred, with its curved legs and gold-leaf accents. Mrs. Sparrow did not sit down. Instead, she picked up a worn leather-bound journal the size of folded letter paper.

"I think you should have this," she said, handing it to Gretchen.

The leather cover was faded and soft and the pages were thick, uneven parchment. Some were stitched with red thread; one had a silver triangular cap on one corner from which hung a tiny bell. When she opened the book, a pressed violet drifted to the carpet. "It's beautiful," she murmured. And it was, in its own tattered way. Someone had loved this book until the bindings were reinforced with gold thread. "What is it?"

"It's a grimoire," the headmistress replied. The sun fell through the window beside them, falling on the white streak at her temple. The rest of her hair was so black it absorbed the light. "It's a magical journal," she elaborated. "Full of spells and bits of folklore. Most families have one they pass down through the generations."

Gretchen looked up from the book. "Is there a Lovegrove grimoire?"

Mrs. Sparrow shook her head. "Your aunt told the Order that Theodora Lovegrove burned it."

That Emma's mother had destroyed a family heirloom stuffed with priceless magic gathered over centuries in one of her mad fits was no surprise at all. Still, it was disappointing.

"I found this one in a bookshop in the goblin markets. I don't know who it belonged to, but the information is sound. If you study and memorize the uses of plants and stones and colors, it will make it much easier to identify the kinds of words you should be listening to when the witches whisper spells in your head."

The pages were the color of tea, with ink that was faded but still legible. Sketches of tree leaves and flowers, and rhymes written in a sweeping hand, crowded next to lists of colors, stones, and herbs and their attributes. There was a drawing illustrating how to gather Saint-John's-wort on Midsummer Night and a rhyme about mullein leaves, and hundreds of symbols and sigils. Gretchen felt a bubble of excitement in her chest. She might not love studying, but she did love having a purpose, a way to stand up to the pressure of this new magical world that threatened at any moment to sweep her and her cousins away. The sting of the embroidery needle's pinpricks on her fingertips suddenly felt like battle scars.

"The other side of your gift is what allows you to create new spells," Mrs. Sparrow told her. "Witches are always attempting them, with various degrees of success and no small danger. But as a Whisperer, you'll be able to hear what others have done."

"Is that why it goes silent when I've found something that works?"

"Yes, the spell memories fall away because you don't need them. Creating spells requires many elements: symbols, harvesting flowers and plants at the proper hour, the alignment of planets, the theory of colors, and so on. A good deal of which you will find in that grimoire."

"I really am dismal at sewing though," Gretchen admitted.

"You're dismal because you don't take it seriously," Mrs. Sparrow replied blandly. "You refuse to practice. But knowing what you know now, does a little embroidery still seem like such a hardship?"

"I suppose not."

"Don't fight your own self." The headmistress looked sad for a moment. "It's a battle you'll never win."

Gretchen tilted her head. "Can I still fight the lads of Ironstone?"

Mrs. Sparrow smiled. "In fact, I would consider it a great personal favor."

Chapter 4

"Do you think these flowers make me look like Ophelia?" Penelope asked hopefully as she added another peony into her chignon. Pearl-tipped pins and a garden's worth of flowers secured her dark curls. She stood in front of the looking glass in a rose-colored gown, frowning thoughtfully at her reflection. She had the only parents in London who didn't care if she rejected the fashionable white of the proper debutante.

"You are aware that Ophelia drowned, aren't you?" Emma teased her. Her slender antlers curved elegantly from her red hair, which was braided around them.

"It's romantic," Penelope insisted. Glowing spiders crawled over her hem, but she studiously avoided looking at them.

"It's soggy," Gretchen said. "And ridiculous. Tossing yourself away for some moody git," she scoffed.

"You simply have no poetry in your soul," Penelope returned

with all the offended dignity of a wounded reader. She adjusted
the rose tucked into the wide ribbon tied under her breasts. "I
hope Lucius is there."

Gretchen raised an eyebrow. "It's Lucius, now, is it? Since
when are you on a first name basis?"

Penelope blushed. "I just meant I hope he attends tonight."
She wrinkled her nose at her grinning cousins. "Oh, hush."

"What about Cedric?" Emma asked.

"What about him?" Penelope said softly. "He doesn't
care for me that way. He never would. Surely, I have to face
that."

"You most certainly do not," Gretchen said decisively.

Emma frowned. "And what makes you think he doesn't care
for you?"

Penelope shrugged. "I didn't say he didn't care for me, just
not in that way. I'm like a sister to him."

When Emma opened her mouth to protest, Penelope turned
away, clearly not interested in discussing it further. Which was
telling in itself. Penelope *always* wanted to discuss love.

They were tucked away in Emma's chambers, preparing for
the MacGregor ball. As usual, Penelope looked forward to the
flirting and the dancing. Emma hoped to catch a moment alone
with Cormac, and Gretchen had already mapped out the location
of the library for her escape. After her discussion with Mrs. Sparrow, she was inclined to take her studies more seriously. Nothing on earth could convince her to take her mother's wedding
plans more seriously though.

"Are you sulking again?" Penelope asked her lightly when

Gretchen's wolfhound sat at her feet, looking pathetic. "You enjoy dancing as much as I do."

"It's not the dancing, it's the dancing partners. Mother's made me a list." She pulled a crumpled piece of parchment from her reticule and tossed it to the floor, where it belonged. She felt better immediately.

A moth flew past her nose. She reached over to close the window. Below her, the statue of Hecate poked her stern head above the hedges of the school gardens. Intriguing shouts and what looked like a small explosion drifted over the fence. Cormac's sister Olwen drifted out of the bushes, her long fair hair tangled in knots. Gretchen didn't see anyone else, but she couldn't shake the feeling that Tobias was out there, waiting for her to come out.

"What do we know about Tobias?" Gretchen slanted Penelope a glance. "And I don't want to hear about his shoulders again." She had eyes in her head, didn't she?

"He's Cormac's partner," Emma offered. "They patrol together for the Order. He was nearly one of the Sisters' victims that night poor Margaret York was killed. I can try to find out more, if you'd like?"

Gretchen nodded. "Know your enemy and all that. I don't like the idea of being spied upon." She drummed her fingers on the windowsill.

"I thought I saw someone lurking at the end of the lane this morning." Penelope turned away from the mirror, having used up every flower in the room. She'd even tucked a rosebud into her neckline. She grinned. "Cedric chased him off with one of the dogs."

Gretchen grinned back. "He gets to have all the fun." She was going to have to get a dog just for the pleasure of setting him upon the very proper Tobias. Then again . . .

Emma turned to Penelope. "She's got that look on her face."

"I just had an idea." Gretchen unclasped the emerald pendant from around her neck.

Emma groaned. "Told you so." She tilted her head. "You're going to teach him a lesson with your jewelry?"

She flicked her an impatient glance. "You must have a map of London in one of those books piled around your bed."

Emma rifled through them until she found a large map of magical London, with the academies and the goblin markets clearly marked. She and Penelope approached Gretchen warily as she stood over the open book, necklace clutched in her fist.

"What on earth are you doing?" Penelope asked.

"Miss Teasdale taught me about pendulums," she explained. "Apparently it's another useful skill for a Whisperer to have. I couldn't convince her that throwing knives would be even more useful."

"I can't imagine why." Miss Teasdale made kittens look cross. "How does it work?"

Gretchen held the necklace over the map so that it swung in a circle. "We ask it questions and depending on which direction it swings, we get an answer. Clockwise is yes, counterclockwise is no. Only she called the directions 'sunwise' and 'widdershins' because witches have to complicate everything."

"And what exactly are you going to ask?"

"I'm going to find out if Tobias is lurking in the bushes."

"He doesn't exactly seem the type," Emma remarked.

Gretchen's smile was more of a baring of teeth. "Precisely. If he's going to follow me about, judging everything I do, I see no reason I should make it easy for him. For any of them. Forewarned is forearmed and so forth. And if he's in the area, I intend to lead him a merry chase." She stretched her arm out over the map. The emerald drop glittered. "Where is Tobias?" she demanded.

The chain swung vaguely in one direction, then the other.

"Where is Lord Killingsworth?" Gretchen tried again, in case magical divination powers were as obsessed with etiquette as her mother. The chain just hung there, swinging like any ordinary chain. She shook it lightly. "Well, come on," she said.

A disdainful sigh came from the doorway. "You're doing it all wrong."

Gretchen didn't even look up. "Go away, Daphne."

Daphne didn't oblige, which surprised no one at all. She didn't particularly care for the cousins. Gretchen figured that was fair enough, as they didn't particularly care for her either. She was bossy and arrogant and convinced she was always right.

"You're not meant to punch at the air." She clucked her tongue at Gretchen's stance. "Give it here." She tucked the clasp in her palm, looping the chain over her forefinger and letting it dangle. "You hold it like this, and be sure to keep your arm steady." She glanced at Gretchen. "What is it you're searching for?"

"Not what," Gretchen mumbled. "Who." Her pride urged

her to snatch the pendulum back, but logic reminded her that Daphne was far better at spells. "Tobias Lawless."

Daphne raised an eyebrow. "You and half the girls in this school are wondering the same thing. He'll be at the ball tonight, I'm sure."

Gretchen rolled her eyes. "I don't care about that."

Daphne smirked. "Of course you don't."

"Are you going to help or not?"

"Fine. But you're still untrained, you should stick to yes and no questions. This is beyond you." Before Gretchen could make a retort, and she had several, Daphne held up the pendulum. "Lord Killingsworth," she said clearly. The pendulum swung very slowly, like the ripples created from a pebble dropped in a pond. She moved carefully, holding it over different parts of the map. The circles stayed wide and steady until finally they tightened abruptly, spinning faster and faster. "There," she said, smugly.

Gretchen's smile was even more smug. "Excellent." She raised an eyebrow at Emma. "Don't you think it feels like rain?"

By the time they hurried through the front door, several of the carriages had already pulled away. Torches lined the lane, leading to the gas lamps on the street. The academy looked like any other finishing school catering to wealthy daughters, with flowers spilling out of urns and rows of immaculately clean windowpanes. From the front gate, no one could see the gargoyles on the roof or the scorched walls of the ballroom where they practiced spellwork. They'd never know a girl had been killed in the alley by the spirit of three vengeful warlocks.

The cousins knew, though, and slowed their steps. Daphne stood on the exact spot where she and Emma had discovered the body of Daphne's childhood friend Lilybeth. They had suspected each other at first, when in fact Daphne's other best friend, Sophie Truwell, was to blame. Daphne's hair was coiled with ropes of pearls, making her look more delicate than the cousins knew her to be. Her arms were crossed protectively over her chest.

"Daphne?" Emma asked softly.

Daphne wiped her cheek savagely before turning around, her expression haughty. "What?"

"Are you quite well?"

"Of course I am," she replied. "I'm the daughter of the First Legate. I'm perfectly able to handle anything."

"All right then," Gretchen said. She considered it great sympathy on her part that she didn't roll her eyes. She was quite sure if she heard the other girl bragging about her father's high position in the Order one more time, her ears would bleed.

Emma stepped on her foot. "Would you like to ride with us?" she asked Daphne.

"Why would I? I have friends, you know." She flounced away before anyone pointed out that of her two best friends, one had been murdered and one was a murderer. It wasn't as though she needed reminding.

"Oh yes." Gretchen sighed as they climbed into the last carriage. "Tonight is going to be loads of fun."

. . .

The MacGregor ball was crowded pillar to post with aristo-
crats in glittering jewels and silk dancing slippers. Lady Mac-
Gregor had recently purchased an impressive collection of
Greek and Roman marbles and was eager to show them off.
Gleaming white, they lined the walls of the ballroom, from
Aphrodite to Zeus. Debutantes clustered together in their
shadows, like cooing doves in their white dresses. It was so
warm and perfumed, fans fluttered briskly and the dessert ices
melted in their cups. From the card room, an occasional shout
punctuated the music.

It was over an hour later by the time Gretchen finally escaped
to the ladies' parlor set aside for torn hems and discreet chamber
pots. Rumor had it the waltz was to be played next and so the
room had cleared down to hairbrushes and half-empty champagne glasses. She found her cousins on a settee, sharing a plate
of iced cakes.

"I thought you'd be waiting for the waltz," she told Penelope as she stole a forkful of her icing.

"And I thought you were in the library." Penelope raised an
eyebrow. "You're all sweaty. Were you bowling on the back
lawn again?"

"I did that once. And no." Gretchen dropped into a chair.
"I may have crumpled up my mother's dismal list but she clearly
hasn't. Every man on it has sought me out for a dance." She licked
the last of the frosting off silver tines, then swallowed slowly, as
though an afterthought. "Emma?"

"Yes?"

"Why are there moths all over your antlers?"

She slumped resignedly against the cushions. "I have no bloody idea."

There were over a dozen of them, from tiny white moths to mint-green luna moths, gypsy moths, apple sphinx moths, and a giant death-head's moth, with its skull pattern watching them carefully. They clung to Emma's honey-hued antlers, like she was the only candle in a dark house.

"They won't go away."

Frowning, Gretchen stood up. She waved her fork menacingly. "Shoo!" "Go on!"

"I can't think why we didn't try that ourselves," Emma pointed out drily when the moths shifted slightly but would not fly away.

"That *is* odd," Gretchen admitted. "Even for a girl with antlers."

"It occurs to me that our definition of 'odd' has certainly changed in the last few weeks." Emma snorted. "But now I can't leave the parlor. When I try, they hover over me, just out of reach of the Fith-Fath glamour."

"It's like a crown," Penelope added. "It's rather a pretty effect. You know, if you're fond of insects."

They watched Emma circle the room, calling up the glamour and letting it slide away. The moths trailed her like the sparks of a falling star.

Penelope stood up so abruptly the plate fell off her lap. "Snake," she said in a particularly calm voice, pointing to the carpet. A small green grass snake slid over the hand-knotted pattern.

Emma stepped out of its path. It circled around, as though trying to seek her out. "What the devil?"

Two more snakes emerged from under the nearest chair, gliding in her direction. Another slithered down the hall, toward the crowded ballroom. The strains of the promised waltz played prettily, punctuated by a startled shout. Behind them, an insistent tap sounded at the windowpane. They glanced over to see an osprey clicking its beak against the glass. The white feathers of its chest glowed.

"Is that . . . a giant bird?" Gretchen asked, bewildered. "I don't remember balls having quite so much wildlife."

Emma gulped, going pale. "Moth, snake, and osprey." Thunder growled outside, a direct result of her anxiety. "The Sisters' familiars," she said. "The ones I bottled."

"What does it mean?" Penelope asked, climbing onto a chair to escape the attention of a large snake with viciously colored scales.

"It means we need to get out of here." Gretchen hazarded a guess. "Now. Before the Order catches wind of this. We'll have to use the window," she added, already striding over to the nearest one not currently occupied by a giant bird. She poked her head out gingerly to make sure there weren't any more ospreys or, worse, couples sneaking kisses in the bushes. Chaperones, in her experience, didn't make one more virtuous, merely more creative. She popped back inside. "It's clear."

Emma nodded, her lips moving as she muttered the Fith-Fath glamour. Her antlers faded, as though they'd been painted over. The moths clung to nothing at all, defying most scientific laws. Gretchen threw a leg over the windowsill and leaped out. Her white gown ballooned around her ankles. She fought her way clear of the daffodils and bounced right off a rather rudely solid shadow.

Tobias.

"Not you again," she groaned when his hands closed around her upper arms. She knew it wasn't to steady her, as she wasn't the least bit wobbly. He was as stern and unyielding as the statues lining the dance floor. "My Lord Killingsworth," she exclaimed very loudly, warning off her cousins. "I didn't take you for the type to lurk in bushes. What would the etiquette books say?"

"Where are you going?" he asked her sharply.

She raised her eyebrows. "That's none of your business."

"I am your Keeper; therefore, you are my business," he informed her.

She pulled free of his hold. The imprint of his fingers was warm on her bare arms. "Nothing about me is yours, my lord," she told him. "So find another occupation."

"And yet I remain."

"Yes, and it's rather rude actually." Rain began to patter through the garden. His gold buttons gleamed in the faint light spilling out of the open window. He looked over her shoulder. If he looked too carefully would he see Emma? A moth drifted between them.

"The rain will ruin your pretty coat," Gretchen said hurriedly, seeking to distract him. He peered down at the water stains with irritation. "You should go inside where it's safe," she added sweetly. Fog curled through the garden, haloing the lights.

"I must insist you accompany me, Lady Gretchen."

The fog was rather insistent too. It pushed against them, clinging to the walls of the house. If she let him lead her away, Emma could slip away. The shadow of another large bird passed over, white as hot ashes.

"Oh very well," she sighed, exasperated. She stalked away, not realizing that Tobias had extended his arm to assist her, like any polite gentleman. Her voice drifted behind her. "Are you coming or what?"

By the time they'd circled the house and crossed the patio to the ballroom doors, the buzzing in Gretchen's head was incessant, overpowering the violins.

Tobias paused, frowning at her. "Are you ill?"

She shook her head even though she was a little queasy. The vibrations in her head made her feel awful. She swallowed grimly and focused on the annoying sound, trying to hear the voices of dead witches as Mrs. Sparrow had told her. She pressed on her temples, trying to alleviate the pressure. She thought she caught the fragment of a word, then nothing.

She closed her eyes. It was just as loud, but it seemed to be coming from Tobias, and not the strange collection of familiars as she'd assumed. She focused harder, following it to its source. It took a long moment and it made her feel disconcertingly brittle. She pointed to his left pocket. "One of your charms is off."

"I think not."

She rolled her eyes, then stopped when it made her head hurt.

"I'm a Whisperer, remember?" She stuck her hand in his coat pocket and yanked out the offending charm. It was a cracked wolf's tooth, leaking magic. "And this thing is like a nail in my skull," she added, tossing it into the bushes. "Now if you're very lucky, I might not cast up my accounts on your very shiny shoes."

"I'd consider it a kindness," he said mildly, following her inside. She didn't notice his outstretched hand, waiting to steady her if she fainted.

She saw Penelope almost at once, chatting with a muscular young man. She smiled cheerfully, looking just like a happy debutante at a ball and nothing like a girl who had just helped her cousin escape through a window. Emma, thankfully, was nowhere to be seen.

"Gretchen," Penelope said. "This is Ian Stone, my very own Keeper. He has read all of Shakespeare, so I think I shall keep him. Also, he is going to dance with me."

"I'd be honored," he replied, not betraying a flicker of reaction to being ordered to dance. "I'm just glad I'm in your good graces. That poor bloke this morning will limp for a month from that dog bite."

Penelope sniffed. "Serves him right for lurking."

"It's probably for the best." Ian winked at Gretchen. "I'm fairly certain he wouldn't have passed your cousin's literary inquisition."

"I wonder if you could fetch us some wine before we dance," Penelope asked. "While my aunt is studiously pretending not to see us."

"Of course."

"I like your Keeper much better than mine," Gretchen remarked once he'd walked away. He was all smiles and amiableness. Nothing like Tobias.

"He can quote *Macbeth*," Penelope said. It was all that mattered to her. He could have smelled like an old shoe and she wouldn't have cared, as long as he had the proper appreciation for Shakespeare and gothic novels.

"What about Emma?" Gretchen whispered.

"She's gone," she whispered back. "I had to distract that pestilent, ill-bred canker blossom Virgil."

"Does he suspect anything?"

"I don't know. An osprey made a mess on his shoulder." She grinned over the top of her fan. Her mother had painted it with a scene from *A Midsummer Night's Dream*, complete with Oberon, Titania, and Nick Bottom, with his donkey's head. Gretchen wondered if her aunt would paint Tobias with a donkey's head. Penelope stood on her tiptoes. "Have you seen Lucius anywhere?"

"I'm afraid not."

"Blast."

Ian returned with their wineglasses before she could find Lucius. Unfortunately, he also returned with Tobias. "Apparently there was a snake in the ballroom earlier," Ian told them. "Everyone is flying into the boughs over it."

Tobias frowned. "That is rather unusual."

"Probably came in from the gardens," Penelope said airily. "You know how dramatic everyone gets. You're not afraid to waltz, are you, my lord?" she asked as the orchestra began to play again.

"Snakes and all?" Ian bowed with a smile. Penelope glanced at Gretchen and Tobias.

"You should dance too," she suggested archly. "So no one suspects why you're really here, Lord Killingsworth."

Gretchen widened her eyes threateningly at her cousin. She was clearly reading too many gothic romances and Keats and those other poets. It was rotting her brain. Didn't she realize that Gretchen didn't want to dance with Tobias? She wanted to *kick* him.

He appeared to feel the same way, if his stiff posture was any judge.

"I'm sure Lord Killingsworth can spy on me just as well from over there," she said.

"And yet why waste a perfectly good waltz?" he returned, holding out his arm in invitation. She saw the dare reflected in the arch of his eyebrow. He didn't think she'd accept. Her hand settled on his arm, slapping down as though to swat an irritating fly.

"Now look what you've done," she said, cheerful despite herself. She refused to let the Order steal her sense of humor away completely. "You've punished us both by daring me to accept."

"It's an honor, I assure you."

The buzzing began almost before he'd started speaking. She smiled at him wryly. "It's no use lying to a Whisperer," she said as he led her to the dance floor. "Surely you must know that."

"I . . ." He looked surprised and, possibly, chagrined. She must have imagined that. Still, she'd flustered him, and it was the most emotion she'd ever seen on his perfect face. He finally looked nineteen instead of ninety.

The music swelled around them, violins and pianoforte braiding together seamlessly. She felt nervous for no good reason, especially when his arm went around her waist, drawing her closer. His eyes, the hard blue of a winter sky, met hers. She thought she heard a wolf howl. She swallowed, suddenly terrified that she was going to start babbling.

The music seemed to get louder but everything else faded. She was acutely aware of the light pressure of his hand on her lower back and his fingers clasped around hers. The candles in the chandelier overhead dripped beeswax, but he steered them effortlessly around it. She'd never really understood the fuss people made over the waltz. But now she was afraid she understood it a little bit better.

And then, because nothing seemed to go smoothly in the witching world, a dull ache built inside her chest. It wasn't the kind of swoony feeling Penelope talked about. It was more like her wolfhound's teeth gnawing on her ribs. She flinched when her witch knot flared briefly, as if traced by an invisible dagger. She was surprised she wasn't bleeding through her white gloves.

She was even more surprised when Tobias whirled her away from the others to press her against the wall.

Moira had just finished stealing mandrake roots from a witch's back garden when she ran into Maddoc. "What are you doing out and about?" he asked.

"The usual," Moira said. "You?"

"Heard Rovers found a body in the Thames and wanted to sell the bones."

She froze, thinking of Strawberry. "And did they?"

Maddoc shook his head. "Near as I could tell they were dog bones."

Moira released her breath. She couldn't bear the thought of her friend being used for foul magic.

"Still," Maddoc continued. "I thought I smelled lemon balm and black magic. Best stick together tonight." He nodded around the corner to a narrow alley that stank of cats and gin. "We're up there."

They ducked into the crooked lane where a ladder was set against the wall, behind a stack of broken barrels. The last three rungs were rotted through, but the rest was sturdy enough. No one ever looked back here, or at least no one sober enough to take notice.

Moira followed Maddoc up to the roof, climbing nimbly over the railing. She straightened just as a posy of purple-and-white violets hurtled at her face. She snatched it out of the air before the petals went up her nose.

"Some bloke left those for you," Cass said, pouting slightly. She was wearing her usual lavender-and-black dress, but she'd taken off her veils. She never did like to share the attention, especially when it came to the other lads. She and Moira only tolerated each other because Moira couldn't have cared less about the lads and because Cass knew they needed each other. It was tricky enough being a Madcap, never mind a girl alone in London.

Moira frowned at the posy, wrapped tight with a fluttering ribbon. Cass would want to weave it into her hair. Moira just wanted to know if she could sell it at the markets. "Who the hell would bring me flowers?"

Cass sniffed. "Exactly my question."

"Easy," Maddoc said lightly, before he had to separate them. He'd learned the hard way just how quickly a comment could escalate to bruises and black eyes. Penn sighed, disgusted with Maddoc. He enjoyed the fights. Moira tossed the posy aside, making sure to clip Penn in the ear with it. She opened her mouth to make a snide remark, then snapped it shut again frowning. The bottoms of her feet prickled a warning, her boots filled with invisible needles. There was the sound of stone on stone and paper tearing.

They turned in unison, just as the enormous gargoyle hunched over the dormer window of the bookshop next door pushed off its perch. It was the gray of autumn storm clouds, roiling with power. It veered clumsily as it animated from stone to magical creature. Its talons raked the shingles, smashing them to bits. It dipped lower, swiping at Moira. She dropped down instantly, already feeling a gash bleeding under her hair.

"What's got him riled?" She cursed, rolling out of the way when a wing point pierced the shingles beside her head. "We aren't even on his roof!" Gargoyles only woke for one reason: magic.

"I told you something was off," Maddoc said as it swiped at Cass, who dove behind Penn, her sense of self-preservation more accurate than any of her predictions. Nigel crouched beside the smoking chimney pot. He rolled an apothecary bottle filled with whiskey and pigeon and bat bones toward Moira. She caught it before it hurtled over the edge or smashed against the railing.

She uncorked it and tossed a few drops in the air, splattering the gargoyle's wing and underbelly. It was better if you could get the whiskey onto the talons or the tongue, but she was trying not to get stabbed with stray bits of rock or chomped by stone teeth. "What the hell's this one called?" she panted, rolling out of the way again. She had to wait for Penn to distract the gargoyle in order to regain her feet.

"It's new," Nigel called out. Since the gargoyles had fled London, the Greybeards had been fetching them back from parts unknown. But it wasn't just the Order; anyone with even a drop of witch blood now had gargoyles somewhere on his or her property. It was getting difficult to keep up. "No one's named it yet."

"Well, that's just great." Names had power, and giving gargoyles their own names was part of the magic that gave the Madcaps their uncanny ability to control them. A gargoyle without a name would turn against any magic, even if it wasn't a warlock's doing.

"We need to tame this one. Give me a name!"

"Tristan," Cass suggested. Tristan and his love, Isolde, were parted and died forlorn. Trust her to come up with something suitably tragic.

Moira didn't have time to argue. "Tether it!" she shouted.

Nigel scuttled forward and drew a symbol on the shingles
with a piece of chalk he fished out of his pocket. It looked like
tree branches. Maddoc pulled a stone with a matching symbol
from his pack and tossed it up into the air, just as the gargoyle
flew over them again, preparing to dive. The stone went over its
head, in perfect alignment with the chalk symbol. Both sigils
flared and the gargoyle stopped in midflight, yanked to a stand-
still by invisible hands. It flapped its wide, leathery wings slowly
and made a rumbling sound.

Moira scrawled the name "Tristan" on a scrap of parchment
with the nub of a pencil. No Madcap was ever without the basic
gargoyle-taming ingredients. She rolled the paper into a miniature scroll around a clutch of bat and pigeon bones and soaked it
all with the whiskey. She tossed it into the air, infused with
magic. The gargoyle, following instinct, snapped at the bundle,
swallowing it whole.

"Tristan I name you," Moira said. "By the name Tristan I
command you!" She scuffed the chalk symbol with the toe of
her boot and the gargoyle lowered slowly, released. "Stand
down, Tristan," she ordered wearily. The gargoyle returned to
its original perch, body hardening to stone.

"Well, that was fun," she added, pushing her hair off her
face. "I wonder . . . ," she trailed off, sniffing the air.

Maddoc reached for his dagger. "What is it now?"

She shook her head and shot him a self-deprecating smile.
"I thought I smelled strawberries. Never mind. I'm going
daft."

"No, you're right," Nigel said, crouching by the chimney

pot. He picked up the broken bowl of strawberries he'd been carefully rubbing free of dirt.

"I found them in Covent Garden," Penn explained proudly, knowing how much Cass loved strawberries.

"Stole them you mean."

He shrugged. "Same thing."

"If they catch you, you'll hang for stealing," Cass said in her singsong voice, the one she used for prophecies and predictions. She fancied herself a prophetess, but only dealt in gloomy, blood-filled predictions. The others ignored her, except for Penn, who was still trying to convince her to let him kiss her. She was smiling, as smug as a cat. She had strawberries, a boy who wanted to kiss her, and the promise of dire consequences. Moira knew the other girl was as happy as she could be, barring some wealthy bloke to shower her with presents.

"I'm going to check on Joe," Moira decided. There was still too much magic searing the air, and she knew if she stayed she and Cass would snipe at each other all night.

"You should," Cass agreed, nibbling on a strawberry. "I sense he's not got long now."

"Oh, shut it," Moira snapped, fed up with the other girl's fortune-telling.

Cass narrowed her eyes. "I have a gift," she said loftily.

"You have a big mouth."

Maddoc sighed. "Cass, hush. Moira, go on."

"Why do you always take her side!" Moira heard Cass shout as she leaped to the next building and the next, losing herself in the familiar feel of shingles underfoot, gas lamps in the fog, and the knowledge that no one could reach her up on the rooftops.

Gretchen's back hit the flowered wallpaper as Tobias shielded her with his body. His shoulders blocked most of her view. She tapped one. "Excuse me, have you lost your mind?"

But her body recognized danger: rapid heartbeat, the roar of blood in her ears, and breaths like tiny caged hummingbirds.

"You feel it, don't you?" he asked, his jawline uncompromising as he surveyed the ballroom.

"I feel something," she agreed, rubbing her breastbone as though it were her wolfhound's furry head. She smelled lemon balm and yawned widely. She leaned her head back, suddenly too exhausted to stand up properly.

Tobias cursed, turning around. He grabbed her shoulders, squeezing hard. "Don't you fall asleep on me."

"What? Why . . . should I . . ."—another yawn, bigger than the first—"do that?"

And yet she was struggling to keep her eyes open. She wondered if someone had slipped laudanum in the wine. An elderly chaperone sitting in one of the chairs set up along one side of the room, tilted right over, snoring loudly. At least Gretchen thought that's what she saw; she couldn't be entirely sure since her eyelids seemed suck at half-mast. They may as well have been cathedral stones for all she could lift them.

Tobias tugged a pendant out of his pocket and slipped it around her neck. The silver chain was unbearably icy, like a winter pond closing around her. But the sudden cold popped her eyes open and dissolved the iron in her bones. The pendant appeared to be made from rose thorns and the teeth of some kind of small carnivore, all wrapped in black thread. It pulsed gently, glittering faintly. "What is this?" she asked.

"Shield charm," he explained. "It will protect you."

"From what, exactly?"

"Magic," he replied grimly.

The witches in the crowd paused, champagne flutes halfway to their lips, or else stumbled over a dance step. A woman scattered salt from her reticule.

The guests began to crumple like discarded paper. Men dropped suddenly. A footman's tray crashed to the ground, glasses shattering. The violinist fell asleep on his stool even as the music from his last-plucked string warbled in the now-silent room. Chatter faded away, laughter died. Ladies fluttered and fell over, flowers wilting on stems. Gretchen's own mother sat down, looking unwell.

Alarmed, Gretchen hurried forward to her mother. She was pale as glass, but her pulse throbbed under her pale skin. "She's asleep," Gretchen said, stunned.

Hundreds of guests had simply toppled over, asleep before they hit the floor.

"Did the Order do this?" she asked.

"No," Tobias replied tightly.

"Are you sure?" She pulled a very small iron dagger from the strap above her knee.

"Be careful with that," he added.

"Believe me, if I stab you with it, it won't be an accident," she muttered.

"A comfort, I'm sure."

Gretchen picked her way among the bodies, clutching the shield charm tightly with her free hand. The icy prickles it shot through her witch knot were reassuring. "Where's Penelope?" Gretchen asked, not seeing her cousin's distinctive flower-strewn gown among the fallen guests. The quality of the silence in such a crowded room was unnerving.

"She has a Keeper to protect her," Tobias pointed out.

She bit her tongue on a sarcastic reply. He was her Keeper after all, and she'd be unconscious like the others if he hadn't helped her. She scanned face after face, dread souring in her belly. "There," Tobias said gently, at her shoulder. She followed his gaze to where Ian was striding across the ballroom, looking just as grim as Tobias.

"Penelope?" she asked, darting forward. She had to leap over two young men and a debutante lying in a puddle of spilled wine.

"She's fine," Ian replied. "But asleep like the others. I didn't have an extra shield charm and it was too late to get her out of range."

"I don't understand," she said, as calmly as she could, making her way to her cousin. Penelope was draped comfortably across two chairs, petals on the floor at her feet. At least Ian hadn't let her fall. She glared around the room, feeling bleak and lost. "What's happened here?"

"One of the magical wards must have disintegrated," Tobias explained. "From these side effects, it must be one of the fail-safes designed to put people to sleep if an excess of sudden magic triggers it. It's meant to keep us secret from regular London folk."

"There are over three hundred people here," she said, trying to wrap her brain around it.

"Magic is leaking through London and it's nothing if not unpredictable. Two days ago a woman in Cavendish Square swore her cat talked to her, and all the crows in the park turned yellow just this morning." He shook his head. "We're in for a rough night."

"Who's doing this?"

Ian shrugged. "Probably just a side effect from the gates being opened and the Sisters. No one knows."

"I've already summoned the Order," Tobias said. Gretchen hadn't even seen him do it. He was rather terrifyingly efficient.

"I'll secure the perimeter," Ian suggested. "Can you track the broken ward?"

"Yes. We'll also need to cast a waking spell, and then memory charms on each of the cowans."

"Cowan?" Gretchen echoed, confused.

"The nonwitch guests. It will take hours."

Gretchen rubbed her arms, guests scattered all around her. They looked like dolls, pretty and pampered and helpless. It made her queasy to look at them. "Are they in pain?"

"No," Tobias replied. "Not as such. But the longer they stay in a magic sleep like this one, the more dangerous it is. Some won't ever wake, others will lose their memories."

She turned to stare at him. "But my cousin is here! And my mother!"

"I know. And I'm sorry. We'll do the best we can." He touched her arm, above her glove where it ended at the elbow. "They're strong. And if we can find a way to wake them soon, they won't be in any danger. If I can track the ward it will be over all that much faster." He turned on his heel, carefully assessing the room.

"It's not in this house," Gretchen said with certainty. "I'd hear it, if it was."

"Bad luck," Ian panted, rushing in through the garden doors. "It's still spreading."

Tobias cursed. "How fast?"

"Too fast. By the time the others get here, it will have contaminated at least two more streets. There's already been two carriage accidents out front."

"And Gretchen says the magic isn't coming from inside this house." Tobias shook his head. "But even when I find it, I won't be able to stop it. I'm not a spell-breaker. We'll have to wait for the Order to send someone to us."

"I can do it," Gretchen offered quietly.

He raised an eyebrow. "Do what, exactly? Even if we knew what's to be done, undoing a spell like this isn't something to take on lightly. It's not like shooting a charmed poppet with your brother's pistol."

"Can't hurt." Ian shrugged.

"I wish that were true," Gretchen muttered.

Chapter 5

The scene outside the MacGregor house wasn't any less disturbing.

The butler was slumped in the doorway. A guest had fallen asleep on the front step, his hat rolling into the bushes. Three ladies were draped over one another in the lane in a pile of fluttering lace and ruffled hems. The road was an impossible tableau, with horses frozen in midstride. The wind touched their manes but they did not react. Lanterns flickered over slumbering coachmen and a woman's arm falling limply out of her carriage window.

It was silent and beautiful and wrong. And it was stealing her family away. What if they didn't wake up? What if they stayed that way, draped artfully and uselessly like decorations?

"This way." Tobias turned sharply down the sidewalk. He walked with purpose, his teeth clenched as though he was in pain. She wondered why the magic he used for tracking would hurt him.

"Are you all right?" she asked. He just nodded. "How will you find the spell?" Gretchen asked, hurrying to keep up.

"I'll find it." He was grimly confident. "It's what I do."

They passed several Keepers who were already blocking the streets so no one would inadvertently stumble into the eerie tableau. She could hear all the ordinary noises of London in the near distance: horse hooves, men shouting, violins from a house window. It made the frozen silence behind her all that much more sinister.

They walked for a long time. Tobias's strides were long and hungry, and he turned left and right according to some inner map she could not see. She followed, unable to do anything but trust him. She couldn't break the spell if she couldn't even find it. The magic snaked its sinister way through Mayfair, leaving the aristocracy sleeping in their finery in carriages, walkways, and gardens.

Tobias eventually led them to a fashionable house with black iron gates. Tobias went down the mews, past the stables and into a garden filled with pink snapdragons and foxgloves. Pebbles crunched underfoot. He stopped in front of a decorative stone pillar framing an opening with banks of lilies on the other side.

Blinding white light burst out of a small fissure in the stone. It widened, sending more splinters of light through the stone. Everything in its path fell away, melting gracefully like ice into water. The shield charm Tobias had given her grew uncomfortably cold. She held on to the pain, knowing it kept her from sagging to the ground like the man in a blue evening coat sprawled half in the lilies. His left hand was flung out toward the pillar, witch knot stark against his moonlit skin.

"Lord Giles," Tobias said, after ascertaining that the other man wasn't harmed. "This is his house. There's a passage under the pillars to the goblin markets. He must have been trying to mend it."

"My aunt has a secret passageway too," Gretchen said. "It doesn't do this."

He turned his head sharply, sensing something she didn't. He crouched to dig through the lilies, pulling out a hollowed adder's stone. The spiraling marks of long dead creatures etched the fossil. It was cracked open like a bowl, the inside painted with gold dust.

"This wasn't an accident," he said. "Someone's gathering this magic."

"For what?"

"This much power? Nothing good. I'll alert the Order." To do that, he added something in what sounded like a cross between Old English and Latin, while drawing a symbol on the stone. He used a piece of charcoal he unwrapped from a scrap of white silk in his pocket. "Ember from a fire that burned at midnight on the grave of a witch skilled with psychical communication," he explained.

In the push of his magic, Gretchen could have sworn his shadow fell over the flowers in the shape of a wolf.

Clearly, she was letting the strangeness of the night get to her. This much magic had the hairs on her arms lifting and the taste of salt burning in the back of her throat. She took a deep breath and closed her eyes. Warily, she waited for the onslaught of voices, for the insistent scrape of pain.

Nothing.

She scowled at the light that seared through her eyelids. It was glowing brighter, rushing more powerfully.

Exactly the opposite of what she was trying to do.

"How do I seal the ward and wake everyone up?" she whispered, imagining all of the witches speaking their spells over the centuries. Surely one of them had dealt with something similar.

The silence stretched from unnerving to downright vexing.

For all her talk of not wanting to be a girl who waited to be asked to dance or who counted the days to her wedding, here she was finally with a chance to prove herself and *nothing*. Just her, awake to enjoy her miserable failures while her cousin and her mother slipped further and further away.

It would not do.

These infernal dead witches seemed perfectly happy to tell her when she was doing something wrong, in great and painful detail, and yet were decidedly less helpful with advice on how to do it right in the first place.

She'd just have to trick them into cooperating with her.

"Do you have salt?" she asked Tobias.

"Of course." He handed her a small glass vial. "What are you doing?"

"Making it up as I go along," she replied with grim determination. She plucked a foxglove blossom and filled it with salt. She pressed it against the crack of light, knowing there was no magic to what she was doing, only random acts.

A cacophony of voices exploded.

Her eyes rolled back but she refused to give up. She sifted through the whispers and shouts as though she were sorting through beads. It was slow and arduous work. Her teeth chattered and her neck muscles cramped. She knew she would shatter into pieces if she so much as moved an eyelash.

She listened for particular words: *sleep, wake, ward.*

"Alas, no witch's rhyme."

That wasn't particularly helpful and she must have bitten her tongue because she tasted blood. It didn't matter, nothing mattered except *sleep, wake, ward.*

There, just under the press of incantations.

"Wake."

She clung to it, refusing to let it go.

"Three red roses."

The voice was soft and it had a lilt. Irish, maybe.

"Like Sleeping Beauty."

Gretchen's eyes flew open. "I know how to break the spell."

"How?"

"With a kiss."

He arched a brow. "I doubt that very much."

She refused to blush. "It's like the stories of Sleeping Beauty and Snow White. A kiss breaks the spell. It's the easiest and quickest way." She pushed aside the snapdragons. "I need three red roses."

Frowning, he leaned over, brushing her elbow to pluck rosebuds from a scraggly bush hidden in the shadows. They were the first of the season, struggling to open. She hoped it would be enough. She tucked them into the ribbons in her hair, feeling foolish.

He watched her, expressionless. He was going to think she was asking him to kiss her. It was mortifying. More mortifying was the horrible pause as he stayed where he was, still watching her. "It's for the spell," she added again. "No need to get missish." There, that was better. She didn't sound as though her heart was pounding at a mad gallop.

"Indeed," he replied, and his tone was just as cool and unaffected as ever.

It really made her want to punch him.

He took her hand gently and politely while she told herself that feeling nervous was ridiculous. He peeled off one of her gloves, untying the tiny ribbon that held it in place and sliding it down to her wrist. He folded it neatly and slipped it into his pocket, ever courteous and proper.

His skin against hers did not feel particularly proper.

His fingers were warm and strong, skimming over her witch knot. There were answering tingles in her belly. She felt as frozen as everyone around them. She couldn't have moved even if she'd wanted to. His blue eyes never left hers as he bowed slowly over her hand and brushed his lips softly over her knuckles.

The light grew brighter until it was painful to look at. It outlined everything in fire—flower, tree, Tobias's cheekbones. It flickered once, contracting, and then shone even brighter.

The wards had not been mended. And no wonder.

"You call that a kiss?" Gretchen mocked, before fisting her hands in his coat and yanking him closer. She pushed herself up on her toes to kiss him fiercely. As her lips touched his, he froze for a brief stunned moment.

"Kiss me back, you idiot," she ordered, her mouth brushing his as she spoke.

His hands slid up to grasp her upper arms, leaving a trail of delicious shivers in their wake. Her eyelids fluttered shut, and there was only darkness and their lips against each other. Gone was the icy restraint, the haughty refusal to show anything but elegance and calm. Their kiss unleashed something beneath the surface, something she would never have guessed could even exist. It scorched her down to her toes.

His tongue touched hers and she forgot about the spell, about proving herself unaffected. She could only kiss him back until their breaths were ragged and entwined.

When they finally pulled away from each other, the eerie unnatural light of the magic spilling out of the broken ward had faded away. There was only moonlight and gas lamps flickering on the street filled with the sounds of horses' hooves, carriage wheels, and violins.

The spell had been broken.

When Gretchen snuck out of the house the next morning, she ran into Godric coming up the front steps, hat in his hands.

"Bloody hell, Gretchen," he said, staring at her starkly. "I just got word. Are you hurt?"

"Not a bit," she assured him.

"Word has it you sealed a broken ward."

She smiled proudly. "I did." So there, she thought to the Order.

"You're preening."

"Only a little." She looped her arm through his. "Can you drop me at Penelope's?"

"I'm on business for the Order," he said apologetically. "I just stopped by to be sure you weren't hurt. There's a swarm of gargoyles on the loose."

"Well, that sounds like much more fun. I'll come with you."

He groaned. "Gretchen. It might not be safe."

"Safety in numbers then," she called over her shoulder, having already scrambled into the carriage. She grinned through the open door. "Come along."

"Mother will kill me if you get caught that close to St. Giles and the Seven Dials. They're not exactly neighborhoods fit for a debutante."

"So let's not get caught." She barely waited for him to sit down before she rapped on the ceiling. "Drive on!"

"You're rather cheerful for someone who was caught in a magic leak."

She shrugged one shoulder. "It was refreshing to be the one with a solution." She very specifically did not mention the kiss. "Instead of the one being blamed."

He snorted. "I'm sure it won't last." She snorted back in agreement.

When the carriage pulled to a stop in front of a lane too narrow for the horses to navigate, Gretchen and Godric got out and walked. She skirted a puddle of dubious origin and tried not to breathe in the stench of cat and cabbages and chamber pots.

The lane narrowed to an alley, leaving only a slice of overcast sky. A shadow crossed between the rooftops, leathery wings extended.

"We'll have to climb," Godric said reluctantly. "To track them."

Gretchen knotted her skirts, and scampered up a wooden staircase, using a small balcony at the top to pull herself up on the roof. Godric followed with considerably less enthusiasm.

"Shite. This is high," he muttered, wiping sweat off the back of his neck with a handkerchief. He steadied himself on the surprisingly large clay gargoyle crouched on the rain-damaged roof. Another circled overhead with the sinister laziness of a vulture.

"I don't see any broken wards or anything," Gretchen said, shading her eyes as she looked around. She'd forgotten her bonnet again.

Moira strode toward them across the peeling shingles, scowling. A small fat gargoyle bobbled behind her. Gretchen smirked at her brother, nudging him to look away from the gargoyles.

He followed her gaze, straightening. "Shut it, Gretchen," he muttered. His cheeks were ruddy.

"You again." Moira raised her eyebrows. "What the bleedin' hell are you doing on the edge of the Dials?"

"Chasing gargoyles," Gretchen replied as her brother bowed politely. Moira just shook her head at him, bewildered by his fine manners.

When the gargoyle beside them stretched, Godric nearly plummeted to his death.

Gretchen grabbed the back of his coat. The gargoyle opened its wide mouth, magic crackling in its jaws. Pigeons shot into the air, squawking in alarm. "Now what have you done?" Moira demanded.

"You tell me," Gretchen gasped as the pigeons wheeled in panic. Feathers drifted by as the gargoyle flew between them, chomping its stone teeth together. "Where is it going?"

The sun threw spears of light, glinting off copper flashing, windowpanes, and the leathery sheen of the gargoyle's wings. "Gargoyles only chase magic, and they almost never leave their rooftops altogether."

"They left a few weeks ago," Gretchen pointed out. All of the gargoyles in London had abandoned their posts the night Emma accidentally dropped her mother's old spell bottle.

"He's tracking something," she said, watching him grimly.

"Perhaps another ward has broken," Gretchen suggested. "Or there's still magic loose from last night. Does magic do that?"

"He's heading east," Moira said, before turning away.

"Wait, we're coming with you!" Godric called out, stepping up on the edge of the roof. He turned green, then gray.

Gretchen grabbed the back of his collar. "You don't even like climbing trees." When he eyed the gap between the buildings she tightened her hold. "You'll never make it. Unless you can grow wings now, as well as talk to the dead."

"For the love of . . ." Moira snapped. "You'll give us away with all your bother. Gargoyles can be shy." She lifted a plank of wood and slid it across the roofs. "Cross on that and keep your bleeding mouths shut."

The gargoyle flew on, graceful despite his bulk, but slow. Something shivered in the air. The hairs on Gretchen's arms stood straight up. Moira's familiar leaped between her shoulders and vanished, hissing. Godric crossed the makeshift bridge with all the alacrity of blind man with a broken ankle. He tottered for a long, sickening moment before his foot slid off the edge completely and he fell. He caught himself with a very painful connection with the board. His hat toppled off his head and was plucked up by the wind. It landed in the road and was run over by a donkey pulling a cart of onions.

"Come on, pretty boy." Moira held out her hand to help him up onto the roof. Gretchen followed quickly. He hoisted the plank over his shoulder and they followed Moira. She ran easily, comfortable with every type of roof underfoot—steep, flat, thatched, or shingled. Her black hair was like a pennant behind her. Godric was so intent on watching her that he tripped and nearly decapitated himself with the board.

"Godric," Gretchen snapped. "Stop trying to impress her and start trying not to get yourself killed."

The gargoyle was joined by another, this one considerably smaller, with dragon wings and scorched talons. They rode the air currents, dipping and soaring until they dove suddenly, like hawks catching sight of a mouse in a field below.

Moira led them two buildings over to a ladder propped against the eaves. They descended into a warren of alleyways and balconies. Laundry fluttered, drying in the reluctant sunlight. A baby wailed from an upper window. Litter chased itself into corners.

"Can you see them?" Gretchen asked, trying to see between the sheets flapping on the crisscrossing lines. They squeezed into an alley barely wide enough to accommodate Godric's shoulders. A gargoyle flew so close its wings scratched the wall, pelting them with bits of brick and plaster. It had a small white bird in its mouth, glowing faintly. "I didn't know they ate birds," she added.

"They don't," Moira replied grimly. Glowing feathers drifted between them. A gargoyle made of cheap river mud broke away from a balcony overhang. Another followed from a soot-stained cornice. "That's curious," Moira said. It was clearly more than curious as she was suddenly holding a dagger, a charm made of iron nails, and a pouch of salt.

And then it became very apparent as to what was agitating the gargoyles.

"Who's that?" Gretchen goggled. Her throat went dry. Godric's hand slipped into hers, and she honestly wasn't sure which of them he was comforting. She held on tight regardless.

Moira let out a sigh that was half reverence and half fear.

Her voice, usually all sharp attitude and sarcasm, trembled. "The White Lady."

A woman glided into the courtyard between several buildings tilting together as though they had secrets. Not a woman, Gretchen corrected herself, a spirit. She glowed violently, outlined in frozen moonlight and fire. She wore an old-fashioned white dress with panniers under the beaded silk, and diamond pins in hair powdered and piled high with ringlets. Ropes of diamonds hung from her hair and looped to chandelier-like earrings. From these chains a white veil fluttered, obscuring her features—all but her eyes, which were lined with kohl and stared savagely. They were gray as ice, nearly colorless with their vicious focus.

Gretchen shivered, even before the white birds followed, flying in from all of the alleyways, the sound of their wings like ice falling from a church steeple. They seared the air behind them as they passed. A cat yowled from an upper window, swiping at one.

"Don't let them touch you," Moira warned.

"Why not?" Godric asked, waving his hat at them when they flew too close.

"Because they'll steal your memories away. Knew a girl once who forgot her own name. She even forgot she was a witch."

Gretchen angled herself shoulder to shoulder with her brother. "Is this more magic leaking from the wards?"

"Reckon so. The White Lady's meant to be confined to the markets, inn't she? And yet here she is." Moira shook her head. "Best pray the others don't get loose too."

"Why, what do they do?" Godric asked, even as he searched for an escape.

"The Grey Lady will steal your thoughts, and the Red Lady . . . Well, you don't want to know what she steals."

The gargoyles swarmed. Chimney pots were clipped by stray wings and talons. They dodged the missiles, covering their heads. "How do we banish her?" Gretchen asked, rubbing her ear where a chunk of brick had bounced of the wall and scraped it. The White Lady turned her head sharply, spearing her with a glare. There was a red heart-shaped patch at the corner of her left eye.

A white bird screeched and dove for Gretchen. Godric yanked her out of the way at the last moment. Moira fumbled in one of the pouches hanging at her belt, withdrawing a shard from a broken mirror. "What's that for?" Gretchen asked as Moira held it up.

"What do they teach you at that school?" she asked, turning the mirror so that it shone the White Lady's reflection back at her. She bared her teeth, a glimpse of a snarl under the delicate fluttering veil. Moira kept the shard steady, even though it had nicked her thumb and blood ran down to her wrist.

"Mirrors can block magic," she explained. "Sometimes."

"This time?"

"We're about to find out."

The birds continued to attack and be attacked in turn. Feathers filled the air. Blood smeared the gargoyle's stone teeth. The sound of so many wings was faintly sickening as it shivered through the tiny courtyard. Gretchen scrabbled on the ground for stones, bits of broken pottery, and glass from a shattered window. She pitched them all at the birds as the White Lady continued to advance.

The sunlight bounced off the mirror and pierced through her veil. Moira craned her neck to make sure the White Lady's reflection was properly centered in the broken mirror. Then she dropped it facedown on the ground and smashed it with the heel of her boot.

The White Lady screeched once, sounding more like a gull than a woman. She shattered into glittering dust and was gone. Her birds faded away.

"Why is she even allowed in the markets, exactly?" Godric inquired, brushing mud off his sleeve. "She's a right nasty piece of work."

Moira shrugged. "Some folk will pay handsomely to be rid of a few memories."

The gargoyles remained, circling overhead. More detritus smashed on the ground. Someone gave a shout of alarm from the street. Before too long they would attract the kind of attention that also attracted the Order. Moira wasn't the only one who wanted to avoid them. Gretchen could do without another lecture. She'd lost whichever Keeper was trailing her this morning, but she wasn't keen on explaining why she'd ditched him.

"How do we turn them off?" Gretchen asked, titling her head back to watch the gargoyles.

"We don't. There's too much magic about." Moira shrugged,

sounding distracted. Her gargoyle tried to perch on the brim of her hat. "They're not bothering anyone and I have things to do."

"We can't just leave them," Godric insisted, touching her arm. She bared her teeth at him. His fingers dropped away. "The Order will come. If what you say is true, won't they suspect Madcaps are behind this?"

Moira swore ripely. Godric waited patiently, too accustomed to Gretchen's outbursts. "What do you suggest, Greybeard?" she finally asked.

"There's a gargoyle trap on the roof of the Ironstone Academy, isn't there? It's in Mayfair by—"

"I know where it is," she cut him off mildly. She pulled a chicken bone from some long-ago supper from her pocket. It was wound around with red thread at one end and designs were painted on the other. She snapped it in half. The gargoyles turned their heavy heads in her direction. Whistling a strange tune, she leaped to the next building.

The gargoyles swooped down toward her. She clearly wasn't afraid of them, but they could inflict considerable damage accidentally. A playful swipe with a stone claw could break her shoulder or send her tumbling to the cobblestones. She ran as fast as an alley cat.

Gretchen and Godric followed, less sure of their footing. Gretchen launched herself over decorative iron scrollwork several stories above the city. Godric looked like he wanted to throw up. When he wasn't looking smitten by Moira.

When they finally reached the roof of the academy, they leaned wearily against the chimney pots to catch their breaths. Even Moira was gasping, her tangled hair damp with sweat. The gargoyles circled them lazily, finally settling on the huge symbol marked out on the roof in bird bones and salt. An open barrel filled with whiskey and milk sat in the center.

"Thank you," Godric said, smiling at Moira. "You're very brave to have helped us. I'll make sure the Order knows to whom it is indebted."

She stared at Gretchen. "Is he daft?"

"No," Gretchen replied fondly. "Just kind."

"Tobias kissed you?" Penelope squeaked an hour later. *"Tobias?"*

"It was only to break the spell," Gretchen insisted as Emma squeezed past her. Gretchen knew Penelope would pounce on it. And if Gretchen blushed she was sure to make a remark. "Never mind that; I just chased off the White Lady and a swarm of gargoyles."

Penelope waved that away. "I want to hear about the kiss."

"It was nothing. What were we supposed to do? Let you all sleep for the next hundred years? Now, are you going to let me in, or what?"

The front hall and main parlor of the Chadwick family townhouse was a hothouse of roses, tulips, and hyacinths. Pink and yellow petals drifted over the marble floor, and pollen clung to the tabletops. They'd run out of vases and had resorted to painted teacups, set out on the windowsills and beside each of the chairs.

"It smells like an old lady in here," Gretchen said. Emma had already arrived and was handing her shawl to the butler, Battersea. A moth flew out of her hair.

"It smells like a garden," Penelope corrected.

"Same thing." Gretchen shrugged, following her into the drawing room. "Who sent you all those tulips?"

"Lord Beauregard," she replied, looking softly at enough tulips to fill Carlton House. "Isn't Lucius just a lovely name? He sent over a pair of pink silk gloves as well to replace the ones he spilled wine on." Penelope held her arm straight out to stop Gretchen when she moved toward the parlor. "Don't even consider it. I want details. Did anyone see you? Your mother will have you married by morning if she finds out about it. I danced with Mr. Abbotsford twice at the Pickford ball and she lectured me for an hour that I was too free with my favors, and in her day I'd have as good as declared my engagement with such behavior."

Gretchen shuddered. "I know. She'd say my reputation was at stake or some such rot and force us to marry." She had no intention of being coerced into marrying Tobias. Even if he was such a surprisingly good kisser. "It's not like people don't kiss all the time. I saw Oliver Blake and Ada Grey vanish into the shrubbery just last week at a dinner party. That was perfectly acceptable as long as no one saw them. It's daft."

"Bah. As if I care a fig for them. I want to know about your kiss. Was it divine?"

Emma's smile was sly. "It must have been, to break the spell so quickly."

Gretchen became suddenly very interested in the tulips. "It was magic."

"Oh ho!" Penelope hooted. "I'll bet it was!"

Gretchen rolled her eyes. "I meant actual magic, you goose." She refused to consider the fact that she'd relived the kiss a hundred times in her head already. She'd been so engrossed in the memory, she'd nearly tripped down the stairs this morning on her way to breakfast. Breaking spells was tiring work, was all. She'd stop hearing wolves howling every time she shut her eyes as soon as she recovered.

"Did he send flowers at least?"

"Of course not. It wasn't romantic, Pen. As if it could be." She half smiled. "Anyway, I kissed *him* actually. His pathetically polite kiss on the back of my hand didn't do a thing to stop the spell."

"*You* kissed *him*?" Penelope beamed at her.

"It was nothing. I'm sure he's forgotten about it already." Even if she couldn't.

Emma's smile was too knowing, too sympathetic. "I thought Cormac was indifferent at first too."

"That was different."

"How?"

"It just was," she said crossly.

"Perhaps I ought to kiss Lucius," Penelope suggested with a wicked smile. "He's taking entirely too long."

Gretchen raised an eyebrow in her direction. "Or Cedric?"

"Why would I do that?" She sounded almost panicked. "He'd laugh at me."

"He would not."

"You're just trying to change the subject," Penelope muttered, suddenly deciding that she preferred to be in the parlor after all.

"And my daughter here would have me believe she isn't a popular debutante," Aunt Bethany said from her favorite Egyptian chair. It was painted black, with cats for armrests and intriguing hieroglyphs along the back. She was surrounded with so many flowers she looked like Titania in her dark green dress, embroidered all over with tiny leaves and white birds. She'd no doubt done the needlepoint herself; it was too extravagant and beautiful to be anyone else's work.

Gretchen grinned at her. "The lads all love Penelope; it's the girls who get all lemon-faced."

Penelope wrinkled her nose. "Those boys only like me because I'm an heiress."

"And because you're kind," Emma put in.

"The same two reasons the girls make lemon faces," Gretchen added, stealing a slice of gingerbread from a silver platter. "And also because you're unfairly beautiful."

"I'm fat."

"You're stupid," Gretchen retorted immediately, with an affectionate pat to the arm. "Not fat."

Penelope stuck out her tongue. "Clarissa called me fat."

"Clarissa is a canker-blossom."

Penelope grinned. "You're cursing in Shakespearean. I'm so proud."

"I try. And since when do we care what a muttonhead like Clarissa says?"

"We don't," Penelope admitted. "I just forget sometimes."

An osprey landed on the nearest windowsill. It pecked at the glass, its dark eye gleaming like the jet beads the Keepers used to break spells. Aunt Bethany set her embroidery hoop down. "That's rather odd."

Another osprey landed next to the first. Moths flew out of the fireplace, in a cloud of dusty wings.

"Blast." Emma sighed. "Not again." She rubbed her arms, chilled. "They were all the familiars of the three Sisters."

Aunt Bethany nodded thoughtfully. "A side effect from bottling them, no doubt. You're not a Lacrimarium and yet you worked their magic. There are reasons they train for so long." She drummed her fingers on her knee, watching the ospreys flap their wings frantically. "We need the Toad Mother," she added finally. "She has spells for this sort of thing. A kind of magical purification."

"She sounds . . . odd," Penelope said with a smile. "I can't wait."

"I want you girls to be exceedingly careful," Aunt Bethany said, the little frown lines between her eyes suddenly becoming deeper. "The Sisters are dangerous."

"But they've been bottled."

"All the same. My father, your grandfather, was a Keeper for the Order when the Sisters went on their last rampage. Decades later, he still had nightmares. And he kept the house spelled against them until the day he died." She rubbed her arms, staring unseeing at the ospreys still pecking at the window. "They killed so many people at a winter ball once that he said the blood never washed off the floors. There's a reason the magpie is their crest. They steal and hoard away magic, using whatever means they can." She turned back to the girls. "Remember your rhymes. *One for sorrow, two for joy, three for a girl, four for a boy, five for silver, six for gold, seven for a secret never to be told.*"

"Isn't that for how many magpies you can count?" Gretchen asked.

"Yes, where do you think children's rhyme and folklore come from?" her mother replied. "And there were Seven Sisters when they were at their most powerful. It took centuries to banish them all."

"We'll be careful, *Maman*," Penelope said soothingly. "Promise."

Aunt Bethany smiled crookedly. "I'm getting as bad as your grandfather," she said. "Go on and take a turn about the garden in the meantime," she suggested. "Before that bird breaks the glass."

The door leading to the garden was flanked with two massive sphinx statues. The Egyptian decorating craze had passed, but Aunt Bethany's love of the artwork had remained. There was a statue of Anubis, the jackal-headed god of the dead, propped in the hallway, which the maidservants avoided. One of the footman swore the statue had blinked once, and then his mother had died of a fever the next day.

The garden wasn't any more traditional, even with the customary pebbled paths and hedges. Silver and glass charms dangled from tree branches, sending out sharp prisms of light. There were rowan saplings in pots lining each walkway and clustered at the gates. Snakes slid through the grass toward Emma, who strode grimly toward the painted shed.

Until a few weeks ago, they'd always assumed it was merely the stillroom where Penelope's mother made perfumes. It was easy to see now how much more was kept here. The dried flowers hanging from the hooks in the ceiling were wrapped in white thread. There were rowan berries everywhere, and jars filled with salt. It smelled like the last perfume or potion Aunt Bethany had concocted, heavy with lilac and amber.

Emma went straight to the small hooked rug under the worktable and kicked it aside to reveal the trap door. "I'm going," she announced.

Gretchen and Penelope exchanged a glance. "Shove over. You're not going alone."

"You might get in trouble."

"Promise?" Gretchen grinned.

"Almost definitely," Emma grinned back.

Penelope slipped between them and scurried down the ladder. "Are you two going to stand there all day grinning at each other like gooses?" She vanished into the dusty darkness. A curse followed almost immediately. It was mostly in archaic Tudor English and made no sense. Gretchen followed, Emma pulling the door shut over their heads.

The darkness swallowed them. It was so palpable, they could have drowned in it. There was barely any room to move, only elbows pressing into one another, and toes being stepped on. The air was damp and dungeonlike.

"I forgot how much I hate this," Emma muttered. There was the scrape of antlers on the wall, and a peevish, "Ow!"

Gretchen ran her hands along the walls until she found the doorknob. "Got it," she announced just as Emma started to hyperventilate.

Even though there was no door, turning the knob created an opening into the goblin markets. This time it didn't deposit them in the alley next to the Three Goblins tavern; it dropped them in the middle of the bridge. Only the large emerald-green snake that startled passersby prevented them from being run over by an ox with silver horns pulling a cart full of swan wings.

"Oi!" The coachman hollered at them, his black cat familiar hissing and spitting at his side. "Move it!"

They scrambled out of the way, letting the bustle of the crowd carry them to one side. The wind carried the scents of salt and flowers, overpowering the stench of the Thames below. The pomegranate lamps swung overhead, pealed open to reveal glowing seeds, hanging on leaf-twined chain, punctuated with red-glass lanterns. There were witches everywhere, sorting through evil-eye beads, dried grass picked inside the circle of Stonehenge, silver apples filled with cloves, and a dizzying array of protective charms in the shape of miniature white horses and gargoyles. Hawkers shouted about amulets guaranteed to stop the Greymalkin Sisters.

They stepped into a gap between a shop selling herbs and another selling gargoyles. The contorted stone faces watched them from behind diamond-paned glass. Moths clung to the shop sign like snow, and clouds of them drifted between the shops. "I don't remember it being this crowded before," Emma said, angling herself so she wouldn't accidentally stab someone with her antlers.

"That's because it wasn't," Gretchen remarked when a woman trod on her foot. The woman looked terrified, spitting on the ground to avert the evil eye and then losing herself in the throngs of witches. Gretchen shook her head. "I suppose I should be glad she didn't spit on me."

Strings of holed stones and rowan branches hung with bells promised to block warlock magic. It was the wind chimes made from silver knives and purporting to keep away the Sisters that gave Gretchen an instant headache. She stepped closer to the stall as Penelope wandered away to look at fruit.

"These wind chimes are faulty," Gretchen said, rubbing her temples.

"Piss off," the shopkeeper snapped.

She narrowed her eyes. "I'm only saying that if you replaced the glass beads there with amber and rose thorns, they might actually be effective."

"As if I can afford amber." He snorted. He leaned forward menacingly. "Now piss off, I said." He yanked a cord, dropping a curtain down to screen his wares from the curious bystanders who were starting to eavesdrop. Gretchen didn't like the undercurrent of suspicion and fear running through the markets.

Emma touched her arm. "We're drawing attention," she murmured. Moths had already covered the curtain. Gretchen nodded and stepped back, but not before she pilfered a miniature chime from the edge of the table. Emma raised an eyebrow.

"It's homework," Gretchen maintained. "I'm going to fix it so it works properly."

They ducked into the shadows. "We'd better find the Toad Mother," Emma murmured, as dozens of ospreys lined the roof across the bridge. "Before someone notices my new friends."

Tobias frowned at a flock of white ospreys flying overhead, their shadows crossing the bridge. "That's odd."

Cormac watched them circle with a shrug. "Goblin markets," he said, as if it explained everything. "Are they connected to the fox-girl trail?"

He shook his head, ignoring the old witch who made a rude sound when she saw his Keeper pendant. He also ignored the lady who fluttered her eyelashes at them. "No, but we're on the right track. I just have to sort through all of the blocking spells." There were so many charms dangling from every shop, stall, and lamppost that it gave him a headache and muddled his tracking. His brother would have told him to wear the wolf and be done with it.

"Fox-girls," Cormac winced. "I'd still rather fight a river demon in my smalls."

Tobias snorted. "As I recall, that didn't end so well."

"For the demon."

"And nearly for you."

He shrugged, grinning. "True."

"Anyway, fox-girls, like all girls, will stop whatever they are doing to flirt with you."

Cormac just grinned again. "Speaking of girls, if you're here, who is trailing after the delectable Lovegrove cousin?"

"Some poor sod who's being punished for falling asleep at the ball because he'd misplaced his shield charm," Tobias replied. "Gretchen will eat him alive." He shook his head. "I just don't understand those girls," he muttered.

"Girls aren't meant to be understood," Cormac returned. "Just appreciated." There was a flash of something in his eyes that Tobias couldn't read, but it was quickly replaced by Cormac's usual lighthearted charm. "Anyway, I suspect they'd say the same about us."

"I'm not even sure Gretchen Thorn *is* a girl," Tobias returned. "I've seen demons with softer manners. She fights everything. All of the time."

"Good," he said. "You could use a little fight in your perfectly pressed life."

Tobias narrowed his eyes. "What do you—"

"You must be talking about my sister," Godric interrupted mildly. "She has that effect on people." Though he looked as cheerful as ever, his wolfhound-familiar had an icy stare.

Tobias bowed politely. "You're late."

"Probably." He didn't seem too concerned about it. Tobias began to see the family resemblance between the twins. Most Ironstone students were keen to shadow Keepers for an afternoon.

Godric just glanced at Cormac and sighed. "There's a dead girl flirting with you."

Cormac grinned at the empty air. "Hello, lovely."

Godric raised his eyebrows. "Don't you find that the least bit disconcerting?"

Tobias snorted. "He'd find it more disconcerting not to have anyone flirting with him at all."

Chapter 6

Penelope couldn't help but admire the baskets of fruit in the stall half-curtained with strands of wooden beads. There were pomegranates, apples, pears, starfruit, pineapples, and sugar-dusted peeled grapes. She reached for a pear, gleaming like sunlight on gold. She'd never smelled anything sweeter. She could already feel the juice running down her chin. The old man behind the stall cackled. Her fingers brushed the fruit tenderly.

And then someone spun her sharply away, and she grabbed nothing but air.

The old man hissed his disappointment. Her own thirst for the fruit made her throat ache.

"You don't want to eat those," Cedric warned her, his fingers still wrapped around her wrist. "Goblin fruit."

She blinked at him. "What?" She felt bewildered and unbearably sad at the loss of the pear. She fought back tears.

"Goblin fruit will leave you addicted, like the blokes in the opium dens," he continued. "Some will even steal years off your life."

"Oh." She snatched back her hand. The clouds skittered over the sun. Cedric pulled her away from the stall, until she stopped stealing glances back at the baskets. She felt as though cobwebs were being pulled from her eyes. Her spider familiars raced around her, glowing irritably. She blinked up at Cedric again.

He wore his usual trousers and white shirt open slightly at the throat. No aristocrat would deign to show his throat in public; he'd wrap it up in a complicated cravat. Cedric was the coachman's son, and he couldn't afford cravats. He didn't wear colognes, either, or pad the shoulders of his coat to make himself seem larger. He was strong and muscular and honest. She had to remind herself that Cedric didn't feel the least bit romantic toward her. "What are you doing here?" she asked, coming out of her bewilderment.

"Your mother doesn't trust the Greybeards," he replied.

"Did he follow me here?" She peered over his shoulder. "Do you know who it is today? Ian said he had other plans, so someone else would be watching me."

"I can't believe you're on a first-name basis with him."

"I like him."

"I'm still setting the dogs on him. Anyway, the other two are still watching the house, waiting for your cousins to emerge. They're just students. They clearly don't think you can get into trouble at home." His smile was crooked and familiar. "And so they've just as clearly never met you before."

He bought a small tin of lemon drops from a woman selling

sweets and marzipan birds. He handed Penelope one of the candies. "Try one of these instead. They taste like sunshine."

She popped one into her mouth while slipping her arm through his. He didn't know it, but she'd keep the little tin in the keepsake box on her desk. She kept all of the little gifts he gave her, even though they meant nothing to him. She couldn't help herself.

"Since you're spying on us anyway, you can help us find this Toad Mother. Emma needs . . ." She paused, eyes widening. "I hear music! In my head!" She tilted her head, shaking it as though there were water in her ears.

Cedric chuckled. "It's the lemon drop."

"It's brilliant!" There was a pianoforte playing music just for her. She listened carefully, trying to memorize the tune. She wondered if she could play it herself, or if it would float away once the candy had dissolved.

"What have you done to Penelope?" Gretchen asked. "She looks barmy."

"Magic sweets," Cedric replied. "She's listening to music."

Penelope closed her mouth with a snap, once she realized it had been hanging open. She swallowed the last of the lemon drop hastily, nearly choking.

"You're not spying on us too, are you?" Gretchen asked.

"Just her." Cedric tilted his chin in Penelope's direction without an ounce of apology. "In case her Keeper is a prat."

"Ian's perfectly amiable."

"Mine's a prat though," Gretchen sighed enviously. "So's Emma's."

"Let's not get distracted," Emma suggested drily. Her antlers were covered in moths. There were more clinging to her shoulders like a fluttering shawl. People were starting to stare. A snake slithered out of a rainspout, trying to reach her. Dozens came down the bridge, spooking a Pegasus. A little girl chased them, scooping them into a wire birdcage mounted on a slender pole.

"Might I be of assistance?"

"Lord Beauregard!" Penelope exclaimed, turning to stare at Lucius. "I didn't know you were a . . . that is . . ."

He smiled at her, the light glinting off the silver buttons of his coat. "Witchery runs in my family too, yes." He blocked a serpent from crawling over Penelope's foot with the end of his walking stick. "We appear to be overrun."

"Aye," Cedric agreed without inflection.

Lucius reluctantly tore his gaze away from Penelope. "I beg your pardon. I see you already have an escort."

"Lord Beauregard, this is Cedric Walker." Penelope introduced them, despite the fact that no one bothered to introduce stable hands and family servants to earls. Cedric nodded a greeting.

Lucius's gaze went back to Penelope. He smiled shyly. "I hope you like tulips."

"They are my favorite," she assured him. "How did you know?"

"Lucky guess."

"Well, they are very beautiful, thank you."

"My pleasure." An osprey landed nearby, black eyes gleaming. His beak looked wickedly sharp.

"I'm afraid we must be on our way," Penelope said to Lucius, disappointment plain in her voice.

"Until we meet again then, my lady." He kissed the back of her hand, winking up at her when the others couldn't see. Her cheeks went pink. She couldn't help but watch him until he turned a corner and disappeared from view.

"This way," Cedric said quietly, leading them in the opposite direction.

Never mind that London Bridge shouldn't be able to host invisible markets; it certainly shouldn't be able to contain the volume of shops, stalls, and alleyways of the goblin markets. Once off the main path, it became a warren of hidden walkways. The cousins followed Cedric down an alley with cobblestones covered in snow even though it was a warm April morning everywhere else. Frost flowers climbed up the rainspouts. Icicles dripped on their heads and the alley stretched on far longer than was logical before ending abruptly at the railing overlooking the river.

Jutting out from the ironwork was a small thatched cottage, no larger than the fruit-seller's stall. Pink smoke curled out of the holes in the roof between a veritable legion of gargoyles. They were only the size of teacups, but they covered every inch, like grass growing on a manicured lawn. A bell hung on a post, more rust than iron. Cedric rang it but it stayed silent. "She'll hear it," he assured them. "It's best not to surprise the Toad Mother."

"How will we know if she . . . oh." Emma interrupted herself when toads emerged from the tiny fenced-off area in front of the green door. There were dozens of them, squatting on the stones and moving slowly between the pots of herbs. They had to pick their way carefully between live toads and glowing toad familiars that gave one an unpleasant shock when touched accidentally.

"Visitors," the Toad Mother said, emerging from her house. Her voice was as earthy and dark as her magic. She wore a simple woolen gown and a shawl over her shoulders. Her hair was unbound, brown, and streaked with gray. Her eyes were a strange pale green. She was beautiful in a hypnotic, slightly sinister way, like a cobra waiting to strike. She tilted her head. "Cedric."

The toads hopped slowly toward him. He didn't seem concerned, but Gretchen saw the way he angled himself so that he was slightly in front of the cousins. His smile was easy and uncomplicated. "Toad Mother," he said with a bow.

"My little ones have missed you," she said. Her voice seemed to multiply, as though there were several of her, all whispering together. She wore a silver toad necklace crouched in the middle of her collarbone, and there were tiny toad bones braided into the fringe of her shawl.

Her gaze drifted to the moths covering Emma's antlers, and her lips pursed. "That's a nasty piece of business, my girl."

"Yes." Emma nodded, not bothering with explanations or excuses. "It is."

"What have you brought me, then?"

Gretchen frowned, feeling for the reticule she always forgot to carry with her. "I don't have any money," she whispered.

"Me neither," Penelope whispered back. She unclasped the ruby pendant on a silver chain around her neck. "Only this."

"But that's not what you want, is it?" Emma asked steadily. "The last time I bought a magic charm, money never changed hands."

"Clever girl," the Toad Mother approved, waiting.

"A lock of my hair," Emma offered.

She laughed. "What would I want with that? I've got my own hair, don't I? And I'm not One-Eyed Joe, collecting trinkets."

"What do you want then?" Emma asked quietly.

"Let's talk, shall we?" The Toad Mother beckoned. Her witch knot was the color of dried blood. The ospreys wheeled away from her house in a panic of feathers. When the moths drifted too near, their wings turned to flames and smoke.

Emma took a deep breath and started to follow. Penelope and Gretchen were right behind her, practically tripping on her hem.

The Toad Mother looked over her shoulder, her glance withering. "Only you."

Emma nodded, her cheeks pale but her posture resolute.

"But . . ." Penelope would have kept walking if Cedric hadn't caught her hand. His fingers twined with hers. Gretchen paused when the toads glowed a vitriolic swamp green.

"Is it safe?" Penelope whispered to Cedric.

"Aye," he said. "Safe enough."

. . .

"Damn it," Tobias snapped as he caught the musky, earthy scent of the fox-girls again. "They're leaving the bridge."

"Fox-girls never hunt in the city," Cormac pointed out for Godric's benefit. "That can't be good."

They left London Bridge behind, following Thames Street along the river. Ships crowded the river and gulls screeched for food. "There are too many broken wards and too few Keepers," Tobias said. "If we can't get it sorted, it will threaten the authority of the Order. The Carnyx are already patrolling every night because we can't cover all of London anymore."

Tobias strode along, trying not to look as though he was sniffing the wind. There was something to be said for having the reputation of being a haughty viscount. People expected his nose to be up in the air.

"Still, you're right," Cormac continued. "My sister Talia is having more nightmares than usual. She keeps screaming about London being covered in ice and bones."

"Have you taken her to the dream temple?"

"She can't sleep when she's there, which makes it difficult for them to truly analyze her dreams."

"Even the ghosts seem out of sorts," Godric admitted. "Scared, almost."

"Makes sense," Cormac said. "They'd feel the magic in the city more keenly than we would."

There was a faint chorus of yips just under the general chaos of the streets as they turned off toward Fleet Street. Dust billowed out from under carriage wheels and street-sweeper boys darted back and forth between the horses. "This way."

They passed redbrick coffeehouses and chocolate houses, the pavements outside teeming with passersby. Burning sugar and roasted coffee trailed from the open doorways, momentarily sweetening the competing smells of runoff, horses, and fox-girls. Still, a gang of fox-girls shouldn't be difficult to track, even without scent markers.

Before they could pass through the Temple bar gateway, where Fleet Street turned into the Strand, Tobias stopped. "They're in the Inner Temple," he said, pushing through the wooden arched doorway of a Tudor-style house. Beyond lay the long brick buildings where barristers did their work, and extensive gardens. He vaulted over the decorative railings with their pegasi and griffins and into a moat of roses. Petals stuck to his shoes as he made his way to the orchards.

Among the quince and walnut trees were five fox-girls in their customary red cloaks. They were tall, with dark flashing eyes and pupils too oval to be strictly human. They yipped and taunted a shadow hiding in an upper branch. Tobias had a sense of quivering but not much else. His wolf stirred, sensing both prey and predator. The fox-girls felt him before they heard him.

They turned their heads slowly, all smiles and snarls. They wore mostly brown or white dresses under their red cloaks, leather belts bristling with daggers, even though in Tobias's experience, they preferred running their prey to ground until they were too exhausted to fight back.

"She stole from us," the fox-girl with the auburn braid said defensively, before anyone else could speak. Godric bowed, ingrained politeness stronger even than wild girls. Come to think of it, he was likely well used to wild girls, being Gretchen's brother.

Tobias peered up the walnut tree, finally catching a glimpse of a girl in a gray dress. She was barely twelve years old, with dirt on her nose and her hem. Tobias the wolf instantly knew her for a rabbit-girl. But she reminded Tobias the gentleman of his little sister Posy. Worse yet, rabbit-girls rarely traveled alone. If the rest of her family came searching for her, it would be next to impossible to hide the altercation from cowans. Especially barristers and solicitors, trained to look keenly. Magic already shimmered around them, glittering in the bright afternoon.

"You can come down," he said softly. "They won't hurt you."

She shook her head mutely.

"Oi, she's ours," the redheaded fox-girl snapped. "We've a right to hunt her, by witch rules and shifter rules both." Unlike Tobias, fox-girls never hid their shifter blood.

"What did she steal?" Cormac asked lightly, as if they were discussing how she took her tea.

"A moonstone," a fox-girl with skin like sweet chocolate answered. She nodded to the redhead. "Kitsu saw her."

Tobias bit back a sigh. Rabbit-shifters never could resist anything to do with the moon, and fox-shifters were notorious for dealing savagely with thieves. They were territorial and fearless.

"I didn't steal anything," the rabbit-girl whispered, voice trembling. "Honest."

"I *saw* you," Kitsu insisted hotly. Tobias had to hold her back and was nearly bitten for his trouble.

"Anyway, didn't think the Order had the time to bother with us," one of the girls said. "Shouldn't you be out there dealing with warlocks and uncontrolled magic?"

"We always have the time," Tobias said sharply, exchanging a grim glance with Cormac. "Especially when you take your hunt out into London. You know it's forbidden."

Kitsu shrugged out of his grip. "It was one of you Greybeards who told us to take it off the bridge."

His eyes narrowed. "I beg your pardon?"

"Said we'd have more sport if we took to the streets."

"You're lying."

She bared her teeth. The others shifted to stand behind her, bristling. Cormac stepped forward with his lazy, charming smile. "Ladies," he said. "I think we can agree there's no sport to a girl up a tree." They scowled at him. He spread his hands, unconcerned. "Chasing a viscount"—he winked—"now that's a proper sport."

The redhead snorted but her stance softened slightly, despite herself. "Not everyone wants a lordling," she said.

"True," he agreed. He bowed, taking her hand and pressing a kiss to her knuckles, which were scratched and bruised from digging through brambles. "But you can't blame me for trying." He straightened. "Let us hunt more pleasurable pursuits. There's a bounty on a herd of piskies running loose and stealing horses. I reckon fox-girls could hunt them down before anyone else."

They glanced at one another, intrigued. "How much?" Kitsu demanded.

"Two guineas."

She whistled. "That's a bleedin' fortune."

"Worth abandoning this hunt?" Cormac asked. "If I tell you where they were last spotted?"

"Aye," she agreed reluctantly. "I s'ppose so."

Tobias gestured to the rabbit-girl. "You don't have to be afraid now."

She climbed down gingerly, her face pale between the leaves. The light glinted off an egg of milky white crystal slipping out of her pouch. It landed in the dandelion leaves, just before she did.

"Oi," Kitsu shouted, making a grab for her. The girl kicked back savagely, slipping the moonstone back into her pouch.

"Thanks, gents." She threw Tobias a smug smile and vanished into the greenery.

Whenever Gretchen took a step in the direction of the Toad Mother's house, the smoke from the chimney turned to green sparks and stank of stagnant water. The toads advanced and the shock they gave when touched made her teeth clench and the taste of copper and burned salt sting her throat. There were welts on her ankle bones and scorch marks on the bottom of her dress by the time she gave up.

Cedric just leaned against the bricks of the confectioner's shop and waited patiently. If the window display was anything to go by, witches preferred their sweets to perform tricks. There were singing marzipan birds and cakes that turned from white to lavender to red every time you blinked. Cats and dogs and even a hedgehog all came to pay court to Cedric. Even the marzipan birds seemed unduly interested, singing loudly and pecking at the glass.

Penelope just rolled her eyes when Gretchen looked surprised. "It's always like this," she said. "The stable has as many stray cats as it does horses."

Cedric just shrugged. "Animals understand me, is all."

Since there was a white mouse curled up in the trouser cuff of his left leg, Gretchen was inclined to believe him. There was even a marmalade tabby, glowing with magic, who approached him and didn't immediately try to eat the mouse. The cat was familiar, but she couldn't think from where. She crossed her arms, staring hard at the cottage again. "She's been in there for ages," she said.

Penelope stood up from where she'd been trying to coax the hedgehog into her hand. Worry flitted across her face. "I know." Her glowing spiders scurried over the stones, trying to sneak around the toads. They flicked their tongues and the same green sparks as had burst out of the chimney singed the spiders. Penelope flinched.

"Stop that," Cedric told her calmly. "You'll only annoy her, and believe me, you wouldn't like her annoyed."

"He's right," Moira agreed from the roof of the confectioner's shop. "Annoying the Toad Mother is a good way to go home with warts. Or a goat's head."

Seeing her there in her patched trousers and battered hat reminded Gretchen where she'd seen the marmalade cat before. It was Moira's familiar. "This isn't your usual neighborhood," Moira said, shimmying down a trellis and landing in a crouch.

"Bit ragged for you, inn't it? Watch your backs, the Rovers are always about lately and they're not the friendly sort. "

"Emma's inside," Gretchen replied.

Moira whistled through her teeth. "After all the trouble I went to keeping her alive, what's she gone and done that for?"

Cedric nodded to the white birds lining the rail and the moths floating between them.

"Oh," Moira said, understanding immediately. "Rotten luck."

"As bad as the time you tried to set fire to Atticus's hat," Cedric said.

Moira elbowed him. "That was your fault."

"Hardly."

"You gave me the matchstick!"

"Well," he said with a wink.

Penelope watched them carefully, her expression unreadable. "Speaking of keeping Emma alive," Gretchen said to Moira. "You helped her buy that cameo to hide her from the Keepers, didn't you?"

"Aye, but One-Eyed Joe's all out. Ever since the Sisters made their reappearance, witches have been coming in from all over. Some as far as the Orkneys, even, to get their charms."

"Don't they have markets of their own?"

"Yes, but the goblin markets are the biggest, and One-Eyed Joe's the best," she answered proudly.

"Can he make more?"

She shook her head. "Not anytime soon. Those are his most complicated pieces, and he can't exactly be obvious about it. Greybeards are always trying to raid his tent."

"Wouldn't work anyway," Cedric put in. "Tobias Lawless is a tracker. Once he has your scent, he can find you."

Gretchen turned to Moira with a conspiratorial grin. "Maybe I can introduce you. I want to see if his icy disdain freezes his head clear through so it falls right off his shoulder."

"Deal. If you can control your brother. He's right daft."

"Probably," she agreed easily. "Why this time exactly?"

"He's been climbing onto the rooftops and leaving red roses everywhere."

Gretchen blinked. "Pardon?"

"It's like a bleeding hothouse up there now. He's going to get himself killed, if he's not careful."

Before Gretchen could reply, a bank of clouds appeared out of nowhere, chilling them. One shaped like a stag ate the sun. "Emma," she said to Penelope just before the ospreys exploded off the rail in a panic.

They wheeled around the cottage, squawking violently. They flew so hard at the invisible wards that white feathers fell as thick as snow. Magic seared the air. More of the white birds filled the sky, until they created a storm cloud of feathers. They dove down at the cottage, using their beaks as weapons, but they were flung aside again and again.

Propelled by the same magic, great slithering knots of serpents came down the alleyway, slipping out of rainspouts and tumbling from cracks in the walls. They moved as one toward the cottage, jewel-toned tails and tongues flicking.

Moths descended on every available surface, from brick to

glass windowpane and crouching gargoyle. They settled in
Penelope's hair and over Gretchen's shoulders and covered
the cobblestones so that to move was to crush papery wings
underfoot.

The clouds raced away, chasing each other into the distance.
Rain fell in a single sheet of cold silver needles, then dissipated.
Frost crept over the cobblestones. There was a pulse of power,
like a storm breaking, and the birds and moths and snakes were
all tossed away from the cottage. They went over the railings,
fell into the Thames, and flew frantically away from the bridge.
The resulting silence was sudden and disconcerting. Feathers
and torn moth wings slowly drifted down to the ground.

The door opened and Emma stepped out, blinking owlishly
at the bright light. She moved carefully, as if she wasn't certain of
her balance. Her hair was a tangle, knotted with dried leaves and
seedpods around her antlers. She didn't look hurt or wounded,
but Gretchen didn't feel particularly comforted by that. There
was something in her cousin's eyes she'd never seen before.

"Did she hurt you?" Penelope asked when Emma just
stepped silently onto the cobblestones.

"No," Emma replied. "Not exactly. But it's done. Let's go
home."

Moira looked at her from under the brim of her gentleman's
hat. "Toad Mother magic packs a punch. You all right?"

"Yes, of course."

Moira snorted in disbelief. "Suit yourself," she said before
climbing back up to the rooftop and vanishing over the shingles.

"Whisperer." The Toad Mother didn't need to raise her voice; it carried easily, rasping like thunder.

Gretchen turned slowly around, goose bumps raising involuntarily on the back of her neck. "Yes?"

"I've a message for you."

Gretchen frowned. "From who?"

"The spirits, the Ancient Ones, the Other Side. Who can really tell?"

"'Cause that's illuminating," Gretchen muttered, approaching warily. She paused on the edge of the toad-lined path. The Toad Mother smiled. It wasn't reassuring. There was something too hungry, too fierce about her. Her eyes might be the pale green of pretty glass perfume bottles, but it was the kind of glass that cut deeply before you'd even realized it was broken.

She tilted her head and Gretchen couldn't help but feel like a fly about to be swallowed.

"There's spirits speaking to you, girl," she said. "Learn to listen before it's too late," she repeated. Her expression turned even more forbidding, and worse, fear lurked under the warning. "For all of our sakes. Because soon, London will freeze."

"Is that their message?" Gretchen asked.

"Can't say, it's for you to learn to listen." And then she slammed the door shut and refused to come out again, no matter how much Gretchen rang the rusty bell.

"That was singularly unhelpful," she muttered. She couldn't supress the shiver that chased up her spine as they made their way back to the portal.

Passage through the dark cellar was disorienting; she was

briefly surprised it wasn't already nighttime when they emerged in Aunt Bethany's stillroom. The sun's bright daggers pierced the dust of the dried flowers hanging from the ceiling. It was still morning. The garden was free of snakes and moths and giant white birds. They should have felt relieved. Instead, everything felt more ominous.

The three young Ironstone students loitering outside the house didn't help.

Gretchen marched up to the carriage even as the curtain twitched hastily shut. She didn't bother knocking, only flung the door open and climbed inside. "So you found me, did you?" The boy stared at her. She sighed. She almost missed Tobias. At least he felt like a proper opponent. This boy looked like he might cry if she said a cross word. "How old are you?"

"Fifteen, sir. Um, miss. My lady."

She flopped back against the cushions. "Just take me to the academy before I'm late for class."

Chapter 7

Gretchen was trapped in a long, tedious class in a stuffy room with a row of small windows curtained against the sunlight, which might freckle the skin. It would be hours before they were liberated for tea. She longed to be in the ballroom with its scorch marks and gouges in the wall from archery practice. That was what witchery should be about.

"It is imperative that you learn to use your magic with the grace and elegance of a true lady," Miss Hopewell lectured. "Just as you would never let yourself be seen eating too much cheese or scratching your nose, you must ever be circumspect about your gifts," she continued. She wore so much pink today, she bore a strong resemblance to strawberry marzipan.

"Why?" Gretchen asked.

Miss Hopewell blinked. "Because it isn't polite to show off. Not to mention that you might put the secrecy of our world in danger."

"Or worse," Clarissa giggled. The plumes she'd tucked into her hair wavered. They were meant to be worn at fancy balls, but Clarissa loved them so much she wore them everywhere. "You might scare off your suitors." She paused, wrinkling her nose at Gretchen. "Not that you have any, of course."

Gretchen rose from her chair with every intention of slapping Clarissa with her own feathers.

"Sit down, Gretchen," Miss Hopewell said, stepping between them. "This kind of unladylike behavior is exactly what we are trying to avoid."

"But making rude comments is considered genteel?" Penelope pointed out archly.

"And I wasn't trying to be quarrelsome before," Gretchen added, sitting back down. "I just happen to like cheese."

Miss Hopewell pinched the bridge of her nose. "Girls should be flowers, not thorns. You mustn't flaunt your power or your cleverness. It only draws attention. And right now, attention is not what we are seeking." Her expression was somber. "The more discreet you are, the safer you are."

"Shouldn't we be learning to defend ourselves then?" Gretchen knew by the flush of red creeping up Miss Hopewell's neck that she'd said the wrong thing again.

"The Order will protect us. The best thing we can do is carry on to show the Keepers that we have faith in them."

It was the same argument Gretchen's mother used about the war with France. Apparently the more Gretchen danced and curtsied, the more patriotic she was. The soldiers would sense it and know they were appreciated. She dropped her chin on her hand. Taking it for acquiescence, Miss Hopewell continued with her lesson.

"Observe." She smiled and curtsied, dropping her eyes demurely. The floor trembled once, as though the earth were splitting open. The girls clutched at their desks, gasping. Miss Hopewell rose out of her curtsy and the ground was still once more. "There, you see? I was polite and modest and no one would suspect me."

Gretchen could have cared less about being modest, but she rather seriously envied their teacher's talent for psycho-kinesis.

Miss Hopewell sank onto a chair and reached for her tea-cup. Above her head, the chandelier rattled. "The trick is to give them something else to observe," she explained. "Something like a flawless curtsy or a simple movement of your hand. It has to be both memorable in the moment and utterly forget-table. You must never forget that you are ladies first and witches second."

Miss Hopewell motioned Daphne to the front of the class. The students whispered to one another, "Lilybeth" and "murder" being mentioned more than once. Daphne used to be famous for being the talented daughter of the First Legate; now she was famous for finding the body of her best friend. It was not improving her disposition.

"Girls!" Miss Hopewell clapped her hands. The desks, chairs, and inkwells trembled warningly. An abrupt silence fell. "You may begin, Daphne."

Daphne lifted her chin haughtily. The delicate cameo she

wore around the neck hung on a gold chain and was carved from abalone shell. It wasn't a rose or a Greek nymph but rather a scowling gargoyle such as the ones crouching on the roof of the academy. The rest of her was as polished as a celebrated debutante could possibly be. Her morning dress was trimmed with lace and printed with mint-green leaves. She lifted her fan, the ivory bones studded with pearls. It was painted with bluebells and the silhouettes of unicorns. No one else seemed to notice the flower fairies pinned under their hooves. Gretchen's respect for Daphne reluctantly increased.

"Duck," Penelope whispered, remembering the last time they'd seen a demonstration of Daphne's magic. Her magic was such that any spell she cast unerringly found its target. She'd flung boiled beets at their heads. With remarkable precision.

"You are not required to speak, Penelope," Miss Hopewell said sternly.

"Clearly she's never had to wash beets out of her ears," Penelope muttered. She held up a thick leather-bound book as a makeshift shield.

Daphne curtsied gracefully, her mouth hidden behind the fan. Properly hidden, she recited a simple spell, then she lowered the fan with a twist of her wrist. It pointed at Clarissa, who had whispered the loudest about Lilybeth. She was determined to fill Daphne's role in the student hierarchy, now that Daphne had lost her best friends to murder and madness.

The inkwell on Clarissa's desk tipped over. She squealed and jumped to her feet. The ink spread and dripped over the edge of the desk, but instead of landing on the carpet, it emerged in black spots on Clarissa's dress. She shrieked as if she'd been stabbed.

"Very well done, Daphne," Miss Hopewell said. "You may resume your seat." She frowned at Clarissa. "That is enough, Clarissa. You know better than to attend spell class without your apron." She surveyed the class slowly. Hands lifted eagerly while others shrank back shyly. "Gretchen," she said eventually. "This is an exercise you could benefit from."

Gretchen stood up reluctantly. Miss Hopewell motioned for her to stand at the front of the room. "I will cast three spells, each slightly incorrect. You will act as though you have not noticed anything untoward, and then you will tell me what is wrong with each spell."

Gretchen braced herself.

"Begin."

She curtsied, feeling like an idiot. Miss Hopewell used salt to create a symbol on the floor. She couldn't tell what was off about the spell, or what it was meant to do, only that it must be something minor. The sound in her head was like waves on the shore, or bird wings, constant but not unpleasant. She strained to hear words, but there was only that murmur. She teetered slightly on her back foot and nearly lost her balance. Daphne and Clarissa exchanged haughty glances, back on the same side. Gretchen gritted her teeth.

"Again," Miss Hopewell said. "This time you will take a turn about the room."

Gretchen circled the room, casting a longing glance at the door as she passed by it.

Miss Hopewell sighed. "I haven't even begun yet, Gretchen, and that is all wrong. You are meant to glide, not march. This is not the militia."

Gretchen contemplated inventing a new spell that would turn Miss Hopewell's hair into snakes.

Instead, she walked, she glided, she positively floated. And she still felt like an idiot.

An idiot with needles piercing her brain.

The buzzing was sudden and painful. The waves were gone, replaced with the grinding of a blade on a whetstone, the screeching of gulls, the relentless grating of rusty hinges. She was instantly queasy.

"Keep gliding," Miss Hopewell ordered, but her voice was very far away. There were too many other voices all talking at once. Sorting through them was like unraveling a knotted carpet. She tried to focus on just one word, one tone, the way Mrs. Sparrow had told her to. It was like trying to hold on to water.

"Unring the bell."

There. A thread. She followed it, her eyes scrunched tight. She'd stopped trying to walk. She almost had it. Pain ricocheted inside her skull. But she wouldn't let go. Neither would they, it seemed.

"We are still here."

"Stop it!" That was Penelope, trying to hold her up. "Can't you see her ears are bleeding?"

Miss Hopewell rushed forward. The other students squeaked with alarm. It was just one more layer of voices.

Gretchen threw up into a potted plant.

"Well, that's not very ladylike," Daphne remarked.

Moira went to visit One-Eyed Joe to make sure the magic leaking through the Dials neighborhood hadn't affected him. His flat was on Pillory Street, tucked into a building that looked ready to fall over. But inside, his room was tidy and sparse, with none of the clutter of his stall in the goblin markets. He smiled at her when she popped her head in. "Well, here's herself," he said.

She shrugged out of her coat as quickly as she could, hanging it on one of the hooks by the door. Though it was warm outside, he had a fire burning in a cauldron and a warm brick wrapped in flannel at his feet. The air was humid and smoky. "Are you all right?" she asked.

"Of course I am," he scoffed, as always. "Why wouldn't I be?"

"Because it's hot as Hades in here, old man."

He cackled. "I've always wanted to visit exotic islands where the sun beats like a fiery heart."

"And a poet today, besides." She shook her head at him, grinning. "Have you been into the gin again?"

"Not a'tall," he said. "What brings you by?"

"There's something in the air," she said. "Even the goblins are watching their backs, and you know them, they've got the delicate sensibilities of a bull. And I had a run-in with the White Lady in the Seven Dials."

"So I heard." One-Eyed Joe coughed into a pink handker-chief.

His dark face was more wrinkled than she remembered, like cracked earth. Her familiar butted her head against his arm. "I'll make you some tea," she said.

She filled the kettle and set it to boil, making a note to gather more water before the end of the week. He was running out again, and there was only half a stale loaf of bread and a hunk of cheese in the cupboard. "What have you been eating for sup-per?" she demanded.

He shrugged. "Not very hungry."

"Well, you'll eat now," she warned him. "I've brought muf-fins and sausages from the street cart and also those dryad-apricots you like so much." She brought him a tray piled with food and strong tea in a chipped mug. He made the steam into somersaulting mice for Marmalade to chase.

The tea brought the sparkle back into his eyes, and he sat up a bit straighter, though she still wasn't fond of the wheeze in his breath. "I hear there's a fine young lad bringing you flowers."

Moira rolled her eyes. "Now who told you that, you old gossip?"

"I've my ways. Will you let him catch you?"

She snorted and handed him a piece of cheese. "Eat this."

Even feeling poorly, One-Eyed Joe was as stubborn as three mules. "You could marry into the fancy and have a roof over your head instead of under it."

She stared at him. "Don't be daft."

"It's not daft to want you safe," he grumbled.

"It is when you're babbling about earls' sons marrying rag-gedy orphan girls," she tossed back. "He's having a go at the wild life," she added dismissively. "It's nothing."

"You underestimate yourself."

"And you overestimate me," she said fondly, bringing him an extra blanket when he shivered. "You've got the ague and it's addling your brain." She kissed his clammy forehead. "I'll bring you some tonic later tonight," she promised. "And have Cedric pop in as well."

"Don't bother the boy," One-Eyed Joe muttered, his eyes drifting closed. "It's just a wee fever." He'd barely finished his sentence before sleep claimed him. She watched for a moment longer, chewing on her bottom lip, before turning away.

She was down the street when her feet prickled suddenly. She was yanked into a doorway before she could even contem-plate changing course.

That's what she got for taking the road like the fancy instead of the rooftops like a Madcap.

She didn't recognize the person who was now gripping her arm behind her back, threatening to snap it out of its socket. She was at an odd angle and there wasn't enough room in the door-way to reach her dagger, even if she could have loosened his hold, which didn't feel likely. It was like being grabbed by an ox. It smelled like it too.

"Oi, leave off!" She struggled, trying to kick back hard enough to shatter a kneecap or, better yet, something he valued a little more highly. He twisted away.

"Someone wants to see you," he said in her ear. His voice

didn't sound familiar. His breath smelled like black ale, and the only places that served black ale were in the goblin markets. He was a witch, she knew that much at least.

"Son of a bitch," she cursed as he forced her up a narrow staircase, the steps splintered and stained under her boots. He slapped his free hand over her mouth, stifling any plans that involved screaming at the top of her lungs. Not that she'd have expected it to grant her much help. In this neighborhood, you saved your own life by pretending not to hear most of what went on behind closed doors and back alleys. Or even out in the middle of the street.

Her mind raced. Procuring rare magical ingredients for One-Eyed Joe and her own paying clientele had its dangers, but she couldn't think who she might have angered lately. She didn't deal with warlocks or Rovers, which didn't win her friends, but she was faster than they were.

Usually.

She was forced into a small apartment with a few broken ladder-back chairs, a wooden table constructed from an old door and stolen bricks, and a shelf with chipped crockery. There were two boys near her age, a girl with long brown hair, and another young man with lavender eyes and a matching violet hat.

Fear turned to fury, lighting like a dry field in high summer.

"What the hell, Atticus?" Moira spat when her captor released her. Her dagger was in her hand before she'd fully regained her footing, but he'd already kicked the door shut and stood in front of it, beefy arms crossed. He couldn't stop her familiar though, and Marmalade swiped at him before leaping through the wall.

Moira shifted so the dirty grate with its old cauldron was behind her.

"Thank you, Ogden," Atticus said, playing lord of the manor despite his Cockney accent and the mended seams of his stolen coat. Atticus turned to Moira and spread his hands out as if he were in the Prince Regent's new Carlton Palace instead of a shabby room with mice nesting in the corners. "Welcome."

Moira didn't know what he was doing here, but she knew it was nothing good. She didn't know who the new bloke was either, but Atticus and his regular gang, Rod, John, and Piper, usually kept to a back alley behind a bookshop in the goblin markets. The last time she'd seen them was when they'd broken Strawberry's wrist.

She bared her teeth. "Go to hell, Atticus."

"And here I was going to offer you tea," he said with his smug smile, the one she always wanted to slap off his pretty face. She lost what little patience she had and made a move toward him. Ogden came up behind her, crushing her fingers until her dagger clattered to the ground. He kicked it away and stepped back, again without a word. Piper bent to pick it up, smiling. She hated Moira as much as Moira hated Atticus. Maybe more.

"Now, now," Atticus preened. "We've come up in the world, Moira. You'll have to show me some respect."

"Like that's going to happen." She rubbed her aching fingers. A cart trundled by outside, shaking the entire flimsy building. Dust trickled from the ceiling. Cold air blew through the cracks in the wall. "What are you doing in this rat's nest, anyway?"

His pretty violet eyes narrowed. He claimed they were proof of his royal Fae bloodline, but he was as much a fairy prince as she was. It was a glamour, pure and simple. "We need a dead witch's teeth. And you're going to get them for us."

"What do you need them for?" she demanded, not even bothering with the rest of his idiotic demand. As if she would ever work for him.

"I don't ask questions, my pretty," he replied. Piper snarled at the endearment. "But we have a fine patron now. A gentleman. You'll be well compensated."

"Get them yourself."

"I would, but it's proving distressingly difficult to procure."

She snorted. "Who are you fooling with those fancy words? I knew you when you begged for coins and rotten leftovers at Leadenhall market."

Atticus was fast, she had to give him that. He never fought his own battles unless he had a clear advantage, and she was cornered and outnumbered. The slap rocked her head back, splitting her lip open so that she tasted blood. Pain bloomed like a red flower, sending roots into her back teeth.

Piper clapped her hands like a child at a carnival. "Oh, well done, Atticus. It's about time someone took her down a peg."

"Shut it, Piper," he snapped, his furious eyes never leaving Moira's face.

She refused to touch the throbbing ache of her cheek, only spat blood on his boots. "You're as stupid as you are mad if you think I'm going to help you," she said, half laughing.

"I don't see how you have any choice," he returned. "There's five of us against little raggedy you."

A cup rolled off the shelf, smashing into pieces.

"Um, Atticus."

"I said, shut it, Piper." He fisted his hand in Moira's hair, forcing her head back. She dug her nails into his wrist. "I can offer you so much more than the old man and your pathetic gang," he said.

She smiled at him even though her scalp hurt. "You could never offer me anything that would even tempt me. I'll take winter hail on a broken rooftop over a house of gold with you in it any day."

A frigid wind rattled violently at the window. Atticus jumped, his hold loosening slightly. Frost filled the holes in the walls and crept down the chimney, limning the cauldron with ice. Winter howled in the narrow room, hurling itself about like icy daggers.

"It's a ghost," Piper said through chattering teeth. "That's what I was trying to tell you!"

Atticus's hat was plucked off his head by an invisible hand. He swallowed nervously. "Do something!" he ordered the others.

Rod and John swiped at nothing, coming away with frost-bitten fingertips. Even Ogden looked nervous, clutching a charm of iron nails and red thread. Moira didn't bother worrying about a ghost; instead she punched Atticus right in the face. He howled, staggering back and letting go of her hair. She leaped out of reach, picking up a chair to use as a weapon.

Pip crashed through the glass behind her, his teeth in his

little gargoyle face surprisingly jagged. He flew straight for Ogden, who was still blocking the door. His leathery wings slapped at Ogden's face and his talons raked at his skin, leaving raw gashes. Ogden stumbled aside, punching at the gargoyle. Pip darted away, angry as a hornet.

Moira rushed to the doorway, pausing briefly. "The Greybeards will never let you trade in witch's teeth, you idiot."

Atticus tossed his blond hair off his face, hiding behind Rod, John, and Piper, who had surrounded him. "Who do you think wants to buy them?"

When her parents finally left for the theater, Gretchen closed herself up in her bedroom with a pot of tea and her new grimoire. She thought she felt a tingle in her witch knot when she smoothed her palm over the cracked leather cover. The tiny bells shivered.

She paused over a spell designed to silence gossip. There was a whisper of sound, like a voice carrying across a great distance. She couldn't help but think the spell would be more effective with the addition of honey and beeswax. She didn't know why the thought popped into her head, but the ensuing silence from the whispering had a decidedly smug quality to it.

She read about iron horseshoes hung over doors for good luck, hagstones on red cords for protection and to see fairies, and putting the name of a disagreeable person in a jar of honey. She considered testing it on Daphne but decided if she was going to experiment with magic, it should be for something more useful. Unfortunately, there was no spell on how to stop your mother from throwing you at eligible bachelors like kitchen leavings tossed in the pigpen. She felt certain she wasn't the first to wonder about such a spell. Surely one of the Rowanstone students over the years had discovered something. She made a mental note to ask around between classes.

She stopped at a page with a black border like mourning paper. It was a protection spell listing salt, an iron nail, rowan berries, and red thread, like most of the magic preferred by the Order. It also called for a thunderstone, the sketch showing a small flint arrowhead like the ones Godric used to collect when they were little. She'd helped dig them out of ancient barrow mounds on the country estate. They'd spent that entire summer hunting for the elves and fairies they were sure had left them behind.

If a Keeper like Tobias intended to follow her around like a bloody hunting dog, it might be a good idea to have a few spells in her arsenal. The instructions were simple enough. And Mrs. Sparrow had encouraged her to study and practice, after all.

And frankly, if it helped stop the constant muttering and headaches, she'd gladly dance naked in a toadstool ring in the middle of Hyde Park.

Feeling instantly more cheerful now that she had a plan, Gretchen went next door to her brother's room. It was still kept ready for him, with clothes, books, and her old sword collection on the wall. It was bad enough that Gretchen had always collected odd things like snail shells, dragonfly wings, and strangely shaped rocks, but Godric had to pretend her sword collection belonged to him in order to keep the peace.

Under the swords was a stack of wooden chests with brass hinges packed with Godric's old toys and knickknacks. The first was a jumble of toy soldiers and broken kites. The next was filled with cedar and lavender sachets to guard against moths and mice. Under a toy boat with a collapsed mast and a paint box was another, smaller box wrapped with twine. It rattled promisingly. When she opened it, it was filled with rocks, acorns, and several chipped arrowheads. The spell had also called for an adderstone, but she decided a hagstone would work just as well, since there were a few already in the box. She picked a small one, the hole in the center worn through by the constant kiss of the ocean.

The house was quiet all around her as Gretchen gathered the rest of the ingredients from the kitchen and her mother's sewing box. Back in her room, she drew a teacup-sized circle out of salt on the floor and placed three rowan berries and a spool of red thread in its center. She added a sprinkle of flower petals from the vase on her desk, just because it appealed to her. She was beginning to realize that her instinct for patterns and collections of items from tiny bird skulls to swords, were as much a magical trait as a personality trait. It was strange to consider how little she might actually know of herself.

She wrapped the blunt end of the arrowhead in red embroidery floss, adding a hagstone and a wrinkled rowan berry struck through with a bent silver pin. It was an unusual assortment that would horrify her mother's elegant taste—which was only part of the reason Gretchen decided she liked it. It tingled briefly, but even so it was only a curious necklace and nothing more.

Magic might be inherent in certain items and combinations therein, but something more had to be awakened for it to have a true effect. Emma's power over the weather was intrinsic—it came from her own self. She could channel it into a spell for healing if she practiced hard; the same way Gretchen's talent for recognizing spells might be channeled. If she learned to control it before it killed her outright, of course.

The thunderstone pendant needed to be awakened. If she'd been a hedgewitch with no ingrained power of her own, she would have to steal that power from the earth, the rain, fire, trees, birds. A warlock would steal it from another witch, or kill for it, as Sophie had done.

Gretchen, being Gretchen, had frustration, disobedience, and impudence to spare, but she wasn't certain it would do her much good in this case. She leaned over the talisman, drumming her fingers on her knees. "Well? Do something!"

She was going to have to remember that speaking idly was no longer a luxury for a witch without full control of her powers.

Preferably before she was struck deaf and her head exploded.

She clutched at her ears as dozens of voices whispered urgently, making gooseflesh rise on her arms. It was a jumble of noise, as disconcerting as hearing footsteps above you when you knew the attic was empty.

She read the spell again. She'd collected everything that was required, but her magic was telling her something was clearly missing. She clenched her teeth. It was remarkably difficult to think with all the disembodied chatter.

The amulet was meant to protect her from harm. It was a shield or, better yet, a sword. The arrowhead needed to remember that it was an arrowhead, not just a trinket. It needed to remember how to be a weapon.

Before she could change her mind, Gretchen sliced through the skin of her thumb with the chiseled point. Pain flared. The cut opened.

"And that is the only pain of mine that you will ever have," she said. "Or allow others to have." She pushed all of the adrenaline and anxiety the whispering caused into the amulet.

"Only a warlock's spell," the voices shouted in a chorus that made her head snap back. She was left with the rasping of her breath and blood trickling from her ears. And no particular clue as to what it meant.

But the magic in the amulet was sound.

When Emma climbed up into the waiting carriage, Cormac grinned at her from the rear-facing seat. Startled, she jerked back, her antlers scraping the side of the carriage. She glanced out of the door quickly as it shut, hoping the school footman hadn't heard her squeak of surprise. She twitched the curtains shut. "What are you doing here?"

"Waiting for you."

"Why?"

"I have a surprise," he said, tugging her closer to him. When the carriage turned off toward the Thames, Emma glanced at him questioningly. "I was supposed to visit Penelope."

He was still grinning, a wicked gleam in his dark eyes. "I know."

She narrowed her eyes. "You look like the cat among the canaries," she said. "What are you up to?"

"It's high time you experienced some of the beauty of the witching world. You've experienced too much of its danger already. There is a debt owing to you, love."

She liked the way he called her "love." Liked it enough that she nearly missed the rest of his sentence. She forced herself to concentrate.

"I'm taking you to Vauxhall."

"The pleasure gardens?" she asked, confused. She'd been once before to watch a balloon ascent. There'd been champagne and strawberries afterward, and a stroll through the picture gallery. "But that's nothing to do with witches."

"On a full moon, I think you'll find you're very much mistaken."

There was a warm flutter in her belly at the promise in his voice. In the close confines of the carriage, his knee pressed against her. She cleared her throat. "What about Virgil?" she asked, hating to break the moment. "Won't he see us together?"

Cormac smirked. "Virgil will follow this carriage to your aunt's house, where Penelope has constructed herself a set of papier-mâché antlers and plans to parade in front of the window for the rest of the evening."

That startled a laugh out of her. She could well imagine Penelope doing just that.

When they reached the Chadwick townhouse, a second carriage pulled down the lane behind them. The family crest had been taken off the door, but the dark wood and the brass fittings gleamed. This was no hired hack with the smell of gin and onions upon the cushions. The door opened and Cormac slipped out, keeping his body between the two carriages so as not to be seen from the road. Emma followed suit.

The carriage pulled away and the front door opened. Light spilled over the front step. Penelope waved from behind the butler, the shadow of her costume antlers crowning her head.

Cormac drew the curtains closed again as they pulled out into the street. "There he is," he said softly. Emma followed his gaze and caught the briefest glimpse of Virgil leaning against the garden wall of the house across the street. He looked bored.

"He doesn't have an umbrella," Emma murmured. "That's not very practical. Doesn't he know how often it rains in London?" Thunder purred overhead, like a lazy jungle cat.

"As much as I'd like to see him as the drowned rat he is, best save your magic for the Fith-Fath glamour so no one at Vauxhall recognizes you." He lifted a mask from the folds of the velvet cloak. "And you can wear this as well."

It was made of supple leather, painted white and decorated with silver beads and spangles. The edges curled into spirals at the corner of each eye, with a fringe of glass beads falling from the bottom to further conceal her features. Cormac leaned

forward to hold it against her cheekbones while she tied the ribbon tightly.

"You haven't been sleeping," he said softly, so near that his
lips nearly brushed hers. Her breath went warm in her chest.

"It's nothing." She didn't want to tell him about the nightmares, not now. Not after he'd gone through so much trouble
to give them an evening without warlocks and curses and
secret witching societies. He didn't need to know that she'd
offered the Toad Mother a secret in exchange for a spell to
allow her to open a portal. The spell required something personal that belonged to Ewan, which was up to Emma to supply,
and a silver bough the Toad Mother promised to procure.
According to the old stories, an apple branch wrapped in silver
bells guaranteed the bearer safe passage to and from the Underworld. The apple tree had to grow on a hilltop, watered with
rain gathered in thunderstorms and cut down under the light of
an eclipsed blood moon. They were, understandably, not easy
to come by.

"You're miles away," Cormac murmured.

She forced her attention back to the present. Cormac leaned
back against the cushions with a kind of lazy confidence, like
nothing could surprise him. The other boys tried to emulate
him, but they always looked bored and peevish, whereas Cormac looked like he was harboring a delicious secret.

When they reached Vauxhall, he paid the entrance fee at the
gate and stepped into the sprawling acreage of London's most
famous pleasure garden. Groves of trees were divided by gravel
paths, waterfalls, grottos, and marble statues. An orchestra played

in the main rotunda where visitors danced or else retired to lavishly decorated supper boxes to eat delicate slices of ham and strawberries.

Cormac led her past the crowds, into the groves where nightingales sang and thousands of glass lamps were strung in the trees. They were set up to flicker into life all at once on musical cues. Emma would have suspected magic, if she didn't know better.

They passed a tightrope dancer wearing spangles and crossing over a courtyard fountain on a rope bridge strung between a temple and a pavilion. Cormac held Emma's hand, and she let herself be carried away with the bright, cheerful chaos of the garden. Fatigue fell off as they made their way deeper and deeper into the woods, where, judging by the furtive shadows, other couples were also seeking privacy.

"There are glamours and illusion charms to keep the others from stumbling upon us," Cormac explained, stepping around a clump of stinking mayweed. "That evil plant keeps all but the most curious out anyway."

Emma's eyes watered. "I can see how."

There was more foliage and fewer lamps, but other than the unfortunate smell, there was nothing else to differentiate this grove from any other grove in the park.

Until Cormac walked between two oak trees and vanished completely.

Emma's mouth dropped open when the space between the trees rippled and gleamed like old-fashioned green glass. It mirrored nothing, did not show her stunned reflection, only the sway of branches beyond, like any windowpane. There was a faint glitter though, like diamond dust clinging to the leaves and branches and the very air itself.

"Cormac?" she whispered. The witch knot on her palm began to feel warm.

Cormac did not reappear, but his arm extended to beckon her from behind the glittering wall of glass. Taking a deep breath, she took his hand and let herself be pulled forward. There was a brief moment of dizziness, a flash of light behind her eyelids, and then she was standing at his side while a swarm of miniature dragonfly maidens flew by.

It rivaled even the splendor of the goblin markets; as the secret garden under the full moon was clearly meant to be a place for celebration. There was no dread of the Order or the Rovers; it was simply witches in their best finery dancing under the stars without fear of discovery. Tables were piled with gingerbread, bottles of strawberry cordial, apple-petal cake, and crescent-shaped biscuits rolled in fine sugar that Cormac called moon cakes. Wind chimes shivered the air, not just with sound but with musical notes, like miniature harps being played up in the trees. Cormac brought her to a cobble-stone maze surrounding a fountain where the stone mermaid had been animated to wash her hair with water being poured from a shell.

"It's perfect here." Emma smiled at him. "Like something out of a poem."

"Nearly perfect," he said. The tips of his ears were red when he pulled a silver chain from a pocket inside his cutaway coat. A small star dangled and spun, the moonlight and lamplight glinting off tiny inset diamonds.

"It's beautiful," Emma breathed, touched.

"This way you always have your stars, even on a cloudy night," he said gruffly.

He understood her. He saw her when so many others had only ever seen the quiet girl at the fringes of the ballroom. She beamed, fastening the clasp around her neck. And when she rose up on her tiptoes to kiss him, he closed his arms around her, lifting her up against his chest. She could have stayed there forever, his lips on hers and nothing else to think on.

When Godric came home a few hours later, Gretchen found him in the parlor, listlessly poking at the dwindling fire. "You have lovely rooms far from parental smothering," she pointed out lightly. "And you're wasting them. It's shameful, really."

"It's merely trading one set of rules for another," he returned. "Not to mention that it's rather crowded with Keepers and their dead ancestors at the moment. Most of them are currently jammed into the parlor, trying to outmatch one another. It was giving me a headache."

Gretchen straightened. "Is that so?"

He turned his head sharply, recognizing her tone. "Lord, no."

"I haven't said anything yet."

He snorted. "I don't need to be your twin to know there's a very bad idea hatching inside that daft head of yours."

"Why does everyone keep saying that?" she grumbled.

"Because we know you."

She wouldn't be gainsaid. Her eyes were shining. "I think it's time you had a visit from your dear old cousin Geoffrey Cove, don't you?" It had been too long since she'd donned a set of Godric's old clothes and ran about town with him with all the freedom being dressed as a boy could offer.

"Most emphatically not." He dropped his head in his hands, knowing the battle was already lost whatever he might have to say about it. Gretchen was bouncing on her toes, like a child about to enter a sweetshop. "Wouldn't you rather sneak into a tavern, like we used to?"

She would actually, but this was more practical. "Not this time. I want to know what the Keepers are saying."

"I could tell you." He already knew it wouldn't be good enough, before she shot him a telling look.

"You're hardly ever there," she added with a snort. "And I want to hear it for myself."

"You want to rub their noses in it later, you mean."

She grinned, unrepentant. "That too."

She took the polished oak stairs two at a time, a habit her mother had been trying to break her of for years. She pulled off her gown impatiently, ripping the seams when she tugged too hard. She couldn't ring for her lady's maid to help her. Marie would never be able to keep such a secret from her mother's gimlet glare. Gretchen pulled on trousers, a linen shirt, and a waistcoat to hide her curves, then buttoned a coat on top of it all. She already felt more like herself.

Godric was still in the parlor, guzzling port while he waited. She grabbed the bottle. "You can't be three sheets to the wind if this is going to work."

"Too late. Let's stay home."

She dragged him down the hall as he muttered about sisters and the ghost of the cat hiding behind the umbrella stand.

They hired a hack out on the street, which took them to his apartments. The building was reserved for the sons of the Order, but on the outside it looked like any other building on the block. This late at night, candles burned at the windows and lit torches flanked the path.

"Are you sure about this?" Godric asked. "It will only make you more cross."

Gretchen knew that for him, it was just another building full of spirits and complications. He was perfectly happy being an earl's son and lad-about-town. He didn't particularly want to be a Keeper, while she might have seriously considered it, had it ever been a possibility. And that was the point. It was never going to be presented as a viable option.

"For God's sake, Gretel, don't swing your hips like that when you walk," Godric hissed under his breath. "It's a dead give-away."

He was a good brother. He might have preferred his ordinary life, but because she didn't, he would stand at her side. He never tried to mold her to his own expectations, not like their parents. And if she wasn't happy, he couldn't be truly happy either. She felt the same way. She kissed his cheek. He frowned. "Have you been dipping into the port too?"

She rolled her eyes. "I was displaying sisterly affection."

"Yes, and you usually do that with your fists."

"Just come on."

The main parlor could have belonged inside any of the gentleman's clubs on St. James. It was stuffed with wealthy, titled young men, card games, food, and bottles of wine.

"Godric, who's your friend?" someone called out.

"My cousin, Mr. Cove. He's likely to join up when he moves to London."

Gretchen gave a theatrical bow, enjoying herself immensely already. After that, no one paid them much mind, as long as Gretchen kept her hat on and tilted so the brim shadowed her features. She leaned against the wall with the studied ennui she'd watched her brother and his friends affect for years.

"Try not to look so happy," Godric teased her as she surveyed the loud and jovial gathering.

The sideboard was well stocked with cheeses, meats, and olives. Rowan berries strung on white thread were wound around the curtain rods, and bowls of salt were scattered around like candy dishes. Someone had cast a white horse, and it cantered around the perimeter of the already crowded room, sparks of light flinging off its tail. It was meant to carry off the spirits of angry warlocks like the Sisters, should they come calling.

"You could cast a white horse too," Gretchen suggested to Godric. "When there are too many ghosts about."

"I considered it," he said, grimacing. "But it seemed rude."

She shook her head. "Truly?"

"Well, that and apparently it's only really effective against spirits who have been banished, not those who plain old died and haven't the common courtesy to stay that way."

"I'm going to circulate," she said quietly.

"Don't get caught."

"Have I ever?" She sauntered slowly, enjoying the subterfuge the way Penelope enjoyed Shakespeare. She watched Oliver Blake lose two hundred pounds on a roll of dice. It would have felt like any other party, if it weren't for the magic sizzling just under the surface.

Until Tobias arrived, of course.

His magical ability must be to sense when she was having fun so he could run right out and put a stop to it.

She circled back to Godric. "Killingsworth is here," she hissed. He choked on his wine. "Very subtle. I can't imagine why the Ministry hasn't encouraged you to become a spy in the war."

"He's looking this way," he muttered.

"Blast." She rubbed her palm on her trousers, her witch knot suddenly feeling sweaty. Godric refilled his glass. "What are you doing? That's not helpful right now."

"I'm creating a distraction," he replied. "Get to the carriage and wait for me."

He raised his glass high, stepping forward into the room. His body conveniently blocked the view of the side door. "A toast!" he announced as Gretchen slipped out into the hall. She hurried toward the back door as her brother toasted some woman's left foot.

It occurred to her that she was in a house full of Keepers. And Keeper secrets.

If they could spy on her, surely turnabout was fair play. Especially as they were all so very thoughtfully gathered in the drawing room. Really, who could resist?

She waited until the butler disappeared into the parlor with a new tray of wine bottles before she darted up the main staircase. She was so busy rolling her eyes at the very buxom mermaid newel post that she was nearly caught out by someone's owl familiar. It sat on top of a potted tree, hooting softly. She stayed close to the wall, hidden by the leaves, and then went through the nearest door.

The room was barely lit by the embers of a coal fire in the grate. There was the usual assortment of tables and chairs and a writing desk. She made a hasty search of the papers and books but couldn't find anything of interest. She left the room disappointed. But at the top of the staircase she noticed Lucius and Ian on the landing, drinking brandy.

"You're watching Lady Penelope, aren't you?" Lucius asked.

Gretchen froze.

"Aye," Ian said. "Why?"

"She's a beauty," Lucius replied. Gretchen grinned. Penelope was going to swoon when she found out two very handsome men had been discussing her. "Would you be amenable to letting me take your place? I'd like an excuse to get to know her better."

Ian grinned, clapping him on the shoulder. His brandy sloshed over the lip of his glass. "Sorry, mate, doesn't work that way. The First Legate assigns the posts."

She didn't notice the glowing fox until it slinked right by her, his phosphorescent tail flicking her leg. "Someone's up there," Ian said suddenly.

Botheration; she wasn't any better at this spying thing than her brother. Gretchen turned on her heel and took off toward the servant stairs. With any luck they would assume she'd been a footman or a servant passing by and Ian wouldn't bother sending his fox after her. She crossed a stone terrace, her breath coming short. Adrenaline tingled through her.

So much better than being at a ball.

"Where do you think you're going?"

She knew those icy cultured tones. She didn't turn around. And she certainly made no comment; he'd know her instantly if she spoke. She didn't bother with the stone steps beside her; instead, she wrapped her hands around the rail and vaulted over it, onto the lawn below. She landed in a crouch in the long shadows cast by torches and the candlelit house.

But by the time she'd straightened up with a smug smile, Tobias was there.

"Who are you?" he demanded.

She took off her hat, bowing.

She rather enjoyed the look of complete shock on his face.

"Gretchen?"

As usual, her plan had turned to chaos.

But wasn't it more fun that way?

"What the blazes are you doing, lurking about?" he demanded. The adrenaline was still singing through her as it must be through him, considering he must have thought he was apprehending a warlock in the shrubbery. His eyes glinted with it, turning nearly silver. Gretchen's mouth went dry, and she wasn't entirely certain why.

"I'm giving you lot a taste of your own bloody medicine," she replied cheekily. "Poorly," she was forced to admit. "But it's the principle of the thing."

"Be serious. Do you have any idea how dangerous it is to be playing games right now?"

"What makes you think I'm not serious?"

He leaned closer. She could see the flecks of pale gray in his blue irises. "The Order doesn't take kindly to spies."

"The Order doesn't take kindly to anything."

"Why do you hate them?" he asked quietly. "Surely after the disastrous ball, you can see we're only trying to protect the witches of London."

"From us?"

"From warlocks, from each other, from themselves."

She tilted her head. "Sounds exhausting. No wonder you look so cross all the time."

"You don't exactly make it easy."

Her smile was crooked and wry. "I know."

He was looking at her mouth. She had the strangest notion that he wanted to kiss her again. On purpose this time and not just to break a spell.

And that she might want him to.

His hair tumbled into his eyes. She lifted her hand to brush it back, then stopped herself. He tensed, his blue eyes snapping onto hers and flaring before he glanced at her lips again. She could feel the warmth of him. Their mouths were so near, even a shadow couldn't have fallen between them. Her lips tingled expectantly.

He dragged himself away, releasing her abruptly. "Go home, Gretchen," he said hoarsely. "Go home."

Chapter 8

Morning in Hyde Park made London bearable. Gretchen could ride her horse over the hills as fast as she liked with no one to scold her. In the afternoon, she was relegated to Rotten Row and hundreds of fashionable people riding at a snail's pace to show off their new hats; but when the sun was burning off the mists and only children and nursemaids were wandering about, she could gobble up the sky. It was a fine warm day already, with a sky as pink as the inside of a peony.

It would have been even better if there weren't a handful of Keepers thundering past her toward the Serpentine. Hearing the faintest of whispers, Gretchen nudged her horse into a trot. She wasn't surprised to find Tobias already there. She'd assumed he was following her but was vexed to discover she couldn't spot him. It was becoming a game to test herself with. Even this early in the morning, he was so put together he could have been on his way to a ball. She wondered if he even knew how to wrinkle.

Or if he thought about their moment last night in the garden.

She slid out of her saddle and approached him. She'd barely tapped him on the shoulder when his hand was around her throat. She froze, breath strangling. His teeth looked suddenly very sharp.

It took him a long moment to recognize her.

He released her abruptly, shame chasing away the light of battle in his face. "I'm sorry. That was inexcusable," he added with a stiff bow.

She swallowed, still feeling the imprint of his fingers on her skin. He looked as though he was going into war, not strolling through Hyde Park just after dawn. His pupils were so dilated, they made his pale eyes nearly black. Blue shadows traced his lower lids as if he'd slept as badly as she had. Worse, actually. "What's happened?"

"Nothing," he said hoarsely.

She closed one eye against the sudden swell of sound in her head. "Tobias, please don't lie to me," she said. "It hurts."

"You shouldn't be here," he said abruptly.

"What's going on?" She peered around him as a vicious stab of sound seared her ears. She flinched, grabbing her temples. There were two Keepers wading into the Serpentine, holding lengths of iron chains. The water bubbled and boiled, like a giant kettle.

The petticoats of a woman's skirt floated to the roiling surface.

She must have been a nursemaid, judging by the two young boys being pushed away from the shore. A toy sailboat bobbed wildly near the woman's body. One of the boys began to scream.

Gretchen had no idea what was lurking in the waters of the Serpentine; she only knew that the magical chains wouldn't hold it.

"They're doing it wrong," she said through clenched teeth. She couldn't stand the poor boys' wailing, or the knowledge that the Keepers were walking into a fate similar to the nursemaid's. She lifted the hem of her riding habit and broke into a run.

"Gretchen, no!" Tobias lunged for her but missed. She'd been outrunning Godric since she was seven years old. By the time Tobias reached the edge of the water, she was already wading up to her ankles.

"Those chains won't work," she told the other Keepers. She struggled to pick out the words in her head and they came a little easier. The words, however, were not comforting: *hungry, run, drown.*

"Of course they'll work," one of the Keepers scoffed, an iron chain wrapped around his wrist. "These were soaked in salt water under three nights of the full moon. After being buried in rowan berries and grave dirt. We know what we're doing."

"It's not enough," Gretchen insisted, even as Tobias reached her. "It won't work."

"You'd best listen to her," Tobias said sharply. "She's the reason all of London didn't fall asleep this past week."

Something began to fight its way out of the water.

A large muscular horse's head broke the surface, green eyes

rolling furiously. It was sleek and vicious, with sharp teeth made for grinding bones. Gretchen had never seen anything like it. Even though it looked like a horse, it was clearly something else entirely.

"What is that?" She stared.

"A kelpie," Tobias said.

She took a step back, slipping slightly. "A what?"

"Water horse," he explained shortly. "They pull people under and drown them."

"If you don't even know a kelpie when you see one," the Keeper said, blood dripping from his chafed hands as water around his legs frothed pink, "how are we supposed to believe you know anything about the chains?"

"Get out of there!" Tobias snapped at him suddenly, hauling Gretchen out of the pond. "Your blood is making it hungrier."

The pond heaved, water slapping at the shores and turning over the body of the woman so she could stare unseeing at the sky.

Still, Gretchen found the kelpie strangely beautiful. Daisies, cornflowers, and wild violets were scattered through its glossy black mane. Its eyes were the exact color of new oak leaves, delicate and mournful. She reached out a hand to touch it, wondering if it was as smooth and velvety as it looked. The nursemaid hadn't understood, she hadn't shown this wondrous creature the proper respect. Anyone could see it only needed a gentle touch.

She stepped closer, the pond lapping at her toes.

"Don't." Tobias's hand clamped around her arm.

Denied another victim, the water horse thrashed resentfully.

Gretchen was suddenly aware of the cold water in her boots and the sodden weight of her riding habit. The material was heavy and cumbersome. It would have been like going swimming with stones in her pockets. She exhaled slowly. "What's a kelpie doing in the Serpentine?"

"A very good question," he replied. "They're only allowed in the Thames, under the goblin markets bridge," he added.

"Like the White Lady?" she murmured, remembering her hungry white birds. "That seems to be happening a lot, wouldn't you say?"

"Yes," he agreed grimly. "I would."

The Keepers flung their chains out. The kelpie lashed back with deadly hooves. The whispering in Gretchen's head turned to the sound of knives being sharpened against each other. The vibration made her feel awful. She thought she caught the fragment of a new word, then nothing. She locked her knees so she wouldn't sway.

"Gretchen, stop," Tobias said in her ear. It took her a moment to realize this voice was coming from outside her own body. "Your eyes." They were bloodshot, irises rimmed with pink, whites veined with tiny burst rivers of red.

"Nearly have it," she insisted, doubling over with her hands over her ears. "Kelpie," she muttered. "Kelpie. Kelpie."

She straightened abruptly. She'd have smiled, if she hadn't also been trying not to be sick. "Ivy," she said finally. "We need to wrap the chains in ivy."

"I'll take your horse and fetch some," Tobias said.

"Not a chance," she shot back, running and vaulting into the saddle. Her stomach tilted unkindly. Tobias swore, going for one of the Keepers' horses. He had to pause to lay out a young man in a puce cravat who wouldn't stop trying to wade into the churning waters. The kelpie screamed and whinnied piteously.

Ivy grew in long vines from the trees and wound around a stone wall left to crumble artistically. Gretchen grabbed fistfuls of it, winding it around her pommel, her waist, and her neck. Tobias worked silently beside her, hacking at the vines with one of his knives. When Gretchen could barely see through the ivy piled in front of her, she turned her horse around, nudging him with her heels. She felt rather than saw Tobias do the same behind her. They pressed their mounts into a gallop, trailing ivy and clods of dirt kicked up by hooves slamming into the ground.

Gretchen leaned forward, the wind pressing against her. She reached the pond a scant moment before Tobias and slid out of the saddle, shoving ivy at the Keepers. They wound the vines as quickly as they could, evading the deadly kicks of the angry kelpie.

The buzzing in Gretchen's head returned. It was more insistent than ever. She concentrated hard, until she tasted copper.

"Stop!" she yelled. "It has to be wrapped around counterclockwise!"

Cursing, the Keepers pulled the chains back, working the ivy with cold, wet fingers. The kelpie came closer and closer.

The chains lashed through the water. The kelpie gnashed its powerful teeth, biting at the waves, the air, a wayward water beetle. The chains tightened and tightened, until finally exhausted, the kelpie went still. It sank slowly down until only its flower-strewn mane was visible. Tears burned Gretchen's eyes.

The whispering slammed into such sudden silence that she flinched. Her entire head felt like a rusted bell. She swayed on her feet. Tobias scooped her up before she could fall. The wet folds of her riding habit draped over his arm.

"Blast," she said blearily. There were three Tobiases, all wavering in front of her, disapproving faces blurring. "All any-one is going to remember now is that you carried me. They'll forget the important part."

"That you helped chain a kelpie?"

"No, that I beat you in a horse race."

Gretchen had fainted.

Fainted. She'd never swooned in her entire life. Not when the Sisters had cornered her and her cousins, not even when she'd fallen out of a tree and right onto her head. She didn't believe in it.

And *Tobias* had caught her.

That just made it so much worse.

She woke up cradled in his arms, just as the carriage rolled into motion. Mortified, she stayed very still. If she was lucky, he wouldn't notice she was awake and she could pretend none of this was happening.

She was sitting across his thighs, her legs dangling over his knees, water dripping from her wet boots. Her head was tucked against his shoulder, and his arm was warm against her back, coming around to rest on her hip. She lifted her eyelids infinitesimally.

She could see the white of his cravat and the fine weave of his coat. He'd removed his ruined gloves, and his skin was tanned, as if he spent more time out of doors than his demeanour suggested. It was intriguing.

The carriage jostled over a bump in the road, and his arms tightened around her, securing her against his chest. He smelled like earth and soap.

She could have sworn she heard one of the dead witches sigh a little.

As if their incessant chatter wasn't bad enough.

The footman opened the carriage door and let down the steps. He made a sound of surprise. "I'll take her, my lord."

"I've got her," Tobias said, his voice rumbling his chest under her ear. He didn't relinquish her, instead contorted himself in what must have been an uncomfortable angle for his neck, in order to step outside while holding her.

The butler hurried to let him in and footmen came rushing to help, dashing any hope of staying discrete.

"My lord Killingsworth!" Gretchen didn't recognize the voice, but she instantly despised the simpering sigh it barely concealed. "How chivalrous you are."

"She's quite ruining your coat." That was Clarissa. "She must be dreadfully heavy being so tall." Gretchen had to remind herself not to bare her teeth. She was supposed to be unconscious.

Tobias carried her into the drawing room, settling her gently down onto the settee. She must have winced at the fevered pitch of girlish giggling because she felt him smile. "I saw that," he whispered against her ear. His breath was warm and tickled the nape of her neck. An expectant silence throbbed behind them. "I'd play dead if I were you," he added.

She couldn't stop an answering smile. "It wouldn't be enough," she returned, barely breathing the words. She cracked her eyes open, not realizing he was still so close. She could see the flecks of silvery gray in the impossible blue of his irises and the faint scar along his cheekbone.

"Ladies," Tobias said, pulling away sharply and turning to bow. "I leave her to your tender care."

"Coward," she muttered.

"I have smelling salts!"

"No, try my vinaigrette!"

The same girls who looked down their noses at her and her cousins rushed forward to show how very helpful and compassionate they were. She didn't open her eyes until she was sure Tobias was gone and the stench of someone's vinaigrette burned her nostrils. Her wolfhound hid under the settee, equally distressed, paws over its nose.

"What the hell is that?" she snapped, glowering at the offending smell. "Demon blood?"

"It's hartshorn and pickling vinegar. My mother swears by it when she's feeling faint."

"It's vile."

"Tobias carried you inside," Emma explained, handing her a cup of hot tea. "After which they all promptly lost their minds."

"He was very dashing," Penelope put in.

"Is he courting you?" A girl sighed, her eyes shining hopefully. Gretchen hoped it wasn't contagious.

"No," she said very firmly. "He most certainly is not courting me."

"He carried you out of the carriage and all the way up the path," someone else put in. "He wouldn't even let the butler help. He took you right to that very couch himself!"

"He was ever so handsome!"

"Do you think he'll call on you?"

"Pity you look so dreadful, Gretchen." Clarissa sniffed. "You've got mud all over your hem!"

Gretchen let her head fall back onto the cushion, sloshing tea into the saucer. "It's not bad enough I had to fight off a kelpie? I have to be gossiped and giggled to death as well?"

"You'd prefer the kelpie, wouldn't you," Emma said with a sympathetic smile.

"Every time."

"You're soaked!"

"Did he rescue you from drowning? How romantic."

The chatter increased to a frenzied pitch. They were like winter sparrows swarming on a single crumb. Her evil-eye ring cracked in half.

"A woman *did* drown," she interrupted. "And I can assure you, it wasn't the least bit romantic."

A hush fell. It didn't last.

"We're safe at the academy, surely."

"And he *did* save you then?" someone else asked tentatively. "Did you kiss him?"

Gretchen threw the cushion at her.

"Oh, go on." Penelope stood up to shoo the girls out. "Before she starts throwing furniture."

Clarissa sniffed. "You don't own the drawing room, Penelope Chadwick."

A sudden clap of thunder rattled the chandelier. One of the girls shrieked in surprise. Clarissa jumped but refused to otherwise react. She glared at Emma. "Don't be childish," she said.

Emma just smiled as a burst of rain flung itself sideways through the open window behind Clarissa. Cold water spattered her, and she stomped away, trailing the others, who were suddenly more eager to stay dry than to hear gossip.

Gretchen grinned at Emma. "I love your magic," she said. She tried to sit up gingerly. When her head didn't fall off, she reached for a biscuit.

Penelope waggled her eyebrows suggestively. "Tobias was very solicitous."

"You're as bad as the other girls." Remembering the soft touch of his breath on her ear, Gretchen's cheeks were suddenly and strangely hot. She must be weak from the embarrassing swooning. She ate another almond biscuit. "I'm sure he was just worried he'd get in trouble with the Order." She made a face. "Or my mother."

"Your mother is rather fearsome," Emma allowed. "But I don't think that's it."

Gretchen refused to look at them. "Stop it, both of you. You're being silly. And we have more important things to worry about."

Penelope did not look convinced.

· · ·

Try as she might, Gretchen could not beat her brother at billiards.

Ever since she was twelve, Gretchen had snuck down to the billiards room regularly in the middle of the night to practice. For years. Faithfully. And yet Godric still trounced her game after game and with apparently little effort.

Gretchen circled the table once more, eyeing it as a hunter might eye a peevish lion.

She muttered to herself about angles and mathematics and vexing twin brothers. Godric leaned on his pool cue, bored but cheerful. The wall behind him was papered in dark blue silk and bristled with spears and swords that were purely decorative, as they'd discovered the afternoon of their infamous duel. The blades had snapped in half, brittle as stale bread. Marble busts of Classical philosophers no one knew lined the walls on either side of the fireplace, as well as gilt-framed painting of horses and hunting dogs and a door that led out to the terrace. Gretchen and Godric's familiars curled up together under the table, watching her pace back and forth.

"If you hit the ball from that angle it will ricochet off the side there and will very likely bounce right off the table. Again," Godric commented. Gretchen had a habit of using too much force and not enough forethought.

She shot him a look. "Don't help me," she ordered. "When I finally flatten you utterly, it will be a delicious revenge entirely of my own making."

Godric nodded to the candles guttering in their silver holders. "Might you make the attempt today? Before Mother and Father return from the opera? I don't fancy another lecture on how I am too lenient with your unseemly habits."

"We've hours yet." Gretchen waved that away. "It's barely one in the morning."

"Some of us like to sleep."

"Please. You're hardly out the door for your evening debauchery at this time." She smirked. "You just want to go out looking for Moira."

He reddened slightly. She smirked harder. "I'm only concerned for her well-being," he muttered.

"Moira can take care of herself," she assured her brother. She took the shot, mostly to distract him from his worry. And the fact that if he left to prowl the London rooftops and the goblin markets, she would be equally worried for his safety. More worried actually, since he wasn't half as fierce as Moira.

Gretchen rushed the shot and knew before the end of the cue struck the ball that she had botched it up, as usual. She stayed hunched over the table, frowning. Her wolfhound scrambled out from underneath, hackles bristling.

"There's no need for dramatics, Gretchen," Godric said. "I already warned you you'd never make that shot."

"It's not that," she said, finally straightening. She pressed a hand to her breastbone. "I feel odd." There was a burning sensation, slowly developing into a painful prickling under her skin. Her breaths went shallow. Her wolfhound growled, just as Godric's wolfhound leaped up beside hers, also growling and with its ears flattened against its glowing skull. "Something's wrong," she added.

Her brother's hold on the cue made it appear suddenly spear-like. "I'll go and see."

Gretchen shook her head wildly. She felt clammy and pale. "It's inside of me." Pain lanced through her, like a sword being driven into her belly. She gasped.

"Are you ill?" Godric frowned. "Shall I call for the doctor?"

"No," she croaked, stopping him when he went to ring the bell to summon the butler. She was both so hollow and so filled with disorienting pain that she could only sink to her knees. Both wolf-hounds circled her, barking madly. "It's something else."

"Is it a Whisperer thing?" he asked, looking helpless.

She shook her head. "The pain's not in my head." She began to writhe, hot needles jabbing her all over. Blood spotted her gown, under her collarbone, on her shoulder, above her belly button. They were small wounds, but they throbbed unpleasantly. "It's magic."

"Hell no," Godric said. "Not with a Keeper likely out lurking in the bushes." He raced out onto the terrace, bellowing Tobias's name.

Gretchen's arrowhead amulet flared as hot as metal on a blacksmith's anvil. Waves of sparkling iridescent heat emanated from it, and the acrid smell of lemon balm forced another dose of adrenaline through her.

Tobias and her brother rushed in from the garden, trailing flowers and rain. Tobias came to an abrupt halt, his expression remained cool and remote. She found it oddly comforting.

"Do something," Godric snapped.

"We need salt," Tobias ordered. Godric left for the kitchens at a dead run. Gretchen tried to push herself up off the floor but couldn't quite manage it.

"Don't tax yourself," Tobias said gently. She had a very good view of the water and mud on the bottom of his boots. She concentrated on them, trying to keep the panic at bay. Tobias pulled rowan berries and iron shavings from the pocket of his greatcoat and built a circle around her. When Godric returned with the salt, Tobias added it to the ring.

Gretchen was able to catch her breath for just a moment. "It's helping," she said, but she knew it wouldn't be enough. The pain was already stalking her. She could practically see it pacing outside the barrier.

An invisible dagger stabbed through her palm. A ragged hole opened on her witch knot, bleeding sluggishly. She cried out, feeling her hand pinned to the floor even though there was nothing physically touching her. The wound throbbed viciously.

"Take this." Gretchen fumbled awkwardly with her free hand for the clasp of her arrowhead amulet. Tobias crouched in front of her, brushing the back of her neck as he released the talisman. He added it to the rest of the barrier spell. He pressed a large chunk of black jet just above the neckline of Gretchen's gown. It was cool against her fevered skin. There was a flash of magic. The candles flared so high and hungry they were extinguished in pools of melted wax almost immediately. Her wolfhound howled, a ghostly sound that wasn't quite audible and yet still managed to chill the blood.

The jet gathered more and more magic into itself until it cracked and then shattered. Shards scattered in every direction.

A small cut opened on Tobias's cheek when he was grazed. Another piece hit a glass case holding a display of bird nests, breaking it. The invisible dagger slid free of her palm. Godric hastily undid his cravat and began to wrap her bleeding hand with the strip of white cloth.

"You'll want to pack it with salt," Tobias said.

"Like hell," Gretchen replied.

"It's a magical wound. It would be safest to cleanse it properly"—he was already walking toward the door—"while I track that spell." He vanished into the gardens.

Godric reached for what was left of the salt in the silver cellar shaped like a swan. He'd grabbed the first thing he could find. Gretchen clenched her back teeth. "Do it."

He may as well have poured acid and fire as salt into her cut. She felt it eating through her skin and flesh, right down to the bone. She couldn't even scream. Pain robbed her voice. Godric tied the makeshift bandage tightly, wincing and chanting, "I'm sorry, I'm sorry, I'm sorry."

When Gretchen could see again, Tobias returned, holding up a doll with stark triumph. "I found this."

"Is that a doll?" Her wolfhound barked at it once, the sound sharp and vicious. She'd felt the same way about dolls when she was little but now she just felt confused.

It was made of brown homespun wool and stitched hastily with dark thread. It had embroidered eyes, yellow yarn for hair, and a witch knot on its left palm. Not only was it stuffed full like a pincushion, but it was poked full of needles too. They bristled from the chest, side, belly, and witch knot.

"A poppet," Tobias explained. "Someone used your hair or blood or saliva and made this of you."

"And then they stabbed it," she finished angrily. She stood up gingerly so as not to jar her hand. Tobias steadied her. "That is *rude*, even by my standards."

"We'll find out who did this," he promised, violence and retribution all but shimmering around him. His eyes seemed bluer, his teeth sharper. Something about him changed when he showed primal emotion. Gretchen couldn't quite put her finger on it. "The poppet was hidden in the bole of an oak tree by your front gate," he continued. "I tracked it but whoever used it must have had a carriage waiting. They left the poppet though, probably meaning to use it against you again."

The salt circle on the floor began to tremble. The tiny white grains hovered, moving together and apart like magnets until they shaped letters. The words burst into green-tinted flames. The fire burned a message into the floorboards.

"I see you, Gretchen Thorn."

She hissed at it. "Why attack me?" she asked.

"To keep you under control?" He hazarded a guess. "To stop you from sealing the broken magical wards and damning up their supply of power?"

"Then they greatly miscalculated." She narrowed her eyes at the warning. "Because now I mean to try even *harder.*"

She slipped off her evil-eye school ring and set it in the middle of the word *see*. She'd read enough of the grimoire to have a basic understanding of sympathetic magic, where a symbol literally became the thing it represented, such as the poppet.

Two could play at that game.

She held out her palm to Tobias. "Iron nail, please," she requested, knowing he would have one on his person. Keepers always carried iron nails.

When he passed one to her, she drove it through the center of the eye.

"Now what do you see, warlock?" she said fiercely.

Chapter 9

By the time the last of the other boarding students had gone to sleep, Emma was still at her desk with her stack of books and a flickering candle. Behind her, the yellow curtains around the bed matched the embroidered coverlet and the silk-papered walls. She pushed the book aside and reached for another. She was going to grow into an old woman hunched over creepy vellum pages detailing the many sinister secrets of the Underworld.

Though few could accurately map out the Underworld, there were enough accounts to give one a general idea. It was filled with the unfortunate souls who were forced to wander endlessly, shut out of the Blessed Isles either by magic or malice. It was also home to warlocks hiding from justice, monsters, and wraiths. Travelers were few and far between, for obvious reasons, and admittance was only to be gained through death or the tricky business of opening a portal. She'd done that very thing just recently, accidentally releasing hellhounds and ghouls and the Greymalkin Sisters. But now that she actually wanted to open a gate, she had no idea how it was done.

Her frustration had thunder rumbling in the distance. One of the other girls had remarked that this spring seemed much stormier than the last, and always in the middle of the night. It was no coincidence that it was the same time every night that Emma's antlers started to give her a headache and she grew discouraged and exasperated with her research. For instance, why did so many witches insist on writing spells in rhyme when they were so very dismal at it?

And the very few spells she could find to open a portal required murder or various parts of dead bodies.

And once the portal was opened, safe passage was another matter altogether.

Orion the hunter, the Plough, Cassiopeia. As always, reciting the names of constellations calmed her nerves.

So did finally finding a clue of some use.

"Portals stain the astral plane, leaving an imprint of themselves wherever they are opened. Even closed and secured by powerful spells, it remains possible to force them open again."

Emma leaped to her feet, yanking off her nightdress in favor of a riding habit that was sturdy enough not to need a corset. She could hardly attempt a clandestine experiment if she had to ring for a maid first to help her get dressed. She filled her pockets with salt and rowan berries and a knife she had stolen off her luncheon tray on her first full day at the academy.

She peered cautiously down the hallway, looking for

Mrs. Sparrow's cat-familiar, who patrolled regularly during the overnight hours. Counting her blessings, Emma eased out of her chambers and raced down the grand staircase. She ducked into the blue parlor because it had the biggest windows. She climbed out, fully aware that every person of her acquaintance would scold her bitterly could they see her. The bushes were thorny and unwelcoming, providing a scolding of their own.

Despite the logical reasons why she should remain safely at her desk, Emma knew she had to test this new bit of information. She had to go at night. She simply could not risk getting caught. No one could see her near the portals, not again. And though she knew her cousins would be cross if she did this without them, she couldn't bring herself to put them in even more danger.

Knowing something was foolish didn't make it any less necessary.

She fought her way free of the shrubbery and ran as fast as she could, through the iron gates and out onto the pavement. Emma had once helped Cormac and Moira close a portal on the rooftop of a bakery off Piccadilly. It wasn't very far, and if she was lucky, a cold spring rain would clear the streets of any loitering pedestrians. The clouds gathered with a swiftness not generally found in nature, but she didn't have the time to be subtle. The rain glistened as it fell through the gathering fog and clung to the windows. Emma wrapped the mists around her like a shield.

She finally found the bakery and recalled that she'd had to climb up onto the print shop next door to access it. Except Moira had put a ladder down for her. Still, she had learned a thing or two from the Madcap, and she managed to find a solid drainpipe and barred windows to climb. It was an ungraceful affair but it got the job done.

Once out of sight, she let the clouds dissipate to reveal the moonlight so she wouldn't accidentally topple off and break her neck. She gingerly crossed the roof, finding a narrow gap to step over to lead her to the bakery. Even in the gloom of the dispersing rain and fog she could make out the grooves left by hellhounds and the scorch marks where the magical fire had been built out of salt and rowan berries. The slash of the iron dagger was charred into the shingles.

She couldn't see anything else though. There was no convenient scorch mark in the air leaking magic. But the gate had once reacted to her blood. From the moment the three Sisters got loose, Greymalkin warlocks paced the other side of the gates, drawn by their shared lineage.

Emma was getting rather tired of bleeding for spellwork.

She took a pin from her hair and jabbed it unceremoniously into her fingertip. She flung the resulting drop of blood at the damage left by the gate. "Ewan Greenwood!" she said. "Ewan Greenwood, I call on you to find me!"

Names had power. Blood had power.

And the Underworld had power of its own.

The first thing Emma noticed was the smell of fennel and dark, wet earth. A tiny pinprick of violet light pierced the haze. It caught like a candle in a draft, its flame lengthening and hissing. The gate wavered into view.

It was faint, like a faded painting left too long in the sun. It didn't burn with the vitriolic lavender light it had before, but it was still tangible, splitting open like ripe fruit. Magic leaked out, flaring brightly. Emma pulled back, squinting.

Until she saw the outline of a man wearing antlers.

"Ewan Greenwood!"

A growl echoed menacingly, raising the little hairs on the back of Emma's neck. She knew that sound. She remembered it vividly.

A hellhound muscled between Ewan and the edge of the gate. It was the size of a pony, with grotesque features that closer resembled a gargoyle's than a dog's. Its black fur prickled with purple sparks. It snapped its jaws around Ewan's leg, above the knee.

Ewan jerked back, holding on to the edges of the gate, the light burning into his palms. He refused to let go, his antlers spearing out into the London night air. Blood dripped from his ragged wound. Two more hellhounds joined the first, snapping and pulling at Ewan's pants, boots, skin.

Emma grabbed his wrist. "No! Hold on!"

"Let go, Emma," he shouted. "You'll be pulled in with me."

"No, I'm getting you out!"

"It's too late," he said, his green eyes meeting hers.

He let go of the gate. The moment his hold released, the hellhounds dragged him back into the Underworld, snarling and growling.

Emma was left alone on the rooftop.

Well, not quite alone.

"Lady Emma, are you up there?"

Blast.

She'd forgotten about Virgil.

"Come down this instant!" he called up, agitated. He was turning bright red. Emma half wondered if he was about to pop the buttons on his waistcoat. "I shall tell Lord Mabon about this, see if I don't."

The last thing she needed was to be brought to the attention of the head of the Order.

Again.

Penelope was in the parlor reading *The Mysteries of Udolpho* with a pot of chocolate when the housekeeper passed by the doorway with her apron still tied over her customary black dress. It was past midnight and she ought to have retired already. Penelope's father was having dinner with friends at their club, and her mother was at a soiree involving some kind of an art show or cornering the judges of the Royal Exhibition about an art show; Penelope stopped listening because the heroine Emily St. Aubert had just been imprisoned at Udolpho by Montoni. Anyway, they wouldn't be back for hours and only Battersea, the butler, ever waited up.

"Mrs. Liverpool"—Penelope marked her page—"is everything all right?"

The housekeeper pressed a hand to her heart. "Bless me, you startled me, miss!"

"Is that Hamish's medicine?" Cedric had driven her parents' carriage to give his grandfather Hamish, the official coachman, a chance to rest. His joints hardened and seized and he found himself frozen at odd angles. Cook made him a tonic that seemed to help, when he could be convinced to drink it.

"Yes," Mrs. Liverpool replied with a sigh. "But you know how he is."

"All too well." They exchanged a knowing, exasperated glance. "Give it here." She waggled her fingers insistently until Mrs. Liverpool handed her the amber glass tonic bottle.

"You do have a way with him," she allowed. "If you're sure?"

"Oh, I'm sure," Penelope tipped the contents of the bottle into the chocolate pot. She tucked her book by the cup and saucer and lifted the tray.

"Let me carry that, miss."

"I've got it." It tilted dangerously to the left. The pot slid a few inches. Mrs. Liverpool winced. Apparently carrying trays was trickier than it appeared. "I've got it," she said again, mostly to convince herself. Battersea hurried to open the door, frowning.

"Hamish," Mrs. Liverpool explained.

"Good luck, miss," he answered promptly.

Mrs. Liverpool quickened her pace to open the door leading to Hamish's room above the stables. The staircase was dark and treacherous but it smelled pleasantly of hay. At the sound of her footsteps, Hamish called out, "Let me die in peace, you daft crow."

"It's not Mrs. Liverpool, you beastly old man," she returned cheerfully, turning sideways to fit through the door with her tray.

"Penelope!" The room was small, with a cot along one wall, a table with two chairs, and a shelf for cups and crockery. The grate was packed with coals, blazing fire. The heat tickled at her throat, but Hamish lay on his bed under a thick blanket. "The daughter of the house, no less. And I'm not wearing shoes." His toes peeked out from his blanket.

"I'm sure I'll survive the shock." He pushed up on his elbows, shifting to try to stand up until she speared him with a look. "Don't you dare."

"It's not seemly." He moved awkwardly, brittle as old paper.

She ignored his protests. He'd sneaked her candies since she was old enough to chew them, taught her how to ride a horse, and even once let her take the reins of the carriage. He was as much her grandfather as he was Cedric's. "You can prop yourself up to take this lovely cup of chocolate I've brought you."

"At this time of night."

"Exactly. I've gone through all this trouble, so you'll drink it." She picked up the cup to pass it to him. She wasn't wearing gloves and she was tired; the combination sent a warning tickle behind her eyeballs. It was all the warning she got before she felt herself pulled in all directions.

She didn't have control over the memories or the order they came in. This time, she was the scullery maid washing the cup very late one night after a dinner party. Her hands were chapped from the hot water and the harsh soap and her feet hurt from standing all day. The smell of the leftover chocolate in the pot cut through the stink of onions and plates sticky with gravy and cheese sauce. She was hoping Cedric might notice her one day and pull her into the hay for a kiss.

The cup bobbled in Penelope's hand, spilling over. A drop

of warm chocolate splashed onto her thumb, jerking her back into her own body.

"You shouldn't be serving me," Hamish was saying.

She just smiled wanly, until the room stopped spinning. He took the cup, his white hair stuck up at odd angles, like a rooster's comb. He must have been lying down all evening, in too much pain to move. "You've put Cook's tonic in here."

"I have. And I sacrificed a cup of perfectly good chocolate to do it." She dragged a chair close to the bed and sat down, crossing her arms. "Drink it."

"It's vile."

"But it will help with the pain."

"It makes me groggy." He liked to bluster, but she could see the lines of pain etched around his mouth.

"It's nearly one in the morning. Were you planning on taking a turn through Hyde Park?"

"Cheeky lass," he muttered, but there was an approving twinkle in his eye. He lifted the cup and drank, grimacing lightly.

"You can't even taste it," Penelope said.

"What book has kept you up this time?" he asked. Penelope's love of novels was legendary in the household. When she was ten years old, she'd run through the parlor in a sheet, pretending to be the ghost of a doomed maiden. She'd frightened some snobby lady with more pearls than humor so that she screamed and threw her plate in the air. The jellied custard had landed in her hair and Penelope's doomed maiden had fallen over in a fit of giggles. Her mother had turned red, not with embarrassment but with the exertion of not laughing herself. After the guest left, Penelope's mother showed her how to paint the edges of the sheet so that it looked even more eerie. She'd been a ghost that entire winter.

"*The Mysteries of Udolpho*," she told Hamish. "I've read it before but it's so delicious. Listen to this."

She read to him until he nodded off to sleep, the empty cup balanced on his chest. She eased it off gently and pulled the blanket up under his chin. His breathing was easier. Pleased, she snuck back downstairs with her book, leaving the tray to be fetched in the morning.

The moonlight gleamed softly on the dark windows of the house, on the copper urns in the garden by the door, and on the open front gates. The wind must have blown them open. She detoured down the lane to shut them.

Ian came out of the shadows.

"I'm very sorry," he said just before clamping his hand over her mouth and hauling her into the carriage waiting at the curb.

"Lady Emma!"

"Oi, someone needs to shut him up." Moira leaned against the black iron railing behind Emma, grinning. Her black hair fell in waves from under her crowned hat. She had a new cameo pinned to her coat.

"Moira." Emma grinned back.

Virgil was swearing beneath them as he struggled to pull himself up the drainpipe. They both looked over the edge and sighed.

"Go on, Pip," Moira whispered to the little gargoyle hovering over her shoulder like a bat. "Give him something to really swear about."

"How did you even find me?" Emma asked Moira.

"You're on my rooftop, aren't you? Madcaps always know." She shrugged. "Besides, I was trailing that one. He looks dodgy."

"The dodgiest," Emma agreed. "And a Keeper."

"As if I couldn't tell that from here." Moira snorted. "What are you doing up here anyway?"

"I was investigating the portal we closed here." It wasn't exactly a lie.

Moira's eyebrows disappeared into her hairline. "Didn't I say debutantes are mad creatures?"

Emma made a face but could not, in all honesty, protest. Instead, she called the mists back, tendrils snaking into the alleys and billowing around the gas lamps. Virgil became an indistinct outline with a tall hat making noises of panic. Magic flared and flickered in the fog around him.

"Blimey, that's a useful talent," Moira said of the mists before leaping away to the print shop. "Quickly, off with you before he manages a tracking spell. There's a ladder three shops down at the back corner."

"Are you sure about this?" Emma asked. It seemed wrong to saddle her friend with someone like Virgil.

Moira looked vaguely insulted. "I can outrun a bleedin' Greybeard, Emma."

"I know that. I only meant—"

"Just run, you daft girl. And quit sending me your old gowns and silk shawls."

"But . . ."

"I know you mean well, but even if I fenced that fancy stuff, someone would get suspicious eventually. I'd be hauled in front of a judge for stealing, make no mistake."

"That's not fair." Emma looked disgruntled. Moira just laughed, slightly incredulously. "Fine, no silk." She was already thinking of what else she could do to help. A round of cheese would be good, wouldn't it? Or new boots?

"Run," Moira repeated. She made a point of stomping loudly away. Virgil scrambled back down the ladder to follow her on foot.

Emma went in the opposite direction, grinning. She grinned all the way back to the academy, up until she reached the gate only to be blocked entrance.

By two Keepers.

The Keepers slipped past the sleeping servants and her parents tucked into their beds, muffled in spells to keep them hidden. Gretchen's mother, having renounced all magic, had no spells to deflect them. She slept on as Keepers dragged her daughter from her room.

Gretchen managed to bite one, but she was outnumbered in the end. They wrapped her in a cloak and kept her arms and legs pinned so she wouldn't do them harm. They dropped her into a carriage, slamming the door shut. Gretchen fought free of the constraining cloak, spitting curses. She kicked her captor hard enough to have him curse back in three languages. She lunged for the door with every intention of hurling herself out onto the road.

"You'll be trampled, you mad little hoyden." Her captor grabbed her wrist. "It's me. Tobias Lawless."

"That does not improve the situation," she informed him between her teeth, just before she tried to kick him again. He was faster this time, and she only glanced the outside of his knee. He slammed his walking stick on the ground between them to protect himself.

"I'm a Keeper," he reminded her.

She tried to kick him again, on principle. Perhaps he really didn't mean her any harm, but it seemed unlikely that he was in the habit of abducting debutantes. She paused in horror. Was he a fortune hunter under all that cold disdain? Had she read him wrongly this entire time? It wasn't unheard of for girls to be kidnapped by fortune hunters and forced into marriage to avoid a scandal. "I won't marry you."

He looked equally horrified. "I don't recall asking."

"Why else are debutantes abducted in the middle of the night?"

He shook his head. "I'm on business for the Order."

She ruthlessly squashed down the niggling hurt that he would turn on her like this. He was a Keeper. He was doing what was expected of him. It was ridiculous to think they'd shared a moment. That he'd saved her from the poppet spell for any reason other than the fact that he was a member of the Order. She settled back against the cushions. "I'll scream."

"Go ahead. There are spells on the carriage."

She really needed to learn to channel her magic, if only to blast Tobias into next week with a fireball. And if there was no such thing as a fireball, she'd simply have to invent one.

The light from the lantern swinging on a hook outside the window did little to help her read his expression. It was as haughty and cool as ever. "I don't mean you any harm," he added.

It wasn't him she was worried about.

She'd heard all about the Order's ship from Emma, but the reality was even more daunting. She was bundled into a row-boat, and the swinging lantern on the prow disoriented her further, showing glimpses of the black water of the Thames, a towering ship beyond, and three Keepers on the bench across from her, neither of whom would look at her. Only Tobias was brave enough to meet her withering gaze.

"Very brave of you, to abduct a debutante from her bed," she snapped. She'd never referred to herself as a debutante, prefer-ring any other moniker, but desperate times called for desperate measures.

The answering silence was broken only by the splash of oars in the water. The rowboat gently bumped the hull of the ship as they came to a halt under a wooden ladder. Bottles were lined along the railing, each with a floating eyeball that watched her as she stood to grasp the lower rung of the ladder.

She began to understand her mother's refusal to have anything to do with the witching world, just a little bit.

The deck gleamed, polished to a sheen under her slip-pers. From the rigging and the mast hung green glass balls, stuffed with bits of string, needles, flowers, and assorted spell ingredients. One rattled with teeth. More nervous than she cared to admit even to herself, Gretchen set a fearsome scowl on her face as she was nudged across the deck to the captain's quarters. Gargoyles crouched over the door. Inside, candles burned in glass lanterns, casting just enough light to reveal both Emma and Penelope standing in the middle of the floor, inside a circle of salt and rowan berries. Gretchen was shoved into the circle beside them.

Lord Mabon, head of the Order, and Daphne's father, the First Legate, sat behind a desk secured to the floor with iron nails. They were stern-faced and imposing; men well used to being the most powerful in any room, both mundane and magical.

Gretchen wanted desperately to prove them all wrong.

Beside her, Penelope muttered Shakespearean sonnets under her breath. Emma was pale, fingers curled around her witch knot. It was black as ink. Until she'd forced the Sisters into a witch bottle, her mark had been the same faded-tea color as Gretchen's and Penelope's. Knots only darkened with the use of magic, and only the very old or very powerful had marks as dark as hers was now. Gretchen slipped her hand into Penelope's, who did the same to Emma on her other side. They would take the Order on together, as they took on everything.

"Just what is this about?" Gretchen demanded, trying to affect her mother's most disdainful tone.

"We will ask the questions here, Miss Thorn," Lord Mabon said.

She knew he deliberately called her Miss Thorn instead of Lady Gretchen, in an effort to subordinate her. There was a

Keeper on either side of the door, and the lights of London beyond the impressive bow windows. Virgil stumbled inside, panting. "Beg your pardon, my lords."

Emma smiled smugly to herself. Gretchen resolved to ask her what awful thing she'd done to make Virgil that alarming shade of puce.

"She was with a Madcap tonight," Virgil accused her hotly, going so far as to point his finger at her like a trembling maiden in a farce.

"She is a friend," Emma replied.

"Do you often meet your friends in the middle of the night on the rooftops?"

"Where else may we be assured of privacy?"

"What do you need privacy for, eh?"

"Why, to talk about boys." Her smile was sweet, with a touch of feigned innocence. It was remarkably difficult to look demure when one had antlers growing out of one's head, but she managed a fair approximation. "Isn't that the only thing girls talk about?"

Since Virgil was the sort to believe it, he snapped his mouth shut, frowning.

"Thank you, Virgil," the First Legate said. "We will make a note of the infraction." He stared coldly at Virgil until the younger man sputtered and left.

"There's nothing illegal about making friends with a Madcap," Emma pointed out, frowning.

"Keeping questionable company does not reflect well on you."

"Then I suggest you let us go," Penelope said with a sickly sweet smile.

The ship rolled gently from side to side. The strings of rowan berries and carved bone beads hanging from the star-painted ceiling clattered together. Lord Mabon gripped the side of his desk to keep his footing. Thunder rumbled, but it was distant and thin. Emma was shaking with the effort, sweat dampening her hair.

Gretchen heard the discordant whispering as magic tried to do its work. Emma's control of the weather wasn't a spell; there were no ingredients to get wrong, so it shouldn't wake the whispering in Gretchen's head. She rubbed her ears.

"Salt for meat, and salt for defeat." Penelope murmured one of her mother's strange rhymes. Gretchen kicked her foot through the ring of salt. Rain pelted the windows like pebbles. Lightning slashed the sky, stabbing at the silhouette of St. Paul's Cathedral.

But it wasn't enough. The First Legate was already throwing three flat black stones on the ground around the salt circle, fixing the gap Gretchen had made. Silence slammed into her as the magical wards strengthened against them. The stones glittered like the eyes of feral beasts ready to devour them if they twitched a muscle.

"Binding stones," Lord Mabon explained tersely. "Emma Day, you worked strong Lacrimarium magic to bottle the Sisters recently," he continued, as if she could ever forget it. "Magic far beyond your ken."

She wiped sweat from her temple before it could run into her eyes. "I suppose so."

"How, exactly, did you manage it?"

"I don't know," she said. "I just assumed it would work since they were *accidentally* linked to me when I *unintentionally* opened the gates."

"Hmmm. Since that Lacrimarium was killed at Greymalkin House, you are now one of the very few people capable of that kind of magic."

Emma rubbed her palms nervously on her skirts. "But I'm not a Lacrimarium. I'm just a weather-witch."

"And yet you bottled three powerful warlocks."

"Is this your way of saying thank you?" Gretchen asked archly, despite the fact that she was trapped inside a magical circle. Or maybe *because* of it. The air was prickly, like wet wool, and it pressed close. "Because you might want to practice."

Lord Mabon's mouth pressed into a thin, disapproving line. The First Legate raised an eyebrow. "You are impertinent."

"Frequently," she agreed. If she could withstand her mother's constant lecturing on deportment, she could withstand a circle of salt and black stone.

"You will be silent."

"I really doubt it."

'This is no laughing matter," Lord Mabon snapped. "The only fully trained Lacrimarium in London died that night. Do you have any concept of how dangerous it is to be without one?"

"Emma *saved* us all, or have you forgotten that?"

"We have not. Nor have we forgotten that you managed to find a way inside the Greymalkin House, something the Order has not been able to do since before you were born. That is highly suspicious, wouldn't you say?"

Since it was, they said nothing at all.

He glowered at Emma. "Since she disappeared, your mother's spell on her own name has begun to fade. We now know she turned against her own father, a celebrated Keeper with the Order, before binding your powers and trapping her own familiar in a witch bottle. Why would she take such drastic measures, I wonder?"

"I don't know," Emma replied. Clearly not all of her mother's spells had faded yet or they'd know it had all been done for Ewan Greenwood. "The spell drove her mad and she never spoke another rational word."

"That kind of history speaks against you."

"That's *Emma* Day you're speaking to," Penelope pointed out. "Not *Theodora* Lovegrove Day. It's easy to tell them apart if you try."

"That is past enough," Lord Mabon snapped. "I have never encountered such defiant girls in my life."

Gretchen and Penelope beamed proudly at each other until Lord Mabon picked up a clay figure of a girl with a witch knot painted on her left palm and jet stones looped around her like a rosary on the Virgin Mary. He threw it into the circle, hard enough to smash it to pieces within the salt boundary.

"I want to know what you're hiding," he said very evenly, the supressed rage in his clipped tones more terrifying than any amount of yelling.

"Nothing," Gretchen replied. "We are hiding nothing."

The black stones heated like embers and glowed red.

"Let's try again. *What are you hiding?*"

"No—" Gretchen broke off. She closed her mouth, opened it again. No sound emerged. She rubbed her throat, feeling panic nibble at her composure. Try as she might, her voice would not respond.

"That's how I know you're lying. Let's try again."

"I sealed the magical wards and woke everyone up from that sleep spell," Gretchen pointed out hoarsely. "And helped chained the kelpie."

"Yes, convenient, don't you think?"

Gretchen stared at him. It didn't matter what questions he asked, he had already decided on the answers.

He shook his head regretfully. "Since you will not cooperate with us, you will have to go before the magisters."

"I think not." Penelope's mother's voice was so icy it burned through the cabin. When one of the Keepers tried to block her way, she glared down her nose at him. "I know your mother, boy." He retreated instantly, conflicted.

"How did you find us?" Lord Mabon did not look amused. "We have spells that keep this ship hidden. Napoleon himself could not find us."

Aunt Bethany lifted her chin. "Napoleon is not a mother."

"Mother or not, you'll have to wait outside, Mrs. Chadwick."

"That is Lady Bethany to you. I have not given you leave to address me any other way," she returned. Gretchen had never known her aunt to pull rank, nor look so much like the granddaughter of a duke she was. She wore claret-colored silk edged in seed pearls, with opal hair pins shaped like peace lilies creating a sort of glittering crown. Her gloves were pale yellow and reached past her elbows, secured with diamond clips. She exuded wealth and consequence.

"Do not presume to order me about, Lord Mabon," she added, steel clipping her words into daggers. "I am not a young girl of eighteen to be bullied." Her badger-familiar prowled the cabin, snarling viciously. "You have abducted my daughter and my nieces, and do not think for one moment that I will not bring the Bow Street detectives into the matter, witching secrecy be damned. Explain yourselves, sirs."

"These girls are to be questioned. Lacrimarium magic is to be under the control of the magisters and the Order." He was so angry, spittle was forming at the corners of his mouth. He loomed over Aunt Bethany. "I want to know how they got into Greymalkin House. And how this one managed to bottle three very powerful warlock spirits."

"And I want to know why you think you can intimidate me," Aunt Bethany replied. "Let's make one thing very clear. You are not welcome in my home, nor are your Keepers. If you have questions for my girls, you may ask them at Rowanstone Academy with myself or Mrs. Sparrow present." Lord Mabon's face turned ruddy. She met his gaze. "I am well aware that you have no authority at the school, Lord Mabon."

"As you have no authority here," he reminded her. "We are charged with keeping London safe and we will do whatever it takes."

"Do you not think I'll do the same for my family? You may

have magical wards and binding pendants, Lord Mabon, but I have something else." Aunt Bethany smiled and knocked over the bottle of brandy on the sideboard. The sweet smell of the liquor stung the air as it spilled over the floorboards. She dropped one of the candles onto the alcohol and it caught immediately. "I have fire."

Black smoke billowed as the flames flickered and hissed. The Keepers jumped forward to smother the fire with their jackets. They coughed harshly, inhaling the acrid smoke. Sparks burned through their shirtsleeves. She flicked her hand, her magical talent sending the fire into patterns not intended by nature. It hissed at Lord Mabon, licking at the toes of his boots.

"Seize her!"

A flaming arrow crashed through the window of the cabin, slamming into the wall before anyone could take a step in Aunt Bethany's direction. Fire raced up a tapestry of St. George and the dragon, consuming it.

"I will set fire to this entire ship if you do not release them at once," she continued, as though the arrow hadn't missed her hair by inches. "Do you understand me?" She raised an eyebrow at the Keeper closest to the cousins. "Release them, boy." He jumped and glanced at Lord Mabon, his Adam's apple bobbing as he swallowed convulsively. "Come along, girls." She didn't have to ask them twice.

"This isn't finished," Lord Mabon warned her, as smoke filled his cabin.

"You can ask politely for our help or make enemies of us."

Aunt Bethany flashed him a dangerous smile. "I suppose the choice is yours. Good evening to you, Rufus. Give my regards to your lovely wife."

"His name is Rufus?" Gretchen whispered as they hurried after her. "No wonder he's so cross all the time."

Chapter 10

"*Aunt Bethany*, that was bloody brilliant," Gretchen said, impressed. "I had no idea you were so fierce."

"Yes, well, the Order prefers supplication," Aunt Bethany replied, tugging off her gloves, which now smelled like brandy and smoke. "But sometimes a show of force is required. And I can assure you that after I visit Lord Mabon's wife, they will mind their manners." She lifted Penelope's wrists, clicking her tongue at the chafe marks left by the rope. "Are you hurt?"

"Ian was rather kind, considering," Penelope assured her mother. "He kept apologizing. The rope burn is because I tried to bite one of the other Keepers. Ian punched him for being too rough."

"How did you even find us?" Emma asked. "I thought the ship was invisible and moves to a different spot along the river daily."

"Cormac heard you'd been taken for questioning," Aunt Bethany explained. "He showed me where it was anchored."

"He's here?" Emma craned her head out of the window to stare into the warehouses and dark alleys in between. It wasn't until they'd turned onto the road leading away from the docks that Cormac stepped briefly out of the shadows. Gretchen saw him tip his hat to Emma as they drove past.

"And the fire arrows?" Gretchen asked. "Since when do you know Robin Hood?"

"Cedric is on the roof of the carriage. He shot a few arrows to make my point."

Emma rubbed her arms, chilled. "Why did they bring us in? They've let us alone for weeks. Why now?"

"Because the Order is quite desperate." Aunt Bethany sighed. "Sophie Truwell has gone missing."

A flicker of dread woke in Gretchen's belly. "What do you mean, she's *missing*?"

Sophie had murdered several girls to use their magic in order to feed the Greymalkin Sisters. She'd nearly killed Emma as well.

"She was confined on the ship while the Order tried to locate another Lacrimarium to bottle her familiar and chain her magic. When they couldn't find one, they decided it would be more prudent to transfer her to Percival House."

Penelope frowned. "What's Percival House?"

"It's an old house on the moors where witches are locked up. It's extremely secure. However, Sophie apparently escaped somewhere en route and is currently at large."

Penelope flapped her hands, agitated. "We have to do something! There has to be another Lacrimarium somewhere."

"There is only one in England at the moment, and he is too young to be of any use."

"Have you tried Scotland?" she pressed. "Spain? Egypt?"

Emma was pale but very calm, far calmer than her cousins. "That's why they want to know how I bottled the Sisters." She shook her head. "But I'm not a Lacrimarium. It was luck more than anything."

Emma's Greymalkin blood allowed her to complete the complicated spell, but the Order certainly didn't know that. It wouldn't help them in any case. Sophie claimed to be related to the Sisters, but her lineage was so diluted there hadn't been enough of a link to get inside the House. She'd needed Emma for that; had nearly killed her in point of fact. And that was before she'd been foiled and arrested. God only knew what she would want to do to Emma now. It would be nearly as bad as what the Order had in mind.

"The Order wants the problem easily solved. That involves either you miraculously turning into a Lacrimarium or else blaming you for the entire mess."

"That's not fair," Penelope said hotly.

"No, but they're scared, and people who act out of fear are rarely fair," Aunt Bethany said wearily. "The Order will keep this secret for as long as possible.

"They are a rather spectacularly ungrateful lot," Gretchen said. "We've helped them and yet they're treating us like criminals." Her eyes gleamed. "And I won't have it. I'll find a way to turn their spleens into spiders if they don't stop."

Aunt Bethany rested her head back against the cushions. "Could you wait until tomorrow, dear? It's been a trying night."

Tobias was in a foul mood by the time he finally made it home.

He'd spent a couple of hours on the ship while Lord Mabon and the First Legate debated on what was to be done to protect the witching world, before being sent to fetch Gretchen. Panic was to be avoided at all costs. The first time the Sisters had roamed London, the sheer volume of magic in the city had nearly caused a riot. Witches threw spells at each other at the least provocation, and even regular folk began to feel the tension. Not only did the Order have to find Sophie, but they had to do so while keeping everyone calm.

Tobias had tracked until dawn but couldn't find any trace of Sophie. If that wasn't bad enough, he then had to make an appearance at the Order's bachelor apartments to make sure the other Keepers knew what to expect. There were too few of them as it was; more Ironstone students would have to be taken on.

And then there was Gretchen.

He simply did not know what to make of her. She was infuriating and yet he still had to remind himself that being amused at her rudeness was not an appropriate response. One of them ought to remain proper. And it clearly wouldn't be her.

It was even more challenging to remind himself that kissing her again was out of the question.

He shouldn't even *want* to kiss her.

She was under surveillance by the Order. Her family had a

history of insurgence. She went out of her way to trample on the manners and etiquette that he found so necessary and important. She was everything that he struggled not to be: impulsive, defiant, chaotic.

But he couldn't stop thinking of her.

The front door to the townhouse opened. "Good evening, my lord." Cameron, the butler, stepped aside to let Tobias in. Cameron bowed, as though Tobias wasn't naked under his greatcoat and hadn't spent the last few hours asleep on the marble floor in the shape of a giant wolf. It was easier than having to stay awake waiting for the family to return for the night. Between Tobias as a Keeper and Ky roaming at all hours and their mother being the Alpha, serving in the Lawless house came with decidedly irregular hours. Besides, Cameron fancied himself more of a bodyguard than a butler.

And butler or bodyguard, shifters had a preference for greatcoats since they were large enough to withstand shifting forms and long enough to hide a body when linen shirts and breeches were shredded to pieces. Tobias preferred perfectly tailored frock coats. Always.

"You didn't have to wait up," he said, handing Cameron his hat and gloves.

"Of course, I did, your lordship," he replied.

Tobias felt, rather than heard, the presence of another wolf and followed the call out to the back gardens. Moonlight gleamed on the fountain and the marble statues. There was a rustle on the other side of the hedges. "Posy," he called out.

A small tawny wolf poked out of the cedars, flower petals

and burrs stuck to its fur. As it approached, it transformed into a lithe young girl. She was sweet and solitary, with thick brown hair and blue eyes.

And a tail.

She was still trying to master her magic and could never quite fully cage the wolf. Sometimes she had ears, once an unfortunate case of whiskers, but usually a rather fluffy tail. Needless to say, she was restricted to the townhouse while in London.

"It's not safe," Tobias told her, tossing a blanket on a nearby chair over her shoulders.

"I'm at home." She patted his arm as though he were an overprotective nanny. "What could happen to me here?"

"All the same," he replied. "It's late, even for you." Posy kept odd hours, even before her troubles controlling her wolf.

"There was a meeting," she said carefully.

"A meeting?"

"Mother called the London pack together," she explained. "When she found out about Sophie Truwell."

"Already?"

She shrugged. "Of course."

"And you should have been there," Ky interjected, coming out of the conservatory. He wore his usual linen shirt with the leather strap across his chest bristling with daggers. He looked nothing like the son of a three-hundred-year-old earldom and everything like a young lad spoiling for a fight.

"Don't start," Posy begged them both.

"The Wolfcatchers are already on the hunt," Ky said, ignoring her plea. "You know as well as I do that shape-shifter

pelts fetch triple the price when there's a warlock on the loose."
He tested the tip of his favorite dagger. "We'll need the Carnyx
to keep us safe."

"That's what the Order is for."

Ky snorted. "It's bad enough they know our secret; I'm certainly not trusting the packs to them."

"And the Carnyx are so much better? A band of boys who
fight for the sake of fighting. Ask Donovan about the human
Wolfcatcher he killed last year."

"That Catcher took his brother's paw. The sawbones had to
take the rest of his hand when he shifted back to human form.
And if you'd let Gaelen join the Carnyx, she might have been
able to save herself."

There was a tense, brittle silence. Posy began to shift, the
tension too much for her. Her teeth elongated and ears poked
out of her hair.

Tobias and Ky were practically nose to nose. Ky was snarling, anger covering the hurt of a little brother. Tobias was icy in
his control, but his fists were clenching despite himself.

"That's enough," their mother snapped from the doorway.
Lady Elise Lawless might have been a silhouette clad in a blue
silk gown, but she spoke with the command of the Alpha, and a
mother besides. The brothers paused, separating.

"Lady Barlow's son was nearly snatched by a Catcher this
evening," she said grimly. "He was last seen by Blackfriar's
Bridge."

"I'll notify the Order," Tobias said immediately.

"Never mind them," Ky said. "This is family business."

"Yes, and I'm family," Tobias pointed out coolly. His inner wolf yanked on its leash. He had to bite back a growl, felt it reverberating in his chest.

"And yet you keep choosing them over us."

"It's not like that." Even if it sometimes felt like it.

"I'm fighting for our pack. For our family," Ky said. "Who are you fighting for?"

Gretchen, Emma, and Penelope crept down the hallway in their nightdresses, the carpet swallowing the sounds of their footsteps. They didn't light a candle until they were inside the last bedroom on the left with the door shut safely behind them.

Sophie's bedroom.

It hadn't yet been assigned to another student, but there was no telling how long that would last. The room was as small as Emma's, with a gilded pier glass over a table meant for perfuming and hairdressing, and furniture painted green with yellow flowers. The requisite rowan berries and salt were set out in the corners and on the windowsill.

Penelope made a circuit of the room. She brushed her fingertips over the tabletop and was immediately assaulted by images that spun by like a lantern show. They made her dizzy with their sheer numbers and speed: a maid with a burn from the fire grate, a footman carrying a trunk and a sizeable grudge against the housekeeper, a student who could talk to birds but couldn't stop them from flying into the windows, another maid, three more students muttering curses over their schoolbooks. She staggered back a step, holding on to the bedpost for balance. "I can't sort through all of the magical residue left behind. There's too much."

"Perhaps all her belongings were taken by the Order," Emma said, peering into the armoire. It was empty of dresses, slippers, and bonnets. "For examination."

"What do you think you're doing?" Daphne snapped from the doorway. She looked out of breath and furious.

Splendid.

"None of your business," Gretchen returned, utterly incapable of ignoring a challenge of any kind. "And must you constantly lurk about? Shouldn't you be trodding on some poor sod's toes?"

"Unlike you, some of us are perfectly capable dancers," Daphne retorted out of habit. Her blue eyes narrowed. "You're in Sophie's bedroom," she added. "And I demand to know why. Before I call the night watchman."

"There's no crime in being in a bedroom," Emma pointed out gently. "You look as if you ran all the way here."

"I set spells to notify me if anyone tried to come in here," she replied, eyeing the cousins carefully.

"Whyever for?" Penelope asked.

Daphne blinked. "What do you mean, why? Sophie was my friend."

"And she betrayed you," Gretchen said bluntly.

"Gretchen." Emma nudged her. "Easy."

Gretchen didn't look away from Daphne's pale face. "You want to know why she did what she did. Why she would choose the Greymalkin Sisters over you," Gretchen continued, not unkindly. She wouldn't have been able to stomach kindness and pity were she in Daphne's shoes. And Daphne had once elected to help Emma when Emma was wrongly accused of Lilybeth's murder, in order to find the real murderer. "We want to know why as well," she added.

"How?" Daphne demanded. "I know she's gone. My father told me, right before he wrapped me in so many protective spells I practically have to move sideways through the doorway."

"She has no reason to come after you," Emma said. "She once told me you were the reason the other girls stopped teasing her when she first arrived at the school."

Daphne nodded bleakly. "She had me fooled."

"She had everyone fooled."

"And for someone who claimed to be an orphan and so lonely she summoned three warlock spirits, she clearly knew someone other than you and Lilybeth very well indeed." Gretchen raised her eyebrows when they only frowned at her, confused. "Well, someone helped her escape before she reached Percival House. The question is who and why?" She glanced at Daphne. "Aren't you going to tell me that is what the Order is for and we should leave it to them?"

Daphne lifted her chin. "Certainly not. They've had every seer and clairvoyant trying to locate Sophie but to no avail. And I have a brother who is going to inherit my father's title and estates, as well as all of the magical knowledge acquired by a First Legate, simply for being born a boy. Even though he is bacon-brained and wouldn't know an amulet from a teacake." She sniffed. "No, I think this is best left to those of us who knew Sophie, or at least knew the world in which she lived. This is still a case best left to debutantes."

"Well, blast," Gretchen muttered. "We agree on something."

"I'm going to read something that belonged to Sophie," Penelope explained, unclenching her fingers from the bedpost. "If there's anything left, that is. I had no luck with the inkwell."

Daphne looked around with a knowing eye, having clearly spent time with Sophie in the room. "She liked that chair by the fire for her morning pot of chocolate."

Penelope shook her head. "That chair's been here long before King George went mad. I'd never be able to sort through that many magical impressions."

"There," Daphne said, pointing to a small red charm bag hanging over the window. It was embroidered with a white witch knot and wound around with a black ribbon. "She'd have added ingredients to that charm bag. They're in all of the bedrooms and last year we were set the task of augmenting the spell."

"Don't touch it," Penelope said quickly when Daphne reached for it. "It will overpower anything left behind as I can read the most recent history the easiest."

Daphne let her hand drop to her side. Penelope plucked the tiny pouch off the nail. The ribbon slipped free, brushing against the back of her knuckles. She was caught in a kaleidoscope, colors and sounds all bleeding together until they sharpened suddenly and she was no longer sitting on the edge of a gilded chair in the front parlor of the academy. For a moment the colors were too bright, pulsing around the edges and making her feel odd inside. Her eyes rolled back in her head.

She was in a thatched house with diamond-paned windows on

the edge of a forest. She was sitting on a cot tucked by the fireplace, holding the hand of a young girl. The girl was pale and clammy, her cheeks burning red.

"Beth," she wept. "Don't die. Please don't die." She rubbed her witch knot until it bled. And still there wasn't enough magic.

There was no stopping it.

Penelope's knees hit the hard floor as she crumpled.

"Did you see her?" Emma asked, helping her to sit up.

"Yes, when she was younger. Before she came here." She shook her head, stopped when it made the room spin. "In a cottage in the woods. Did she have a sister?"

"She never mentioned it," Daphne replied. "Though she did have an old doll she refused to part with. She said it belonged to someone she knew once."

Gretchen looked suddenly and darkly gleeful. "Do you know how to make a poppet, Daphne?"

"What does that—oh. Yes," Daphne said slowly, as the idea germinated. "In fact I do. But the Order burned all of her belongings, in case they were laced with dark magic. It never occurred to them that she might get away." She opened the drawers of the desk, rifling through abandoned ribbons, pencils, and writing quills left by countless students.

"What are you two planning?" Emma asked.

"A poppet like the one that was used against me," Gretchen replied grimly. "By Sophie, I imagine. Who else would attack me?"

Daphne snorted. "Anyone who'd met you, and half the girls at this school since Tobias carried you into the parlor in his very manly arms."

"Thank you, Daphne," Gretchen said. "That's very helpful."
She shrugged. "Still, you're probably right. Sophie would be
vexed that you undid a few of her spells this week alone."

"Did you say I was right? Can someone write that down so
she can sign it?"

"Never mind that," Penelope interrupted. "Can't we use the
charm bag? Since we know she handled it?"

"No, it has to be something personal, not something that she
merely touched. It has to have been a part of her." Daphne moved
to the vanity table, pausing over a silver tray holding a silver-
backed hairbrush made to look like a braid of foxglove flowers
and a crystal bottle of rosewater. "Can you find out which ones
belonged to Sophie?"

Penelope felt limp as old lettuce but she straightened her shoulders with determination. "Yes." She went to the bed and stretched
out. "So I don't fall on my head," she explained before she closed
her eyes tight, the same way she always did before having to swallow unpleasant medicine or jellied sweetmeats at a formal supper party. Luminescent spiders lowered from her hair in glowing
webs. She pulled at one of the hairs clinging to the bristles of the
brush. "Once more unto the breach, dear friends, once more,"
she said finally.

*She was sitting in front of the mirror, brushing her hair in even,
constant strokes, staring at her reflection. A yawning loneliness nibbled at her, consuming more and more of her until she was hollow as
a pipe reed. The wind could go through her and sing a song. "Soon,"
she whispered desperately. "Soon."*

Penelope opened her eyes. The bed's embroidered canopy
was a pale arch above her as she waited for the dizziness to pass.

At least the room wasn't spinning as quickly as it had before. She sat up on her elbows. "This one," she said finally, her voice hoarse with exertion.

Daphne plucked it from her hand. "Good," she said grimly. "Let's get started. We need dried lily stalks."

Gretchen flinched, pressing a hand to her temple. "Reeds would be better. I'll fetch some from the apothecary closet."

By the time she returned, clutching dead flowers, Emma had taken down one of the curtains. Daphne found scissors in the desk and was cutting out enough of the heavy cream-colored brocade material for two dolls. "There's only enough here for two poppets," she said. "One for us and one for the Order." When Gretchen opened her mouth to protest, she continued haughtily. "My father's the First Legate."

"Not this again," Gretchen muttered, but she didn't pursue it.

"I'll sew them," Penelope offered. "It will be faster. Hand me my reticule." She pulled out a small kit with needle and thread and began to stitch the edges of the poppets together. She left the head open enough for Daphne to stuff it, adding Sophie's hair to each. She used ink to mark the left hand with a witch knot, and added two eyes.

They were simple dolls, smelling like flowers.

"Sophie has the ability to make us suffer all our past injuries, a connection to the Greymalkin Sisters, and she has four murdered girls to her credit. And we have a doll," Gretchen said drily. "I feel safer already."

. . .

Penelope decided to stop for ices at Gunter's in Berkeley Square. The sun was finally out and it felt like a proper summer afternoon. Mayfair even smelled like flowers instead of the hot Thames and horse droppings. They had a poppet to protect them against Sophie, and she'd just bought three novels and Lord Byron's new collection of poetry. It was as good a reason as any to celebrate.

And since it was ridiculous to ignore Ian, who was standing outside the shop, trying to look nonchalant, she bought him one too. They stood under the awning and discussed her new books, and he apologized three more times for his part in bringing her in for questioning.

"Lady Penelope."

Penelope recognized Lucius Beauregard's voice instantly. She widened her eyes at Ian, who, not being Gretchen or Emma, just looked confused. She stifled a sigh. Until he wiped the corner of his mouth pointedly but subtly. She licked the corner of her lips, tasting sticky sugar. Having her own Keeper was proving to be quite useful. Never mind a warlock on the loose, he'd just saved her from the embarrassment of greeting Lucius with food on her face.

She turned on her heel and bobbed a curtsy. "Lord Beauregard." He was as handsome as ever, in a green coat and buff trousers.

He bowed, eyes twinkling appreciatively. "Might I say you look very fetching in that dress." She wore a mint-green muslin dress with a striped pelisse with cap sleeves overtop. The shade was almost exactly the same as his coat.

She blushed. "Thank you."

"I wonder if we might talk awhile," Lucius said, dropping his voice until it was like warm caramel. "I have—"

"Did you really buy your jailor a lemon ice?" Gretchen interrupted, her shadow falling between them.

"It's burnt filbert, actually," Penelope returned. "Because we like *him*, remember?" She peered behind her cousin. "Where is Tobias, anyway?"

Gretchen shrugged. "It was another student from Ironstone following me today," she said. "I lost him ages ago."

Ian just sighed. "It's embarrassing, really," he muttered.

"Shameful," she agreed. "You lot could do better."

Lucius looked surprised. "Surely you're not saying you defied a Keeper."

She rolled her eyes. "Of course I did. He was two years younger than me, and he blushed every time I glanced in his direction. He was like a puppy."

"You'd think they'd learn to put a full guard on you," Penelope teased.

"You'd think."

"Where's your maidservant?" Ian asked. Gretchen patted his arm with a kind but patronizing smile. He shook his head. "Never mind."

"Now you're catching on." She grinned, stealing a spoonful of Penelope's ice. "Parmesan." She grimaced. "You always choose the worst flavors."

"Shall I have them bring you out an orange ice?" she suggested. "They were kind enough to deliver one to Cedric over there." She waved at Cedric, who was leaning against the wall, arms crossed and expression unreadable. Three sparrows, a cat, and a stray dog had already found him, sitting peacefully on the pavement at his feet. No matter how many times she asked him to join her, he never would. Was it any wonder she was so certain he did not have romantic feelings for her, despite her cousins' constant suggestions otherwise?

"No thank you, I—" Gretchen broke off, pinching the bridge of her nose.

"Headache?" Ian asked, concerned. "I'll get you a chair."

"It's not that." She squinted at Penelope's embroidered reticule. It was a dark earthy brown velvet with birch tree branches forming magical runes. She was quite proud of the effect. "You dropped a stitch."

Penelope raised an eyebrow. "As if you even know what a dropped stitch looks like."

She grimaced. "Right there. That little line there changes the pattern of the protective spell so it's not effective." She rubbed her temples. "Believe me, I know exactly what it looks like." She wiped a trace of blood off her ear.

Penelope paled. "Gretchen!"

Gretchen just waved away her concern with a smug grin. "I'm improving! It's just a little spot and I wasn't sick on anyone's shoes."

Lucius surreptitiously moved out of reach. "Might we find someplace . . . quieter?" he suggested to Penelope with that wicked smile that made her toes curl in her silk slippers.

"Sorry, mate," Ian said. "I'm watching Penelope, and he's

watching me." He gestured at Cedric with his thumb. "This is as quiet as it gets."

He looked frustrated. "Why don't we walk in the garden then? Berkeley Square is lovely this time of year."

Penelope took his arm when he offered it gallantly. She ignored Gretchen's exchanging a pointed look with both Ian and Cedric, who had straightened away from the wall. Penelope was left relatively alone with Lucius, trailed by Ian, who was trailed by Cedric and Penelope's own maidservant. Lucius glanced over his shoulder, amused. "You're like a lovely swan with a train of lost ducklings."

She laughed. "It is a rather odd situation." She eyed him askance. "You're not concerned for your reputation? I feel honor bound to point out that although Ian is a wonderful person, he's here because the Order doesn't trust me."

"Then the Order is run by fools," he said much more severely than she might have expected. Something must have shown in her face because he added lightly, "When a beautiful lady such as yourself is hounded, I believe the system is deeply flawed."

Her cheeks warmed at the compliment. They crossed into Berkeley Square, which was five acres of paths through grassy lawn, sculptures, and a row of smooth plane trees with wide leaves and their peculiar spiky seed balls.

"I hope you'll forgive my forwardness," Lucius said. "But I have a gift for you."

She peered up at him, from under the brim of her bonnet. Society would say that accepting gifts, exchanging letters, and dancing more than two dances were declarations of your intent to marry. Gretchen's mother would have demanded Penelope refuse the gift. "That's very kind," she said instead.

His smile widened. "When I found it, I thought of you," he explained, guiding her to a bench under a tree. Dappled sunlight fell through the leaves. He pulled a small paper-wrapped parcel from the pocket of his great coat. "I've been carrying it around for days now, hoping I would see you."

The package was only slightly larger than her palm and felt like a book. She tore into it eagerly, trying not to notice Cedric watching her from the other path. It shouldn't have made her feel guilty and uncomfortable. She was enjoying the company of a young man who might return her interest. Surely, that was mature of her? Wouldn't it be worse to pine hopelessly after someone? It was all fine and well for novels, but it was decidedly unpleasant in real life.

The tree above her filled with sparrows, watching her. Forgetting her assertion to be mature, she made a face at Cedric, knowing full well that he was using them to spy.

She undid the red ribbon and pushed aside the torn paper to reveal a small leather-bound book. *Shakespeare's Sonnets* was stamped on the cover in elaborate gilded letters. She ran her fingertips over it. "Oh, it's beautiful." She flipped through the pages and partly dried rose petals tumbled into her lap.

"Take off your gloves," he suggested. "The leather is soft as silk."

She knew she shouldn't do it, but it would be odd to refuse. And to touch something that might have been made during

Shakespeare's own lifetime was too tempting. She tugged off her gloves. Lucius's fingers were warm as they trailed over her wrist and across her palm, tracing her witch knot. She couldn't look away, couldn't move, could barely swallow. He dipped his head so that his mouth was close to her ear. "Go on, Penelope. Books are meant to be loved, aren't they?"

The use of her given name sent a delicious shiver through her. She felt shockingly bare without her glove, something she would have considered absurd not five minutes ago. Licking her lower lip, she stroked the book. It was lamb-soft and smelled of dust, sunlight, and the curious sweet vanilla of old paper.

"You're right." She smiled up at him. "It's so much bet—"

The world smeared, like paints on a palette.

Rain made the cobblestones slick, so she ducked into a nearby bookshop. The air was pleasantly dusty and dry. She smiled at the clerk. No, not her. Lucius smiled at the clerk. She had a moment to feel the tightness of his cravat and an impatience simmering below the surface.

"Where is your Shakespeare?" he asked. "I've a mind to get a gift for a beautiful girl."

He was talking about her.

The vision fell away abruptly. She gave a start.

"Are you unwell?" Lucius asked, concerned. His eyes searched her face.

She smiled weakly. It was one thing to know about magic, and another thing to know that the girl you just gave a present to stepped into your head for a moment. He thought she was beautiful.

"I'm well," she said, pressing the small worn book to her chest. "Perfectly well."

"Are you sure about this?" Gretchen asked dubiously as the rain pattered though the leaves of the oak tree outside her house. "You should let me come with you."

Emma shook her head. "We'd never shake Tobias off our trail. You know it as well as I do."

Because she did, Gretchen scowled. "But who knows if that spell I made will even work properly?"

"I know it will." Emma tucked the lodestone into her reticule, next to the poppet of Sophie. She stayed hidden inside the unmarked carriage so Tobias wouldn't see her.

"Are you sure Virgil won't follow you?" Gretchen wasn't convinced.

"I slipped belladonna tincture in his tea, which I had Olwen bring to him outside the school. She told him she was worried he'd catch cold in all this rain. She's pretty, so he believed her."

"But she's Cormac's sister. He hates Cormac."

"She's *really* pretty."

Gretchen shook her head. "Serves him right then." She handed Emma a rolled piece of parchment. "If the first spell doesn't work, try this one. They both need your blood."

"It will work."

"Emma, I'm only just now starting not to bleed out of my ears when I work my magic," she pointed out. "Your faith in me is touching and all, but it won't do you much good when you're alone in Windsor Forest."

"I'll be fine. I'll wrap a Fith-Fath glamour around me and no one will see me at all. And I'll be back in time for breakfast. You're fussing."

"It's much easier when *I'm* the one concocting foolish plans," Gretchen grumbled. "Waiting at home is rubbish." She stomped back up the lily-bordered path to the front door and disappeared inside. The carriage rolled away, and she had to stop herself from pressing her nose to the window to watch her cousin go. Worry gnawed at her. Or it would have done, if a shriek from the kitchens hadn't interrupted.

Godric came out of the back parlor to join her as she rushed down the stairs to investigate. Smoke choked the air, drifting slowly up the steps. Two maids and a footman were in the hall, coughing. Light flickered ominously in the doorway to the kitchens.

"Fire!" Cook hollered, sounding more confused than scared. Godric tucked his chin into his cravat, and Gretchen unwrapped the bandeau in her hair and used it to cover her mouth and nose. The smoke was acrid and persistent.

Cook threw a bucket of wash water at the fire licking out of the hearth, but the flames ducked and split around it. She wiped sweat off her face, bewildered, before spotting the twins. "Get back! 'Tisn't safe."

Godric reached for another bucket from one of the scullery maids, who was pumping water as fast as she could. When he stepped around Cook to toss the contents, the fire growled, shooting up the walls. Something small but remarkably bulky tumbled out, swiping at Godric. Godric stumbled, landing on his arse. "What the bloody hell was that?"

"Must be something stuck in the chimney and the wind is pushing all around it," Cook guessed, trying to beat back the flames with a dishtowel.

"That's no draft," Gretchen whispered as the flames responded by coalescing into a squat goblin with red hair and feral eyebrows. Cook clearly saw the fire leaping about and behaving altogether oddly, but not the goblin. He cackled, voice scratchy from constant heat and smoke. He stomped his foot and the fire exploded in all directions. He cackled again before taking off, singeing the floor under his boots as he went.

"That little blighter." Gretchen gave chase, leaping over Godric, still sprawled on the ground. She followed the fire goblin, trying desperately to remember if she'd read anything on how to defeat them in her grimoire. She settled for pelting him with whatever object came to hand: a teacup, a small potted fern, and three of her mother's decorative crystal swans.

She eventually cornered him in the living room. The tassels on the footstools were smoldering. Smoke billowed mysteriously from under a settee. "Oi," she said, borrowing one of Moira's favorite words. The wards were in dismal shape if fire goblins were roaming Mayfair now. Cook might have been seriously hurt. And the next house might go up in flames if the inhabitants didn't know a fire goblin when they saw one. "You're not meant to be outside the markets."

"I won't go back," he cawed, lunging for the marble fireplace with its stone lion heads. Fire licked out of their jaws. The dead coals in the grate crackled.

"Oh no you don't." Gretchen grabbed for one of the vases of flowers her mother liked to crowd on every available surface. If she didn't have magic to use against him, she'd use common sense.

And a great deal of violence.

She threw the vase as hard as she could. White lily petals sailed through the air. The vase tipped, spilling some of the water. Gretchen watched it spatter uselessly over a chair. Finally, it struck the goblin on the back of the head with enough force to fling him into the marble fireplace. He slumped, groaning. Smoke sputtered from under his shirt. His eyebrows sparked but not enough to cause any real damage.

Godric ran into the parlor, skidding on the floor. "Did you get him?" He spotted the goblin teetering dizzily.

"We need to secure him," Gretchen said, "before he catches his breath."

Godric glanced around the room. "The urn," he said. It was large enough that it had served as one of their favorite hiding spots when they were little. It was currently stuffed with ostrich and peacock feathers.

It took both of them to drag it from the corner. Gretchen's arms were quivering by the time they reached the goblin. She used her entire body to push it until it toppled over the goblin with a thump, trapping him inside.

"Now what?" Godric leaned against it.

"Now we wave Tobias out of the bushes so he can come and deal with it." Since he was the reason, unknowingly or not, that she hadn't been able to join Emma, he ought to make himself useful. "Before Mother comes home."

Godric paled, looking frightened for the first time that night. "Bollocks."

Emma settled back onto the cushions, having already instructed the coachman to take her to her father's townhouse after she'd visited Gretchen. She'd told Mrs. Sparrow she was spending the night at home and hadn't bothered telling her father anything at all as he would be at his club and wouldn't know the difference anyway. She hadn't even told Gretchen the real reason she was visiting Windsor Forest again. It wasn't to search for her mother this time. She needed something that had belonged to Ewan if she was going to bring him out of the Underworld.

She waited until the carriage rumbled away again before slipping into the stables. She stole the horse in the end stall because he was the farthest away from the stable hands asleep in the hay. The tapping of the rain on the roof covered any noises she made. She was actually looking forward to the hard horseback ride through the night to Berkshire. It would be a nice change from wondering about her father, worrying about Ewan, and dreaming about the Sisters.

Invisible in her glamour, she was safe from the dangers of the road, from curious eyes to highwaymen. It sapped her magic until she was limp in the saddle, but it was worth it. On the outskirts of the family country estate, she slid to the ground on soft legs.

Windsor Forest was dark and moist, like the inside of a giant's mouth. She shivered, finding she needed more courage than she'd thought she would, just to take the first step. The trees whispered all around her, scraping at her antlers. She risked the light of a lantern. It might give her away to poachers but she'd wander in circles without it. She held a dagger in her other hand, the blade washed in thunderwater and pepper, to cut through all danger.

She used the tip to poke her finger, smearing a drop of blood on the lodestone Gretchen had given her. A crude stag outline was painted in white, with two "E's" back to back on its belly. She assumed it was for "Ewan" and "Emma." Her blood was his blood and the spell would show her the way to his hut, the one her mother had visited once.

The blood smeared the letters. Nothing else happened. There was no spark or flash of light. She didn't suddenly see a map printed on the inside of her eyelids. She was still just a girl lost in the forest.

Frowning, she turned on her heel, looking for clues. She spoke the words Gretchen had taught her. *"Sun and moon both light the way, sun toward and moon away."*

The lodestone grew uncomfortably cold. When she kept turning and was facing south, it warmed. Curious, she took a step in the opposite direction. It grew frigid and coated with ice. Another step back where she'd been facing and it warmed like sunlight. "Sun toward," she murmured, holding out the lodestone on her witch knot and the lantern in her other hand.

It led her between the trees, over a creek, and through thickets of ivy and wild raspberry. She kept walking until it was like holding a burning coal.

By the time she found the remains of the hut, her witch knot was burned in the center. The lodestone went quiet, just another chunk of stone.

The hut was just like she remembered from the memory trapped in her mother's spell bottle, though obviously more neglected. The gargoyle in the tree was missing an ear, and the circle of stones out front was filled with old ashes and rainwater. The willow door was splintered and off one of its hinges.

She stepped carefully inside, picking her way around a broken chair, ruffled with mushrooms. The blankets on the cots were moth-eaten and mouse-nibbled, and there was moss growing on the oak trunks that served as beams to hold up the roof. She wasn't sure if Ewan's father was even still alive, but he clearly hadn't stayed here after Ewan vanished.

She searched under the beds and in the corners for anything that might have belonged to Ewan. She found spiders and beetles and wood shavings from a whittling project. She investigated all around the shavings until she found a discarded piece of willow wood carved into the likeness of a deer decorated with bluebells. On the back, in crude letters: *For Theo.* He'd have spent hours making it for her mother. It was no doubt soaked in his sweat and blood. She tucked it into the reticule tied around her wrist and turned to leave.

Outside, a branch snapped.

Startled, Emma pressed against the doorjamb. Lightning slashed the sky. She wasn't even aware she'd called it until it briefly illuminated the deer in the clearing. The doe was sleek and red, the tip of her white tail glowing whenever lightning flashed. She stomped one foot imperiously, in warning.

Not just a deer.

"Mother?" she asked softly, hesitantly.

The deer flicked her ears. The lantern light showed wide liquid eyes, too human for the delicate deer face.

"Please," Emma said, hope and sorrow battling inside her. It was a vicious fight that left her trembling and stumbling around her words. Snow drifted between the branches. "You need to turn back into Theodora Lovegrove."

She stepped forward slowly. The deer tensed. Emma froze.

"Please," she added. "Sophie is back, which means the Sisters might not be far behind. I *need* you."

The deer watched her for a long impossible moment before turning away.

"Ewan needs you."

The deer paused.

Emma ignored the snow on her lashes and the mist of her breath in the cold. Wind tore at the leaves around them. "He's trapped in the Underworld. I can't get him out alone. And if Sophie tries to open Greymalkin House again, she'll need me to do it. Ewan sacrificed himself to make sure that didn't happen."

The deer flared her nostrils, scenting the snow and the Greymalkin blood in her daughter, just as it scented Ewan in the hut. Emma noticed the hoofprints in the dirt around the shelter. She'd been here for a while, long enough for Emma to know her mother wasn't entirely lost.

"*Maman*, please."

The deer bounded away, sailing over branches and undergrowth without a sound.

Lightning stabbed at the ground behind her, trees burning like torches.

When Emma returned to the academy, Virgil was waiting for her. He looked groggy and furious, his eyes still dilated from the herbal tincture. His cravat and coat were creased from sleeping in the bushes. "Where have you been?" he demanded.

"I went out for a walk," she replied with a bland smile. "I couldn't sleep."

"What did you do to me?" There was mud in his hair. "I woke up in a rosebush." She might have felt badly if he wasn't always so awful to Cormac.

"It's hardly my fault if you can't fulfill your responsibilities," she pointed out. "Perhaps you should drink less wine."

"I wasn't drunk!" He advanced, infuriated. "I demand to know what you were doing."

"I've told you," she replied dismissively. "Now if you'll excuse me, I have lessons to prepare for."

He grabbed her arm when she started to walk away, leaving a bruise. She narrowed her eyes at him, just as thunder shook the sky so hard the ground trembled. "I wouldn't," she advised softly.

"I am a Keeper for the Order," he seethed. "And you will answer me."

He yanked a length of black cord from his pocket, uncoiling it like a snake. Rain speared between them, silver and sharp. She tried to break his hold but he was maddeningly strong. She contemplated using her antlers, but instead of tying her up, he let the end drop to the ground and measured it to her length.

Before she could ask him what in the world he was doing, a night soil man spotted them.

"Oi, you let her be," he shouted from the road, his cart stopped behind him. "Before I call the guard."

Virgil released her reluctantly, but there was a smugness to his smile that filled her with cold trepidation.

Chapter 11

Tobias knew the exact moment it went wrong.

Cormac glanced at him. "Where?" He knew perfectly well that particular expression on Tobias's face, coupled with his own amulets all but sending smoke through his buttonholes, did not bode well.

Gritting his teeth against the pain, Tobias started down the sidewalk, senses open, nostrils flaring. Tracking was both a physical thing and one bound by magic and therefore less definable. London stank of coal smoke, rain, and horses. He tried to focus on the physical: the waft of scorched lemon balm that always followed a warlock's spell, or the more common salt and fennel from the magical wards set all over the city. Magic twanged like a broken violin string.

They emerged onto Piccadilly, gas lights burning fitfully through the yellow fog. Men hurried to the pub and street sweepers waited on corners with raggedy brooms. Ladies peeked through the windows of their carriages. It was a most inconvenient place for a warlock to practice nefarious deeds. Dark magic had after-effects, after all, just as more benevolent magic did.

"Are you sure this is right?" Cormac asked, peering through the dandies gathered in groups along the sidewalk. The crowds at this time of night always made things more difficult.

Someone screamed.

"Quite sure," Tobias replied drily.

They broke into a run, dodging around two gentlemen so deeply in their cups they swayed together. The scream had come from a woman pressed against the wall of a fruiterer shop. A pyramid of pineapples trembled behind the glass at her back. She was pale, her chest heaving as she gulped in air. A few young men stood nearby, mostly to admire her impressive cleavage. One of them had pulled out his pistol but wasn't entirely sure who he was supposed to aim it at.

"He'll shoot his own foot off," Cormac muttered, approaching the group with an easy smile. He had the charm and patience to deal with people, not to mention an arcane ability to flirt. Tobias was too tightly controlled to appear as anything but what he was: a young lord with a healthy respect for rules and proper conduct.

While Cormac convinced the gentleman to put away his pistol, simultaneously getting the woman to purr a greeting, Tobias concentrated on pinpointing the source of the forbidden spell.

The woman screamed again, clutching Cormac's sleeve. "There! Did you see it? Did you?"

"Oi," one of the lads gulped, abandoning any pretense at heroism to hide behind Cormac.

Tobias followed the trajectory of their stares to a shape in the tattered mists. And another. Malevolence oozed, stretching out invisible fingers. "Shadow people," he muttered.

The dark shapes stayed just out of the corner of the eye, no matter how quickly one turned one's head. It was like feeling the hot breath of a rabid dog while blindfolded. They had no shape beyond that of a shadow that had peeled itself off the ground to walk upright. They carried no weapons and had no physical form, but their mere presence caused a bubbling cauldron of adrenaline and terror in anyone in the vicinity.

The pistol reappeared. They'd have a riot on their hands within moments.

"Stay back," Cormac said. "Looks like a gang of pickpockets," he lied. It wouldn't distract them from their fear for very long.

The shadows grew more insistent and more poisonous. Tobias lifted his left hand and his witch knot glowed with a white-blue fire, spearing them with light. Their nonfaces elongated in silent screams.

"What's that light?" a passerby wondered.

"Broken gas lamp," Cormac improvised, dropping handfuls of salt on the ground between them and the shadows.

The shadows recoiled slightly, just enough that heartbeats stopped racing wildly and terror abated to an ordinary fear of pickpockets.

The shadows turned on Tobias and Cormac, who moved into standard defensive formation. Cormac had his weapons of iron and salt, and Tobias pushed his personal magic through his body, like jagged spring ice tearing at the banks of a river.

The shadow people exuded bleak and morbid hunger. The gentleman with the pistol fainted dead away. Tobias flung more magic light, even though it cost him to do it. He was starting to feel the way he'd felt after being bedridden with a fever. The shadows parted slowly and fled. They left a taint to the night air.

Tobias caught the scent of scorched lemon balm before he could indulge in even a brief moment of triumph. He followed it into the alley, iron dagger at the ready. Tucked behind a crooked water spout he found a smooth black stone and a bee trapped in a glass jar with broken opals in the dirt around it.

The shadow people were returning, taking advantage of his distraction.

The spell was calling them to the area, but it wasn't the dark magic he'd sensed earlier. And it wasn't a broken ward or a wayward spell.

"It's a diversion," he told Cormac in furious undertones. He lifted the jar and the bee drifted away, befuddled. The shadow people flickered. "Something else is happening. Something worse."

Gretchen was on her way home from Rowanstone when the voices began to wail and screech in her head.

She knocked on the carriage ceiling and tumbled out of the door before the horses had come to a proper halt. People pushed past her on the pavement. A woman snapped at her to get out of the way. She ignored them all, trying to locate the cause of the warning cacophony in her head. It was different this time. Not so much a chaos of spells being spoken, more like a coven of witches chanting a warning. She couldn't make out what they were saying, only that it was coming from St. James Church, across the street. The stone walls, worn smooth as butter by centuries of wind and rain, threw their shadow across the street.

The gate was locked, but the wall was pitifully easy to climb. The spire pierced the sky and the windows were dark, glassy eyes watching her progress through the graveyard. If Godric were here, she knew he'd have seen ghosts drifting across her path. She tried not to think about it.

"A ring to be wed, and a ring for the dead."

"As if I even know what that means," Gretchen muttered.

"Cast off your widow's weeds."

She rather hoped that at some point, these bothersome dead witches would start to make sense.

Bracken-green smoke oozed between the headstones. She gagged, choking on the acrid sting of it. It was slimy and unpleasant, like a film of green water from a stagnant pond. She staggered as it clung to her, shifting to envelope her like poisonous mist. She was immediately ill and light-headed. She had to find a way to contain it before it spread, but she couldn't see where it came from, could only see more of that bracken-colored fog.

"Run."

That wasn't cryptic at all.

She struggled to separate the rising cacophony of voices. They were urgent, scared, cautionary. As if she didn't already know random magic that soiled the very air was unwelcome.

"We are still here."

"Who are you?" she asked. She could have sworn one of the voices was vaguely familiar. She wrapped her hand around a branch of the nearby yew tree and held on tight. Pain made spots dance in front of her eyes. Bile burned in the back of her throat. She felt something pop, and her nose started to bleed. The pain in her head intensified, but she refused to give in.

"Gretchen, stop!" Tobias was suddenly there, holding her up. "You have to get out of here!"

She shook her head. She couldn't stop. She was too close now. She just needed to sort through the last of the voices assaulting her. *"A warlock's spell. We are still here."* "Almost got it," she croaked.

"It will kill you," he insisted, his fingers digging harder into her arms. "It's warlock magic." He took a pouch from his coat pocket, fingers trembling slightly. "Angelica leaves, mullein, and pepper," he said through clenched teeth. "Burn it."

Gretchen made a little pile of the herbs on the dirt and used a matchstick Tobias gave her to carry the flame from one of the church torches. The mixture smoked and smoldered, scented smoke pushing against the unnatural fog.

Tobias meanwhile was shaking and had turned away from her, shoulders hunched. Remembering his reaction when she'd startled him the day they'd bound the kelpie, she approached him cautiously. "What's wrong?" she asked.

He didn't turn around. "Take this flask," he said, thrusting it at her. His voice was strangled and breathless. "Salt water," he explained. "Pour it over your feet and your witch knot."

She did as he asked, trying to keep an eye both on the receding poisonous fog and Tobias. There was an alarming crunching sound that made her abandon the warlock's magical residue.

Tobias wasn't entirely Tobias.

His teeth had elongated and his eyes burned the color of the sky on a parched summer's day. The irises were too large and a strange sound ululated from his throat.

Right before he fell to the ground, his hands shifted into fur-covered legs with paws. Claws scraped the dirt.

By the time Gretchen had blinked in shock, he was back to being Tobias again, the seams of his coat ripped but with nothing else to show for the change. She might have imagined it all.

She took a step backward, trying to find her equilibrium.

And fell right into a hole.

No, not a hole exactly.

An open grave.

Tobias crouched to peer over the edge. "Are you hurt?"

"No," she finally wheezed. She'd landed on her backside and the force of the fall had knocked the breath from her lungs. She was offended more than actually hurt. "Just winded." Soil crumbled onto her, skittering over her clothes like ants. Her tailbone throbbed lightly as she struggled to sit up. More dirt rained down, covering her legs.

That was when she realized she hadn't landed on a coffin or a collection of bones. Whoever had rested here was gone. "Bloody hell," she said, scrambling up.

Tobias reached a hand down to help her out of the grave. "This body was deliberately dug up," he said.

"Grave robbers?" she asked dubiously. "In Piccadilly?"

He only pointed to the iron nails driven into the ground. If Gretchen squinted she could see the salt scattered in the hole. Both were clear signs of magic. *"A ring for the dead."* Salt. The whispers meant the salt ring around the grave.

Tobias circled it, looking even more stark than usual. His focus was so intent and predatory, it was clear he was hunting for something. She took a closer look at the area but couldn't see anything other than the broken earth and the glint of the nails.

"Why would someone do this?" she asked. She stepped over to the headstone that had been left where it toppled. It was carved with a weeping angel.

"I'll have to turn it over," Tobias said, crouching down to grip one end. Gretchen hurried to help him. He glanced at her, startled. She didn't have the breath to make a cutting remark; she was already red in the face from trying to budge the stone. Tobias applied himself hastily and flipped the marker over. It landed with a thud. She brushed the dirt off the lettering. Her hand stilled as her blood went cold.

"Lilybeth Jones," she read aloud.

Tobias rose to his feet, swearing softly. "The wards haven't been leaking magic on their own. They're meant to keep the Order occupied so Sophie could gather magic." He pulled a scroll of parchment from his pocket and unrolled it. "More grave robberies," he said. Gretchen watched over his shoulder as names began to burn themselves into the paper.

Margaret York.

Alice.

The names of the witches Sophie had murdered for the Sisters.

"Not again," Gretchen said grimly.

Even after midnight, the goblin markets bustled. Usually, only the taverns and the seedier shops stayed open after dark, unless it was a full moon or a Threshold day, which were times of power like solstices or May Day and midnight. But the witching world was most decidedly on edge. If any more wards broke, One-Eyed Joe would be able to retire on the profits. And London might run out of salt altogether.

Moira poured some into a tiny glass bottle, trying not to scatter the grains over the table, with little success. She was better at leaping between buildings than she was at fiddling with delicate spells, but One-Eyed Joe needed the help, despite his protests. She couldn't carve his cameos for him, but she could put together the other charms he sold at his stall.

The trade in protective amulets was even brisker than it had been after the kelpie was found in the Serpentine right in front of the Beau Monde. They'd had to shut the brocade curtain on the side of the tent that dealt with regular shoppers looking for cameos. One-Eyed Joe's illusion talent was easily strong enough to hold the tent open between both worlds, but there was just too much magic to be done and he already looked tired. On the other side of the stall, goblins, witches too poor to own shoes, aristocratic witches, spirits, hags, Rovers, and Madcaps mingled together uneasily. Protective witch knots and other symbols were painted onto walls, chalked over the cobblestones, and embroidered on dream pillows meant to safeguard familiars while you slept. Evil-eye beads stared back from every corner.

But at the end of the day, if you weren't stronger, you could only hope you were faster.

Moira intended to be faster. Marmalade sulkily prowled the confines of the stall. He wanted to run but she just couldn't risk it. She wasn't even entirely sure it was safe enough in One-Eyed Joe's tent, but she couldn't stand her restless familiar's scratching inside her chest to get free.

One-Eyed Joe hunched over a delicate shell cameo. He wore his usual purple cravat and gray coat, even though it was stiflingly hot in the tent. A brazier of coal and incense smoked at his feet. His knotted fingers worked carefully to carve a relief of a knight holding a shield decorated with a witch knot. He'd pack salt, crushed rowan berries, iron dust, and lady's mantle leaves behind the backing when he finished it. It was both magically protective and pretty, and therefore popular with the young ladies Emma and her cousins went to school with. Cedric had purchased one for Penelope just this morning.

Moira wrinkled her nose. "You're pungent today, Joe." He usually smelled like gin and lettuce, another illusion to keep the curious away. It was especially strong today, even under the incense. "Are you mad at me?"

"Never you, ferret," he chuckled. "No warlock wants to tangle with an old man who smells bad. Best protective magic there is."

She rubbed her nose with the sleeve of her shirt. "I can see why," she grumbled. She turned back to her work. "What's this one for?" she asked, adding three hairs to the mixture of mistletoe berries and mirror dust in the mortar and pestle.

"Shape-shifters use it to keep hidden. You can look right at one and never quite see his face," One-Eyed Joe explained.

They worked in silence for a long moment, and Moira made a mental note to gather more mistletoe for the cabinet. She watched Atticus swagger across the street, pale hair gleaming like gold threads. Piper followed, as she always did. She wore a new dress, with pink ribbons on the sleeves.

"Since when can they afford fripperies?" Moira wondered.

One-Eyed Joe looked up. "Eh?"

"Atticus," Moira explained. "He's up to something. Even the Rovers are leaving him be."

"He's like a child," One-Eye Joe muttered dismissively. "He chases every shiny thing and then cries when he breaks it."

She snorted in agreement. "But he says a Greybeard hired him to find a dead witch's teeth."

Joe narrowed his one eye speculatively. The incense smoke transformed into owls and ferrets as he thought. "Don't like that much," was all he said. He sorted through one of the baskets on his table and tossed a tassel of evil-eye beads at Moira.

"I don't need more charms," she said. "Sell them to the next country witch who comes to the table."

"Humor an old man," he insisted.

She made a face but attached the tassel to the end of her braid and then flipped it behind her shoulder. "There. Happy?"

"Aye." He coughed as he rose from his chair. She hurried forward to take his arm. When he didn't snap at her, she worried more. "I think I'll sleep on the cot tonight," he said, shuffling to the narrow bed behind a standing screen. She helped lower him down on the straw-stuffed mattress, pulling the blankets up over him. "Don't fuss," he grumbled, but he patted her hand gently.

"I didn't say anything."

"You think loudly," he said.

The bridge didn't feel right. The wind was too cold, the sounds too sharp. She didn't need Cass to know something was happening. She glanced outside. The dragon he conjured up to coil around the tent didn't have the usual ferocity that kept Rovers, thieves, and Greybeards at bay. She didn't think it would keep anyone over the age of six away tonight. It was thin as mist and looked as old and tired as One-Eyed Joe.

Moira waited until he was snoring before settling in his chair to keep watch.

The fact that Sophie was gathering the bones of the witches she'd murdered did not bode well.

Gretchen should probably fixate on that instead.

But it wasn't every day someone half turned into a wolf in front of her.

Especially not someone she considered to be the most tight-laced and unbending gentleman of her acquaintance. Frankly, she could more easily imagine herself accidentally turning into a wolf before Tobias Lawless, Viscount Killingsworth, Lord of All Things Proper. And yet he looked as haughty and calm as ever. One would never guess he had just grown fangs. And fur.

He didn't let go of her arm until he'd hailed a hackney and she'd hopped inside. He gave the driver the address and climbed in to sit across from her. She rubbed her arms, slightly chilled now that the adrenaline and bravado were fading. "You're not taking me to the Order?"

"No."

She licked her lips. "Not that I'm not grateful, but why not?"

"Did you do this?"

"Well, no."

"Do you know where Sophie is?"

"No."

"Then why split what little manpower we have left into questioning you when we could be hunting a warlock instead?"

"Oh." It was logical. Still, she'd expected him to follow the letter of the law when it came to his duties. The carriage lurched into motion and she winced, bumping the bruises currently forming on her backside.

"You're hurt," he said sharply.

"Just a few bruises from the fall," she said.

"You were lucky you didn't crack your head open."

"You're a wolf," she blurted out.

He went ominously still, except his gaze snapping up to her face, blue eyes as wild as the rest of him was civilized. "Yes," was all he said.

She stared at him. "A *wolf*," she repeated. "I didn't even know such a thing was possible."

"You are rather new to this world," he pointed out. "And we prefer to keep it private." He leaned forward. "Very private." His expression was too mercurial to read accurately.

"The Order knows, I assume." Although, come to think of it, she'd never heard any suggestion of wolves, and the girls at Rowanstone did love to swoon and fuss over him.

"The First Legate knows," he replied. "And Cormac. No one else."

She shook her head. "No one else? Why not? And how on earth can you keep it a secret?"

"Because I must," he said.

She looked at him carefully, searching for signs of who he was truly was. He wasn't just a Keeper, nor just a tracker, nor even just an aristocrat. He was someone else, under all the rules, but she couldn't figure out who that someone was. The mask of a proper gentleman was firmly, and maddeningly, back in place. "Can you do it again?" she asked. "Turn wolf?"

"No," he replied shortly.

Tobias was thinking about Gretchen when he nearly walked into his own murderer.

It was his own fault. He knew better than to walk around London reeking of the wolf.

He hadn't lost control like that since he was thirteen years old. One unguarded moment and he was at another witch's mercy. She could tell anyone, despite her promise not to. The word of a reckless debutante who was always at the wrong place at the wrong time was a tenuous guarantee at best.

She smelled like snow and pine, like home. Like a wolf. He simply couldn't figure her out. He reined in his inner wolf with the kind of violent precision usually reserved for an encounter with Napoleon himself.

But she wasn't the only thing his wolf was reacting to.

London held many predators for the unwary: pickpockets, cholera, gaslight leaks, the Thames in August. But shapeshifters, wolves especially, had only one true predator.

Wolfcatchers.

He couldn't say what alerted him this time, only that it was like hackles bristling on the back of his neck. He kept walking, trying to keep his wolf from pressing too hard at the inner wards that contained him. He could smell rainwater in the gutters, fish pie from a kitchen window, and a dried spill of black ale on a coat sleeve. He didn't hear footsteps, only the faint clatter of teeth strung on a chain.

And then out of the shadows a man passed by him, dressed in sturdy trousers and a leather coat with a stained cuff. Tobias smelled iron, blood, incense.

He was a fool for having dropped his guard, even for a moment. Wolfcatchers never dropped theirs. They were never satiated and considered their work holy, not savage. His own mother bore the marks of their handiwork: a scar from throat to collarbone, a nick on her upper lip where one had tried to rip her canine teeth out for a talisman. A growl reverberated in his chest at the thought.

"Beg pardon," he said instead, in his most cultured and

haughty tone. The one most unlikely to be associated with a wolf.

Tobias called on his legendary self-control to keep his pace unhurried, his breaths even. If he was lucky, the hunter would keep on walking, seeing only an aristocrat in an expensive crowned hat. He was aware of every raindrop, every creak of every cart wheel, every scratch of the cat in the nearby alley. Adrenaline prickled under his skin, sharpening to jabs as he fought the instinctive magical response building in his blood and bones.

The illusion of being invisible, cast by fog and shadow, shattered.

The Wolfcatcher didn't say a word, didn't even pause, but Tobias knew when he was being hunted.

They launched into a run at the same time. Tobias could outdistance him if he shifted, and they both knew it. Wolfcatchers counted on the fear of their quarry. The pelt, bones, and teeth of a shifter in animal form was where the magic lived. It was what the Wolfcatchers wanted, and they laid violent and cunning traps to that end.

Since they seemed to have surprised each other, the hunter was likely alone. It was a small advantage. He'd still have all of the spells at the ready; it was how they lived. They were more animal in the hunt than the wolves were. They gave themselves over to it like a lover.

Tobias ran faster. At least his face was partially hidden under the brim of his hat. The Wolfcatcher was tracking him by instinct, not by name or reputation. He wove through the streets until they became crowded with women huddled under streetlamps to finish their sewing. Candles were dear in this part of London. Children ran back and forth, playing some sort of game. Men stood in doorways, talking. It was as good a cover as he was likely to get.

He glanced behind once, catching a glimpse of his pursuer. The wolf teeth he used as a toggle on his coat gleamed. In the country, the Catchers wore strips of fur cut from pelts. Tobias felt his own teeth sharpen, elongating to canine fangs. His wolf was both jubilant and desperate. Tobias snapped his traitorous jaw shut, tilting his head down to hide another momentary lapse of control.

He tried to figure out where he was exactly. Near Fleet Street, perhaps. There was a safe house nearby. He and his siblings had memorized all of the shifter burrows in London the very moment they were old enough to escape the attentions of their nanny. There were three between Seven Dials and Westminster. Surely he was close.

Not quite close enough.

The Catcher's first charm glanced him, slicing through the mist and blasting it clear away. It reeked of pepper and pond water, disorienting his sense of smell. The second cracked like glass, the sound shivering in his sensitive ears.

But the Wolfcatcher wasn't accustomed to pursuing someone like Tobias. His shackled magic did more internal damage on a daily basis than any hunter spell. Pain meant nothing to him.

The dagger came next, slender and wickedly pointed. It sliced through his jacket, cutting through the thin shirt to the skin beneath. The cut was shallow, a mere annoyance.

But the wolfsbane now seeping into his bloodstream was something else altogether.

All wolves knew the plant intimately. Its purple blossoms flowered late in the season and were made into tinctures and powders to torture wolves.

Effective tinctures.

He was already slowing down. The Wolfcatcher would be on him in moments. He stumbled, his arm full of fire and vinegar and rust. Sweat dampened his hair immediately. The pain licked down his arm to his hand, which curled into a paw. Fur spiked with more sweat. His nails turned to black claws. He choked on the taste of salt and wolfsbane flowers.

He was too slow. Too tired from fighting shadow people and Gretchen.

An iron chain dosed in wolfsbane water lashed him across the cheek, coiling around his neck. The Wolfcatcher yanked savagely, sending him sprawling on the pavement. His cheek was already split from the chain. The poison was making him clumsy and light-headed. The chain tightened again, and he scratched at it desperately, twisting this way and that. Coins and iron nails tumbled out of his pocket.

He paused, blinking rapidly to make his eyes focus properly. He fumbled more coins out of his pockets and the gold cuff links out of his shirt. They seemed impossibly bright. His cravat pin decorated with sapphires was easy, even with the thick frozen fingers of his still-human hand. "Alms!" he cried out, tossing them into the air.

The gaslight flames caught the unmistakable glitter of gold and jewels. People converged, children squealing and adults grim with silence, hoping to keep the others from noticing. The ones too suspicious to fall for his ploy at least didn't get in his way.

It wouldn't buy him much time but it would have to be enough. The wolfsbane sent darts of acid into his chest, robbing him of breath. He shoved the chain off.

He wouldn't die. Not like this. His family needed him. Without the protection of a viscount and a Keeper, they would be vulnerable. His mother might rule the Lawless Pack, but society rules were vastly different.

The Wolfcatcher would not have him.

Neither would his wolfsbane.

He tripped along, stumbling to a stop across the street from the grim façade of a workhouse. They were set up to discourage people from lingering, and they succeeded with dismal success. Folk naturally avoided any contact with such a place, knowing them to be mirthless boxes where the poor were forced to toil with little hope of improvement.

This workhouse was different, and not just because it was cloaked from any eye that couldn't see as a beast. Even witches would walk right past it. The only clue to the presence of the Hoof and Horn burrow were claw marks scratched into a brick at the corner. Tobias fell, more than walked, inside. The oak door was so heavy it may as well have been still a tree, rooted to the earth.

He managed to make it to the bar where he half collapsed. The door thumped shut behind him, and the resulting draft sent the candle flames dancing. They left trails of purple light and Tobias watched them, knowing the wolfsbane was well and truly in his system now.

"Please," he croaked to the woman behind the bar. She had a braid wound around her head and the kind of no-nonsense stare that was comforting. Comforting or not, he didn't have any money left. He'd tossed it all onto the street. "Lawless . . ."

"Oh, I know who you are, love," she said. "Jonquil!" she called over her shoulder.

A woman emerged from behind an elaborately carved wooden screen in the corner next to the bar. She wore a thick linen-and-leather apron over a dark brown dress. Dozens of amulets and charms hung around her neck, and pouches clung to the wide leather belt around her waist. The brooch of a dagger crossed with a needle proclaimed her to be a magical healer. The wolf tooth dipped in silver and wrapped in a ring of rabbit teeth meant she specialized in shifter healing. She frowned at him, nose twitching. "Wolfsbane poisoning," she said with a sigh. "Your pupils are as big as ponds."

"Beg your pardon." He wasn't sure why he was apologizing.

"Drink up, Greybeard."

Three tincture bottles floated in front of him, and after watching him pluck at the air, the healer slapped the bottle into his palm. She guided it to his lips. The first sip was gritty with salt. The rest tasted exactly as awful as it sounded: a concoction made from salt, peppermint, cloves, and mallow leaves steeped in the water of a Welsh healing well.

"Thank you," he said to Jonquil. "I am much obliged."

She snorted, pushing him back down when he tried to stand up. "You're far from healed, my lord."

When his pupils finally retracted enough that his vision stopped blurring, he was able to get a better look at his surroundings. What had been fuzzy outlines and too-bright lights became a collection of wary shifters and firelight.

Burrows clung to a wary peace at best, fostered by a mutual enemy more than any mutual affinity. In any other place, rabbit, wolf, cat, and the other various shifters could not have shared drink together. The smell was smoke and musk and fur, with a heavy overlay of rosewater to cover the more animal traces. Magical sigils had been painted on the walls with a paste of red ochre, soot, and herbs. Rowan berries strung on white thread wound through the iron chandeliers and hung like Yule garlands on the windowsills. The floor was scattered with salt, apple seeds, and lavender.

Above the main fireplace hung a shield made from the teeth of every kind of shifter—from wolf, boar, rabbit, and fox, all the way to mice and voles. Wolfcatchers and other magical hunters took the teeth for their magical properties, but these had been freely donated and their power manifestly tripled.

Three men swaggered in his direction. One wore a necklace of human teeth in a grisly imitation of the wolf-teeth trophies Wolfcatchers wore. These were hardened hunters, the kind Ky and his friends admired.

"Who poisoned you, friend?" he asked.

"I didn't catch his name," Tobias replied, his voice raspy from where the chain had pressed against his throat.

He snorted. "I don't need his name to kill him, mate."

Tobias tried to stand again, even as Jonquil clucked at him. "He's long gone," he said. "Leave it."

They laughed, practically barking. Two rabbit-shifters in the corner buried their heads nervously in their hoods. Tobias pushed back with weary determination at his own wolf, scenting a challenge. Jonquil slipped her arm around his throbbing shoulder to steady him. "Easy," she murmured.

He breathed through his nose, concentrating on the sting of salt, the residue of so much shield magic in the burrow. "You're in no condition to stop them," she continued as the men thundered out of the burrow. "Even if they weren't Carnyx."

"If they track him, they'll kill him," he protested. He was still feeling fuzzy from the poison, but he felt like that was something he should care about.

"Probably." Jonquil didn't sound nearly as perturbed.

"He's human."

"And so not my concern," she returned with a pragmatic shrug. "I don't know anything about human medicine." She placed a pillow under him as he began to topple. "But I do know if you go out there right now, you'll get yourself killed and waste a perfectly good wolfsbane remedy."

Tobias wanted to protest but the healing potion had been laced with belladonna and valerian. He fell asleep, slouching in a most undignified manner.

Chapter 12

When Gretchen arrived at the academy, she found Emma at a small table in the dining room with Catriona, the Scottish girl everyone else was too afraid to befriend. Her habit of foretelling a person's death was alarming. As long as Catriona didn't eat all of the strawberry tarts, Gretchen didn't care.

She slid into a chair, commandeered two tarts and a roll, and poured hot, strong tea into a cup. Her eyes were gritty and sore from lack of sleep. Still, she was tired, not blind. The others had all stopped to stare at her, teacups and forkfuls of coddled eggs suspended halfway to their mouths. Gretchen slathered butter on her roll. "I gather word is out, then?"

Emma made a face. "Did you doubt it? Lynn crossed herself when I walked by, and she's not even Catholic."

"Did you save any of the graveyard dirt?" Catriona asked.

Gretchen blinked at the non sequitur. "Um, no. Should I have?"

"Pity. It's quite powerful." Her expression was rather disconcertingly hard for a girl who tended to float about half smiling at nothing at all. When she didn't elaborate, Gretchen went back to eating her breakfast.

"Daphne's father was here earlier to speak to Mrs. Sparrow," Emma told her. "And three of the girls' parents have already pulled them out of school to take them to the country."

"Is it any safer there?" Gretchen wondered.

"There are more people to kill in London," Catriona put in calmly. "And witches are easier to find here."

"Splendid," Gretchen said. "You are cheerful, aren't you?" She smiled to take the sting out of her words. Catriona didn't giggle or gossip so Gretchen was inclined to like her, despite her morbid pronouncements.

There was a hitch in the general dining room chatter before it exploded again.

"Now what?" Gretchen said. "Honestly, it's like being in a room full of mad little sparrows."

Daphne paused in the doorway. She wore her usual day dress, trimmed with ribbons and flounces, and her hair looked as much like spun sugar as ever. The set of her mouth, though, was more about swords and sabers than sweets. The other students went silent again, save for one of the girls, who burst into hysterical sobs.

Daphne straightened her shoulders and sailed into the room, like a ship going out to war. The girl wept harder, hiccuping, "Poor Lilybeth," until Gretchen wanted to throw the rest of her bread roll at her. Daphne swallowed hard, searching the expectant faces staring at her. She finally slid into the empty chair beside Gretchen as the others began to whisper behind their hands again, eyes round.

"Daphne?" Gretchen asked gently, equally surprised.

"Yes."

"You don't *like* us, remember?"

Daphne sniffed. "At least you don't fuss about like I'm a china doll." Her eyes were red, but she held her chin high. Emma poured a cup of tea and slid it toward her.

"Fair enough," Gretchen added. "But if you eat the last strawberry tart, I will stab you with my fork. I don't care how sad you are."

A smile trembled on the edge of Daphne's mouth.

"And don't worry," Catriona added. "You don't die from pity."

As Mrs. Sparrow had elected to cancel classes for the day to better accommodate the parade of distressed parents, Gretchen took her grimoire and left for the apothecary to purchase supplies for more protective amulets. She wore her arrowhead, but she'd taken off the hagstone to give to Penelope and the rowan berry for Emma.

She walked out into a morning that had grown bright and warm, utterly at odds with the fear lurking in every cranny and corner. She saw it in the gargoyles snarling at every passing shadow, in ropes of silver bells hung from iron gates, and in rowan branches tied to door knockers with red ribbon.

She hadn't bothered with a lady's maid or a footman; what was the point, when Tobias was surely stalking her even now? And she found it rather liberating to walk alone, despite the state of affairs in magical London. She couldn't imagine Sophie would risk being in such a busy thoroughfare, not now that every Keeper in the Order was hunting for her. She'd given herself away by stealing Lilybeth's bones. The Order wasn't able to keep her escape a secret, not while still pacifying witching society. And with the sunlight slanting through the columns and the freshly washed shop windows, it was easy to imagine it entirely impossible for someone to steal the bones of dead girls in the first place.

The shop was bustling with customers, crowding elbow to elbow against the counter. Two clerks rushed back and forth, weighing herbs and measuring out tonics. The shelves of the apothecary were crowded with glass bottles of tonics, flower waters, dried rosebuds, and one cat. She inhaled the comforting scents of lavender, mint, and something more medicinal.

She turned sideways as a clerk approached her, her hair half falling out of her chignon. "We are entirely out of salt and rowan berries," she said before Gretchen could speak.

"Quickly, I want to get home," a shopper interrupted, eyes darting from side to side. He and nearly everyone else inside the shop was thinking about protective spells, some more successful than others. Gretchen heard it in the escalating whispering.

"This young lady was before you, sir," the clerk said apologetically. Gretchen handed her list over. The clerk scanned the parchment quickly. "I can help you with everything but the Saint-John's-wort. It can be gathered only on Midsummer's eve, if you're using it for spellwork." She lifted the lid off an enormous glass jar filled with dried leaves and used a decorative wooden spoon to scoop some into a cloth bag. "Metal spoons have iron in them sometimes," she explained at Gretchen's examination of the spoon. It was covered in tiny carved lotus flowers. "Or silver. Both of which can interfere with a plant's magical properties."

The clerk's steady voice soothed the whispering in Gretchen's brain. She took a deep breath. *Hush*, she thought at them. *These aren't my spells and you're driving me mad.* Surprisingly, the volume dimmed.

"You there." A woman in a fringed velvet pelisse snapped her fingers imperiously. Gretchen recognized her as a countess but couldn't remember her name. Her mother had memorized all of *Debrett's* and knew every peer in England. She'd made Gretchen recite them before dinner every night the summer she was twelve. She'd promptly forgotten them all as soon as possible.

"I am sure you meant to say please," Gretchen remarked loudly. "Being a lady of such elegant refinement."

The countess sucked in a breath, her nostrils constricting so that they looked pinched. "I *beg* your pardon."

"Is that Gretchen Thorn?" someone whispered loudly. "She found one of the empty graves!"

The resulting chatter made Gretchen sigh. She leaned on the counter, resting her chin on her hand. "Wonderful, it's just like being back at the academy."

"I am sure I am more deserving of your attention than a Lovegrove," the countess insisted haughtily. "I require a full jar of rowan berries and several herbs your assistant says you have run out of. That is simply unacceptable."

"I am sure we can find something just as effective," the clerk assured her. "If you'll wait just one moment, your ladyship." She was brisk and efficient and slid several paper-wrapped packages across the counter. Gretchen handed her a coin. "Shall we have these delivered, my lady?"

Gretchen tilted her head. "Actually, if you could give them over to the gentleman with the very disapproving blue eyes waiting just outside, he'll carry them for me." If Tobias was going to continue to follow her about instead of walking at her side, especially after what they'd just been through, she intended to put him to good use.

The countess launched into an immediate and condescending lecture when the clerk didn't offer help quite to her satisfaction. "I'm sure my grimoire said hyssop. And it's been in my family since Hastings fell, young lady. I certainly trust it more than some shopgirl."

"Your grimoire's wrong," Gretchen said, pinching the bridge of her nose, trying to alleviate the sudden chorus of a dozen hysterical witches in her head. "Hyssop won't work," she told the countess. "You should listen to her."

She let the door shut firmly behind her, glad to be back outside. She hurried across the bridge, avoiding the curious glances and outright pointing of those who recognized her as the girl who'd fallen in an open grave. The regular streets of London were equally crowded with shoppers and vendors selling every-thing from buttered muffins and baked potatoes to posies of spring violets. She couldn't see Tobias over the sea of crowned hats, nor Sophie nor anything untoward.

In truth, she was a little disappointed. Not over Sophie, of course, but because she had a hundred questions for Tobias. How did one go about changing into a wolf? Did it hurt? Did he retain knowledge of himself? Was it delicious to run as fast as four legs could carry you?

She glanced in the shop windows as she passed, noting a huge umbrella stand in the shape of an elephant. If she purchased something unwieldy and heavy and sent it out for him to carry, would it needle him into talking to her?

On second thought, why wait?

Determined, she turned sharply, hoping to catch him off guard. She managed to knock into a footman with a stack of parcels and an old woman who poked her savagely with the tip of her umbrella. She couldn't see Tobias anywhere. He must have already stepped back into the shadows. "Well, we'll just see about that, won't we?" she muttered to herself.

She marched back down the street, peering into all of the alleys and each shop, even the tobacconist who was not pleased to see a woman in his doorway.

Still no Tobias, and no other Keeper.

Feeling suddenly concerned, she quickened her step. She knew enough about Tobias to know that if there was no one else following her, he was on duty. And if he was on duty and not to be found, then something was terribly wrong.

The carriage sitting quietly by the side of the curb shouldn't have caught her attention.

Except that Tobias leaned against the window, eyes squinting at the single ray of sunlight that found its way between the edges of the curtains he twitched shut. She flung open the door and clambered into the carriage before the driver could stop her. "Tobias Lawless, you scared me half to death, you—" She broke off, outraged. There was stubble on his jaw and his cravat was half falling out of his pocket. His throat was exposed, as was the smooth skin under his collarbones. "Are you *drunk?*"

He scrubbed at his face. "Not now, Gretchen."

She sniffed the air gingerly but didn't catch the sharp burn of whiskey or gin. She knew precisely what Godric smelled like after a night of drinking in gaming hells and men's clubs, and Tobias didn't smell like that in the least. He smelled like some kind of flower and rain. His hair was tousled and wild and his linen shirt was wrinkled and untucked. Horrified, she sat back hard against the seat, embarrassment burning her cheeks. "Were you with a *girl?*"

Not that it was any of her business, of course. It shouldn't matter in the least to her. In fact, it *didn't*. She was only curious. She'd have been curious about anyone she found in this state, especially taking into account his usual elegance. Her traitorous heart sped up, calling her a liar. She didn't need the smirking smug dead witches in her head to tell her.

He clenched his teeth suddenly, his jaw clenching violently. "Go away, Gretchen."

She raised an eyebrow. "I thought you bled good manners, Lawless."

He shuddered, a strange sort of growl rumbling in his chest. There was the sound of fabric ripping and the seam popping on his sleeve. His teeth flashed white and sharp.

"I mean it," he barked, bracing himself with one hand against the window, and his booted feet on the seat beside her. *"Get out!"*

Too late.

She was suddenly trapped in a small, plush carriage with a wolf with burning blue eyes.

Under normal circumstances, if those even existed anymore, Gretchen would have been overjoyed to see Tobias transform into a wolf. He was beautiful—pale fur and eyes too blue to be natural. His legs were surprisingly long; his fur brushing her skirts as she tried to inch away. He was so large he took up the entire seat and towered over her. His white paws were as big as her hands.

The transformation happened so quickly she'd barely had time to process it. He shimmered like heat lightning. The violence of it lingered in the small space between them. She could hear the driver struggling to control the horses, who clearly sensed a predator. The carriage rocked back and forth, tilting dangerously. Gretchen flattened one hand against the side. His lips lifted off sharp teeth that made her cringe. It took no imagination at all to picture them grinding deer and rabbit bones.

Her bones, if she wasn't careful.

She considered leaping for the door, but all that would

accomplish would be to release a wolf into the streets of London. And she'd promised Tobias she'd keep his secret safe.

Still, she'd leaned toward the door without realizing it, and he barked once, sharply. It was so loud and sudden, it was like a slap to the face. She froze, trying not to stare at him openly. Hadn't she read in some library or another that dogs attacked when stared at? She had no idea if dogs and wolves reacted the same way, and she really had no desire to find out.

There was something of Tobias the man in the blue eyes, even surrounded with fur. Her heart thumped a little less like a cannon and more like a misfiring pistol. He moved restlessly, uncomfortably. The cramped carriage smelled like a forest, like snow and pine and danger.

But she wasn't frightened anymore.

Especially when he whimpered. Swallowing, she reached out a hand, moving as slowly as she knew how. Please God, don't let her lose her fingers. He whined in his throat again, shifting. She froze. "Don't be cross like Tobias," she whispered. "Nice wolf."

He was panting, front paws scrabbling on the floor as he tried to find purchase. The carriage rattled violently, stopping and starting. His ruined clothes tumbled onto her boots. The horses whinnied and snorted. "Don't mind them," she said gently, stripping off one of her gloves. "They think you're going to eat them. Possibly, I shouldn't give you any ideas." She itched to touch him, his fur looked thick enough to sink into. His black nose flared. "But I know you're a nice wolf," she continued soothingly.

Her fingertips sank into thick fur, brushing warm, muscular flesh underneath. He was as warm and soft as she'd imagined. His breath was hot on her arm. He nudged her with his wet nose. The carriage lurched again. Her stomach dropped, sickeningly.

"I think I like you better as a wolf," she murmured. "But unfortunately, I really need you to be Tobias again."

Her fingers were stroking soft thick fur. She froze as it retracted and then she was touching warm skin.

The wolf was Tobias again.

And he was naked.

They stared at each other.

She was in a carriage with a naked man.

And not just any man, but the most proper one in all of Mayfair.

A giggle burst out of her. She slapped her hand over her mouth to stifle it.

"Bloody hell," Tobias said, his voice hoarse as though he'd been a wolf for weeks instead of mere moments. He grabbed at the torn remnants of his shirt and pants. Gretchen giggled again. "It's not funny," he said sternly.

"It really is," she insisted, even though her cheeks were red. Her gaze bounced to the brocade curtains, the mahogany paneling, his chest, the tip of her boot, his shoulders, her dress, his face. His mouth twitched. She nearly missed it. Their gazes collided again, and they burst out laughing. His chuckles were like honey wine, smooth and surprisingly sweet. She'd never heard him laugh before.

"Most girls wouldn't think it so funny to be trapped in a carriage with a wolf," he finally said.

"Never mind the wolf, you're still naked."

"I'd be most obliged if you'd hand me the change of clothes stored under your seat," he added. He reached up and thumped the roof of the carriage with his fist twice, paused, and again. There were two quick answering raps from the driver.

"I take it this has happened before?" Gretchen asked, standing up to lift the cushion away to reveal the hinged lid of the hollow seat.

"No," he said starkly.

"And yet you are so well prepared." There was a woman's dress and two sets of men's clothes as well as a woolen blanket. She handed back a pair of dark brown trousers and a white linen shirt, telling herself not to peek. She caught a glimpse of his chest in the windowpane before she'd even finished lecturing herself. When she turned back he was more decently attired, if also more casual than his usual selection. He looked perfectly healthy, as if whatever it was that had plagued him when she'd found him had been exorcised by becoming a wolf. Only his eyes were still wild, dangerous.

"I do beg your pardon," he said stiffly, resorting back to his usual excruciatingly polite self.

"Oh, don't do that," she fairly begged.

"But I put you in terrible danger," he said. "And I am very sorry for it."

She waved that away. "I wasn't scared. Mostly."

"Why didn't you try to leave?"

"You might have been found out," she replied. "I did promise."

"Yes, you did, didn't you?" The way he was watching her made her want to squirm and she wasn't entirely sure why. She was suddenly more nervous than when she'd been trapped with over a hundred pounds of wolf.

His blue eyes never left hers, as he bowed over her hand and brushed his lips softly over her knuckles. "Thank you, Gretchen."

She had to clear her throat to find her voice. "You're welcome."

He opened the curtains, glancing out into the sunlit street. The light and bustle seemed like an intrusion. "I'll take you home. . . ." He paused, looking out the window and swearing softly. "Change of plans." Gretchen leaned forward to see what had alarmed him, but he pulled her back. "Don't. You mustn't be seen."

She raised her eyebrows at him. "Are you worried for my reputation?" Her wits must be addled by seeing a man turn wolf and back again, because for some strange reason she found that sweet.

"Of course," he replied. "But that's not all."

"There's worse for my reputation than open graves and wolves and naked men?" She sounded as dubious as she felt. The tips of his ears went very red. And that was sweet too. Bloody hell. She cleared her throat decisively and determined not to be such a flibbertigibbet.

"What do you mean, Tobias?" His eyes touched hers when

she spoke his given name. She smiled ruefully. "You'll say I ought to call you Lord Killingsworth, but I think we can dispense with the usual courtesies, wouldn't you say? Considering?" She couldn't help but notice the wolf fur sticking to the seat. "What is it?"

"I told you that the wolf families prefer to keep to themselves." He pulled a wooden wheel from his pocket. It looked like it had once belonged to a toy cart.

"Yes."

"For reasons of security, you understand."

"I can't see how it's so very different than being a bone-singer or one of those women who sword-dance." Truth be told, she was rather jealous of them.

"Believe me, it's different." He snapped the wheel in half and thumped on the roof again. "Faster, Hale!" he shouted through the paneling at the driver. "There are men who call themselves Wolfcatchers. Their sole pursuit is to hunt us down for our pelts because they allow a witch with no shape-shifting ability to transform."

"But that's barbaric!"

He nodded grimly. "There's magic in bones and teeth too. It happens more often than you'd think. So I'm afraid you'll have to come home with me."

She was instantly burning with curiosity to see how he lived. "Of course." She hoped she hadn't betrayed her indecent eagerness.

"I've spent the night recovering from wolfsbane poisoning," he explained. "And the same man who attacked me is following me still. You will have my wolf scent on you, Gretchen. And they will come for you as well, if they catch it on you, if only to discover my identity."

"I would never tell them," she replied quietly.

"They are not gentle in their persuasions."

When the carriage turned left, Tobias reached for the door handle. "It's here. Are you ready?"

A glance out of the window showed that they weren't in a residential area. "For what exactly?"

"We have to switch carriages," he explained. "I called for a second one with that wheel charm. We've a system of summoning and escape routes in place. Any Wolfcatcher will follow the first carriage, while unbeknownst to them, we ride away in the second."

When he pushed the door open, the sound of the wheels rattling and the wind snaking into the sudden opening was deafening. The carriage rolled along at a great speed, parallel to another unmarked carriage. "This one's too easy to track now that it has the scent of my change on it. And we can't afford to delay," he said. "Not for a single moment." He watched her carefully, as if he expected her to fidget with nerves. "Can you manage?"

She just shot him a haughty glance and braced herself in the doorway. "This is nothing. I fell into an open grave, remember?"

"I'm not likely to forget."

The ground was moving at rather an alarming pace beneath her. If she slipped, she'd get trampled under the horses behind her. If she didn't crack her head open on the cobblestones first.

Pebbles and dirt sprayed up between the two vehicles, stinging when they hit her ankles.

"Never mind," Tobias said behind her, his hands on her waist to steady her over a bump in the road. The carriages diverged for a moment. "We'll stop. It won't take that long. I don't know what I was thinking."

Gretchen shook her head, remembering running across the rooftops with Moira. How different was it, really?

Which gave her an idea, actually.

She turned back, shoving the cushion off the seat. Tobias blinked at her as she lifted the wooden board off. She secured one end at the edge of the door and waited for the carriages to align again. When they were as steady as they were likely to get, she dropped the board between them, creating a bridge such as the one Moira had made for Godric.

"Let me test it first," Tobias said, sounding reluctantly impressed. He braced himself with one hand on each side of the opening, stepping out with his right foot. He gingerly applied weight, the wind tangling his hair and plastering his shirt to his side. Gretchen held her breath. "It holds," he shouted back, but his voice was snatched away by the rattling of the wheels.

She stepped up, dragging her gaze away from the uneven road beneath them. Tobias was lodged halfway in the second carriage, his leg hooked inside to secure him in place as he reached for her. "Look at me," he called out. "Only at me."

His eyes held her fast as any rope. There was confidence and strength in his face, under the haughty politeness that she now knew hid so many wild secrets. It was the secrets that made her trust him. She stepped out into the buffeting wind as the carriages lurched over the street. His hand closed over her wrist, warm and steady, and he hauled her inside.

The carriages parted way and she fell against him as they leaned sharply to the right, compensating. The wooden seat board fell into the gap and broke into pieces. A coachman shouted abuse, yanking on his reins to avoid the sharp fragments.

She was still in the circle of Tobias's arms. She seemed to be spending an awful lot of time there recently. She pulled back, embarrassed, and he released her abruptly. "Won't someone have noticed that?" she asked, to cover the awkward silence. "It was hardly subtle."

"The board, certainly, but not us. They'll think it was a broken panel or a package that wasn't properly secured to the roof," he replied as she sat down. "There's an illusion charm that fools the eye into thinking this carriage is wider than it actually is." He noted the houses and the black iron scrollwork fences. "It won't be long now."

"Did we lose them?" Gretchen asked.

"Yes, I believe so. Still, I'll have a bath drawn for you to wash off any of the wolf on you. We have charms we wear as well, of course, but with the magic being so unpredictable in London lately, it's best we err on the side of caution. It may take some time to find a charm that works well enough to keep you safe. You may have to stay the night."

"If you show them to me, perhaps I can help," Gretchen offered.

He looked at her consideringly. "I hadn't considered that.

Whisperers are rather rare." He tugged at the collar of his shirt and she caught a flash of the bronze skin of his throat. He pulled a thin strip of leather from under his shirt. "Iron and metal interferes with the magic," he explained, showing her the smooth birchwood pendant. "Only natural items tend to work for shifters, and for wolves especially."

She leaned closer, until his shadow fell over her. She ran a finger over the disk, following the sigil inscribed there. It looked like a combination of ancient runes. "It's soaked in moonlight for three nights," he continued, his voice slightly hoarse. She felt his breath on her cheek. "And rainwater gathered in a wolf-shifter's paw print. That water can change a human into a wolf."

"What does it do exactly?"

"It's meant to cover our scent and confuse a Catcher's tracking. We also use a drop of a human witch's blood on the back."

"Sounds messy for you," she teased, but there was no rancor to it. "What happens if you lose your charm?"

"Some of us have the symbol tattooed on our skin."

She was suddenly wildly curious to know if he had such a tattoo and where it might be placed. "Can't you use the Fith-Fath spell Emma uses to make her antlers invisible?" she asked instead.

He shook his head. "It's not strong enough to hide a full shifter from Catcher magic. That's the trouble. They have as much magic as we do."

His house was in Berkeley Square, not far from her own parents' mansion. It blended into the neighborhood, being neither demonstrably larger nor smaller, more beautiful nor less. It had fashionable fanlight windows, flagstone paths, and what looked to be extensive gardens at the back. A footman waited just inside the gates to lock them shut behind the carriage. As she emerged into the daylight, Gretchen half expected it to be nightfall already. It seemed impossible that so much had happened in less than an hour.

Tobias's brother rushed toward them, his jaw set angrily. He looked to be about the same age, but he had none of Tobias's refinement. He wore trousers and scuffed boots and a belt with loops to carry daggers. "What—" He broke off, noticing Gretchen. "Who the devil are you?"

"You'll keep a civil tongue," Tobias said mildly, but the ice was back in his voice.

"I can't believe you're courting at a time like this!"

Tobias's cheeks went a dull red. "I assure you, that's not the case."

Fighting an absurd twinge of disappointment, Gretchen smiled. "Your brother doesn't care for me, actually." She tilted her head. "You're a wolf too, I assume?"

"Ky, this is Lady Gretchen Thorn," Tobias said drily as Ky goggled at her.

"You told her?" He gaped.

"I had little choice," he answered.

"I saw him change shape," she explained. "He couldn't very well pretend it never happened after that."

If anything, Ky looked even more stunned. "You wore the wolf?"

"Not now, Ky," Tobias said sharply. "Let it go."

"Are you—"

"Tobias is right." His mother descended the front steps. "This is hardly the place. Though I can assure you, we will be discussing it." She wore a dark blue morning dress with little embellishments. She was tall and elegant and Gretchen instantly knew which parent Tobias took after. Although he had nothing of the savage glint in his mother's pale blue eyes. Ky submitted, which would have surprised Gretchen if she hadn't felt like she ought to submit as well, even though she hadn't done anything wrong yet. The countess was impressive, to say the least, even without the faint scar on her upper lip.

"Who was it then?" Ky barked. "Who dosed you with wolfsbane?"

"I don't know," Tobias replied calmly.

"As if I believe that. The Carnyx told me you wouldn't speak of it last night. I want a name."

"And I want a cup of coffee," Tobias returned without inflection.

"You could have died." Frustrated, he jerked a hand through his hair.

"Let's take this conversation inside." It was an order, not a suggestion, and the countess turned away with every expectation of being obeyed. She wasn't disappointed.

Barking greeted them from the other side of the door. When it opened, Gretchen was enveloped into a pack of enormous wolfhounds and mastiffs. Her familiar bounded out of her body in a streak of light and raced in mad, delighted circles. She slid

Tobias a sidelong glance, wondering if she was breaking some sort of witching etiquette. Probably. Why change now?

But Tobias's mother only laughed.

"Oh, I like this one, Tobias," she said. "She has animal spirits."

Godric could understand why Moira preferred the rooftops.

He was above the worst of the city—the disconcerting odors, the mud, and the dust of road construction. He was so high above, in point of fact, that his knees felt decidedly jelly-like.

He might enjoy the view, but he didn't care for the height. His body knew perfectly well what it would do should he fall from such a distance. Despite logic reminding him that there was a railing between him and gravity, a cold sweat tickled the back of his neck. His wolfhound-familiar flatly refused to step out of his body. He had only a few inches of whiskey left in his flask and he couldn't even drink it. He was several stories up and he was sober.

All for a girl.

A mad, surly girl who would as soon chuck him over said railing as smile at him.

He'd tried every romantic spell he'd come across, had risked his neck delivering red roses over the rooftops hoping she'd find them; he'd even walked the goblin markets three nights running hoping to see her. Instead he'd been bitten by a carnivorous cabbage, drank enough black ale to have him seeing spots, and lost his new pocket watch to a Rover built like a bloody bull.

And here he was, once again on a rooftop, sacrificing the last of his whiskey to the gargoyle beside him so that it wouldn't eat his face off.

He felt a faint shift in the air behind him. Had he found her at last? He forced himself to turn slowly when all he wanted to do was whoop with joy. Gentlemen ought not to whoop. He was certain it was one of the many rules his mother enforced. His rules were extensive and bothersome; Gretchen's rules were epic. The one time their mother had tried to write them all down, Gretchen had burned the resulting tome and nearly started a house fire.

But here he was, far outside the realm of rules and responsibilities, alone with a girl he barely knew but already loved. "Moira," he said. "Finally."

Only it wasn't Moira standing behind him after all.

It was a ghost.

The gables shimmered through her. Godric sucked in a breath and it iced his throat.

"Bollocks," he muttered, a far cry from the poetry he'd memorized for Moira, even though she didn't seem the type to like poetry. Wasn't that what you were supposed to do to prove your love? Make an ass of yourself? And how better than with a sonnet?

He wanted to be anywhere but here with another ghost staring at him with hopeful, hungry eyes; but his training as a gentleman forbade him to do anything but bow a polite greeting, even to a dead girl.

She smiled faintly, her long curls so pale he could barely see the ends where they turned to snow. There were dark smudges of bruises on her wrists and red welts on her collarbone. A small white mouse perched on her shoulder. He assumed it was her familiar before she even raised her left palm to show him her witch knot. She beckoned him forward. He groaned. "I'd really rather not."

She beckoned again, insistently.

When he smiled apologetically and started to walk toward the attic door he'd snuck out of, she slammed into the air in front of him, sparks and ice flinging off her wispy form. The shingles frosted under her feet. Icicles stabbed off the railing like daggers.

He pulled back sharply, but her fingers closed over his wrist, blistering him. His teeth chattered involuntarily as the cold slapped at him. She looked melancholy but undeterred. And then she floated away, hovering briefly in the space between the two buildings. Snow fell from the hem of her dress.

He shook his head firmly. "I'm no Madcap to be running the rooftops. If you want me to follow, it will have to be on the ground."

He missed her flare of excitement as he ducked into the tavern to exit on street level, like a normal person. He passed girls selling bunches of watercress. The leaves froze briefly when the ghost found him again. Pedestrians shivered, wondering if they were falling ill. She flickered like a candle caught in her own unnaturally cold draft, in danger of guttering out.

She turned down an alley between a haberdashery and a ribbon shop, leading him to a pile of broken crates and a snout-nosed gargoyle who blinked at her once. She floated up to the gables, staring down at him impatiently.

"Splendid," he said. "More climbing."

Tobias could never have imagined the incongruity of Gretchen in his London townhouse. He was surprised to discover he wished he had a moment to enjoy it.

The Lawless mansion was elegant and fashionable, with silver sconces, silk wallpaper, and a curving staircase with a mahogany banister. He knew, without being told, that none of it would impress her. There was nothing in this part of the house to hint at the family character, except perhaps for his brother stalking through the front hall, rattling the crystal drops of the chandeliers and bristling with challenge. If he betrayed much more aggression, their mother would give him a set down he'd not soon forget, stranger in the house or not. It didn't do to challenge the Alpha of any pack, never mind Elise Lawless. Tobias might be a young gentleman of considerable social power in London society, but behind these doors he was one of four children, and subject to pack law.

"Mother," he said, hoping to distract everyone from Ky's temper. "May I present Lady Gretchen Thorn."

Gretchen bobbed a quick curtsy. The dogs pressed around her, eager to catalogue her scent. "How do you do?"

"Welcome," Elise said. "The wolf is on her," she added to Tobias.

"Yes, that's why I had to bring her here," he explained. "I couldn't leave her to the Catchers."

"Certainly not."

"The Carnyx needs to answer this insult," Ky seethed.

"Ky, hush," their mother said. "I'll decide what needs answering, if you please."

There were soft footsteps on the stairs as Posy rushed down, her nose tucked into a book as always. She didn't notice their guest until she was on the last step. She started, looking trapped, before cringing. "It's all right, Posy." Tobias smiled at her encouragingly.

Their mother watched Gretchen carefully for a long silent moment, nostrils twitching before she said, "Don't be shy, Posy. This is Gretchen."

Tobias and Ky exchanged a glance. Whatever their mother had sensed on Gretchen, it was enough to trust her, and Elise trusted no one easily. She half turned to Gretchen. "You don't mind me calling you Gretchen, do you? Lady this and Most Honorable that, it gets rather tiresome and takes up too much time, don't you think?"

"I couldn't agree with you more."

Posy pushed timidly away from the banister. "Are you not shocked?" she asked as her tail became obvious. She'd had to alter some of her dresses for comfort, her tail flicking against the sprigged lemon-yellow muslin.

"My cousin has antlers," Gretchen replied with a cheerful shrug.

Tobias knew in that moment that he could never go back to seeing her as a dangerous rebel who flouted the Order. Well, a rebel and flouter of rules, yes, but not dangerous. Certainly not vindictive.

"Tobias, why don't you show Gretchen up to the family parlor and then clean yourself up so we can discuss last night's events."

"Can you send word to my mother and Rowanstone that I am at Aunt Bethany's overnight? And to my cousins with the truth, as well, please?" Gretchen asked. "They'll be able to circumnavigate everyone so no one sends out the guards to find me."

"Of course."

Tobias motioned to the staircase with a sweeping gesture. "After you."

Gretchen climbed the steps, no doubt wondering why they weren't entertaining her in the formal drawing room on the ground floor, as expected. He showed her to the parlor, with its dark green walls and scattered rugs. There were sturdy chairs, bowls of pine needles Posy collected as potpourri, and books scattered on every table. He knew how it must look with fur on the cushions and gathering under the furniture, all of the windows open, and the bits of greenery that Posy insisted on bringing inside.

"I know it's not what you're used to," he trailed off, suddenly awkward. Any gently bred debutante would have been horrified.

As usual, she defied expectations.

She looked up at him with a grin. "It's perfect." She beamed.

At least the ghost had the good sense to bring him to a ladder, even if it was rather rickety. Snow drifted over his head as he climbed, teeth gritted against the instinctive need to look down. The ghost hovered impatiently until the rungs of the ladder iced and cracked. Frost burned his fingertips. He hauled himself over the edge, rolling onto the shingles.

He sat up, scowling. "All right," he muttered at the agitated girl.

She took him across two more roofs, around a gargoyle with eerie painted eyes, and finally to a small rectangle of shingles and chimney pots.

And Moira.

He'd know that long black hair and her cameo-studded striped waistcoat anywhere. She rose slowly to her feet, dagger in her hand. Her orange tabby cat-familiar hissed. He held out his palms to show he was unarmed. When she finally recognized him, she sighed. "What are you doing here?"

"I was led here," he replied.

"If you say you were led here by love, I will stab you."

He chuckled despite himself. "No, not quite by love. By a ghost."

Her eyes narrowed. "Sorry?"

He admired her, even as she eyed him suspiciously, balancing on the balls of her feet as though she were ready to fly. He knew she could outrun him without even trying. "You're so beautiful," he blurted out.

"You're sotted," she returned blandly.

"I'm not drunk," he said, even as the ghost circled her.

"Well, you're not right in the head," she muttered. "Get back to the bit about the ghost."

"She has long blond hair and a little mouse on her shoulder."

Moira's mouth open and closed but no words came out. She was pale as milk suddenly. The dagger trembled in her fingers. He took a step toward her. "Are you all right?"

She swallowed and it looked painful. "I knew a girl like that," she finally said, her voice raspy. "She was killed by the Sisters. Her name was Strawberry. She was the one the Rovers tried to snatch that night under the bridge."

The ghost nodded at him with so much excitement the shingles under her feet iced and cracked into pieces. Moira shivered under the blast of cold. "Is she here right now?"

"Yes," Godric replied. "Take my hand." He stripped off his glove and held it out. "If you touch me, you can see her for yourself."

He could see her fighting some kind of inner battle. She probably didn't believe him. He didn't exactly blame her. She finally took a step closer and slipped her fingers into his. "If this is a trick . . ." She let the threat trail off in favor of gesticulating with the very sharp, pointed knife still in her other hand.

"It's not a trick," he said softly. "Look."

She turned away from him as an icy breath blew on the back of her neck. Her hair lifted in a cold breeze and then the ghost was standing right in front her. Her cat-familiar pawed at her snowy hem. "Strawberry?" Moira stepped forward, dropping his hand. She stopped, glancing wildly all around her. "What happened?"

"You have to hold my hand," Godric reminded her, slipping his palm over hers. "To see what I see."

Moira released a long, shaky breath when Strawberry fluttered into view once more. She tucked her dagger into her belt and reached out to her friend. Her hand went right though her. Strawberry's lip trembled in response. "You shouldn't be here." Moira used her shoulder to impatiently wipe a tear off her cheek.

"Maybe she just misses you," Godric suggested.

"You don't understand. We burned her bones," Moira explained. "We gave her a proper Madcap boat burial. She should be in the Blessed Isles. The fact that she's here can mean only one thing. Something's gone wrong."

Strawberry nodded. Moira frowned at Godric. "Why can't she speak?"

"None of the ghosts speak," Godric said apologetically, even though it was hardly his fault. "Only spirits can speak, apparently. My professor told me that in the old stories the dead cannot speak so that they cannot tell the living what's on the other side. But mostly I think ghosts just don't have enough power. They use it all up trying to stay visible."

There was the crack of stone and a leathery hiss as the gargoyle behind them was awakened by Strawberry's presence. Moira didn't even glance back at it, just snapped her fingers at Godric. "Give him your whiskey."

He didn't bother denying he had any, just struggled to open his flask one-handed. He tossed an arc of amber liquid at the gargoyle. "Stand down, Tristan," Moira snapped.

The gargoyle settled back on his perch with a grumble. Strawberry's outline sharpened brightly before turning misty.

She pointed at her bruises and the welt on her collarbone. Her mouse flared red.

"Is this about Sophie?" Moira asked, pouncing like her cat-familiar. "I know she killed you for the Sisters. But she's escaped." Her mouth hardened. "Do you want me to kill her instead?"

Strawberry shook her head, looking gently reproachful. She pointed at herself.

"You want to kill her yourself?"

Now, the pale ghost-girl just looked disgusted. Moira laughed through the tears Godric wasn't sure she knew were streaming down her face. "You know I've always been harder than you," she said.

Strawberry rolled her eyes before her expression turned serious again. She pointed to herself again.

"I'm sorry I couldn't save you," Moira said quietly.

Snow hurtled into her face, dusting her eyelashes.

She blinked it away. "You didn't have a temper like this when you were alive."

Strawberry opened her palm, and on her witch knot, haw-thorn flowers formed from the misty ectoplasm. The misty phosphorescence turned to icy blue flames, until she was made of fire. Snow and ice formed a boat from the hem of her dress. Godric had been slowly growing used to deciphering the way ghosts spoke, which was mostly through images or cryptic meta-phors. He might not know about the flowers, but the fiery boat meant something. "Is this about your funeral?"

Strawberry nodded. Her flames faded back to glowing mists.

"And the Rovers," Moira guessed. "The ones who wanted your bones."

She nodded frantically, frost blooming all around her and creeping up to touch Moira's boots. It clung to her like lace. "They have something to do with the Sisters? With you?"

Strawberry faded away, still nodding.

"Where did she go?" Moira squeezed Godric's hand desperately. "I'm still touching you! Where is she?"

"She's gone," he replied.

"Bring her back!"

"I can't. I'm sorry. She's not strong enough." Moira let go of his hand and turned away furiously. "She might come back on her own though," he said. "Eventually."

"Not before I find those Rovers," she promised darkly.

Godric knew that kind of rage intimately. One didn't grow up with a twin like Gretchen and not understand the drive to fight against the world before it fought against you. He took his own Ironstone-issued knife out of his boot and sawed a lock of hair from his head. "Here," he said, moving to her side and offering it to her. "This way you have a part of me to see her with if she comes back. It's worth a try."

She took it carefully, frowning. "You could have made me depend on you instead," she pointed out. "You have all the power as a bone-singer."

"I could," he agreed. "But that's not love. And I love you."

She pointed at him with the dagger. "Stop that."

"I mean it," he insisted.

Her shoulders hunched. "Godric, I don't want to hurt you, but . . ."

He shook his head, smiling sadly. "You don't feel the same way." He stared off over the rooftops of London instead of at her impish, clever face. *"If music be the food of love, play on; Give me excess of it, that, surfeiting, the appetite may sicken, and so die."*

Moira paused. "Um. What?"

"Sorry, Shakespeare. Penelope's hard to tune out." He shrugged one shoulder. "I can wait for you, Moira."

"Godric—"

"Let me wait for you," he cut her off. "Just for a little while."

"I've never met anyone like you." She sounded endearingly confused.

He smiled. "Nor I, you."

"I am sorry, you know," she said gently. "Truly."

He heard her walk away, running lightly over the shingles and over to another rooftop, but he didn't watch her go. Maybe she'd change her mind. Maybe she wouldn't. That part was none of his business in the end. There were worse things than unrequited love.

"What are you doing?"

Penelope knew it was Cedric, even before he'd spoken. She was in the back corner of the conservatory, where her mother had set up a cluster of settees on brightly colored rugs, surrounded by orange trees, pineapples, jasmine, and orchids. Moments earlier a dozen sparrows had landed on the glass roof, pecking at her through the glass, and three cats pressed against the windows in anticipation.

"Mugwort is meant to stimulate the magical senses,"

she informed him. Her voice was muffled, her face pressed entirely into the plant. It made her want to sneeze so it must be working.

"I'm not sure you're meant to suffocate yourself with it," he remarked. His linen shirt was undone at the collar, the skin tanned like toasted hazelnuts; so much richer than the studied paleness of the gentlemen she usually encountered. His Romani blood made him as exotic as they were plain.

She peered at Cedric through the foliage. "Did you bring them?"

"Aye," he said, holding out three identical ivory-colored buttons. They could have belonged to anyone in the house, earl or gardener, man or woman. The only identifying marks were a spot of color in the center and only Cedric knew to whom they corresponded.

"Can you lay them on the table, please?" Penelope asked. She wasn't wearing her gloves and if the experiment was going to work properly, she needed to be thorough. He laid them out in a row between a silver candlestick holder and her cup of tea before stepping back to lean against one of the windows. He could lean just like that for hours, arms crossed and patient as a tree in winter. He smelled faintly like hay and soap. His presence was familiar and grounding, as were his steady dark eyes watching her silently.

She reached for the first button, and as expected, the world tilted sideways. Her stomach pressed against her spine, as though she was in an overturning carriage. Colors and textures slid together and apart again, forming new shapes.

She smelled onions frying, and she was sweating through her dress. Her feet ached. There were blood and grease stains on her apron and a heavy meat cleaver in her hand. She brought it down in one savage thunk, hacking straight through a cabbage. The sound echoed, jarring her out of the moment.

When she came back to herself, the first thing she felt was Cedric's strong arm at her back. He was crouched by her chair, unfazed by the spiders crawling up his pant leg. "I've got you," he murmured. She shivered. "Are you dizzy?" he asked, misreading her reaction.

"Spiders," she squeaked.

He glanced down, then back up with a grin. "You'll have to get used to them. You're the one who called them out, not me." He brushed them away gently. She wished he'd stomp on them instead. "They won't bite you," he said, reading her thoughts exactly. "And they were snug in their webs until your familiar drew them out."

"It wasn't on purpose," she muttered. His hand was still pressed against her back, warm through the thin muslin of her dress.

"What did you see?" he asked, drawing back.

"That button belongs to Cook. I had no idea swinging a cleaver could be so invigorating."

He chuckled. "I reckon the Beau Monde thinks you're all moonbeams and poetry. They have no idea how bloodthirsty you really are."

"Gretchen is the violent one," she said with mock primness. "I am a lady."

Cedric snorted. "Try again."

"Everyone else believes me."

"That's because none of them was ever on the receiving end of a bucket of cold water and worms balanced over the door," he pointed out.

She grinned with more mischief than remorse. "You deserved it."

"Probably," he agreed, handing her the next button.

The conservatory was a whirligig of greens and purple orchid petals, spinning then stopping. She blinked down at Cedric, who was still next to her chair. One of the neighborhood dogs had made it into the back garden and was licking the glass behind him, tail wagging.

"Nothing," she told Cedric. "I couldn't see anything at all that time."

"Try the last one then," he said.

She folded it into her palm, obligingly. She was dandelion fluff, spinning every which way until she finally landed in the stables.

She was brushing down one of the horses and a cat purred at her from a patch of sunlight in the rafters. She enjoyed the simple work of caring for an animal, but there was worry in the back of her head for Hamish. He hadn't been able to get out of bed this morning, and his fingers were starting to curl into painful, permanent claws.

And then she stepped into the stables.

It was disconcerting. Penelope was someone else, watching herself in the doorway, limned with light. Her hair was a tumble of curls and she was waving a new book of poems excitedly. She smiled at herself and that was when she realized she was Cedric. He was thinking that he didn't particularly care for Byron's poetry, he preferred Shelley, but since Penelope loved it so much, he was willing to listen to it. He preferred it when she played the stable piano, the music speaking words he couldn't find. He knew she'd leave one day, some fancy prat would sweep her away with badly quoted Shakespeare. Well, that wasn't precisely true. She'd never fall for badly quoted Shakespeare. Still, he'd miss her. But he was a stable boy and she was the great-granddaughter of a duke. He had no illusions.

The light intensified, even as the walls of the stables grew so dark they faded away. For the first time since Penelope's gifts had awaked, she tried to stay inside the vision. She wanted to know what else Cedric was thinking, why there was a hint of sadness to him that she'd never noticed before. And what, exactly, did he have no illusions about? She already knew he'd never answer her if she asked.

She held on as long as she could, but it wasn't long enough. When she opened her eyes, she was only slightly disoriented and he was leaning against the windows again, out of reach and expressionless.

"That was your button," she said softly. She wanted to say something else, but she wasn't sure what. She didn't like that he was sad, for whatever reason. She was tempted to tell him how she felt, that he just made everything better. But she'd told him that once, when they were fourteen. She'd said she wanted to marry him and he had laughed. She'd never forgotten that moment. She'd wept into her pillow for days. Even now, she used it as a medicine against her too-romantic heart. He didn't love her. Not in that way. No matter what her brief foray into his thoughts had produced, he still wouldn't marry her. He was already marrying her off to some "fancy prat."

She cleared her throat and determined to sound normal. She didn't have a chance to prove how very calm she was. He cut her off before she could speak. "Beauregard is waiting for you at the front gates."

"What?" She stared at him for a moment. It was for the best, surely. "And you just left him there? Why didn't you tell me sooner?" She leaped to her feet. "Why didn't Battersea show him into the parlor?"

Cedric's smile edged toward a smirk. "Bloke couldn't get through the gates, could he?"

"Blast," she said, hurrying out into the garden and up the lane. She didn't notice one of the cats following behind her.

Lucius stood on the other side of the fence. His green eyes were mesmerizing, even from a distance. He wore a dark green coat again, and it made his irises shine like light through green glass. She picked up her hem and ran the last few yards. "Lord Beauregard," she said. "I'm sorry to keep you waiting."

"Not at all." There was a flash of irritation under his smile. She didn't blame him for being put out. Her mother had hired a witch to spell the gates, and the result was an ugly scorch mark on his sleeve and burns on his knuckles.

She winced at them. "Oh, I'm so sorry. The house was recently spelled to deny entry to the Order. It must be faulty."

He shook his head, suddenly amused. "So much for my nefarious plot."

"Nefarious plot?" She tilted her head questioningly. "That sounds promising."

"I served with a similar secret society in France these past two years," he explained with a self-deprecating smile. "When the Order found itself dealing with the onslaught of magical anomalies currently plaguing London, I offered my assistance." He stepped closer to the fence, even when it started to spit warning sparks at him. "When they mentioned you needed a magical escort, I insisted."

"A magical escort." She wrinkled her nose. "That sounds so much more genteel than being under surveillance." She paused. "But where's Ian?"

"I'm afraid he had an accident and won't be able to continue at his post."

"Is he hurt?"

"He broke his leg when he was attacked by a Rover who didn't wish to give up his claim on a fairy cow wandering through Covent Garden." He saw her stricken expression. "I am assured he will fully recover."

She released her breath. "Good. I'll have Cook brew up some of her pain tonic for him."

"You have a good and gentle heart, my lady." He bowed, pulling a pink tulip from behind his back and offering it to her between the bars.

She accepted it, burying her nose in its petals for a moment. "Well, if you can't come inside to me, I suppose I shall have to come outside to you." She unlatched the gate and stepped through.

"Shall we visit the park?" he suggested, offering his arm.

She accepted, feeling his muscles move under her fingertips. "Let's."

Cedric slipped through the gates behind them, his legendary patience wearing thin.

Chapter 13

Gretchen sat on the floor of the guest room in a circle of salt, holding a wolf charm. She curled her fingers around it, picturing herself turning into a wolf and running through the London streets nipping at the heels of proper ladies in silk gowns. She visualized Emma's Fith-Fath spell and the Feth-Fiada mist Aunt Bethany had once used to cloak her and her cousins from sight. The dead witches in her head were content. "The spell needs to be better," she snapped. "Talk to me."

There was no searing pain, no iron clang of sound, just a simple whisper. *"Wear a wreath of amaranth flowers to be invisible."*

She couldn't quite picture Tobias chasing down warlocks for the Order while wearing flowers in his hair.

"What else?" she asked. "Please," she added, just in case politeness counted as much as her mother and Tobias seemed to think it did.

"Chicory flowers gathered with a gold sickle at Midsummer."

"Seven poppy seeds."

She'd never used her powers so easily and effectively. Feeling giddy with success, she decided to press on. She'd studied enough to know what she was about to attempt was dangerous and fool-hardy. It was like picking out a single thread in a tapestry, when you finally knew what color you were searching for, but as she'd barely begun to control her gifts as it was, trying to listen in on a spell cast by a live witch was a hundred times worse. Still, she had to try.

"Come on then, Sophie," she said. "What are *you* planning?"

She closed her eyes, straining to listen. A whisper of sound, like a summer breeze, and nothing more. She waited long enough to be thoroughly bored.

She opened one eye, annoyed. "Blast." She scrounged for a scrap of paper and scrawled Sophie's name across it. She brought a candle into the salt circle and fed the paper into the flickering flame. "Sophie Truwell, talk to me."

Jagged noise slashed at her. She cringed, ducking her head out of instinct. The voices were an avalanche of rocks threatening to bury her.

"Turn back."

"Not a chance," she muttered through clenched teeth. It wasn't Sophie's voice. It was that damn chorus again.

"We are still here. Still here."

"Turn back."

Gretchen put some of the salt on her tongue and the pressure eased. The more she learned to follow her first instincts, the more she was able to expand her magical abilities.

"Rise up."

"Rise up or turn back?" she snapped. "Make up your mind."

"Warlock's spell."

"Yes," she said, impatiently. "Which one?" She paused. "Hang on." She was almost certain that had been Sophie's voice.

"Warlock's spell."

Try as she might though, she couldn't hear anything else of use. No incantations, no mention of herbs or stones or cloying rhyme. Nothing but the blood in her ears and her pulse jerking fitfully, and, finally, nothing at all.

She woke up with Tobias kneeling beside her on the floor, even though it would crease his buff trousers. Her wolfhound sat beside him, tongue lolling out of his mouth. She smiled at them groggily. "Hello."

"Are you hurt?" He bent over her, looking concerned.

She shook her head, pressing a hand to her ears. When they didn't come away bloody, her smile widened. "I'm improving."

"You call swooning an improvement?"

She wrinkled her nose. "I never swoon. I don't even like the word."

"Falling into an unconscious heap, then," he amended drily.

"Much better." She sat up on her elbows. "I really hate her, you know."

"Who?"

"Sophie."

"Is that what you were doing? Trying to hear her whispers?"

She nodded, grimacing. "I caught her voice, but nothing else."

"It's dangerous," he said, reaching out to gently push a curl off her forehead. "You ought to be more careful."

She swallowed, staying still as his fingers brushed her brow. "I have to do something. She nearly killed my cousin the last time she was messing about with spells and whatnot."

"I can't even track her," he said, his thumb resting on her temple. Neither of them moved. "Whatever she's doing, it's complicated."

"My solution is simple," Gretchen said. "Kick her until she stops."

He smiled. "You're as fierce as any wolf-girl I've ever known."

She smiled back wistfully. "I think I'd make a brilliant wolf."

"Don't even think it," Tobias said hoarsely. "It can turn into a curse in the blink of an eye."

"But I can break curses, remember?"

Gretchen was in a house of wolves.

Was it any wonder she couldn't sleep? It was long past midnight when she left her room, feeling positively buoyant. The very things Tobias worried about in the upstairs portion of the house, the fur and the charms and the baby wolf teeth strung on ribbons as sentimental keepsakes, made her comfortable. The first floor with its gleaming silver and marble floors and sweeping staircases made her feel exactly as itchy as her own house made her feel. But she was fairly certain that there was no such thing as running too fast in the halls or being too loud here. She padded down the carpet runner in her bare feet, knowing it wouldn't scandalize anyone, and followed her grumbling belly to the kitchens. The door to the library was open slightly, light slashing across the floor. She paused, glancing inside.

Tobias was pacing the not inconsiderable length of the room, a frown between his eyebrows. There were bruises showing where his sleeves were rolled up his forearms. She assumed they were a result of his altercation with the Wolfcatchers. His head snapped up. "Who's there?" he demanded, stalking toward the door.

She poked her head in. "It's just me, sorry to startle you."

That brought him up short. "Gretchen."

He looked wretched and sad and lost. That decided it and she stepped farther inside. "I was just going to see if I could find some sweets."

He stared at her. "Sweets."

"Yes, they're for eating," she replied, teasing him. She'd known enough black moods to know that sometimes nothing would do but to be startled out of one.

"There's gingerbread on the tray over there."

"Excellent," she said briskly, marching past as though she wasn't wearing a nightdress she'd borrowed from Posy. It was just slightly too short, flashing her ankles as she went. She imagined Tobias would be scandalized instead of distracted. More's the pity.

Now really, where had that come from?

"Yes, we'll have cake," she said firmly, cutting generous slices of the molasses-dark gingerbread. She added some dried apricots from a china bowl. She handed him a plate and a silver fork, the tines glinting in the firelight. He accepted it, manners kicking in, no matter his current emotional state. She'd considered that kind of control a weakness, but now she wondered.

"They say you'll be the next First Legate, you or Daphne's brother. How will that work with all of your other duties and . . . secrets?"

"Uncomfortably, I'm sure." He offered her a ghost of a smile.

"Your family doesn't seem the type to bow to the Order."

He snorted. "You've the right of it."

"I knew I liked them for a reason." She had another bite of the cake, mind swirling with wolves, witches, and warlocks. "Why would Sophie steal Lilybeth's bones?" she asked. "If it was even her?"

"She must be gathering power for a spell," he answered.

Something about it tickled at the back of Gretchen's mind but she couldn't quite figure out why. It sounded familiar somehow.

"She'd have to be storing the magic somehow, wouldn't she?"

"Yes, but we can't seem to find her anywhere. It's like she's disappeared." He swallowed another mouthful of gingerbread. "We assume she's hiding inside Greymalkin House, where we can't reach her."

"How would she have gotten in?" She'd needed Emma for that, last time.

"Another good question."

Gretchen surveyed the room as she ate. It was grand and imposing, full of books with gilded lettering and the smells of leather and smoke. A globe stood in one corner, along with a backgammon table and several chairs clustered around the stone grate. There was only the fire to light the room. She noted the empty coffee cups lined up on a shelf and wondered what made him fear to sleep.

"You don't approve," Tobias said softly.

She looked at him in surprise. "What do you mean?"

"Of the library. You practically skipped through the family parlor upstairs with its dog-chewed table legs and clutter."

"It's comfortable. This is very grand, I'll grant you, and believe me I've seen all the libraries in Mayfair, but how can you prefer it?"

"It's simpler," he replied.

"Is it?" She licked a grain of sugar off her lip. Tobias's fork clattered against his plate. "Why's that, I wonder?"

"It just is."

"There's something I've been wondering, listening to your brother talk."

"I should warn you, my brother is . . . radical."

Gretchen snorted. "You're just as radical, Tobias. It's only that your opinions differ."

"I suppose." He paused. "I'd never thought of it that way."

"He made it seem as though you only rarely 'wear the wolf,' as he put it."

"True."

She stared at him. "You can't be serious," she said, as shocked by that as by any of the rest of it. More shocked, actually. "I'd be shifting all the time."

He nearly smiled. "Yes, I imagine you would." He stared

unseeing out of the dark window while she stared at his pale reflection. "But I have never truly worn the wolf before today."

"In London, you mean." She thought of the cramped carriage and the agitated horses and the oblivious crowds pressing all around. "Yes, I can see why."

"No. I mean, ever."

She moved to stand in front of him. "How can that be possible?"

"I shifted once on my thirteenth birthday," he said. "It's tradition. But never since then, not until the wolfsbane potion. It interferes with control, but shape-shifters must wear their animal to drive poisons and dark magic from their bodies."

Gretchen's head fairly spun. "I don't understand. Why would you waste such a gift?" she asked, inadvertently echoing the same question his family and Cormac had been asking him for years.

"A curse, you mean."

"Do not tell me that you are all conflicted and brooding over this. Why wouldn't you just enjoy it? You're daft."

"You wouldn't understand."

"Explain it to me then," she insisted quietly. She wasn't sure why it was so important. Except that something about the conflict with his own nature, touched with sadness, reminded her of her brother when the ghosts drove him to drink too much. "Please," she added when he still didn't speak. "I'd really like to understand."

"The wolf wears you as much as you wear it," he said tightly. "You can forget yourself."

"Is that such a bad thing?"

"You can forget your duties, as well."

"And for you that would be terrible indeed," she allowed. They were so near she could feel the warmth of him, contrasting with the cool draft from the window behind her. The coals shifted in the grate, sending up sparks.

"You noticed the scars on my mother's face?"

She nodded.

"They were put there by Wolfcatchers."

"Well, surely that says more about humans than wolves."

"Perhaps. But the danger is the same." He pointed to a small family portrait hanging between the bookshelf and the window. "That's my older sister Gaelen," he said, pointing to a girl with dark brown hair and gray-green eyes. She was as pretty as a porcelain doll. "My family prefers to stay in the country. It's much easier that way. But Gaelen doesn't have a choice."

"Why not?"

"She's gone feral. She barely bothers to return to human shape, and when she does, she can't stand to be around people. She's not able to cope with them."

"What happened?"

"Four years ago, she found her lover's bloody pelt strung on a tree branch to be tanned. A Wolfcatcher had found him in the woods. He was still collecting his trophies when Gaelen stumbled across them."

Bile rose in the back of Gretchen's throat. "No."

"She killed him. And she's never been the same since." His voice was rusty as the story spilled out like iron nails from an old tacking box. "I swore that night that I'd do whatever it took to keep my family safe. Our kind can't risk attending the academy unless we have iron control. So I trained hard to contain my magic."

"And then you joined the Order," Gretchen said, understanding. She assumed his brother had decided to join the Carnyx at the same time, to protect the shifters from the Wolfcatchers. "Oh, Tobias, I'm so sorry for you and Gaelen, both."

"Why me?" he said. "I wasn't wronged."

"Weren't you?" she asked simply. "Weren't you robbed of the joy in your true nature?" He looked as though he didn't know what to say to that. "Still, how can you have kept it a secret? You are not exactly anonymous. All the Wolfcatchers in London must have a bounty on you." She shivered at the thought.

He only shrugged. "As a Keeper I smell like magic every day. To detect wolf on me is difficult. And there are the charms, of course." He shook his head. "I've never told anyone any of this, aside from Cormac and the First Legate."

"What's so wonderful about control anyway? To hear you and my mother talk, it's a magic shield against bad manners, pestilence, and disease."

"It's what separates us from the beasts."

"Hmm, pity."

"There is an entire city depending on me, not just my own family." The fire had dwindled and the darkness of the library held them in its palm. They could pretend they were anywhere. "Without control," he added hoarsely, as his eyes locked onto hers and his hands slid up to grasp her upper arms, leaving a trail of delicious shivers in their wake, "anything can happen."

"Isn't that the point?" She didn't pull away. Couldn't have.

He brought her closer, up against his chest, even as he lowered his head to kiss her. His hand tangled in the cropped curls at her neck, his thumb resting along her jaw. He nipped at her mouth, and she stood on her tiptoes to get closer. She felt everything—the fire, the taste of gingerbread on his tongue, the secrets between them. He pressed her back against the wall until wolves and warlocks were forgotten, until it was only two witches and a stolen moment before the battle breaks.

When the kiss ended, too soon, he rested his forehead against hers, struggling to reclaim his usual discipline.

Her breath trembled when she finally released it. "I'd say control is overrated, wouldn't you?"

Gretchen spent the early morning hours in the gardens, still unable to sleep. She drank tea on the terrace until the sun was too bright and the spring flowers too cheerful to ignore. She wandered the paths, making note of the kinds of plants she found and their magical application. Why, it was practically like taking an exam. She felt positively virtuous.

The gardens, much like the house, started off formal, with a fountain made of leaping fish, box hedges, and dainty benches set on pebbled paths, before it deteriorated into a pretty sort of wilderness.

It wasn't long before Gretchen came across Posy in one of the shadows, sitting up in a poplar tree with a book and a half-eaten apple. "Hello." She tilted her head up, shielding her eyes with her hand. That she hadn't been wearing the customary bonnet when she'd stumbled onto Tobias's carriage went without saying.

Posy smiled shyly. "Hello."

"I haven't climbed a tree in a dismally long time," she announced. "That must be rectified immediately."

Posy goggled at her. "But you're a lady."

"All the more reason to climb trees, if you ask me." She hauled herself up onto the lowest branch, steadying herself.

"I'm not sure that's a good idea," Posy said dubiously. "Are you sure you know how?"

"Oh, Posy, you've just dared me to do it now. And I never could ignore a dare." She pulled herself up from branch to branch, pausing to tie her skirts into a knot between her knees when they got in her way. "This is much easier in breeches," she huffed, wriggling into the crook where the main trunk split into two. Catkins dangled like braids of golden hair.

She peered through the branches to the pebbled paths and the mossy wall at the edge of the property. "Lovely," she declared. She gestured in the direction of the wall. "How have the neighbors not found you out?"

"There are spells and wards," Posy replied, her voice small, as though she wasn't accustomed to speaking easily with other girls. "And we have so many dogs about, if they were to glimpse anything, it's easily explained."

"Clever."

"It was Tobias's idea," Posy said proudly.

"Yes, I imagine it was."

Posy's tail curled over the branch, soft fur ruffling in the breeze. When she saw that Gretchen noticed, she flicked it out of sight.

"Did you know I'm a Whisperer?" Gretchen said lightly. "I'm still getting used to it. My ears bleed sometimes. It's not very attractive. I'd much rather have a tail."

Posy's smile was shy and sweet, like sugared violets. She fairly shone when she forgot to cringe away into the shadows. Gretchen caught sight of Tobias walking the paths below them. She wondered how often Posy laughed. And if Tobias even knew how to.

She plucked a handful of catkins, which were soft and slightly sticky. "I think I can hit him from here."

Posy giggled before clapping her hand over the mouth to stop herself. "You wouldn't."

"Oh, Posy." Gretchen grinned. "There you go, daring me again."

She waited until he'd turned the corner before lobbing them. They flew into the rosebushes on the right, missing him completely. He turned his head sharply.

"You missed," Posy pointed out.

"That was a little misdirection," Gretchen disagreed. "Now I have him exactly where I want him. Looking the other way." She sent another volley of missiles. They pelted him like sticky green rain.

She hadn't counted on his proximity to the fountain though.

He ducked the attack, pulling up the hose lying in the grass, currently filling the stone basin. And aimed it directly at them. They scrambled down the tree, shrieking with laughter. Cold water dripped from their hair and Gretchen sputtered out a mouthful. Tobias leaned against the fountain, grinning.

"You knew we were up there," Gretchen accused.

"You're rather hard to miss."

Posy wrung water from her hair and looked from Tobias to Gretchen and back again. She wandered away, still giggling. Gretchen felt awkward. Not because she was soaked through or because Tobias was a wolf, not even because they'd kissed, but because she didn't particularly feel like punching him in the face.

"My sister has been lonely. You seem to be good for her," he said. A catkin clung to his arm like a giant caterpillar.

"I've never been accused of that before."

"It is rather unprecedented."

Chapter 14

Gretchen was going down to breakfast when Ky arrived, blood-stained and grinning. He smelled like violence and the Thames, with that hint of pine she was starting to associate with wolves. "Did you find him?" she asked.

"Who, love?"

She rolled her eyes. "The Wolfcatcher who attacked your brother, of course."

"I'm sure I was out drinking with the lads," he replied. "Isn't that what aristocratic boys do?"

"And I was working on my needlepoint," Gretchen returned. "Because that's what gently bred ladies do." He snorted a laugh. "Tell me about the Carnyx," she added, fascinated by all the aspects of this new hidden world.

"My brother will have told you we're savage."

She grinned. "Yes, but he's said the same about me."

"We protect the wolves from the Wolfcatchers and the warlocks. Someone has to," he added defensively.

"I agree."

"Do you have any idea how many of us are tortured and killed for our pelts or teeth? We're not even animals to them, only magical trophies."

"So you fight."

"Often and well." She saw the swagger in him, so different from her own brother's easy affability. "We can't all bow to the Order like Tobias."

"He fights for you as well," Gretchen said, suddenly feeling the need to defend him. "For all of us, really."

"He's ashamed of his heritage."

She shook her head gently. "I don't think that's true. His way is just different." She nodded at the daggers on his belt. "Are those magical? May I see one?"

He lifted his eyebrows at that but handed her one. "It's sharp, mind."

"Wouldn't be much use if it wasn't," she remarked, testing its weight and wicked point. It wasn't ornamental in the way of antique or ritual daggers, but there was a certain beauty to the ironwork on the wooden handle.

"It's quite nice." Gretchen handed it back reluctantly. She bent to retrieve the dagger she'd worn tied above her ankle since the night they'd stumbled across a kelpie. "Tobias's hat on the side table," she announced, before throwing it. It flew with little flourish, but it flew true, puncturing the tall, crowned beaver-pelt hat.

"Blimey." Ky whistled. "You'd make a fair Carnyx."

She grinned. "I know."

Gretchen lingered over breakfast but she knew it was time to go home. Rain gathered, perfectly reflecting her mood. The first few drops hit the windowpane like fat silver coins. The clouds were mounds of whipped cream, edged with blackberry icing. She could just make out the shape of Posy as a small wolf racing between the trees, fur in wet spikes, tongue lolling. She bounded and leaped about, looking so pleased with herself it was impossible for Gretchen not to smile as she watched.

Remembering what Tobias had said about wolf-charms, Gretchen hurried out into the garden as the carriage was brought round. She kept to the hedges, water trickling down the back of her neck. She circled the garden until she found a paw print in the soft lawn on the other side of the ornamental garden. She waited for it to fill with rain before collecting the water in a small vial. She tucked it up into her sleeve and returned to the house.

Tobias found her entering through the conservatory, using her shawl to rub the wet from her hair. Her dress was thin and damp, and she was grateful for Posy's dark blue spencer keeping her arms warm. The glass house was redolent with the perfume of lilies and waxy white jasmine flowers.

"The carriage is waiting," Tobias said. She hoped she heard a twinge of disappointment in his voice, to match her own. He was impeccably dressed in a morning coat and simple cravat.

When he glanced at her mouth, she felt the heat start in her belly and travel up into her rib cage. She shivered, suddenly flushed within and chilled from the rain without.

"You're different here," he added quietly, turning to stare at the row of orange trees and the wet hedges beyond.

She tilted her head. "As are you." Though he still looked so solemn and serious, at some point it had gone from being irritating to sweet.

"I thought you argued and challenged everything as a matter of course."

She shrugged one shoulder. "Sometimes I do, but it's only because I'm continually constricted by my birth or my gender or social etiquette. I have always known I am not a pretty dress who happens to speak and move, but here I have finally felt that to be true. You have no idea how liberating it is."

He finally looked away from the gray rain. "No one would choose this life, Gretchen."

"You're wrong. I would."

"You say that now. But the secrets would eat away at you. You have an open nature. I don't think it would sit well."

She shook her head. "Being quiet and proper because you are hiding a beautiful secret is vastly different from being quiet because it is assumed you must have nothing to say."

He quirked a smile, softening his stern beauty. "It was much easier when I didn't like you, you know."

She smiled back. "Why, Tobias, that was positively romantic," she teased.

The rain continued to beat on the glass roof, like a stampede of horses in the sky. It swallowed up the words they could not say. Tobias was the first to straighten, as if going to war.

"Are you ready?"

She thought of the rainwater safely hidden in her sleeve.

"I am now."

Godric was waiting at a discreet distance from the Lawless townhouse, leaning against a lamppost and scowling. Rain dripped from the brim of his hat when he surged forward, spotting her. The Lawless gates were barely open when he was pounding on the carriage door. Gretchen opened it and stepped out, grinning.

"What the hell is going on?" Godric demanded as their wolfhound-familiars chased each other in happy circles around them.

"I thought Emma and Penelope told you," she replied, dropping her voice so as not to be overheard.

"They did." He looked at her steadily. "I'm assuming they left out all the important bits." He turned to glower at the house. "I've half a mind to drag Tobias out here for an explanation."

"Don't you dare," she said. She smiled up at the coachman. "Never mind. I'll walk home."

"In this weather?" He sounded more resigned than aghast. She had a feeling Tobias was the only one in the family who didn't run about in all types of weather and at all hours. He nudged the horses into a backward walk, easing the carriage back into the drive.

Gretchen slung her arm through Godric's, the rain already

soaking through her dress. Mud splashed up under the wheels of the other carriages on the road. The sky was a bland uniform gray, nearly low enough to touch. "I'm perfectly fine," she assured her brother. "Or will be as long as you tell me Mother doesn't suspect anything."

"No," he grumbled. "She thinks you're at Aunt Bethany's house."

"Good."

"I was going to come fetch you myself," he admitted. "Until Penelope tackled me."

"Also good."

He slid her a sidelong glance. "She's stronger than she looks. And she's vicious. She bit me." When Gretchen laughed he smiled begrudgingly, but only for a moment. "What happened, Gretchen?"

"I can't tell you," she said apologetically.

He stared at her incredulously. "You tell me everything."

"I know. But this isn't my story to tell." She nudged him with her elbow. "They only took me in to keep me safe."

"From what?"

"I can't tell you that either."

He made a sound of frustration. "You can't be serious."

"Just trust me, Godric. Everything is fine."

"You said that the time you convinced me to set that rowboat on fire for your mock Viking funeral. I lost my left eyebrow. It took all summer to grow back."

. . .

Gretchen dreamed of wolves every night.

Her mother dragged her to the dressmakers to look at bolts of fabric, and even as she was stuck with pins, all she could think about was wolves.

She attended the opera and heard not a word of any song, only howling.

She walked down Bond Street with her cousins, looking at ribbons, oranges, jeweled hair pins, and glove buckles, but all she could see in the windows were wolves.

She stayed up late at night, craning her head out of the window to hear howling. She wasn't sure if she was hearing dogs, foxes, or wolves, but she listened anyway.

She read everything she could find on wolves and shapeshifters. Wolfwater would allow her to shift into a wolf, but only once. She took to carrying it tucked into her corset, just in case.

She sought glimpses of Tobias at balls and soirees and interminable supper parties, but the Order had taken its Keepers off surveillance. Every available Keeper was needed to fix broken wards and ground wild magic that lashed out like an electric storm. Mostly they were needed to track down Sophie.

News of Sophie's escape reached all the witching families, right down to the hags scratching a living selling tinctures in Whitehall. There were so many protective spells hanging from every door and garden gate, carriage lantern and horse bridle, that they made the fog sizzle. Gretchen sneezed once and a swarm of gargoyles attacked her bonnet.

Oracles and soothsayers worked day and night to locate

Sophie but couldn't narrow it down beyond London. The area around Greymalkin House was strictly patrolled and off limits. The Order had even taken to searching homes and interrogating witches at random. When Gretchen noticed a sudden surplus of milky white pendants the size of marbles, Emma told her they were meant to glow when in the presence of a Greymalkin. Emma spent most of her time dodging anyone wearing a necklace, which was proving difficult.

Gretchen watched a herd of sleek black pegasi fly over the street. Or was it a flock? Either way, it didn't bode well for the success of the Order's attempt to control the magical backlash. Neither did classes on defending oneself against curses and dark magic, though Gretchen enjoyed the latter a lot more.

Penelope stepped down out of the carriage, a thick linen apron wrapped around her dress.

"We're not baking cakes," Gretchen told her, grinning.

She adjusted her gloves. "Daphne is the one throwing the spells today," she said. "I mean to be prepared this time." There was a lace fichu tucked into the neckline of her dress, covering every inch of her chest and throat.

The school halls were unusually quiet, the floor creaking as they made their way to the ballroom. The smell of smoke and burned salt prickled in Gretchen's nostrils. They joined Emma. "What did we miss?" Gretchen whispered.

"Nothing yet." Emma glanced at Penelope. "Are you planning to gut fish in that outfit?"

"Laugh now, but when you get boiled beets all over you, I'll be the one laughing," Penelope replied primly. "Isn't that what this class is all about? Being prepared?"

Daphne took her position at the front of the room, next to Miss Hopewell. Her chin was lifted haughtily, but Gretchen was learning to read the uncertainty under the gesture. It wouldn't help her duck boiled beets though.

"Girls, your attention, please." Miss Hopewell clapped her hands. "Today we will be casting shield spells, just like the Ironstone students did at the demonstration." She paused when one of the younger girls raised her hand. "Yes, Agatha, what is it?"

"My pendant is glowing!" She held up the crystal, wide-eyed. The girls around her stepped away, as though she were contagious. Frantic whispering erupted. Emma paled, even as Gretchen and Penelope surreptitiously stepped in front of her.

Miss Hopewell sighed. "Never mind that. Protective spells like that always go off in the ballroom," she explained. "If you'd been listening in class, you'd know that. There's too much magic residue and spells actively seeking you out. Look around, most of your pendants are glowing."

Emma released her breath. Gretchen and Penelope parted, looking innocent. Miss Hopewell had already returned to her lecture.

"You want a shield of light that will envelop you. A bubble works best, but we'll start small and work our way up to that. Blue light is preferable. Take a moment to picture it in your mind's eye and then pull magic from yourself. It helps to concentrate on your witch knot. It can act as a conduit."

"What about daggers?" Gretchen asked. "Throw one of those and you're right as rain."

"A lady does not go about stabbing people," Miss Hopewell said severely.

"But ladies go about being murdered, is that it?"

"You are not going to die, Gretchen," Miss Hopewell said, exasperated. "I do wish you'd stop being so violent. There is no need for it. We have the Order to keep us safe."

Gretchen scowled. "But——"

"And should you miss with your beloved dagger," she continued, "then you've just handed your opponent another weapon, haven't you?"

"I don't intend to miss."

"No one ever does," she said. She nodded to Daphne. "Begin."

Daphne tossed a handful of red wax wafers into the air, the kind used to seal letters. Each had a word scratched into the surface. They hovered for a moment, before transforming into hornets, magpies, and red sparrows with sharpened beaks.

With a flick of her wrist, Daphne released them all at once. Her magic hurled them with lethal accuracy. The girls fell back a step, throwing up energy shields with varying degrees of success. Blue light flared up and down the ballroom. The smell of burned fennel and apple was thick. Catriona and Clarissa had the best shields, repelling all spells until the wax wafers melted away. Cormac's sister Olwen flickered in and out of view, though her shield remained, glowing brightly.

"Good," Miss Hopewell interrupted when everyone was red-faced and panting for breath. "Daphne, you may join the others now and work on your shield. If you are tired, draw power from the earth, from the trees in the garden, and from the water falling in the fountain. But never, never, from each other."

"Why not?" one of the girls asked.

"Because it would drain a person of his or her power and energy. Not to mention that it is very rude indeed."

Miss Hopewell marched up and down the line like a general, flinging elf-bolts. They left welts when they made contact, leaching energy until one felt feverish and ill. One of the girls fainted. Gretchen had to put her own hair out when it accidentally caught fire. Emma's antlers got tangled in a volley of elf-bolts and bled green sap. Furious, Emma fried the bolts with lightning bolts that shot from the chandelier.

Gretchen's magic fizzled out before the others. She tried to force her shield to stay active, but it fell apart in a rain of blue sparks. They hit the floor, leaving pockmarks. She wiped sweat off her brow crossly.

"Shields won't do any good against Sophie," Daphne said beside her, sounding as frustrated as Gretchen felt. "I told my father as much."

"And what did he say?"

"That the shields are only meant to protect us long enough for a Keeper to finish the job."

"Bollocks to that," Gretchen said, reaching down to unhook the dagger tied to her ankle. She threw it at one of the hay-bale targets.

"Now that, I want to learn," Daphne said, when she'd retrieved it, even as Miss Hopewell glared her displeasure.

Gretchen tested the dagger's tip on her forefinger with a grin. "It's not like needlepoint."

"I should hope not. Pass it here."

"Never mind Sophie," Penelope whispered to Emma. "Those two getting along so well is what's really scary."

Chapter 15

Dancing the waltz at a May Ball seemed even more ridiculous than usual.

The first of May was a Threshold day, as powerful as All Hallow's Eve and the summer and winter solstices. Everyone was certain that Sophie would make her move, having gathered enough magic to cast any spell of her choosing.

Which made dancing an odd choice, to Gretchen's mind.

But witching society believed there was safety in numbers, and several Keepers had been dispatched to the event. Gretchen would attend, like everyone else, because it was expected. But better to put on a silk gown and topaz earrings and gloves that refused to stay up around her elbows than feel helpless. She tucked salt into her slippers and the wolfwater vial into her corset just in case.

She went by the academy first, determined to make yet

another attempt at listening in on Sophie's spell. Perhaps being inside her room again would help. Most of the students who boarded had already left or were in a frenzy of last-minute hairdressing. Emma was already gone and Penelope was being escorted by Lucius.

Before Tobias had kissed her, Gretchen would have found it odd to be escorted by a Keeper. Truthfully, she did still find it a trifle odd, but mostly she just wondered if Tobias would be there. He hadn't followed her to the school ever since the Order had pulled the Keepers off surveillance of the cousins. Finding and stopping Sophie had become the only goal.

Gretchen marched into Sophie's old chambers with a determined step. This time she would get it right. She sat on the bed and closed her eyes. She breathed slowly and deeply until her heart wasn't hammering in her ears. She listened but could only hear the same words again and again.

"Only a warlock's spell."

"I need more," she said.

"Only a warlock's spell."

"Yes, I got that bit, actually."

"Only a warlock's spell."

"Honestly, you could try being helpful," she snapped peevishly. "*Which* spell—"

"What are you doing?" Daphne demanded, closing the door behind her. Her magical talent for targeting spells exactly where they needed to be brushed over Gretchen. The resulting chorus of dead witches snapped her head back.

"Alas no witch's rhyme."

Gretchen clamped her hands over her temples and tried not to be ill. "Alas no witch's rhyme," she repeated, her voice tinny and distant.

Daphne froze. "What did you say?"

"To turn back time."

There was more, but they were talking over each other, like singing a round.

"To turn back time?" Daphne guessed, interrupting the psychical litany. "I know that spell."

And just like that the chanting ceased. Gretchen blinked at her. "You do?"

"Well, it's a rhyme, really," she said. "Everyone knows it."

Gretchen raised her eyebrows. "I wasn't a witch until very recently, Daphne. I wasn't raised in this world."

"Oh, right. Anyway, it goes like this: *'Alas, no witch's rhyme to turn back time; only a warlock's spell unrings the bell. To rise up those that fell, court thee the Seven Sisters well.'"* She paused as it sank in. Gretchen still didn't think the rhyme in its entirety made that much sense. Daphne began to pace, wide-eyed. "Sophie means to raise the dead."

Gretchen stood slowly. "She can do that?"

"Yes," she replied quietly. "But it requires sacrificing a witch so that the spirit of the dead person she is summoning has a place to dwell. Among other things."

"Like the bones of a murdered witch?" Gretchen hazarded a guess.

"Yes. And the Seven Sisters," she added. "The Greymalkin Sisters were at their most powerful when seven of them roamed together. She must have originally summoned the three who were easiest to control or anticipate."

"I think it was convenience, actually. When Emma opened the gates, they happened to be there to take advantage of it."

She shivered. "There haven't been Seven Greymalkin Sisters together since the Great Fire of 1666. They say there was blood in the streets." Daphne drew her shawl closer around her shoulders. "She needs to summon all Seven Sisters in order to work the spell."

"Can she do it?"

"Yes," she said tightly. "I'm very much afraid to say I think she can."

"But she won't," Gretchen said, steel in her voice. "Because we're going to stop her."

Daphne met her gaze and nodded. "You're bloody right we are. My father's at the ball; we'll warn him about the spell."

"I don't even know why they're bothering with this ball," Gretchen muttered as they rushed down the hall.

"Because the Threshold day will amplify our magic just as it amplifies Sophie's." Daphne lifted her chin haughtily, which was an impressive feat seeing as she was half running. "And because we do not bend to villains."

Carriages were dispatched to and from Grace House, to take the students to the ball. Gretchen shouldered aside a clump of giggling younger girls about to step up into a carriage pulling up the lane. "Sorry, urgent business," she said.

The girl fought back. "That's our carriage!"

Daphne just glared at her until she gave in, sulking. Daphne climbed inside and Gretchen was lifting her skirts to follow when a streak of silvery mist leaped between her and the steps. She stumbled back.

Her brother's wolfhound.

Again.

He was even more agitated than the last time he'd found her, leading her to Godric drunk on London Bridge while Sophie sent Rovers to steal the bones of a murdered Madcap that were about to be burned. She cringed to think of what trouble Godric was in now.

"Bollocks," she said. "Daphne, my brother's in trouble. I'll catch up when I can."

Daphne just shut the door, shouting for the coachman to drive on. Gretchen was going to find her brother and rescue him.

And then she was going to hit him over the head with his flask of whiskey.

When a bird with strange toad-green eyes landed on her windowsill and dropped an apple seed from its beak, Emma knew it was time to visit the Toad Mother.

She packed a satchel with the whittled deer, the poppet of Sophie, and various traveling supplies. The bridge was quiet, with most witches preparing for their May Day festivities. Clouds scuttled across the sky and the pomegranate lanterns swayed under a steady wind. Salt and rowan berries clogged the gutters on either side of the road. Wind chimes made from knives and scissors dangled from shop posts, catching the light and clinking together like cutlery at a dinner party.

Nerves danced in her belly as she counted three alleys down and turned right, then left and right again onto Bonesong Alley. The Toad Mother's hut looked the same, if less lively. There was no pink smoke coming from the chimney today. The last time she'd been here every aspect of the hut buzzed with magic. You could cut yourself on the grass, choke on the pink smoke, lose yourself in the army of acid-green toads. But now there was only one single toad hopping across the path as Emma crossed the stones to the front door. And the legion of gargoyles who watched clients approaching to ring the bell were gone. The ground was littered with bits of shingles.

Something was wrong.

"Hello?" she called out hesitantly, pushing the front door open. Anxiety sang through her. "I received your message." The only reply was the squeak of rusty hinges.

A small hole in the wall served as the hearth, with most of the smoke belching back out to hang in the rafters. Smoke wasn't the only thing bumping against the ceiling. Dozens of small gargoyles hovered overhead, jolting together, scraping the walls and leaving dents. They buzzed toward her, and she dropped the glamour hiding her antlers. The less magic they could smell on her, the less likely they were to attack. They drifted away, confused. One turned to stone before he made it up to the wooden beam and fell with a *thunk*.

Shelves climbed from floor to ceiling. The jars of herbs, dried flowers, sea salt, graveyard dirt, eye beds, iron nails, bones, and braids of hair that usually stood in orderly rows were opened, upended, and broken over the floor. There was a table, a tipped-over bench, and a cot in one corner.

And the Toad Mother.

She was on the ground, her long hair fanned out over the hearthstone, behind a spinning wheel. The toad bones stitched into the fringe of her shawl had been crushed under a boot tread. They left a fine powder that glowed faintly yellow, like fireflies. When Emma reached her side, the Toad Mother opened her eyes. They flared green.

"Emma," she croaked. Her silver toad pendant floated in the blood collecting in the hollow of her collarbone. Luminescent toad-familiars crouched around her, gleaming wetly.

"What happened?" Emma asked. She didn't know how to help her. There was so much blood and her skin was already waxy and clammy. The hilt of the knife protruding from her rib cage was made of jet. "What do I do?"

When she went to pull it out, the Toad Mother shook her head. "Don't. It's too late."

"It's not. I'll fetch a doctor."

"Too late," she insisted. "Couldn't take my magic," she coughed, smiling smugly even through the pain. "Not the first to try. I cursed myself back when I was your age when my lover tried it for himself. I decided anyone else who tried would just end up with a dead witch."

"But who did this to you?"

"I didn't recognize him. Just his wheel pendant."

"A Keeper?" Emma sat back on her heels. "Not a debutante? Sophie Truwell?"

"Don't let the Greybeards find you here," she said, grimacing as she pressed at her wound.

"What was he looking for?" Emma asked, surveying the spell ingredients scattered in the dust. The Toad Mother's eyelids fluttered as she fought to keep them open. Emma wasn't even sure if the other woman could still see her.

"He wanted the silver bough I promised you," she wheezed, blood bubbling on her lips. "But I hid it. You need to use it tonight. It's a Threshold day. I hid it—"

Her eyes rolled back in her head. The phosphorescent toads glowed red and then fell apart.

She was dead before she could finish her sentence.

Godric's wolfhound took Gretchen to a cluster of shops at the edge of Mayfair. She glanced around for a tavern, or a gentleman in an ignominious heap on the ground, reeking of gin. She found him sprawled under the shadow of a gargoyle.

"Damn it, Godric," she muttered, hurrying to his side. He was lying at an odd angle and she had to crouch down to turn him over. "When are you going to stop drin—"

He was covered in blood.

"Oh, God, Godric, can you hear me?" He didn't have bruises on his face to suggest he'd been in a fight. She patted him down frantically, looking for wounds. His pockets were still full of coins, and his gold watch was tucked into his waistcoat. He hadn't been robbed or stabbed.

Then why was there so much blood?

"Godric, wake up. You have to wake up."

It was then that she noticed the strange angle to his neck and the bulge under his knee where his leg was broken. She looked up, trying to see through her tears. He must have fallen off the roof.

His wolfhound faded away. "No!" she cried out, grabbing for it even though she knew magic couldn't be caught that way. The familiar's silhouette glittered red for a moment before there was nothing left of it at all. Godric's witch knot flared as red as crushed berries.

He hadn't fallen. He'd been pushed.

Godric wasn't just dead.

He'd been murdered.

A shadow fell over her. Someone was speaking to her, but she couldn't hear over the roaring in her ears. Nothing was real, not the pavement under her knees, not the darkness of the alley or the warmth of her brother's blood on her hands.

Even she wasn't real without Godric, not really. She was a paper doll, dust, ashes, nothing.

He had kept her from breaking under the crushing weight of fine society and their mother's expectations, and she had kept him tethered when he threatened to float too far from reality into daydreams.

In the end he hadn't floated.

He'd fallen.

Her brother.

He'd always stood up for her, defended her against accusations of improper wild behavior. He'd loaned her his toy weapons, his clothes, even his name when she got herself into trouble. He understood her like no one else. He was the only person in the world who truly, truly understood her.

And he was gone.

Emma pushed to her feet, hands shaking. The Toad Mother's blood was soaking into the ground, staining the dried flowers and the dusty hearthstone. She looked around, feeling even more helpless. The Toad Mother had died protecting the silver bough, and Emma had no idea where it might be hidden. She sifted through some of the broken crockery and bottles filled with strange thick ointments before deciding that if the thief hadn't found it in the hut, it likely wasn't here.

Which left all of the goblin markets.

And the entire city of London.

She searched the garden before the futility of the situation set in. She pulled the clouds down until they tattered into mists, which she wrapped around herself. She used a stick to poke into all of the potted herbs and under the flagstones of the path to the door.

Nothing.

The last toad in the garden croaked at her.

She paused, staring down at him. He wasn't made of magic the way a familiar was, but he'd been steeped in magic in this particular garden for so long he shimmered. His eyes were the same pale green of the Toad Mother's—hungry, bright, and deadly. He hopped away into an elderberry bush pressed against the window.

Emma followed, mostly on instinct and curiosity. The toad hid in the cool shadows, staring back at her when she got on her knees and crawled under the branches. Beside him was a small stone gargoyle, tilted on its side as though it had fallen off the roof.

She reached for it gingerly, ready to snatch her hand back if it decided to bite. It stayed silent and stern, with its veined wings and gray snout. Its talons curved tightly around nothing. There was a small crack running along the bottom of the clay. She slid her thumbnail into it and tried to loosen it. When that didn't provide any results, she pulled out one of her hairpins and used it like a knife. She jammed it into the clay and wiggled it fiercely until the crack widened slowly, crumbling away to reveal a silvery apple leaf.

The silver bough.

She closed her fingers around it, backing out of the bushes and looking around. The mists still clung to the hut and the railing. She could hear the water of the Thames lapping at the bridge, gulls crying, scissor wind chimes tangling together.

And footsteps.

She leaped up, heart racing.

Cormac loomed suddenly out of the haze.

"Emma!" he exclaimed. "Thank God."

She blinked at him, aborted panic making her choke. "What are you doing here?"

He held a pouch of banishing powder and an iron dagger. The amulets he wore around his neck flared and flickered like embers. The implacable hardness to Cormac's features was chilling. "My little sister sent me. She said you were in danger."

Moira had tied the lock of Godric's golden hair with thread and placed the curl inside a battered tin locket she found in one of One-Eyed Joe's baskets. She wore it around her neck even though the glint of a gaslight lamp on the tin might give her away. The risk was worth it. She'd only seen Strawberry once, though she hunted for her constantly. She'd stayed awake the entire first night, searching the shadows. She caught a glimpse of her pale hair on the corner of the building where she'd died. Once, she smelled ripe berries while balancing over an unsteady rain pipe on Cat's Hole Street, where no one had been able to afford strawberries in over a hundred years.

After that, Moira assumed she couldn't be taken by surprise.

She was, of course, wrong.

Ice clogged her nostrils and she choked, nearly losing her footing.

Strawberry hovered just out of reach.

"Strawberry," she said, reaching out to take her hand even though she knew it was a fruitless gesture. Strawberry faded in and out, her outline flaring like molten silver as she struggled to show herself.

Moira clutched the locket so tightly that it cut into her palm. She squinted hard. "Godric's token can only do so much."

Ice crawled over her boots even as hawthorn blossoms were pulled from a tree too far to see, to pelt over Moira. Strawberry flickered and flared like a candle's flame under a strong wind. She was clearly trying to tell Moira something.

"Is it about Godric?" she asked.

More hawthorn petals. The flicker of her silhouette appeared three buildings down. The glass lamp nearby shattered and the gas-fed flame shot up high like a beacon.

Moira followed, running as fast as she could.

"We need to get out of here."

"But the Toad Mother is dead," Emma said. "Shouldn't we report it?"

"Believe me, the Order will find out soon enough," he said. "And if she's already dead, there's nothing we can do for her right now." He peered warily through the thick fog. "Let's go." He took her hand, noticing the silver bough. He froze. "Why do you have that?" He met her gaze before she could reply. "Never mind. You mean to use it to go to the Underworld and find Ewan."

He knew her perhaps a little better than was strictly helpful at the moment. She hadn't wanted to admit her plans to him. He raised an eyebrow at her. "Fine," she sighed, not bothering to construct a lie he wouldn't believe anyway. "Yes."

"Because you're completely mad," he continued with that false calm that signaled anything but. "Do your cousins know?"

She shook her head. He stared at her. "You were going to go alone?"

"Yes. It seemed safer."

"For whom, exactly?"

"Everyone else."

"You're the only one I care about," he said evenly. "We need to get you somewhere safe."

They emerged onto the bridge. The haze was thick enough that only the glint of windows and the iron chains of swinging shop signs pierced through it. She could only see the vague shadows of people making their way through the markets, but she could hear the cart wheels and the clanging of the blacksmith's hammer. "Shouldn't Virgil be storming in right about now, making an ass of himself?" she wondered out loud.

"With any luck he'll get so turned around in this fog, he'll fall over the railing."

They passed under the archway leading out of the markets, with its magical symbols and enormous gargoyles snarling from the towers. The mists followed them. Cormac had to step out onto the road to flag a passing hackney. She pulled the glamour up over her antlers before he stopped. "Just drive around," Cormac told him.

He smirked at Emma. "Aye."

Cormac's jaw clenched at the implied insult, but he only opened the door to help her up. "If we don't know where we're going, then no one can find us. But we need a plan."

She glanced out of the window, grimy with fingerprints and noseprints. The fog was yellow and soupy. The carriage had slowed to a crawl as the horses tried to pick their way through the gloom. "That, at least, I can fix," she said.

She closed her eyes and imagined a sharp wind blowing through the mists. They tattered but didn't dissipate. Wind rushed through the small carriage like a herd of wild beasts.

She'd never realized how gently magic flowed through her, until it turned against her.

What should have been a subtle shift under her skin, a gathering of energy inside her belly, a tingle in the witch knot on her palm, went vicious. It was burning needles and searing pain jabbing at her from the inside.

The magic built, and with no outlet, turned on itself. It prowled through her, feasting and tearing with sharp, jagged teeth. She didn't know how long she screamed, only that her throat was sore, and Cormac was holding her up, eyes wild and desperate.

"Don't use your magic," he was begging her. "Emma, stop. Stop!"

She collapsed against him, trying to find the strength to keep breathing. The pain receded slowly, inch by inch, like the tide going out. She was hollowed out and bruised. He passed a hand over her hair and she flinched, the skin around her antlers tender and inflamed. He drew back immediately.

"You've been bound, love," he said softly, helping her to sit up against the cushions. The fog pressed against the window. "When the hell did they take your measure?"

"I don't even know what that is," she said hoarsely.

"It's a tradition passed down from covens of old. During the

Inquisition, people were assured secrecy because with a black rope measured to your exact length, a person can bind your magical powers," Cormac explained grimly. "And work magic against you if they decide you're a threat."

Emma's eyes widened. "Virgil took my measure."

Cormac swore. "When? Why? Why didn't you tell me?"

"I didn't know what he was doing," she said. "He was angry because I drugged him."

"He must have tied a knot in the cord," Cormac explained, still watching her cautiously, as if she might start screaming again.

"Or else my mother's concealing spells have finally faded and they know who my father is now."

"Or that."

"How do I get it back?" she stared at him, wide-eyed. Her entire body could have been trampled on by wild horses and she'd have felt less pain. "I need to open that portal tonight, Cormac. It's a Threshold day. And I need to be able to fight back if Sophie comes looking for me!"

"We have to undo the knot," he told her. "It hasn't been done in a very long time. It must be on the ship, where all measures are kept."

She needed her magic back. She needed the lightning and the fury of wind. "Let me try again," she said, fisting her hands and clenching her back teeth. She concentrated on making her-self a conduit, on the feel of wind tearing at her hair and hail tearing through spring leaves.

Pain.

"Emma—"

The needles were sharper, longer, more malicious. They scraped inside her skull. Cormac was only slightly gentler, shaking her by the shoulders. Her eyes flew open, sweat prickling the back of her neck. The pain was making her slightly queasy. The fact that he was shaking her didn't help.

"Stop it! You're only hurting yourself."

She panted, her skin cold with sweat. She pushed damp hair out of her eyes. "I guess we know where we're going now. The ship."

He cursed.

"You don't need to come with me," she said softly. "I can go by myself."

"It would make more sense if I went by myself." His dark eyes pierced her. "But if you think I'm letting you out of my sight now, with a silver bough in your satchel, you're daft, woman. And we'll find the cord faster if you're there."

"Well, you did say I needed to go someplace safe," she pointed out, smiling weakly. "Can you think of anyplace safer than the ship of the Order of the Iron Nail?"

"How about anywhere else ever?"

"At least it's the last place they'd look for me."

The May Eve ball was crowded with witches eager to prove they weren't afraid of a young girl, warlock or not. Blooming hawthorn trees were painted on the walls and green garlands wound with foxgloves, bell flowers, and spider orchids hung from the chandelier and draped from the ceiling. Blue cameos dangled from the garlands, providing a glamour in the form of ghostly, sprightly nymphs and shaggy-footed satyrs dancing between the guests.

Red-and-white ribbons dangled from the enormous crystal chandelier in the center of the ballroom, creating a maypole. Hanging from the center was a crown made of pale white hawthorn flowers. Sugar sculptures of famous lovers circled the guests, from Cleopatra and Julius Caesar to Romeo and Juliet. Penelope couldn't help but cluck her tongue at that.

"That's not a romance," she muttered. "It's a tragedy. Has anyone actually ever read the play?"

Ordinarily she would have enjoyed such an extravagant ball, especially with the handsome Lucius as her escort. He brought her lemonade, offered her smoldering glances and a tour of the sugar sculptures. She wanted to revel in it, to lose herself in his green eyes and the beautiful setting, but the festivities were brittle. It was all false bravado and dead eyes.

Lucius stood closer to her, smelling of sandalwood and champagne. "Are you well?" he asked softly, his breath tickling her ear and sending shivers of a far more pleasant sort across the back of her knees.

"This seems strange, is all." She rubbed her arms against a chill. "I can't see my cousins anywhere. And the music is lovely . . . but it feels like icing. As if it's coating everything." She shook her head with a self-deprecating smile. "You'll think I'm a goose."

"Not at all. May Day can have that effect." He bowed and

offered his arm. "Perhaps if you danced, it would not feel so odd."

She let him lead her onto the dance floor, where the other couples made room for them as a waltz swirled and billowed from the balcony where the orchestra played. The perfume of hawthorn flowers was heavy and made her feel cheerfully sleepy, like too much wine. Lucius's arms went around her waist and she placed her hand on his shoulders, holding tight as he began to whirl her around in graceful circles. The colors of the ladies' dresses, the white silk of debutantes, the black suit coats of gentlemen, and the striped candy-colored waistcoats of dandies blurred together. She focused on Lucius, on his fierce glass-green eyes and wicked smile. She laughed, finally feeling the spell of May Day wrapping its languorous, shining coils around her.

When the music finally stopped, she was out of breath and pressed against Lucius's chest. Someone was making a speech about crowning the May Queen, and there was applause and snatches of a song. Penelope barely noticed. The world had narrowed to Lucius's whisper of a smile, to the angle of his cheekbones, to his mouth covering hers. She almost didn't notice when the light changed and his face was in shadows.

He was still looking at her tenderly, thinking he wanted to kiss her. But he was also concerned, wondering if she would ever get over her grief.

Which made no sense.

The kiss took over, the flashback slipping away under the touch of his tongue along hers.

He was kissing her in the middle of the ballroom, for all to see. The scandal would have her turned out of the fine houses of the Beau Monde by morning. She didn't care. This was the kiss that found her own true love. His lips were soft and clever and he savored her like a sugar-dusted pastry. She kissed him back, her head full of music, just like when she'd eaten the lemon candy Cedric bought at the goblin markets.

Cedric.

For some reason the thought of him made her pause and then pull back slightly. She was still close enough that she could see the flecks of amber in Lucius's eyes.

"Penelope," he whispered.

She couldn't look away. "Yes?"

"They've crowned you the May Queen."

The guests had made a circle around them. Lucius had steered them under the hawthorn crown hanging from the chandelier, and she hadn't even noticed they'd been moving. Unease trickled through her.

Something was wrong.

A footman used a long pole to unhook the crown. Lucius took it, the long ribbons floating as though they were underwater, animated by some charm. They reminded her of the snakes that had followed Emma. They were as yellow as the poisonous fog that plagued London.

She tried to take a step backward, but his hand was on her lower back, holding her in place. She didn't even have a chance to speak. The crown settled on her hair. It made her feel exactly like the day she'd eaten too many sweets at the country fair and even her teeth had ached.

But she smiled, unable to do anything else.

Moira found Gretchen just inside the mouth of an alley. She'd have run right past her if Strawberry hadn't cracked all the gas lamps, like Hansel and Gretel leaving a breadcrumb trail. Pip flew frantically, trying to gobble up all of the magic.

"Don't you know better than to—" Moira broke off with a soft curse. Gretchen was kneeling beside Godric's broken body, her face expressionless. She might as well have been carved out of ice; cold and beautiful and without a flicker of animation.

"Bollocks, what happened?" Moira glanced up at the edge of the roof. "He was rubbish at rooftops," she added, surprised at the clench of anger and sorrow in her throat. She might not have been in love with him, but he'd been kind. "What was he thinking?"

Gretchen didn't reply. She simply stayed on the dirty ground, her cheeks dry and her eyes red as embers.

Moira didn't need Strawberry's warnings or the sudden prickling pain in her feet to know it was time to leave.

"Gretchen, we have to go. *Now.*"

When Emma and Cormac stepped out of the carriage, twilight was wrapping blue shadows around the city. Emma stared across the river to the massive ship with its painted scrollwork and figurehead. She pushed at her magic faintly, whispering the words of the Fith-Fath spell to glamour her antlers. Pain raked over her, singing under her skin. Her bones melted. She gasped, sweat dripping into her eyes.

"I wish you'd stop doing that."

"I can't help it." It was like the most painful loose tooth ever, and she just had to poke it. Still, the bleak inevitability of her situation lent her a sort of courage.

"Ready?" He held out his hand and she slipped her fingers through his. "Remember, if anyone asks, I'm interrogating you. Pretend you're scared of me."

She squeezed his hand tightly before letting go. He took her to a narrow dock, half sliding into the dark, fetid waters of the Thames. A rowboat was tied up, a single blue eye painted on the prow. Cormac loosened the rope, which gleamed briefly, like silver.

The ship bobbed on the water, wood polished to a sheen and cannon mouths gaping darkly through the gunports. The eyeballs set in bottles along the rail turned in unison to watch their approach. Cormac rowed them to the ladder where he tied off the little boat. He climbed up first, disappeared over the railing, and after a long, tense moment, popped his head back over and gestured to her. She climbed carefully, her leather satchel across her shoulders and her riding habit skirt billowing around her ankles. Cormac helped her over the side and then stood apart, chin tilted and legs spread arrogantly. Two Keepers on the deck looked up from the game of dice they'd been playing.

"You got the short end too, did you, Blackburn?" one of them asked. "Sitting here while the others drink themselves silly with pretty girls. Some May Day for us."

"Caught this one lurking about," Cormac replied easily, with a jerk of his chin in Emma's direction. She swallowed and tried to look frightened and fragile.

"Blimey," the Keeper whistled. "Look at the antlers on her."

Cormac's hand closed over her upper arm. "Move it," he barked at her, tugging her roughly. When the others didn't follow or raise a cry of alarm, Emma released a long, shaky breath. There were other Keepers on the ship but they didn't pay them much mind. Cormac was one of them after all, and he'd gone to considerable effort to conceal his regard for her.

He took her down another ladder and into the hold. She saw the familiar carved wooden screen behind which the magisters had sat to proclaim judgment on her. The hold was empty this time, except for the cages, chains, and nets securing witch bottles. Feathers, paws, and eyes pressed at the glass. The bottles made from clay were sealed with wax, with only a leering gargoyle to hint at their contents.

They ducked under the low ceiling, passing piles of ballast stones for the cannons, coils of thick ropes, and the general clutter of the underbelly of a massive ship. Cormac stopped in a cramped narrow space with an apothecary cabinet built into a cubbyhole. It had dozens and dozens of slender drawers with unicorn horn handles.

"This was meant to be the shot locker," he explained. "But it was converted. Measures are worse than witch bottles. Those will just make you mad, but if the wrong person damages your cord, they can work magic directly against you. They can kill you."

"And mine is in there?" she asked, adrenaline making her stomach drop. There were only a few hours left until midnight. She had to get to the portal before then. "Which one is it?" she asked, looking for brass name plates or painted letters.

"That's the thing," Cormac said. "Only Lord Mabon knows for sure. The rest of us aren't technically allowed to handle the measures." He peered around once more to make sure they were alone. "But they keep underestimating me because I have no magic," he said. She suddenly knew exactly how he felt, and she found she really didn't care for the feeling of being so vulnerable. He tossed her a self-deprecating smile. "The magical wards down here won't react to me."

He pulled a drawer open to prove his point. The ship continued to rock gently, the water barrels stacked in the hold creaking faintly. There was no burn of magic, no bells ringing or gargoyles suddenly attacking.

Inside the drawer was a black cord, exactly like the one used to measure her, only judging by the layer of dust on it, it had been here for considerably longer. He opened another drawer and another, revealing more black cords. There was something sinister about them, like venomous snakes that might wake at any moment.

She swallowed. "How am I supposed to know which one's mine?"

"I'll open all the drawers and you hold your left hand over the ropes. Your witch knot will glow when we've got the right one."

"And then what?"

"And then we untie it and run like hell, because that will definitely set off the alarms." He shrugged, grinning comfortingly. "I told you it was a bad idea."

She grinned back, feigning insouciance. "I've known Gretchen all her life. This doesn't even rate as a bad idea."

She wiped her slightly damp left palm and then held it over the rope. Nothing.

Cormac opened another drawer, revealed another rope. Still nothing.

It went on for a dozen more drawers, until he was yanking them out as fast as he could. Twilight darkened outside the port holes, and they could barely see. He rifled the cabinet until panic beat at her like bat wings.

The drawer in the bottom left corner held a black rope with a knot tied in the center. Just seeing it made her stomach clench. Bile burned her throat. She knew even before her witch knot glowed faintly, searing her hand, that it was the right one.

Cormac stopped her when she went to grab it. His fingers were warm around her wrist. "Wait." She tugged impatiently. "The moment you touch that, the wards will break. They'll know we've been tampering with it. Let me carry it until we get to shore."

She knew he was right but everything in her protested. The need to untie the knot was physically painful. "Hurry," was all she said.

They skirted the barrels and the ropes and the sacks of salt. Lamplight fell down the ladder, a single small shaft of light that bled brightly into the quiet shadows of the hold.

"Well, well," someone sneered. "What have we here? A traitor and a thief."

Virgil.

Chapter 16

At first Gretchen barely noticed when Moira slipped a long chain with a locket over her head.

"Gretchen," Moira snapped. "Don't let her win. She killed Strawberry and your brother and don't you bleedin' dare let her win."

Gretchen blinked slowly, realizing that her eyes were burning. Ice glittered on the walls of the building in front of her. Frost covered Godric's coat, creeping up his neck. His hair froze like needles. Her fingernails ached, turning blue until she stopped clutching at his shoulders. A flash of light scalded the snow drifting around them. It melted almost as fast as it formed.

Gretchen looked up, seeing Strawberry's flickering silhouette. The snow turned to hawthorn petals.

"Your brother cut a lock of his hair so that I could see her whenever I wanted to," Moira explained softly. "I keep it in the locket."

"Godric?" She sat back on her heel, hope slashing through her like a dagger. Desperately she searched the alley, the frigid air above his body, the pavement running along the road beside her. When she didn't see his spirit, she nearly gagged on the disappointment.

When her shoulders sagged, Moira spoke again. "He said that sometimes ghosts aren't strong enough to show themselves fully."

She nodded, biting down savagely on her lower lip so she wouldn't cry. A cold wind, cobbled together of snow, frost, and hawthorn petals, slapped at Gretchen so hard she was shoved away from Godric. She staggered to her feet. Her arrowhead pendant was fringed with tiny, delicate icicles. It wasn't protecting her the way it had when she was attacked, it was more that it was recognizing it used to belong to Godric, that he was using it to signal to her that he was still here.

And that he wanted her to leave his body behind and follow Strawberry, who whirled around her and Moira, screeching silently, her mouth full of icicles.

Strawberry's edges blurred, and Gretchen couldn't be sure if she was leading the way or being dragged.

Cormac stepped in front of Emma. "Back off, Virgil."

"Oh, I don't think so. Not this time," he said. "I know everything now. She's a Greymalkin, you fool."

Emma froze. "What did you say?"

"You heard me," he snapped. "I know your secret." He produced a folded letter from his pocket. "I was sent word. And as your Keeper, it was my duty to stop you."

"You *bound* her," Cormac hissed. "You left her vulnerable when Sophie is out there." He lunged suddenly and Virgil staggered back, his nose cracking with the sound of splintered driftwood. He grunted in pain but didn't fall. They grappled viciously, fists smashing into kidneys, ribs, cheekbones. Cormac was a better fighter, but he had no magic.

When Virgil's fist hit Cormac in the face, the blow smashed his head back against the wall. It wouldn't have stopped him for long if Virgil hadn't followed with a puff of powder that billowed, all pink fire and the smell of burning.

"Emma, run," he coughed out, even as Emma pushed the magisters' screen into Virgil. It clipped his shoulder but didn't knock him down. He kicked Cormac in the kidney.

"If you run, I'll kill him," Virgil said.

Emma, who had been lunging for Virgil, stopped dead.

"Sod him," Cormac said, trying to get up, but he kept slipping on his own blood. The cloud had faded, but he was covered in a fine gold powder. It was leeching strength from him. He was already turning an odd shade of gray.

"You stay right there," Virgil ordered her.

She had no magic. She couldn't sear him to ashes with lightning. She couldn't even make it rain on his head.

Yet.

As Cormac fought the effects Virgil's spell, he thrashed in agony. The black cord slipped off his shoulder.

"I can tie him up or I can kill him, it's your choice," Virgil warned.

Emma wove on her feet.

"What are you doing?" he snapped. "Stop it."

"I'm—" She let her eyelids flutter and then crumpled. She let her arm fall at just the right angle, covering her face so she could open her eyes just enough to see him. He was turning red. The black cord was by her hand. She could nearly reach it. She stretched out slowly, carefully, as Virgil closed in on her. Cormac used the last of his strength to kick at Virgil's ankle, tripping him. It bought Emma just enough time to catch the end of the cord.

The ship rocked violently to the left, then righted itself. Cormac slid a few inches toward the ladder. Virgil fell hard to one knee, his footing already compromised by the hit to his ankle.

Emma clawed at the knot until magic exploded inside her. It filled her up until her rib cage may as well have been made of paper. Her skin stretched, her veins burned, her bones creaked. She wasn't able to move, let alone fight Virgil off.

He yanked Emma up by the back of her riding habit. She snarled at him but too much was happening inside her own body. Magic shackled her before it could release her. Her antlers glowed so fiercely they might as well have been made of fire. Virgil squinted but did not let go. He dragged her toward the collection of witch bottles.

Cormac pulled a talisman off the chain around his neck, trying to break it into pieces off the wooden floorboards. He moved weakly, slowly, his eyes rolling back as he fought to stay conscious. The amulet finally cracked, blowing away the poisoned mists.

As magic continued to shudder through Emma, the bottles responded, shivering in their cages. Emma tried to push her power out, tried to turn the Thames into a stormy ocean, tried to bring lightning down into the hold, tried rain, sleet, anything. Her magic wasn't ready, all it did was pour more light into her antlers. Virgil hauled her up against a bird cage wrapped in iron chains. There was a dagger in his hand.

The iron lock was open. The chains were loose, rattling against each other.

Inside was a single clay jug.

She recognized it and was instantly full of pain again, as she pushed her magic into its proper place. Her teeth chattered.

Cormac hauled himself up by using the ladder. He looked dizzy and nauseous. And furious. He lurched toward them. "Get away from her." The amulets around his neck sparked and hissed.

Virgil forced open her left hand and sliced through her witch knot with his blade. He pushed her forward, dragging her palm over the witch bottle. Her blood smeared the clay.

The jug rattled and shook. Misty light leaked through the cracks like icy needles. The iron stopper vibrated, as the force of the magic inside slowly pushed it out of the neck. Silvery smoke followed the light, forming luminescent moths, snakes, and a giant white bird with jagged talons.

Emma tried to back away, but Virgil still had hold of her. She drove her elbow sharply into his sternum, even as Cormac grabbed the back of his collar and hauled him off her. Virgil used the momentum to drag Emma off balance as he fell, shoving her into Cormac so that they had to steady each other.

"What did you do?" Cormac spat at Virgil, using his arm to keep Emma behind him. She crouched to snatch the black cord off the floorboards and stuffed it into her satchel.

Virgil smiled, blood on his teeth. "I released the Sisters," he said. "I suggest you run."

This time, Cormac's punch knocked him out cold.

Penelope wasn't certain how she came to be inside a carriage.

It was difficult to think clearly. All she could smell were hawthorn flowers. Lucius sat across from her, smiling his charming smile but a new kind of anticipation vibrated through him. She could see it in the glint in his eyes; she just didn't know what it meant. Or why he'd insisted they leave the ball.

They didn't go far. Penelope tried to memorize the movement of the carriage, one right turn, one left, and then a stop. Hyde Park crouched on one side, full of flowers and secrets and kelpies.

On the other side, Greymalkin House.

A part of her recognized that it was a gray and dismal house, one that had nearly killed Emma, but she still felt drawn to it. It might have been a palatial mansion with grand columns and manicured gardens instead of warped wood, chipped stone, and peeling paint. A gust of wind caught the shutters, banging them against the wall as if to prove her point.

Frost crept over the inside of the carriage window, tendrils of ice unfurling like pale fingers clutching at everything in their path. Penelope's breath misted. Snow pelted them as the carriage shuddered and they rattled like coins in a cup. Lucius kicked the door open, fighting his way free. There was ice on his collar and in the nooks of his cravat.

The petals of her hawthorn crown frosted and froze until they shattered into silvery dust.

She was no longer bewildered and befuddled.

"Penelope, come with me," Lucius ordered, holding his hand out to her through the open door.

"No," she said, slowly.

"I beg your pardon?"

She removed one of her gloves and he watched her carefully.

"Come with me now," he repeated imperiously. He gripped her wrist tightly, ready to haul her outside. Instead of fighting him, she curled her bare fingers over his knuckles, holding on tightly, the gold ring on his finger digging into her skin as she willed her powers to show her what he was really thinking.

Her eyes rolled back in her head.

The shards of the broken witch bottle lay on the ground, leaking magic. The substance was somehow smoke, liquid, and light all at once, coalescing slowly into the shape of three women. They were hazy at first, barely a wisp of an outline, growing stronger and stronger as Emma and Cormac watched, helpless and horrified.

The eldest, Magdalena, was full of glowing beetles, wasps, and moths, blending together to finally form the spirit of the Greymalkin warlock in her medieval gown and unbound hair. Lark was next, with her bloodstained plaid and tragic smile. Rosmerta was scarred by the poisonous plants draped over her, the same berries and flowers Cormac's sister Colette had turned against her. Even her sickle looked rusted, and it was still simple ectoplasm.

"You," she hissed at Emma. Magdalena and Lark paused, turning their heads.

"I guess they remember me," she said. Fear and anxiety had her swallowing an inappropriate and slightly hysterical giggle.

"You need to run!" Cormac pushed her up the ladder.

"What about you?" Emma asked, clinging to the rung but not climbing any farther.

"Someone needs to stop them," he said.

The Sisters had enough power between them, even after having been trapped, to rattle all of the other witch bottles in their cages. They pulled energy from the atmosphere so quickly and greedily that frost clung to Emma's eyelashes. Ice sheeted the floor and stole her breath. Her teeth chattered under the frigid blast of unnatural winter.

Witch bottles shattered, sending glass and clay shards throughout the hold. A familiar in the shape of a fat rabbit bounded away. A cat with a scar across its eye snarled, hackles raising as it slunk away.

"They're releasing the others," Cormac said, grabbing a

sword from the wall beside the ladder. It had knotwork etched onto the hilt and was inlaid with jet. A crystal sphere filled with salt and rowan berries sat in the center of the pommel. "Get out of here, Emma!"

The jagged pieces of the bottles and jugs hovered, glittering with malevolent magic. The Sisters flung them at Emma and Cormac. Cormac swung the sword, using the blade like a shield. When the shards struck the metal, they exploded and crumbled to sand. "Magic sword," he explained tersely.

Emma gathered the magic in her, and it only prickled slightly. Wind whipped and howled through the hold, dragging at the Sisters, tearing at their hair and their clothes until it took all their concentration not to dissipate like mist. Cormac fumbled for a red pouch inside his jacket and tossed the banishing powder inside onto the snow-stung floor between them and the Sisters. A white horse coalesced, hooves striking sparks as it reared. The Sisters backed away, howling curses.

"It won't be enough to hold them," he said with grim certainty. "Not one horse."

"Come with me," Emma demanded.

"I can't leave the ship to them. Don't argue with me, Emma. Go!"

"That wasn't an argument, it was a statement. You're coming with me," she said, as her hair whipped into her eyes. "Because *they're* coming with me. Isn't that right?" she yelled over the wind and the curses. They turned toward her as one, necks unnaturally long, heads swiveling too far around.

"Shite."

It was all Cormac had time to say.

Strawberry led Gretchen and Moira to the May Ball.

"Why's it always at a ball?" Gretchen muttered, racing up the steps to the front door. The windows of the lower portion of the house glowed with lamplight. The smell of roses and lilies was strong. Everything seemed normal.

"I don't think she's here," she said, even as snow assaulted her and she stumbled over the stoop into the front hall. The marble floors gleamed, slippery with ice. Moira followed gingerly, her shoulder hunched protectively.

"A bleeding Society dance with Greybeards." She pulled an iron dagger from her belt. Her fat little gargoyle circled over her head, snapping its jaws. "I'd rather be in the stews of the Seven Dials."

Gretchen snorted. "I don't blame you."

The butler stood at his post, staring straight ahead. Moira raised an eyebrow in his direction. "What's with him?"

"He's being a butler," she explained, frowning slightly. "Sort of." Apprehension tickled her spine.

They followed the hungry gargoyle down the hall to the ballroom. The perfume of flowers and melted beeswax hung in the air. Hawthorn petals and snow blew in behind them. The guests danced the waltz even though there was no music. Others stood by the walls, mechanically drinking champagne. Footmen continued to circulate though their trays were empty.

"They're bewitched," Moira said softly. "Bollocks."

Gretchen wandered between the guests, feeling ill. They smiled frozen smiles, their eyes wild. Even the Keepers stationed by the garden doors stood at attention, unable to move. She shook one of them, slapped another across the face. There was no reaction. Gretchen screamed, hoping to startle them out of their stupor. It wasn't the dainty yelp of a lady startled by a spider, but a full-on war-bellow.

No one noticed.

She screamed so loudly the dog next door barked in reply, and Moira's gargoyle hid in the chandelier until she stopped.

Moira rubbed her ears. "Are you done with that?"

"It was worth a try." And yet no one so much as glanced her way. The guests waltzed in circles like music-box figurines. The scuff of their shoes on the parquet floor was the only sound. It send shivers skittering over her even as part of her wished she could join them. She could stay here, frozen, and pretend that Godric was still alive.

She forced herself to stay in the moment, to blink away the image of his blood on her hands, and pushed through the guests.

"Why won't they stop?" She saw Daphne whispering in her father's ear. And a few feet away, Tobias stood by a sugar sculpture of two entwined lovers, as equally chained as the others. He looked as cold and controlled as ever, but it wasn't discipline pinning him in place this time; it was dark magic. She knew him now, knew him well enough to read the despair in the taut lines of his body. She grabbed his arm. "Tobias!" She shook him, even though she knew it wouldn't help. "Can you hear me?"

He couldn't reply of course. There was a burning lump in the back of her throat. There was too much inside her—grief, fury, worry. She might explode. Her fingers dug into his coat. "Wake up, damn it!"

"We need to find the spell," Moira said, patting down the gentlemen's coat pockets. She didn't find any amulets or witch bundles, but she did come away with a handful of coins and three gold cravat pins.

Gretchen stepped away from Tobias to dig through the potted plants. She tore the flowers and leaves off the garlands. She didn't find anything, couldn't even find her own cousins, never mind a hidden spell bundle. Fear soured her belly like it hadn't at the sight of the silent ball. They could be anywhere. Anything could have happened to them. She doubled her search efforts frantically.

Moira's gargoyle began to attack the chandelier, sending a shower of crystal shards over the whirling guests. Moira watched him for a moment before dragging a chair across the floor and setting it under the chandelier. "I think Pip's found something," she said, climbing onto the chair. She stretched, wobbling. "Can't quite reach it." She cursed.

Gretchen followed the silk-wrapped chain from the chandelier to where it was looped on a hook behind one of the brocade curtains. "Watch out," she called, waiting for Moira to step out of the way before unwrapping the chain and lowering the entire chandelier to the ground. It rattled as it dropped, breaking more crystal beads. A candle rolled away and nearly lit a lady's hem on fire before extinguishing. Pip darted at the chandelier like a viper.

Moira nudged him aside, digging through the broken glass until she came away with bloody fingertips but nothing else.

Gretchen closed her eyes, her fists clenched even she tried to relax. "How do I wake them?" She listened hard for the whispered answer, but she could hear only the heavy, sick thud of her pulse.

"Ask Strawberry," Moira suggested. "She's clearly been keeping an eye on Sophie."

"Strawberry," Gretchen murmured. "Help us again. How do we break this spell?"

"Alas no witch's spell."

"Not that one," she snapped. "Concentrate. How do we break this hypnosis?"

"Cross running water."

She shook her head. "Not possible. What else?"

By the time Gretchen had a reply she could work with, she was trembling and pale, her hair damp with sweat. Her ears burned. "We need malachite stones," she said. "And wormwood for the magical infection, and salt. All of it needs to be mixed with thunderwater." She shrugged bleakly. "I don't know how we're supposed to gather thunderwater; it's not even raining."

Moira grinned cheekily. "I can find you all of those things. It's what I do. And we're in a witch's house, after all. Folks this rich, they'd have everything on hand."

She left to prowl the house, leaving Gretchen alone with hundreds of silent guests. She tried to ignore the soft sounds of their forced mechanical dancing. "We're going to break the spell," she told them out loud, wondering if they could even hear her. "I promise you."

She was just starting to believe it when Tobias grabbed her from behind, pinning her back against his chest. The betrayal made her freeze for a moment, unable to process what was happening. She felt his breath on her cheek. He still couldn't speak, but he could prevent her from breaking the spell.

"*Oi*," Moira yelled, thundering down the stairs. She skidded into the ballroom, holding two round bottles filled with water and herbs. "We have bigger problems."

Gretchen, trapped in Tobias's iron-hard, dead-eyed hold, wasn't entirely sure how that could be possible. •

Emma twisted to the side to avoid colliding with the frantic Keeper hurtling toward the ladder down to the hold. Cormac emerged behind her, magic sword glowing.

"Call the white horses," he ordered, thundering past the stunned Keepers following the first. "And hide!"

The malice emanating from the hold convinced them, even before the Sisters began to float up through the deck. Glowing beetles and wasps filled the air, lending an eerie pale blue glow to the Keepers as they ran for cover, fumbling for banishing powder. Emma and Cormac were already sliding down the ladder into the rowboat. The Sisters had the advantage; they could float over the water.

But so could the white horses.

They rode the waves like it was a field of grass. One of them clamped strong teeth over the edge of Lark's plaid shawl, tearing it. She went from moon white to a sickly shade of gray.

Cormac rowed as fast as he could, muscles straining. Emma stood at the stern of the small boat and faced their pursuers, calling the wind to attack them and the waves to confound them. She wore the lightning like a crown. The boat bobbed dangerously and she nearly fell over the edge. Rain fell in sheets, turning to snow and ice the nearer it came to the Sisters.

They reached the shore, and Emma pulled the fog back down. She sent it clinging to the shadows, the houses, and the carriages, hiding everyone from the Greymalkin Sisters. They would see no warehouses, no dockside taverns, no clogged London street, only her.

Cormac cut the traces of the first horse he found, freeing it from the carriage it was meant to pull. The coachman was asleep and didn't wake in time to stop him. Cormac leaped onto the back of the horse and pulled Emma behind him. The sword was dimpled with rainwater, still gleaming unnaturally.

Lightning struck the ground behind them like spears. She could just make out the Sisters racing to catch up, light trailing off them like shooting stars. Frost formed and melted, closing its fingers around lampposts, street signs, and unwary pedestrians. Windows shattered under the violent and sudden pressure.

Behind the Sisters, a herd of white horses galloped madly. No one else saw them, but they knew enough to get out of the way when ice formed on the first of May and the sound of ghostly hooves spooked even the rats nibbling at the garbage in the gutters.

Magdalena vanished and reappeared beside them, trailing icy light. The horse's sides heaved and ice crackled in his mane.

He ignored Cormac's pull on the reins, turning right to get away from Magdalena.

"She's herding us," Cormac shouted above the whirling storm. He struggled to control the frightened horse.

"Where?" Emma asked, though she thought she knew the answer.

"Greymalkin House."

"Tobias, what are you doing?" Gretchen struggled in his arms, making the same noises a wounded badger would make. Tobias held on tighter. "You have to stop!"

"Gretchen," Moira's voice was strangled. "There are Rovers closing in."

"I don't care if they rob the place," Gretchen said.

"That's not what they're here for," Moira replied grimly. "Someone's sent them here while the Greybeards are useless. And we can't hold them off, not the two of us."

"We just need to hold them off long enough for me to break the spell." Gretchen struggled harder against Tobias's grip.

"I'll have to break that one's arms to make him let go of you," Moira said.

"I have a better idea," Gretchen said. Or possibly the worst she'd ever had. Or the best. It was hard to tell.

Tobias was a shape-shifter. They needed him to fight the Rovers and rouse the others. He'd once told her that shifting into wolf shape burned any malevolent magic out of a shape-shifter. She could free him. She just had to force him to wear the wolf. The pull of his own magic had to be inexorable, had to fill him up so there was no room left for any other magic.

She reached into the front of her corset, where she'd hidden the vial of wolfwater. She'd half-expected the potion to taste like snow or fire or wild herbs. Instead, it tasted like what it was: muddy rainwater. For a frozen moment, nothing happened.

He continued to hold her pinned against his body. The Rovers kept on advancing. The guests danced on and on.

It was a tickle at first, then a cold burning down to her belly, as if she'd eaten too many ices too quickly. A shiver raced under her skin, pricking painfully.

The change was fluid and excruciating. She was ice melting and reforming. Her bones dissolved. She slid like rain down a drainpipe and Tobias released her. There was nothing left of her to hold on to.

She landed on four legs, disoriented. She was still Gretchen, but everything looked and felt different. Her vantage point was so much lower, all hips and legs and frock coats billowing. Her joints worked differently, her center of balance shifted. And when her tail moved, she nearly fell over. She smelled everything— beeswax, lemon balm, sweat, hair oil, floor polish.

The wolf trapped inside Tobias.

He backed away from her, blue eyes wild. She prowled toward him, hunting him.

A Rover crawled in through one of the windows. Pip attacked him, smashing into the back of his head until he slumped over the sill, unconscious. Two more thundered into the ballroom. Gretchen snapped at one, her teeth closing over his leg, tearing through linen and flesh. The taste of his blood should have sickened her, but it didn't. He howled, stumbling. Moira broke a chair over his head.

"Bloody hell," she added, giving the giant wolf that was Gretchen a wide berth.

Gretchen lunged at Tobias, knocking him back. He landed on his back, and she slapped her paws on his chest, growling.

Finally, finally, his wolf answered.

Chapter 17

While Gretchen was clumsy and disoriented in her new body, instinct gave Tobias a undeniable feral grace. He slunk around a couple still whirling in their own frozen moment, barely brushing the woman's skirts. He leaped over the broken chair and landed on the third Rover, who had a fistful of Moira's hair. Pip dove for the Rover's face, breaking his nose so it bled down his chin, but he still wouldn't let go. Tobias swiped at his thigh with his claws, tearing through pant leg and muscle. He fell, clutching at the claw marks. The ragged wound was so deep it showed glimpses of the bone beneath. Moira yanked herself free.

"I saw at least six more of them in the garden," Moira warned. "Gretchen, you need to be Gretchen again."

It felt better to be a wolf. She didn't feel the loss of Godric so keenly; it didn't burn into her marrow because even her marrow had shifted. She was finally as wild on the outside as she felt on the inside. She could stay like this forever.

Tobias changed back; she could smell the human in him overpowering the wolf. He crouched beside her, naked and calm. "Gretchen," he said gently. "You saved me. Now we have to save the others."

She whined, longing for long nights spent running through the forest with nothing but the stars for company. Her ball gown was in tatters on the floor, where it belonged.

"You're stronger than this," he insisted. "And you're the only one who can break the spell. Change back."

She didn't want to.

"Please, Gretchen. We need you."

The combination of his plea and the feel of ice crystals forming under the pads of her paws convinced her, but only because she imagined Godric was the one freezing her toes with his displeasure.

Fur turned to skin, bones reshaped, fingers formed. She let the wolf in her retreat, let the human girl take over with her grief over her brother, her fear for her cousins, her frustration that she would never find her place in a world where the girl always won out over the wolf.

She nearly howled at the loss of it.

Tobias tugged the tablecloth off the refreshment table and wrapped it around her before ducking into the privacy of the shadows. Teeth chattering, she felt the heaviness of her legs, the fragile confines of her body. Dully, she took one of the bottles from Moira. Chips of green crystal and salt swirled around the angelica and wormwood leaves. "We need to put it on their third eye," she murmured. Her voice felt strange in her throat.

Tobias returned wearing a linen shirt and buff trousers he'd stolen from their hosts's bedroom. He carried another set of clothes for Gretchen. "I thought you'd prefer these," he said quietly, handing her trousers. "They belong to the young son of the house. They should fit you."

"Thank you," she said, touched.

Moira rolled her eyes. "Could you flirt later? We're about to be overrun here."

Telling herself she wasn't blushing because there was simply no time for that kind of foolishness, she stepped behind the curtains to get dressed.

A lit torch crashed through a window.

Moira stomped it out as Gretchen rushed to anoint the First Legate, rubbing the potion between his brow. He jerked like a marionette whose strings had tightened abruptly. While Tobias explained what he could of the situation, Gretchen woke Daphne. She jolted into consciousness, looking furious.

More smoke from the hallway and the smell of scorched carpeting.

"They're going to burn the place down around us, with everyone frozen inside," Tobias said harshly. "We're the sacrifice."

Fire continued to consume the house, closing in on the ballroom. The curtains went up in flames, snapping and crackling as they belched black smoke. Moira coughed, pulling her cravat up over her mouth and nose. "It's spreading," she said, peering down the hall.

They only managed to release a few more Keepers before the next wave of Rovers closed in. They stood in the gardens, blocking escape and throwing more torches into the house. Moira and Gretchen continued to dispense the potion as quickly as they could.

The first few Keepers went out the broken windows to fight off the Rovers. Disoriented witches woke to a house filled with fire. Smoke hung from the ceiling and the yellow-and-orange light flickered violently. Shouts and the clash of swords and daggers drifted in from outside. The First Legate dispatched more people to fight or find water. "And a way out," he snapped. "For God's sake, clear a path."

"We need to find the linking spell," Tobias said as the chaos of guests trying to escape the fire reached a crescendo. "We have to break the connection so Sophie can't feed on the sacrifice."

"Get everyone out first," he ordered. "Start with her." He gestured at his daughter.

Daphne shook her head, even as a cough racked through her. "I can help you find the spell."

"Don't argue with me, girl," her father shouted. "Get outside!" A Keeper picked her up around the waist and tossed her over his shoulder.

Gretchen had used up the last of her potion, and there were only a few more people in the ballroom and the various servants of the house to release with the remains of the second bottle. The real danger now was the panicked jostling and the inexorable smoke, impossible to fight. The windows in the conservatory were being broken as an escape route. She saw a grandmother hoisting a candlestick like a club to use against the Rovers. She looked keen to bash someone's head in.

"The Keepers are getting the last people out." Tobias handed Gretchen a wet strip of tablecloth to tie over her nose. "Run!"

The dark of the smoke pressing in on them and the brutal flashes of fire made it feel like they would never get out. The screaming gave way to choking and coughing and stifled sobs as people tried to feel their way out. Gretchen brushed against a metal door handle, branding a vicious welt into her arm. Burning debris rained from the ceiling, and Tobias bent over her, using his body as a shield.

They crawled through the jagged window, the door secured shut from the outside by a Rover. The air was sweet and clean and Gretchen gulped it down like a dessert ice.

Daphne shoved through the frantic crowd toward them. "I'm better with a pendulum than anyone else here," she insisted. She unclasped the opal pendant from around her neck. "No matter what my father thinks, I can help."

She dangled her necklace like a pendulum with her right hand, letting it swing over her witch knot. "Is the connection spell anchored in Grace House?"

The pendulum circled clockwise.

"Is it in the ballroom?" Daphne asked.

The pendulum circled in the opposite direction.

"Grace House must have twenty bedrooms alone," Gretchen said. "This could take hours."

"Then don't interrupt," Daphne snapped. "You'll only make

it worse." She went back to staring intently at the pendulum. "Is the connection spell in the library? The kitchens? The attic?"

The pendulum circled both ways, then swung side to side, confused.

"Try the roof," Moira interjected, soot on her face. "Where else would it be safe long enough to be used while everyone and everything burns?"

Daphne opened her mouth to object to being ordered about by a Madcap, then shut it with a snap. "It does make sense," she said grudgingly. "Is the pendulum on the rooftop?"

The pendulum made wide clockwise circles.

Moira nodded. "Right. I'll go."

"Let me," Tobias said. "It could be dangerous."

Moira snorted disdainfully. "A Greybeard balancing on a ridge pole? You'd fall on your pretty head. No, this is what Madcaps do, remember?"

"Help Greybeards?" Gretchen said with a commiserating smile.

"Don't tell the others," Moira retorted before tightening her cravat securely over her nose again.

Fire shot through the house windows like dragon tongues licking the sky. The light pulsed hungrily. The neighbors evacuated their own houses for fear the fire would jump from building to building. Most of the guests were running out into the road to find their carriages. The Rovers, outnumbered, had run off.

Gretchen should have felt relief.

She felt only a deeper, colder fear.

"Has anyone seen Emma?"

"She wasn't here," Tobias replied, soot marks in his hair. His shirt was pockmarked with burns.

"And Penelope?"

Daphne looked at Gretchen. "I thought you knew."

"Knew what?"

"Lucius Beauregard did this to us," she replied. "He mesmerized us all somehow. And when he told us to, we became music-box dolls, stuck in a pattern."

"Son of a bitch," Tobias ground out, his blue eyes turning arctic. "I didn't see him activate the spell. And he was just made an honorary Keeper. Who else has he hypnotized?"

"He took Penelope," Daphne said.

Gretchen turned to go without a word, the broken glass from the conservatory windows crunching under her shoes.

"Gretchen, wait," Daphne called out. She pulled the poppet they'd made of Sophie from her reticule. "I took this from my father's pocket," she said, tossing it to her. "You'll need it."

Penelope fell into Lucius's memories. As always, they were out of order, and she spun through them like a kaleidoscope, all colors and patterns that made sense only for a brief moment.

He hurried down an underground tunnel. He had to hunch over in order not to hit his head on the damp stone. The old mines of Paris had been converted into catacombs for the dead during the French Revolution. The cemeteries were emptied to make space for buildings and houses. A river of bones had decanted down into the mine tunnels.

Knights, cheesemakers, wine sellers, dancing masters, merchants, and old kings all gathered here, heedless of titles and wealth.

More importantly, so did the bones of those who'd died in the riots at la Place de Grève, and those who'd laid down for "Madame la Guillotine."

Seraphine, one of the Seven Sisters, had died in Paris during the Revolution.

It took Lucius a full year to find the right gatekeepers and street urchins to mesmerize into helping him, and then another to explore the catacombs.

The burble of water from the aqueducts and springs was his ever-constant companion. Fossils gleamed in the wet limestone before it opened up into the catacombs. He passed walls made of leg bones, skulls lined along the top. Finger bones and cracked jaws made patterns delicate as lacework. He barely noticed. Finally, finally, he had what he needed.

Seraphine's finger bone was tucked safely inside his coat pocket. He wasn't able to find anyone to read the bones, but three bone-singers assured him that her ghost lingered, hungry and desolate. "You'll be with your sisters soon enough," he murmured, his voice echoing in the tunnel as he climbed back up to the city streets. "And I'll be with my love."

It took another year to navigate the Channel, made too dangerous to cross by the war and Napoleon. He missed home. He missed the green hills, the silver rain, the yellow fog of London.

He missed her.

The colors smeared on the palette in her mind, and Penelope tumbled and bounced between memories.

Lucius was told of an old man who lived in the alley behind la Place de Grève. He talked to himself all day and night, laughing and offering wine to the empty air. Lucius knew a bone-singer when he saw one. His faded eyes tracked movement Lucius couldn't see. Lucius crouched down beside him, ignoring the pungent smell of unwashed cloth and hair. He placed a jug of wine and a basket of cheese, grapes, and sausages in front of him. "J'ai besoin de ton aide."

The man looked at the food, then squinted up at Lucius. "Va-t'en, salaud."

He wasn't friendly or willing. It didn't matter.

He'd looked into Lucius's eyes.

Lucius smiled, his witch knot flaring. He grabbed his left hand, pressing their witch knots together. "You'll do as I say, old man."

Even knowing she couldn't change the outcome, Penelope tried to warn the old man, but the memory was already changing.

The ring slipped on his finger, put there by a girl with tears on her cheeks. Not just any girl.

Sophie.

She smiled up at Lucius, lower lip trembling. "This way we'll always be together. I'll wait for you."

He gathered her close, already missing her. "I'll find the bones," he murmured in her hair, which always smelled like lavender. "We'll bring her back."

"I love you," she said, rising on her toes to kiss him. "Come home soon."

Penelope opened her eyes, seething.

"You toad-spotted varlet."

. . .

"Don't try and stop me," Gretchen snapped as Tobias loped by her side.

"Give me a little credit," he said quietly. "I can track her, remember?" His nostrils flared as he catalogued scents she couldn't smell. She felt the loss of her wolf again, sharply.

"What the hell does Lucius have to do with any of this?" She ground her teeth. "I can usually tell when someone is hiding that big of a lie."

"You're still learning how to use your gifts," Tobias pointed out. "It's as new to you as wearing the wolf is to me."

She shook her head. "Still, I . . ." She thought about each time she'd seen Lucius. At the musicale when he'd spilled wine on Penelope's gloves, at the goblin markets, outside of Gunter's when she'd heard the warning buzz but had assumed it was a reaction to the dropped stitch on Penelope's reticule. "It was him all along." Frustration boiled inside her. "What does he want with her?" she asked. "Or Sophie? And where's Emma?"

"We'll find them," Tobias promised her. "This way."

Tobias's tracking led them to Greymalkin House. It was as dilapidated as ever. Even the ivy clinging to the walls looked gray. It tainted the very air, all dust and cobwebs and darkness.

Lucius was outside the gate, holding Penelope's arm behind her back. Keepers stood on either side with blank expressions. Gretchen didn't think; she just grabbed the nearest object and lobbed it at Lucius's head. The stone glanced his cheek. It took him by surprise, but not long enough for Penelope to dash away. He yanked her back and she yelped in pain.

And then Sophie emerged from a waiting carriage. The roof was thick with sparrows and pigeons. She wore a pale yellow muslin dress with a row of topaz buttons. She floated with all the grace of a debutante, her smile politely bland. She wore a necklace of pearls and diamonds that glimmered prettily. Gretchen looked closer. It wasn't just pearls she wore. Godric's locket gave her the ability to see what was really chained around her neck, and it wasn't pretty stones. The pearls glowed blue and violet, unfurling chains of light that stretched out behind her.

Leashed to that virulent light were the ghosts of the people she'd murdered and whose bones she'd stolen.

Gretchen recognized Margaret York, Sophie's first victim. She still wore her silk ball gown, stained with blood.

Beside her, Alice the seamstress with her pinpricked fingertips and plain homespun dress.

Lilybeth, with her sad, surprised eyes, clutching at the leash that burned around her wrist.

Strawberry was there as well, though not chained. The whips of light snapped at her like serpents, but she fought their pull. Her edges were smeared, nebulous. Sophie hadn't managed to steal her bones before Moira burned them in the funeral boat. Godric was there too in his striped waistcoat and pale hair. The whips slashed hungrily and impatiently.

"We are still here."

Gretchen stopped breathing.

"*You* killed him," she finally croaked, swaying as her vision went red. Tobias's hand on her arm kept her from shattering into pieces. She wondered if she hadn't fully shifted out of wolf form, because all she could hear was desperate howling.

"It was meant to keep you distracted," Lucius said. "We did warn you, but you reversed the poppet curse onto us. It had to go somewhere, didn't it?"

"What's she doing here?" Sophie asked Lucius. "She's the worst of them. I thought we agreed to keep them occupied and separated."

"Why?" Gretchen asked flatly.

"To keep you out of the way," she snapped. "You and your cousins ruined it all for me. And I won't fail again. I can't."

"So raising the dead is an excuse for killing my brother?" she spat. "For killing all of those girls?" She was dimly aware of Tobias holding her back, mostly because every time she surged forward, Lucius's hold on Penelope tightened painfully. His hand was around her neck now, immobilizing her. There were hawthorn petals in her dark hair.

"What do you mean, Godric's dead?" Penelope asked, her cheeks going pale.

"*Alas, no witch's rhyme to turn back time; only a warlock's spell unrings the bell. To rise up those that fell, court thee the Seven Sisters well,*" Gretchen quoted.

Tobias forgot that he was preventing Gretchen from attacking Sophie and took a step forward himself. "You can't be serious. You could never control all Seven Sisters."

"I've been gathering power, or haven't you noticed? I can do anything."

"Ignore him, love," Lucius said softly. "He doesn't understand. He never will."

"But you courted me," Penelope whispered. "You said you loved me."

"He loves me," Sophie broke in savagely. "*Me.*"

"Lucius, let the Lady Penelope go," Tobias said softly. "Or I can guarantee it will end badly for you."

"You can't do anything to me without doing it to her as well," he said. "She's mine now."

"Oh, I really don't think so," Gretchen said. "You're as mad as Sophie is. And you'll be equally dead if anything happens to Penelope."

"I'm not mad," Sophie insisted. The ghosts of her victims floated behind her. Frost clung to the cobblestones. "And I *am* sorry, you know. But I'm doing this for love."

"Love?" Gretchen spat. "For a man who courted my cousin?"

Her eyes glittered. "My *sister* died of a fever when I was twelve years old. She was only ten. And I couldn't heal her. Me, with my healing gifts. But at least I can bring her back now."

"That's who I saw in the vision," Penelope realized softly.

"My brother for your sister?" Gretchen seethed. "By sacrificing a house full of witches?"

"By sacrificing anyone. Anything," she replied acidly. "That's what family is. Can you honestly tell me you wouldn't do the same? For your brother? For your cousins?"

"Where's Emma?" Gretchen and Penelope demanded in unison. Penelope's voice was more of a rasp.

"She'll be along," Sophie said. "The Sisters are fetching her even now."

"But why? Why the Sisters again?" Penelope asked. "Why are you doing this?"

"Who cares?" Gretchen said. "She's selfish and insane. Someone punch her in the eye already." Instantly, her knee flared with pain. She felt the bruise forming, just as she had when she was seven years old and had fallen from her pony. A gash opened on her arm, blood seeping into her sleeve. There was a rush of dizziness and a headache burst in her left temple. She'd hurt herself in this exact way falling from a horse.

"Oh dear, it looks as though you were rather clumsy as a child," Sophie said. "You'll find that regrettable."

"What are you doing to her?" Penelope struggled. Lucius tightened his fingers and she stilled, going pale. "Gretchen, get out of here!"

Tobias half stepped in front of her, but it didn't stop Sophie's magic. Gretchen grit her teeth against the aches and stabs assaulting her like a swarm of invisible hornets. She remembered Sophie's poppet tucked into the pocket of her borrowed trousers, but she had no pins. And no breath left as her body remembered exactly what it felt like to fall out of an apple tree in the family orchard.

"Don't you remember?" Sophie explained with her pretty debutante smile. "I can revisit all of your past illnesses and injuries upon you. It's much more useful than healing them, I can assure you. And once Emma is here to open the gate, this will all be over." She watched Gretchen's struggle, amused. "You might think you're strong enough to ignore the pain, but when all of those injuries hit you at once, you'll do what everyone does. You'll faint."

"I never faint," Gretchen replied, tasting copper and lemon balm.

"But what do you need with me?" Penelope croaked, trying to distract Sophie. "I can't bring back the dead."

"No, but you can tell me which are the bones of the Sisters in the Greymalkin ossuary. Lucius found Seraphine in Paris, but the others are in this house. I need them if they're going to be more than mere spirits."

"The Shakespeare book," Penelope realized.

"I had to be sure your powers were strong enough," Lucius said quietly, his breath stirring the hair on her neck.

"Spilling the wine on my gloves that night was no accident either." She bit back tears. "How can you do this, Lucius?"

"You're a romantic girl, Penelope. Surely you understand doing anything for love."

"Not this," she said. "Not murder."

"I spent years searching for Seraphine's bones, separated from Sophie. All to ease her grief. If this were one of your books, you'd call me the hero."

"I'd call you a—" His thumb dug into her windpipe, cutting off her voice just as the First Legate arrived with a small unit of ash-and-soot–stained Keepers. They carried jet-inlaid wheel pendants, iron daggers, and spell bundles.

It wouldn't be enough.

Other Keepers came out of the shadows to join Lucius. They stared straight ahead, weapons ready. They had the advantage, by being completely indifferent to fighting their brothers. The others paused, confused. They were forbidden to fight each other. But Lucius's Keepers weren't bound by those laws anymore. And there were more of them.

And then Lord Mabon, the head of the Order.

And Theodora Lovegrove, Emma's mother. She wore a ragged, torn dress and there were leaves in her black hair. Her eyes flashed.

"Where the hell is my daughter?"

Moira raced up the grand staircase, trying to see through the gloom and keep her footing. The fire was still contained to the ground level, but it raged unabated and it was only a matter of time before it nibbled up the steps and at the ceiling. Smoke pressed in on all sides, rising through the cracks in the floor-boards.

Coughing, she kept climbing, keeping one hand on the wall. She'd never been inside a nobleman's house before, but she imagined that attics were attics, no matter the neighborhood. She crossed acres of plush woven carpets to reach the servants' stairs to take her to the top floor. It was cramped and crooked, the steps too narrow for her feet. She couldn't imagine climbing them with a basket of laundry or coal. Better to live as a Madcap, ducking pigeons and Greybeards.

She smelled the smoke but it was thin enough that she could lower her cravat. She went through a maid's bedroom and used the fire poker to smash the glass so she could climb out the window. It was a simple thing to haul herself up over the over-hang and grasp the railing. It was decorative iron, adorned and painted black even though she'd wager no one ever came up here. The household gargoyles had been beheaded, hulking bodies ending in jagged stone.

"Go on, Pip," she urged. "Find the spell."

The fat little gargoyle flew fast and deadly, suddenly fierce with his sharp teeth and curved talons. He circled the roof, dipping low and rising up again. He finally led Moira to the far corner.

On a round mirror sat a nest made of three yew twigs bound with red-and-black thread. In the center of the web sat a rob-in's egg, blue as the summer sky. A circle of black salt sur-rounded it. When she went to brush it away, the grains flung themselves at her like stinging insects. Bloody marks rose instantly on her skin. Pip growled and snapped at the salt, plucking it out of the air like a toad with a swarm of flies. Moira rubbed feeling back into her numb fingers. When Pip had cleared the way, Moira undid the spell. She didn't use fancy rhyme or herbs picked at midnight. She just used her boot.

She stomped down hard, breaking the egg and cracking the mirror into shards. She ground it into dust under her heel.

Below her, the fire had consumed too much of the house. She felt it shift as floors gave away. She clung to the railing, cursing. Smoke snuck between the shingles. Her feet burned. She couldn't swing back down to the window. Flames licked the broken glass, cutting off her escape. She peered down the length of the building to the flagstones below. An oak tree scraped its branches against the stucco.

She'd have to jump.

She leaped, soles of her feet prickling. She landed precariously, the branch dipping low under the sudden weight. She twisted and grabbed onto another branch, before the first could drop her. She pulled herself along to the trunk, the bark scraping the inside of her elbow and her jaw. Once she'd steadied herself, she climbed down into the ruins of the garden, darted over the wall into the lane, and ran right into Atticus.

"Can this night get any worse?" she muttered. Marmalade hissed as he emerged from her rib cage.

Atticus smirked, his lavender eyes pale as water in the hungry light of the house fire. "Where are you off to, love?"

"Piss off," Moira said. "I'm not in the mood."

Ogden stepped out of the shadows, and before she could react, he'd cuffed her on the back of her head. She crumpled, pain clouding her vision.

"We're not done with you," Atticus said as Ogden hauled her over his shoulder. She bounced painfully as he ran, swearing once more that she would never visit Mayfair again.

"The bakery by Hogarth's Print Shop," Emma yelled in Cormac's ear. The moment he realized why she'd suggested that particular rooftop, his shoulder stiffened. "It's the only way to get away from them," she insisted. "They won't stop. And if they need me to be at Greymalkin House, then I need to be any-where else."

She called down more and more lightning. She was exhausted and hollow but she refused to stop. They couldn't risk getting caught. And they couldn't risk letting the Sisters loose again.

Cormac guided the horse down the dark alley even when it balked. They slid out of the saddle, and he went straight to a pile of wooden skids used for transporting stacks of parchment and jars of ink. He moved them against the wall to the print shop, perpendicular to the drainpipe, as makeshift steps. The ladder Moira had lowered down for them the first time they'd been here clattered to the ground. They hadn't seen it shoved in the corner.

Cormac slammed it against the bricks. "Go!"

Emma scrambled up the rungs, trying not to trip on her skirts. Cormac followed, just as the ice began to make the shin-gles into a skating rink. The gargoyle shifted and woke, grum-bling when it smelled the Sisters' magic. More ice cracked as the gargoyle unfurled its talons.

Emma tried to recall all of the Toad Mother's instructions from the day she'd been cleansed of the Sisters' familiars. She dropped the half-carved deer she'd taken from Ewan's hut. She glanced around wildly, looking for something she could use to grind it into dust. The gargoyle would just as easily swallow it as crush it for her. The hilt of Cormac's dagger wasn't strong enough.

"What are you waiting for?" Cormac yelled. The sound of ghostly hooves shivered through the alley.

"I need something strong enough to crack this," she said frantically. The wooden sculpture was sturdy and surprisingly heavy for something so small. The hooves were carved in perfect half moons.

Hooves.

Thanks to Ewan's blood and Theodora's magic, Emma had grown antlers. Once, briefly, her leg had also transformed, while standing in a herd of deer. A hoof would be strong enough to break the carving.

She wrapped her hand around her antlers, pressing the witch knot to the tines. She stared at the deer figure, remembering her mother shifting shape, her father turning into a stag, the painful push of the antlers when they grew out of her hair. She thought of grass, trees, the sound of hooves on the ground.

Her bones elongated and her foot hardened, fusing together. It was painful and strange. She brought her hoof down in one sharp motion, shattering the wooden deer. She ground down with enough force to splinter it into dust.

The Sisters shot up the side of the building, screeching.

"Now!" Cormac shouted. "Do it now!"

She released the magic and dropped to her knees, too weak to stay upright. Her hands shook as she piled salt, crushed apple seeds, graveyard dirt, and moonwort fern onto the wooden remains. She lit it, hunching over the small flame so the sleet wouldn't blow it out.

The alley below was full of stampeding spirit-horses. The cold stung, leaving tiny bloody bites on exposed skin. The gargoyle attacked, tearing through the ghostly moths and beetles that surrounded Magdalena. Cormac slashed at Lark's bird. The horses began to appear, scorching through the ice.

Emma shook the apple branch, the silver bells chiming softly. The sound shimmered, leaving trails of sparks.

The fire glowed faintly, sucking in the energy from everything in the vicinity. Emma wilted. Cormac staggered, nearly losing his footing. The gargoyle thunked inelegantly to the shingles. The Sisters washed out, tendrils of thick fog being pulled from them.

The flame shot up like a flashing sword, cutting through the cold shadows. The center widened, pushing at the darkness of the rooftop. The edges unfurled, made of purple lightning.

The portal opened like the mouth of a beast.

Luminescent snakes slithered over the shingles. There were so many of them, they tangled into knots around Emma's ankles, trapping her. Their magic burned, leaving welts as it ate through her stockings. Cormac stabbed at them until they parted, hissing. She pushed feebly to her feet. Cormac caught her around the waist as they teetered on the edge of the portal. Violet sparks caught and flickered. There was blood on his chin and on his collar, and he held a vicious sword in his other hand. "Emma?"

"Yes?"

He smiled, dipping his head so close to hers she could see the flecks of amber in his dark eyes.

"Marry me?" he asked, just before they fell into the vortex.

.   .   .

Gretchen and Penelope exchanged a glance as the aunt they'd never met stormed across the road toward them. The illusion spells that kept Greymalkin House and the argument occurring on its doorstep hidden did not hide them from another witch. Theodora Lovegrove was furious and muddy. She'd spent months as a deer only to finally shift back in time to save her daughter. But Emma wasn't here.

The three Sisters, however, were.

The unnatural spirit winter followed them, closing its cold fingers into a ruthless fist. Gretchen's lips chapped with the drop in temperature. Her fingernails ached, turning blue.

Lucius's Keepers attacked first, slashing at their brothers with iron daggers. Magic lanced between them, sparking with sour greens and virulent yellows. Spell shattered against spell. The gas lamps in the area exploded all at once, even as snow fell thick as rain. Tobias tried to separate his brothers, using a branch to shove between them. Gretchen tripped as many as she could, trying to reach the fence.

Icicles dripped from the railing, glittering like silver knives.

She stayed low, crawling between the Keepers and trying to avoid being stomped on. She nearly lost a finger to a boot, jerking out of the way at the last second. A Keeper tripped over, sending her sprawling. She hit the fence hard. She reached up and snapped off one of the icicles.

"Where's Emma?" Sophie demanded, her back pressed to the gates.

"She has fled," Rosmerta hissed. Serpents slithered from under her dress.

"Well, get her back!" Sophie snapped. "I need her."

"She's in the Underworld now." Lark shrugged sadly. There was blood on the ends of her hair.

Sophie's pretty face fell.

"Hush, love," Lucius murmured. "We'll find another way."

Sophie's gaze snapped onto Theodora. "You're right. We will."

Theodora stiffened as bruises bloomed on her skin and wounds opened like tiny, hungry mouths. Blood dripped down her arm and she held it gingerly. She looked confused for a moment, as if she didn't know where she was.

Gretchen used the icicle like a pin, stabbing into the poppet.

Sophie screamed, clutching her side.

Gretchen smiled grimly and stabbed again. Sophie staggered, moaning.

"Stop," Lucius commanded. "Stop or I'll snap her neck." He tilted Penelope's head back until she mewed.

"You need her," Gretchen said. "You said so yourself."

"Stop her," Lucius ordered his Keepers. The two nearest to her abandoned their attack on the others and turned toward her. Tobias leaped over two grappling Keepers to slide to a stop in front of her.

Gretchen kept stabbing. Unfortunately, so did Sophie, in her own way.

Theodora fell to her knees. Her torn sleeve was soaked with blood. Whatever wound she'd suffered had been deep.

Gretchen's icicle melted to cold water. She fumbled for another one with numb fingers but the railing only glistened wetly and did not freeze. The Sisters whirled through the battle, scattering snow and hail. She couldn't reach any of it.

Beside her, Godric's pale shadow closed his hand around the iron fence. Frost gathered, bristling like moth-eaten lace. Sophie's imprisoned ghosts strained at their chains, reaching out luminescent fingers. A thin film of ice traveled over the filigree until the black iron gleamed white. They didn't have enough power left to create icicles. Instead, she pressed her fingers to the furred frost until they ached and water collected. It was slow, excruciating work.

"You bore a Greymalkin, after all." Sophie crawled forward to rip a strip off Theodora's sleeve. "Your blood might work just as well."

"Gretchen breathed on the frost until more water collected, enough to make a puddle that might fill a teacup. She pressed the poppet's head into it.

Sophie gurgled in surprise.

Gretchen willed herself not to feel the weakness of the fever she'd caught three years ago. Her hands trembled as she held the poppet down. Lucius took a step forward. Penelope jabbed her elbow into his sternum and stomped on his instep at the same time. She stumbled out of his grasp.

Sophie spat water, clawing at her throat. She threw a hateful glare at Gretchen, who tried not to feel guilty as she drowned a girl.

It still wasn't enough.

Choking, Sophie managed to press the blood-soaked fabric

against the scorched magpie crest joining both sides of the iron gate together.

They flew apart in a burst of lilac fire.

Sophie fell forward and vanished, dragging her ghosts behind her.

Lucius stalked Penelope, unconcerned with the magic and the blood all around them. Greymalkin House loomed behind her like a troll. She flattened against the fence, not quite trapped but not quite free either.

"Penelope, come with me," Lucius said, pushing the magpie gates open wider. They creaked, rust flaking into the dead grass. Sophie had been transported inside, using the spell that still clung to the gates. Gretchen was sprawled on the ground, covered in bruises and old injuries. Earlier in the evening Penelope would have followed him anywhere. She was a fool.

"You mesmerized me," she whispered.

She inched away, trying to see through the confusion of Keepers fighting Keepers. The Sisters abandoned them, flying into the wilted gardens.

"You leave me no option then," he said. "If you don't come with me right now, Gretchen will die. Emma will die, and all of these Keepers trying so valiantly to rescue you will die. And, dear girl, your tenacious little Gypsy friend will die."

She shook her head. Glowing spiders crawled fanatically over her hem. "I don't believe you."

"Cedric, who has kept you from me for too long now, has had a rather regrettable evening. Look for yourself, Penelope."

Cedric was pulled from Sophie's carriage. He was gagged and his hands were lashed together. Worse, he was unconscious, carried over the shoulder of a stern-faced Keeper built like a bull.

Penelope launched herself at Cedric, but there were too many Keepers between them.

Other Keepers were dying at her feet.

Her cousins were in danger.

Cedric was in danger.

Lucius smiled at her expression. "There it is. Hopeless capitulation. So much easier than any spell."

Penelope did the only thing she could do.

"Penelope, don't!" Gretchen yelled, knowing her too well.

She took Lucius's hand and let him lead her to Greymalkin House. The gates slammed shut together behind them. The house flared once, shooting arrows of light between the shutters and under the mended door. It flung everyone back, blinding them. Penelope could only watch, half shielding her eyes, as it changed.

Instead of broken shutters, peeling paint, and the dark hunger of the house as it had been, it now gleamed, all elegance and sophistication. The gardens shed their shroud of weeds for dresses of candy-colored petals. Daffodils, lilacs, tulips, and violets bloomed cheerfully from urns, box hedges, and out of the mouth of a satyr's head set into the artfully crumbling stone wall separating the house from the lane to the stables.

The trim around the windows and the fanlights had blue, cream, and plum accents. The iron scrollwork railings on the balconies were freshly painted black, decorated with magpies in flight. On each corner of the roof hulked two giant gargoyles, two more holding up the third-floor balcony on its outstretched wings. A brass knocker in the shape of a magpie was affixed to the front door, which was now a vibrant blue.

The white stones might well have been carved of marzipan and meringue, with icing for mortar. The roof was a collection of sugar biscuits. It no longer looked like the house of a family of banished warlocks. It was welcoming and warm, like a fairy-tale witch's house—the kind made out of gingerbread, meant to lure the innocent until they were caught like flies in a spider's web.

"Welcome, Penelope," Lucius said with a smile that shivered her insides.

Epilogue

Gretchen watched Penelope step inside the Greymalkin House and disappear.

A trail of ice and frost clung to the railing and spilled over onto the stone path, all the way to the door. She couldn't see Godric anymore. For all she knew, he was trapped inside as well, dragged by Sophie's spell.

Fear and rage made the back of her throat burn. She lunged for the gates, but she was too late. The spell that locked them in flung her away in a shower of yellow sparks. Tobias caught her before she hit the lamppost. Keepers stood around them, stunned. Their brothers on the other side of the fence were expressionless and cold.

And then the London night was broken into shards of light. Fire shot into the sky, like columns of fireworks and Catherine wheels, spinning violet sparks over the Tower, Temple Bar

Gate, and Blackfriars Bridge. Lavender smoke billowed to eat the stars.

"Portals are opening," Tobias said grimly. "She's nearly got all Seven Sisters through now. With their bones, she can materialize them fully."

"London is doomed," one of the Keepers whispered.

The last portal opened on the sidewalk in front of them. The light from the opening portal was too bright to look at directly. Gretchen shaded her eyes, waiting for the jagged forks of light to dim. It didn't disgorge one of the Sisters. Instead, the silhouette of an antlered man stepped through the violet light.

"Ewan!" Theodora's voice was fragile. Her bird-familiar dropped red feathers all around her.

Ewan froze, clearly both desperate and terrified to believe he'd found her at last. He turned his head. Theodora struggled to get to her feet, not yet recovered from Sophie's magical attack.

"Emma's in the Underworld," Gretchen broke in. She might have felt badly for them if there was any space left inside her body not currently devoted to fear for her cousins and brother. "You have to get her out."

Ewan paused. The air around him seemed to shiver, so cold was his expression. Blue lighting arced between his antlers. The portal wavered, starting to seal itself. "I'll be back for you, princess," he said to Theodora, bowing his head to her before stepping back into the portal. The fissure closed behind him.

"No!" Theodora yelled, crawling brokenly toward him. "Take me with you!"

Gretchen turned away, mind already racing with plans and plots.

Tobias's hand was warm on her shoulder. "We'll get her out," he promised.

Gretchen lifted her chin. "We'll get them *all* out," she corrected.

Author's Note

The witchcraft in this book is purely literary. It is not intended to represent modern or ancient belief systems.